REALITY CHECK

REALITY CHECK

CHRISTOPHER G. NUTTALL

ISBN-13: 9781544261607
ISBN-10: 1544261608

http://www.chrishanger.net
http://chrishanger.wordpress.com/
http://www.facebook.com/ChristopherGNuttall

All Comments Welcome!

AUTHOR'S NOTE

As an odd-numbered book in the series, *Reality Check* is stand-alone. I believe that you should be able to read it without reference to the earlier books in the series. However, if you wish to read about the Fall of Earth, you may refer to *When The Bough Breaks*, Book III in the series. The next mainstream book, *Retreat Hell*, is already available in eBook, paperback and audio format.

Chronologically speaking, *Reality Check* takes place at the same time as *The Empire's Corps*.

If you enjoyed this book, please review on Amazon and consider joining either my mailing list or Facebook page (or both). I post regular updates on my Facebook, along with free snippets, political commentary and other stuff. (And the more followers I have, the more impressive it seems to potential publishers.)

As always, if you spot any spelling errors and suchlike, drop me a note. I offer cameos! Please let me know about any problems in context, however. Kindle locations aren't always helpful, sadly.

Thank you for your attention.
Christopher G. Nuttall

DISCLAIMER

I am not a survival expert. Some of the actions taken by the characters in this book can be dangerous if not done properly. If you want proper advice, please consult a survival manual or ask someone with genuine experience.

CGN

CHAPTER
ONE

It may seem absurd or unnecessary to point out that the core purpose of education is education, teaching children what they need to know. Indeed, there are people who would argue with that definition, or point out that education rarely ends when a child becomes an adult. But it is largely true.
- Professor Leo Caesius, *Education and the Decline and Fall of the Galactic Empire*

"Settle down," Miss Simpson said. "Please, settle down."

Darrin Pearson rolled his eyes as he moved towards his seat, neither fast enough to mark him as one of the nerds who actually *liked* learning nor slow enough to pose as one of the thugs who preferred being rough and violent to actually being in school. Coming to think of it, he was definitely closer to the latter than the former, but he actually enjoyed playing sports and the schoolyard was the only place they were allowed to play without being harassed by the Civil Guard.

He took his seat and pretended to study the blank screen. Miss Simpson was younger than the last teacher Form 11B had had, a man who had left three months after he had arrived. Rumour had it that he'd been caught in the closet with a schoolgirl, but Darrin suspected that he'd actually been defeated by the teenage boys and girls he'd been supposed to teach. Few teachers actually lasted longer than a year, if they were lucky. He'd seen pranks where teachers and students had been badly injured, even killed.

Miss Simpson was young, too young. With her long brown hair, tight top and pale face she looked barely older than the kids she was meant to teach, which made it impossible for her to maintain discipline. Not that age or even physical bulk mattered, Darrin knew; a teacher who laid a hand on a student, or even raised his or her voice too high, would be off to the nearest penal world as soon as an official complaint could be filed. It hadn't taken him – or most of the other children – long to realise that there was little the teachers could actually *do* to them. The only children they could threaten with meaningful consequences were the ones least likely to cause trouble.

He caught Judy's eye as she sat at the next desk and winked at her. She smiled back at him, rather nervously. The last time they'd gone to a party together, they'd wound up having sex in a private room...and, since then, they'd barely talked. Darrin had merely noted her as another conquest and suspected that she felt the same way too. It wasn't as if there was room for real love in his life, no matter how the girls might swoon at bad romantic flicks. No one in the CityBlocks had time for real romance.

"Please, sit down," Miss Simpson pleaded. "The test will begin shortly."

Darrin snorted to himself. There were one hundred and fifty children in the classroom – few of them were allowed to skive off, not when their parents were paid by the government for sending their children to school – and there was no way that even the most effective teacher could pay attention to all of them. He glanced around and saw a dozen conversations taking place, even when the teacher stared at them desperately.

Judy leaned across to whisper to him. Darrin stared in admiration as he saw her breasts pressed against her tight shirt. She hadn't bothered with a bra, he saw, and the memory of touching those breasts in a loveless night of passion sent heat surging through his groin. He could reach out and touch them, he knew...

"This test," Judy hissed. "Do you think it is actually *important*?"

Darrin shrugged. They were tested every three days, as far as he could tell; the tests ranged from important to completely pointless. If the test was important, the teachers would have worked over the previous two days to teach them how to *pass* the test; Miss Simpson hadn't, so logically the test was unimportant. It was just another wasted day in a whole series of wasted days. He couldn't wait for his next birthday.

One more year and I will be out of here, he thought. The nerds and geeks might stay in the system until they were twenty-one, but Darrin had no intention of remaining in school one second longer than he had to. At seventeen, he could leave school and have all that time to himself. *One more year...*

"I don't think so," he said, out loud. Behind him, a sudden fracas broke out between two boys, neither of which seemed to care about Miss Simpson's tearful pleas. "They didn't tell us much about it in advance."

Judy let out a sigh of relief. "Glad to hear it," she said. "I don't want to be grounded again."

Darrin smiled as she sat back and stretched, a movement that automatically drew his attention to her breasts. Judy's parents were odd; they believed that their daughter should actually try her hardest in school and grounded her if she didn't perform to their standards. In her place, Darrin would have filed a motion for emancipation from his parents; he didn't need that sort of pressure in his life, not when he was trying to drift through life with as little effort as possible. But Judy seemed to actually *like* her parents. Darrin couldn't have said that about his stepfather. The bastard had made it clear that he would be kicked out of the family apartment when he turned seventeen.

He briefly considered asking her out again, but he'd already had her one way and he didn't want her as a girlfriend. It wasn't something people did, not at his age. The folk in the CityBlock might not care about casual sex, but they would talk if they formed a proper relationship. Not that they wouldn't talk anyway – if there was one lesson Darrin had learned, it was that everyone lied about sex – yet it would bother him. Having a girlfriend was the first step towards having a wife...and the dreary mundane life endured by the older residents of the CityBlock.

"The test will now begin," Miss Simpson said. "This test is crucial to your future, so please answer each question carefully. Very carefully."

Darrin smiled to himself as the screen in front of him lit up, showing the name of the school - Rowdy Yates Centre of Educational Excellence

Forty-Two – and the logo of the company that had designed the test. He'd heard that schoolchildren stalked the halls of the CityBlocks looking for the test companies, intending to vandalise their premises, but none had actually *found* them. Rumour suggested that the teachers themselves actually came up with the tests, a rumour Darrin personally doubted. Very few teachers he'd met actually wanted to make their lives harder.

"There will be an important announcement at the end of the class," Miss Simpson said, desperately. "Please, take your seats and prepare for the test."

The class settled down, just long enough for the first question to appear on the screen. Miss Simpson flinched at the groan that ran through the room, then sat down at her desk. Darrin smirked to himself at her defeated expression, then looked at the question. It looked impossibly difficult, as always.

> *Person A gets into his aircar and travels at a speed of 30mph. Person B gets into his aircar and travels at a speed of 60mph. They pass each other after 10 minutes. How far apart were they when they started?*

Darrin gritted his teeth. Below the question itself, there were a set of possible answers. He skimmed them quickly, then took a guess, stabbing his finger at the first solution. The screen changed, revealing the second question, which demanded to know why the solution was the correct one. Darrin rubbed his forehead as he examined the handful of possible answers, feeling his head starting to pound. Why did they expect him to answer such questions?

Desperately, he picked another answer at random and then moved on to the third question.

———

Gary Seaman felt sweat trickling down his back as he kept his eyes on the screen, carefully not glancing either left or right. To the right, there was Moe; to the left, there was Barry...both of them obnoxious bastards who delighted in tormenting the weak and powerless. Gary knew himself to be smarter than both of the assholes put together, but somehow that wasn't enough to keep them from picking on him. And he already knew from bitter experience that complaining about it to the teachers didn't help. Barry and Moe were so strong and fearsome that even the teachers were scared of them.

The coldly logical part of his mind suggested that the teachers were right to be scared. He knew that teachers had been injured or killed by their pupils before. And yet it still gnawed at him that they would permit some of their charges to harm or even kill their other charges.

One more year, he told himself, as the first question appeared on the screen. He'd worked hard to build up his grades, working towards the moment when he could get into Imperial University and leave the CityBlock far behind. *One more year and I can get out of this death trap.*

His family had been CityBlock residents for centuries, according to his father. They'd moved in somewhere in the dim mists of prehistory, then stayed there...but Gary intended to be the first to leave. He had the brains, he had the grades; all he had to do was stay alive long enough to make his escape. Besides, it wasn't as if there was anything tying him to the block that might induce him to stay. He had no friends, not when anyone who talked to him might be picked on by the bastards. And he certainly had no girlfriend. He was a virgin and, in a class where almost everyone had lost their virginity already, it rankled.

He looked down at the question. It was surprisingly simple for their age, which confirmed his suspicion that the test wasn't actually important. God alone knew what the tests were actually intended to measure, but the students were barely allowed *any* time for self-improvement.

Person A travels three miles in ten minutes, he thought. It was logical; Person A would travel thirty miles in one hour, so he would travel...

No, that was wrong. Person A would travel five miles in ten minutes; Person B would travel ten miles in the same space of time. Logically, therefore, they were fifteen miles apart. But that assumed that they were travelling directly towards one another, or that there was nothing in the way. He knew better than to assume that the simple answer, no matter how logical, was the correct one. There were times when he'd seen the marking sheets give the wrong answer to questions, as if no one bothered to check them before they were sent to the schools.

He reread the question, looking for hidden surprises, then skimmed through the list of possible answers. There *was* one marked fifteen. He pushed down on it and jumped to the next question, which demanded to know *why* that was the correct answer. Again, there were five possible answers, so he picked the one closest to his line of thought and then moved on to the next question. It was something completely different, nothing to do with maths at all.

Snorting inwardly, he answered the question as best as he could. It was important, desperately so, for him to keep his grades up. The person who graduated with the highest ranking would win a scholarship to Imperial University, he knew, and that person had to be him. His family wouldn't make any investment in his future, certainly when they didn't think he *had* a future. But then...he looked over at Barry and shuddered. The over-muscled buffoon – the nasty part of Gary's mind wondered if his ugly appearance was due to incest – was perfectly suited to live in the Undercity. Gary had other ambitions.

Barry looked up and leered at him. Gary shuddered at the expression, knowing that he would have to run when class ended or face yet another beating. At first, they'd demanded money, but after Gary's father had stopped giving him pocket money they'd just settled for beating him up at every opportunity. And there was nowhere he could be safe, after all. They were forbidden to leave the schoolyard during the day – the electronic wristband he wore would alert the teachers if he left – and there was nowhere he could hide.

Just one more year, he told himself. *And then I can be gone.*

———

Kailee Singh didn't bother to try to answer any of the questions on the screen. She could barely read, let alone write; for her, sounding out a single question would take more time than she had to complete the entire test. Instead, she studied her appearance in the screen and smiled to herself. She looked perfect. Long black hair framed a pert face and fell down to her shirt, which exposed just enough cleavage to make the boys stare. Good enough, she told herself, to pass through the early auditions to become an actress. Good enough, she prayed, to get her out of the CityBlock once and for all.

She knew that staying in the CityBlocks was effectively a death sentence. If she were lucky, she might marry and start pumping out children, just like many of her peers. God knew that a third of the girls in the class had had kids of their own – and that there were girls in the CityBlock who were grandmothers at thirty. And if she wasn't lucky, she would wind up raped and murdered, her corpse abandoned in a dumpster and left to rot. Or married to someone who beat her on a regular basis. Her father wasn't a bad guy, as fathers went, but she knew that he had hit her stepmother more than once. She didn't want to wind up in the same boat.

Miss Simpson might have been admirable, under other circumstances. But Kailee could see the predatory glances from some of the boys and knew just what they were thinking. A young teacher – a young sexy teacher – who knew just how far they could go? And, if the poor bitch dared to complain, Kailee knew that her attackers could simply claim that she led them on. A teacher was always presumed guilty, particularly when challenged by her students.

Kailee allowed herself to slip into a daydream of life as an actress. She knew it would be hard, but it would also be something worthwhile. The very best actresses earned millions of credits in a year; by the time she retired, she would have enough money to ensure that she never had to go back to the CityBlock. A home in an upmarket part of Earth, maybe even one of the luxury orbital apartments she'd seen so often on the entertainment flicks...who knew how far she could go?

"Wake up," Dawn muttered to her. "The test's over."

Kailee made a face, but sat upright. Dawn was the closest thing she had to a friend, although she kept trying to convince Kailee to come out with her and Judy. Kailee, who had no intention of allowing anything to damage her looks, generally refused to go anywhere unless it was in a large group. But she didn't really trust her friend's boyfriend and *his* friends either...

"There is a competition coming up," Miss Simpson said. "It has been decided that a handful of students from Earth will be sent to a colony world to see how the colonials live their lives. You are all invited to submit an essay of five hundred words explaining why you would like to go to the colony world; the best-written pieces of work will be rewarded with a free trip."

There was a brief buzz of excitement as the news sank in. Kailee rolled her eyes at Miss Simpson's expression. For the first time in her life, she had the undivided attention of almost the entire class. But Kailee found it hard to care. Everyone knew that the colonies were poor worlds, populated by criminals and those who couldn't get a job on Earth; *she* certainly had no intention of submitting an essay. And besides, given that there were over ten thousand pupils in the school, who was going to *read* them all?

"Class dismissed," Miss Simpson said. "I..."

Her next words were drowned out as half of the class fled. Kailee saw Gary running for his life, with his two tormentors walking after him in a calculated manner they'd learned from countless bad entertainment flicks. Gary wasn't bad-looking, she knew – his short brown hair gave him a kind look - and he was nicer than most of the boys in the class, but he couldn't have hoped to protect her. Pity, really.

But given the way he stared when she was near him, perhaps it was for the best.

The girls waited until they were all ready, then left the room and towards the canteen as a body. Kailee glanced back, just in time to see Miss Simpson slump into the chair and cover her eyes with her hands. She felt a moment of sympathy, which was washed away in a flood of cynicism. Miss Simpson would have been through the same school system as Kailee and the others, hadn't she? What had she been thinking when she'd applied to become a teacher?

Maybe she thought it could be better if she was in charge, Kailee thought. *And she was wrong.*

She scowled, bitterly. As always, she felt hopelessly vulnerable while at school...

Because she knew that, whoever was in charge, it wasn't the teachers.

CHAPTER

TWO

The secondary purpose of education is to imbue the child with the values, ideals and social mores of the surrounding society. No man (or child) is an island; sooner or later the child will have to leave the family home and interact with outsiders. When he or she does so, education provides the training to navigate such a potentially hostile minefield successfully.

- Professor Leo Caesius, *Education and the Decline and Fall of the Galactic Empire*

Another fucking essay, Gary thought, as he stepped into the canteen. *Another goddamned fucking essay.*

Swearing in his head didn't do much for his feelings. He had too much work to do already, starting with the standard coursework and moving on to the extra credit materials he did in a desperate attempt to boost his grades. Thankfully, the essay didn't seem too complicated...but there was a nasty sting in the tale. The sensible answer might not be the one they were looking for.

He considered, briefly, just refusing to enter the competition. Most of his fellow pupils would do just that, he was sure. Few of them had the determination or the drive to leave the CityBlocks where their parents and grandparents had lived out their lives; they knew, as clearly as Gary himself, that it was possible to live without good grades. After all, there were no real consequences for bad grades, unless it was remaining in the towering CityBlocks. But if one wanted to leave, one had to have near-perfect grades. Gary didn't dare get a black mark on his record, not now. And not entering the competition might well earn him a markdown from whoever was in charge of collecting the essays.

There was no sign of Moe or Barry as he joined the line of students waiting to be served their food. Gary let out a sigh of relief, although he knew that the two bullies were probably on their way. It was forbidden to bring food in from outside the school and parents could be fined if their children were caught with non-school food, something that was surprisingly effective in keeping it out of the compound. Gary could only wonder why the authorities didn't use similar methods to keep the worst pupils under control. After all, some of them picked on tutors and teachers as well as their fellow students.

He took a plate of food and eyed it doubtfully. It was little more than a plate of algae-based stew, which they had been told provided everything that a growing child needed to stay healthy. After twelve years in the school system, Gary knew that it was almost completely tasteless, even though it would have been easy to add a flavour to the gruel. He'd once tried to find out why the food was never flavoured, only to draw a complete blank. The only answer he could think of that made sense was that there was no money in flavouring school food. If the people in charge – whoever they were – thought nothing of allowing bullying to run rampant through the school, they probably didn't care about making the food tasty as well as healthy.

If it is healthy, he thought, as he took a bite. It was lukewarm and felt unpleasant against his tongue, so he washed it down with water. He remembered all too clearly the first time he had been introduced to school food. Swallowing it as a boy of four had been a thoroughly unpleasant experience. *I wouldn't put money on it.*

He placed his reader on the table beside him and started to think, hoping to distract himself from the tasteless food. The essay would have to be completed as soon as possible, perhaps in the afterschool classes that were compulsory for all students. But what answer were they actually looking *for*? The truth – that he didn't want to go to a colony world, even for a few short months – wouldn't go down well with whoever was marking the essays. But what answer did they actually *want*?

Why would they want me to go to a colony world? The question buzzed through his head, he turned it around and around. *They'd want me to show the locals how to live.*

It seemed a plausible answer, he decided. They hadn't been told much about the colony worlds, but what they had been told wasn't very encouraging. The colonies were founded by settlers from Earth, yet they lacked the true civilisation that made Earth such a wonderful place to live. Gary, who knew perfectly well that Earth was *not* a decent place to live, found it hard to imagine anywhere worse. And yet the images they'd been shown had told them of men scrabbling to pull foodstuffs out of the soil and women desperately trying to survive the pangs of childbirth. Earth's vast social security network was simply not present on the colonies.

Carefully, he shaped the answer in his mind. He would like to go so that he could show the value of living on Earth. It was toadying, he knew, but there were quite a few teachers and professors who appreciated it when the student recited official dogma back at them. He made a mental note to look up the textbooks on the colonies, then add quotes to suggest how Earth's solutions would fit the colonies and solve all of their problems. It would be completely absurd, he suspected, but that wouldn't matter. If there was one thing he had learned after years of schooling, it was that the right answer was the answer they wanted, not the one that made the most sense.

The only danger, he decided, as he stood up and carried his tray over to the waste disposal tube, was that he might actually *win* the competition. But it seemed unlikely. Assuming that only ten students could go – and Miss Simpson hadn't been precise about the exact number – and only a third of the school entered the competition, there would still be hundreds of thousands of possible winners. The odds of not going were in his favour. Somehow, he doubted that the teachers would actually *read* the essays and mark them, not when the poor bastards barely had the time to handle their classes. They used the readers and examination machines to save time...

Shaking his head, he walked out of the canteen and down towards the history classroom. If he were lucky, he would be able to get inside and wait for the teacher there. Neither Barry nor Moe were likely to go to the classroom a moment before they absolutely *had* to go, not when their parents would probably be fined too. Gary had occasionally wondered why the teachers simply didn't let them skive off from school – everyone would win – but it wasn't the teachers who monitored the students. That was the job of yet another department.

He slipped inside the classroom and sat down, pulling his reader out of his pocket. All he could do now was wait – and, perhaps, start working on the essay.

————

"A trip to the colonies," Sally proclaimed, as the girls picked at their food. "Can you imagine it?"

Kailee could. A week or two away from civilisation, away from sophisticated medical treatments that helped keep her face flawless and her body slim. None of the images she'd seen of the colony worlds had suggested that they were good places to live, although they'd all shared a giggle at the sight of topless men in the fields, bringing in the crops. She took another bite of her food, then pushed the rest of the tray towards one of her friends. She'd be hungry for the rest of the day, but it was better than overeating. Dangerously slim was *in* at the moment and she didn't dare put on weight.

"Just enter a blank piece of paper," Joanne suggested. "They never bother to read these essays anyway."

"But then they wouldn't know who *deserved* to win," Sally objected, with mock horror. "Imagine going out there and breaking a nail."

Kailee tuned them out and started to daydream about her future career. One more year of schooling, then she could start applying to talent scouts and casting agencies. She knew, without false modesty, that she was beautiful, very much like the current crop of celebrities who dominated the entertainment channels. All she would have to do was impress the scouts and she would be on her way. It was a shame that they weren't allowed to act in school, but the one time she'd asked about putting on a school play she'd been told that they were elitist and threatened with having her grades marked down when she'd asked *why*. After that, she'd given up and practiced her acting at home.

She could easily see herself in a dozen different roles. Stellar Star, Queen of the Spaceways; there were over a hundred entertainment flicks based around those stories, starring twenty different actresses in the lead role. Or galactic super-spy Jonny Barracuda...maybe she couldn't take the lead role in that franchise, but she could play the incredibly hot female agent who was assigned to him whenever he landed on a new world. She'd be reluctant to take part in a soap opera – she had always found them boring – yet one of them might launch her career into high orbit. Or...

The daydreaming kept her occupied as the girls finished their meals and dumped the remainder in the disposal tubes. At first, they'd been lectured on not wasting food, even though they had struggled to finish their meals. Later, they'd discovered that there were no real consequences for throwing away half their trays and just carried on – or given the food to the handful of students who actually *liked* it. In theory, that too was forbidden, but the teachers tended to turn a blind eye. Whenever Kailee bothered to think about it, the dull illogic of the school puzzled her. But she had long since chosen her own course, one taking her well away from her CityBlock.

She walked with the other girls down towards the history classroom, keeping one eye out for trouble. It just wasn't safe, even in what was meant to be a supervised environment. She still recalled the shock of a gang of boys invading the girls toilet, four years ago. The immature little brats had run in, catcalled at the girls and then fled before anyone could catch them, although she knew that they would probably have escaped punishment. If pupils could get away with harming their teachers, they could get away with being creepy and invading toilets.

Inside, they sat down and chatted about nothing. Kailee tuned them out effortlessly and went back to daydreaming. It was so much better than reality.

Darrin hadn't bothered to give the question of why he would want to go to the colonies much thought. The truth was that he couldn't decide if he actually wanted to go or not. Part of him thought that it would be an adventure, just like those he saw on the entertainment channels, but the rest of him suspected that the teachers would find a way to suck all the interesting parts out and leave them with dry dust and boredom. It was astonishing just how subjects that might have been interesting had been drained of life by the schools.

"Class, be seated," Mr. Rogers said. "We shall resume our study of the Unification Treaties that ended the wars."

He went on without waiting for the class to quiet down. "In 80EE, the third set of treaties were signed between the Empire and various interested parties. Those treaties ensured that the Empire would remain unchallenged in the sectors surrounding Sol and laid the groundwork for the assimilation of those parties into the Empire..."

Darrin rolled his eyes. The Unification Treaties – and the importance of Unification – were probably important, but he knew almost nothing about them. Who had been fighting the Empire – and *why* had they been fighting? The lectures were vague, almost completely imprecise, until he could regurgitate facts without having any idea of their context. And when he'd asked about the Unification Wars, as a young child, he'd been sent to a counsellor for an examination. The wars were largely a forbidden subject, barely touched on and almost always in passing.

He would have liked to know the truth behind the entertainment videos. There was no shortage of war movies freely available on the planetary datanet. But the schools refused to talk about the whole issue, leaving him bored out of his mind. Who gave a damn about the treaties anyway? Surely the wars before them were much more exciting.

"These treaties were important because they established a framework of law that they used to build the Empire," Mr. Rogers continued. "For the first time in thousands of years, there was a unified code of law. This was important because previously there were many different codes of law; what was permitted on one planet might be forbidden on others. This led to problems when someone committed, all unknowing, a crime that caused a diplomatic incident. Now, those problems were eliminated at the stroke of a pen."

Darrin snorted to himself. The boredom was threatening to overwhelm him. He glanced around and saw that several students were taking advantage of the class to catch up on their sleep, placing their heads on the desk and closing their eyes. Judy was sitting with the other girls, sadly; Darrin tried to catch her eye, but she either missed his glance or ignored it completely. He briefly considered trying to get some sleep himself, before deciding that he needed some other entertainment. Carefully leaning forward, he kicked the back of Gary's chair. The nerd let out a surprisingly loud yelp.

"Yes, Mr. Seaman?" Mr. Rogers asked. "Is there a problem?"

The back of Gary's neck turned red as the class tittered. Darrin smiled; it was just the nerd's rotten luck that he had a name that could be turned into an object of easy mockery. But if he would only stand up for himself once or twice...not that he could. Gary wasn't strong or tough or determined to hurt his enemies even if he were to be hurt worse. He was just a wimp and the CityBlocks had no place for wimps.

"No, sir," Gary said. He shuffled forwards, although with the chairs bolted to the floor it was impossible to move out of Darrin's reach. "No problem."

Darrin saw Barry and Moe smirking and grinned to himself, then sobered. If there was one lesson that everyone learned quickly in the CityBlocks, it was that you had to look after yourself or submit yourself to someone else who would look after you. It was why Darrin's mother had married his stepfather, trading the occasional beating from him for safety from everyone else. The man was a sadist – Darrin wanted to kill him one day – but he did manage to protect his wife from everyone else. Gary... had no such protection, nor did he have any friends who might help him defend himself.

"Glad to hear it," Mr. Rogers said. He exercised his sarcasm on the students who didn't have the nerve to fight back, either directly or indirectly. "Please be quiet while we resume our study of history."

He clasped his hands behind his back as he addressed the class. "These treaties also gave the Empire the legitimacy to unify the remaining inhabited worlds, even if their inhabitants objected to becoming part of the Empire. In addition, vast numbers of people who wished their own colony worlds were shipped to new places where they could live, subject only to the Empire. The First Emperor..."

Darrin rolled his eyes as the teacher droned on. He'd actually read several biographies of the First Emperor after watching an entertainment flick about his life, but it hadn't taken him long to realise that each biography had contradicted the others. The man's life was more myth than reality, with some books claiming that he had been born on Earth and others that he was a superior being who had descended from the heavens to rule the human race. If he had so much as stubbed his toe, it hadn't made it into any of the biographies. Maybe Darrin was just cynical, but he couldn't help wondering if the First Emperor had really existed. How did they *know* he'd lived?

"For homework," Mr. Rogers concluded, "you will write an outline of the basic treaties and submit it at the end of the week, then log into the school datanet and answer the questions on the test. Class dismissed."

Darrin rose to his feet, hastily. He hadn't been paying attention, but Mr. Rogers was one of the teachers who rarely bothered to collect homework; if it wasn't handed in, he just didn't care. Nerds like Gary would hand it in, he was sure, but nothing seemed to happen to the children who didn't give a shit. Besides, there were more important matters than homework, particularly *history* homework. His name was down for playing basketball after class, during the mandatory afterschool classes. It was about the only thing they did at school that interested him, even though none of them were actually allowed to *win*.

And we keep the scores in our head, he said, turning so he could see Judy as she stood up. He could ask her out for the weekend, if he moved quickly. She would be willing, he was sure...or maybe he should ask one of the other girls. Perhaps a *real* challenge, like Kailee. There was no shortage of bragging among the boys over their conquests, but Kailee had never been lured into bed by anyone. Maybe he could try...

Grinning at the thought, he followed the other pupils out of the room, towards their next class.

CHAPTER
THREE

In addition, the child must learn how to interact with his or her peers. This is not easy; children are, by nature, selfish. They must learn to come to terms with the fact that they are not unique and that society does not, must not, put them first.

- Professor Leo Caesius, Education and the Decline and Fall of the Galactic Empire

Gary let out a sigh of relief as he made his way into the classroom that was reserved for afterschool studies. Few of his fellow pupils would willingly come into the classroom, not when they bitterly resented having to remain in school for an additional two hours. Gary himself resented it; he could work just as easily at home, without having to worry that Barry or Moe would come after him. Even *they* would hesitate before breaking into an apartment complex.

Only because dad pays off the gangs, Gary thought, bitterly. The gangs that controlled the CityBlock took payments from the residents, in exchange for leaving them alone and even providing protection from unauthorised thieves. No doubt Barry and Moe would go straight into the gangs as soon as they left school, if they weren't gang members already. They were always bragging about their connections, about how they could get anything their fellow students wanted – for a price, of course.

He pushed the thought aside. The day's humiliation had been bad enough, but he knew that there was worse to come, unless he managed to dodge Barry and Moe on the way home. Not that he was surprised that Darrin had attacked him; when his classmates were bored, Gary was often their favourite target for mischief. His schoolwork could be deleted at any moment, his few possessions stolen and hidden – if he was lucky. If not... he remembered, his cheeks flushing with shame, the day he'd had to walk home naked. They'd stolen his clothes, then left him alone.

Bitterly, he pulled out the reader, cursing the person who had come up with the whole idea of the competition. They didn't care, did they, that the students might have other work to do? Or that there were some students who were so desperate to escape that they were working frantically to earn the highest marks? No, all they cared about was...what? No matter how much he considered the question, he honestly couldn't think of how they benefited. Unless they actually *wanted* a group of students to go to the colonies...but even that made no sense as far as he could tell.

One more year, he told himself, firmly. As long as he kept his grades up, entry to Imperial University should be a snap. And then he could leave Barry and Moe and all of Rowdy Yates CityBlock behind, for good. Wherever he ended up had to be better than spending the rest of his life in a tiny apartment, hiding from the gangs. *One more year and then I can be gone.*

He accessed the datanet, downloaded a copy of the formal instructions, then started to work on his reader. At least he *could* write, unlike the students who had to dictate their work to the computers, which would then transcribe it into something legible. There wasn't a specific word count, thankfully, but he knew that meant they wanted at least a thousand words. Piece by piece, he put the essay together, reread it for obvious mistakes – although he'd never noticed anyone get marked down for poor spelling or grammar – then tapped the submit button.

And then he got back to *real* work.

———

Darrin caught the ball Hamish tossed to him, then passed it to Sadat before Charlie could try to snatch the ball out of his hands. Sadat threw his ball at the hoop and, after a brief heart-stopping moment, scored for the team. The PE teacher blew a whistle, acknowledging the point, then waved cheerfully as Charlie grabbed the ball and threw it back towards the far end of the court. One of his teammates caught it, then lost possession as he was tackled by another player. The ball bounced towards the edge of the court; Darrin gave chase, trying to get his hands on it before the ball could strike the wall. That would have given the other side a free shot.

He grinned as he snatched up the ball a moment before it could strike the wall and threw it over Charlie's head, towards Gavin. Gavin fumbled the catch – there was a groan from Darrin's team – and lost the ball to Yoda, who threw it back towards the other end of the court. There might be no official scorekeeper – for some reason, scoring was officially forbidden in school – but his team were definitely in the lead. Sweat trickled down his back as he followed the rest of the team after the ball. As long as they held the ball in their possession, they were in the lead.

The PE teacher blew his whistle again, tapping his wrist meaningfully. Darrin shared a disappointed look with the rest of the team, but they filed off the court anyway. Mr. Howarth was the only teacher most of the pupils respected, if only because he skirted the rules on scoring and rewarding the better players as much as possible. Darrin couldn't understand why team captains weren't allowed to make their own decisions – or why they couldn't actually have a declared winner and loser – even though the games were obviously set up to allow just that. But Mr. Howarth bent the rules in their favour and Darrin was grateful for that, sometimes.

"Have to play outside the school tonight," Joe muttered, as they lined up outside the protective bars. The boys were sweaty and smelt horrid, but few of them would willingly refuse to watch the girls playing afterwards. "See who actually wins."

Darrin nodded. There were no sports centres for young teenagers that allowed them to play properly, but they'd located quite a few abandoned storage compartments that were large enough for a full – and sometime quite violent – game. They had to pay a bribe to the gangs, of course, yet apart from that it was perfect. Hell, the gang members sometimes came to watch – or shout advice from the sidelines. And they did a roaring trade in illegal alcohol, drugs and VR flicks too.

He allowed his smile to grow wider as the girls began to play. Whoever had designed their outfits was an absolute genius; the girls who wore shorts showed off the shape of their buttocks, while the ones who wore skirts flashed their panties from time to time. The boys catcalled, leered and jeered whenever they saw something interesting, until Mr. Howarth finally told them to get lost. Darrin was the first to leave when the PE teacher started bellowing orders at them; Mr. Howarth might have as little disciplinary power as the rest of the teachers, but he was capable of banning someone from the sports field if he felt like it...and no one would dare complain. After all, if they got Mr. Howarth sacked, his replacement might well be worse.

The showers were smelly and unpleasant, but he was used to it by now. He stripped off his shorts and shirt, dumped them in the basket to be washed, then stepped under the water and allowed it to wash him clean. As always, it was lukewarm and there was never enough of it for anyone. The one time he'd asked, he'd been told that water was carefully rationed and given a lecture on the importance of conserving resources. It hadn't been until much later that he'd realised that every drop of water that was flushed into the waste disposal system was recycled, cleansed and fed right back into the distribution network. There wasn't any waste at all.

He dried himself under a gust of hot air – once again, there wasn't enough air to dry him completely – and stepped out into the changing room, where his clothes were waiting for him. The bracelet he wore opened the locker, allowing him to remove his clothes and dress quickly. It was irritating to have to secure everything, wherever he went, but even the toughest kids were not immune to having their possessions stolen. He glanced in the mirror, decided he looked reasonably clean, and then walked out of the changing room. Kailee wasn't a sporty girl, not like some of the others. She valued her good looks too much to play sports.

Darrin paused as he walked back through the viewing gallery. A girl was sitting there, crying. She was chubby, chubby enough to make playing games or attracting a boy difficult, if not impossible. And she hadn't seen him...Darrin hesitated, held in place by an impulse he didn't fully understand. Part of him wanted to go to her, to comfort her...and the rest of him knew that it was a waste of time. Helping a social outcast was a good way to become a social outcast yourself.

The girl's shirt had been torn, he saw, and there was a nasty bruise on her face. She had to have been pushed into the railings, he decided; he'd seen similar injuries on boys, when the struggle for the ball had turned into a shoving contest. He'd been told, time and time again, that girls were no different from boys. When it came to bullying, he'd seen, it was perfectly true. The strong girls picked on the weak girls and everyone in the middle supported the strong, for fear of being made a target themselves.

And the girl still hadn't see him...

Shaking his head, he walked away. There was nothing he could do for her.

————

Alone in the classroom, Kailee sat in her chair, staring down at the images on her reader. The latest models were strutting their stuff on the catwalks, each one wearing a dress that was worth more than the combined yearly income of everyone on her apartment floor. They all looked completely perfect, their faces free of any blemishes that might mar their careers. Kailee felt envy swelling in her heart, even as she worked out how best to approach the talent scouts. For one reason or another, they were rarely permitted to come to school and recruit openly.

She made a face as she downloaded yet another page of advice, then listened as her reader read the words to her. Everyone seemed to have different ideas of what to do; one suggested merely sending a photograph and contact details, others suggested full videos and even nude shots. Kailee wasn't sure she wanted to do *that*. If it was a requirement, she would do it, yet she wasn't comfortable with it at all. And yet she knew that many models were required to wear skimpy clothes...or no clothes at all.

Stellar Star had plenty of nude scenes, she knew; she'd watched every flick religiously, searching for the secret behind the actress's success. The famous starship commander had slept with so many people that it was hard to understand how she had managed to get command of a starship at all, unless it was through the goodwill of the senior officers she'd allowed into her bed. And then there was the famous *Stellar Star XXVI: In Enemy Chains*, where Stellar Star had fallen into enemy hands and endured a long BDSM session which had ended with the torturer falling in love with her and helping her to escape.

Maybe I will have to do it, she thought, *but I want to put it off as long as possible.*

Mentally, she composed the letter she intended to use to approach the agents. She was young, attractive, willing to do whatever it took to succeed...surely, they would appreciate someone like her. And there were no shortage of agents; if one refused her, she would just go to the next one and the next, until she found someone willing to take her on.

She clicked off the images as someone stepped into the classroom. Her plans for the future were hers and hers alone; she knew, all too well, just how easy it would be for one of her classmates to sabotage her dreams. Those who let their dreams become public knowledge made themselves vulnerable. Instead, she flicked the reader to the instructions for the colony essay and turned around. Darrin was standing there, admiring her back.

Kailee shivered, inwardly. Darrin wasn't one of the truly bad or dangerous boys – although the girls knew that every boy could be dangerous, given the right situation – but she still didn't trust him any further than she could throw the entire school. Maybe he didn't cop a feel when he had a chance, yet that meant nothing. He'd been quick enough to get into bed with Judy when she'd offered – and equally quick to refuse to become her official boyfriend. But then, that *would* have forced him to protect her.

"Darrin," she said, as coolly as she could. A hint of invitation would have him in her face before she knew what was happening. "What can I do for you?"

Darrin smiled. "I was merely wondering why you were here," he said, unconvincingly. "Are you all right?"

Kailee didn't smile. "I'm working," she lied, turning the reader so he could see the essay instructions. "I need to have this finished before tonight."

"Oh?" Darrin asked. "What's tonight?"

"Flicks I want to watch," Kailee said, cursing her own mistake. She wanted to end the conversation as soon as possible, but she'd given him a hook to keep it going. "And my parents won't be happy if I don't get good grades."

"Sucks to have parents like that," Darrin said. He gave her a look that was probably meant to be sympathetic. "Do your grades really matter?"

Kailee shrugged. Her parents, in truth, didn't really care *what* she did; they'd long since lost interest in their extended family. If she was kicked out of school – which almost never happened - they were unlikely to say anything to her. And besides, good grades weren't important in the acting world. All that mattered, as far as she could tell, were good looks and a determination to work hard to get the best roles.

"I was wondering," Darrin said. "Would you like to come to the party with me this weekend?"

No, Kailee thought. But would he accept it if she just refused? Some of the boys would, she knew, but others believed that if they asked again and again the girl would eventually give in. And then there were the ones who thought that 'no' actually meant 'yes' or that being firm with the girl would be enough to make her submit and open her legs. She braced herself as best as she could, hoping that she could hurt him if he tried anything. There would be no help from anyone if he tried to force himself on her right there and then.

"I'm going to be busy this weekend," she said, untruthfully. Her only real plans had been to spend more time studying the famous models and actresses and working out how they rose to such dizzying heights. "I won't have time, I'm sorry."

Darrin gave her a toothy grin. "Come on," he wheedled. "You'll have a good time."

Kailee shook her head, trying to look regretful. She knew from other girls how those parties generally went; there would be some dancing, some alcohol...and then the boy would start trying to get into their date's panties. Sometimes the girl welcomed it; sometimes she was too drunk to care – or offer resistance. It wasn't as if anyone else would help her, even if she was trying to fight. The whole idea was laughable.

"I have to work," she said, firmly. "Sorry."

Darrin smiled at her. "Maybe next week?"

Kailee gritted her teeth. She wanted to say no directly, but who knew how he would react to that? Would he accept it or attack her? There was no way to know.

"Ask me nearer the time," she temporised. "My parents are being quite demanding this year."

Darrin looked disappointed, but nodded and walked off. Kailee rolled her eyes at his back; he was walking in a manner deliberately calculated to show off his ass and leg muscles. He looked thoroughly ridiculous, although she knew better than to say it out loud. Being alone, even long enough to indulge her dreaming, was foolish. She picked up the reader, followed him out of the room and headed down to where she knew the other girls were chatting. Even their brainless chatter would be better than a conversational minefield with a boy.

She caught sight of Joanne's bruised face as she entered the common room and winced inwardly, keeping her reaction hidden. Joanne shouldn't be playing basketball or anything else, but her parents had insisted that she play with the other girls...which was nothing more than a hellish experience for the chubby girl. She might look better if she lost some weight, but she wouldn't lose anything through playing games. And someone had torn her shirt.

Feeling an odd moment of pity, Kailee removed her bag from the locker and produced her spare shirt, tossing it over to Joanne. The chubby girl stared; Kailee tapped her lips hastily, before Joanne could say a word. Helping someone, no matter how badly they needed help, was often taken as a sign of weakness. It wasn't something she could afford.

Sitting down, she produced her reader and submitted a blank essay. Really, what did it matter if the essay was blank or not? It wasn't as if *she* was going to a colony world, not when they would have no place for her...

And she had her own life to think about, on Earth. Who cared about the colonies, really?

CHAPTER

FOUR

But, most importantly of all, the educational process must teach a child how to think and solve problems. Most skills can be mastered through practice, once the purpose behind them is reasoned out.

- Professor Leo Caesius, Education and the Decline and Fall of the Galactic Empire

Gary stepped into the security gate, cursing the designer under his breath. They were so obsessed with school safety...and yet they cared nothing for *his* safety. The child who brought a knife or even a pen to school might face hours of questioning from the teachers, security officers and even the Civil Guard, but they didn't take away *fists*, did they? He could never defend himself against bare fists, not without a weapon. And weapons were banned, while they did nothing to keep out the attitudes that caused violence.

There was a buzz as the scanner swept his body. "Place your reader in the drawer," a toneless voice ordered. Gary sighed and obeyed, passing the reader over for safekeeping. It was better, he supposed, than having it stolen, but it still grated on him. "Place your bracelet against the scanner."

There was a click as the bracelet unlocked, falling away from his wrist. Gary dropped it in the basket, then braced himself to run. The other gate opened, allowing him to escape; he ran, passing a handful of other students as he fled towards the stairs leading to the upper levels. If he was lucky, he might just manage to put a space between himself and his tormentors before they made it through the gate. He was rarely grateful for the security precautions, which he knew to be completely ineffective, but they did slow down Barry and Moe. The idiots had a habit of trying to steal from the school.

But the whole process was just annoying. They were meant to be in school from nine to three, then two more hours of mandatory after-school care. In reality, they had to arrive at the school early enough to pass through the security gates, then wasted more time in the evening waiting to pass through the gates in reverse. Pushing the thought aside, he reached the stairs and sprinted up them as fast as he could, then into the long overpass that led to his apartment block. There was hardly anyone else about, not when they knew that the school pupils were coming out of school. They wouldn't want to be mugged or molested by angry students.

"Hey, Semen," a voice called.

Gary skidded to a halt as Barry stepped out of the shadows, ahead of him. For a moment, his mind refused to process what he was seeing. How the hell had the bastard managed to get *ahead* of him? It should have been impossible...maybe he'd just sprinted the long way around. Gary didn't need to look behind him to know that Moe was standing there, just waiting for him to try to run. The two bullies worked as a team.

"We are truly sorry to call on you," Barry said, with mocking polite-ness. He'd taken the act from a flick they'd had to watch in school, one where the villain had been chillingly polite and the heroes had been ridiculously rude. "But I'm afraid you have to pay the toll if you wish to proceed."

Gary took a step backwards as Barry advanced, threateningly. The overpasses were neutral ground as far as the gangs were concerned; they served as useful barriers between their areas of influence. No one was likely to come help him, as Barry and Moe knew very well. He took another step backwards and crashed into a solid form, who grabbed his arms and twisted them behind his back. Barry walked up to him, coming so close that Gary could smell something unpleasant on his breath, and started to go through Gary's pockets. There was nothing, apart from a sheet of paper with a handful of notes he'd made for himself.

"Trying to show off, are you?" Barry demanded, as he waved the paper in front of Gary's eyes. "Trying to prove yourself better than us?"

Gary kept his mouth shut. Learning to read had been difficult, but once he'd mastered the skill he'd discovered a whole new world of literature and entertainment that would be forever closed to those without the ability to read. Barry, Moe and two-thirds of the class had never learned how to read a book. They were completely dependent upon the readers. In a fair world, that should have put Gary at the top and them at the bottom. But the world was far from *fair*.

"And you didn't even bring anything for us," Barry said. "Why not?"

Gary glared at him, mutely. He was too frightened to move, but he was damned if he was going to give Barry the satisfaction of admitting that his father had stopped giving him his allowance – even if it was mandated by law – so it wouldn't be stolen by the bullies. Barry didn't wait for an answer, he merely punched Gary in the stomach, hard enough to leave him choking helplessly. Moe let go of him a moment later; Gary crumpled to the ground, gasping in pain. No matter how often they hit him – and it was a rare day that he wasn't hurt by someone – he never quite got used to it.

"Leave him," Barry said. He bent down to speak directly to Gary. "And you'd better have something for us next time, you little shit."

Gary barely heard him through the pain. It took all of his determination to stand upright on bendy legs, then stagger through the overpass. Barry and Moe seemed to have vanished completely; Gary silently cursed them, wishing that someone – anyone – would come to his aid. But no one would help a stranger, not on Earth. There was no profit in getting involved and a great deal of risk.

Somehow, he managed to make it through the overpass and into the apartment block. It was safer than the rest of the CityBlock, even if they *did* have to pay off the gangs. Even Barry and Moe would hesitate to start something there, or to break gang law when they left school and joined the gangs. From what Gary had learned, mainly by listening and keeping his mouth shut, the gangs knew better than to push their victims too far. There was no point in killing the goose that laid the golden eggs.

"Hey," Sammie called. "Are you all right?"

Gary shuddered. Sammie, his nine-year-old sister...and, just like him, a victim at school and everywhere else. She was pretty enough to be noticed; he dreaded the day when she grew into a young woman, for he knew that she would be picked on by her fellow classmates. Or she would have to put out for someone who could protect her...he'd seen it happen, more than once, but it always ended badly. The protector got bored or annoyed; if bored, he moved on to the next woman; if annoyed, he took it out on his former girlfriend first.

"No," he muttered. "Piss off."

Her face paled; Gary felt a twinge of guilt for snapping at her, which he pushed aside as he stumbled into his room and sat down in front of the computer. It was mandatory for every schoolchild to have a computer, which were supplied free of charge by the government; naturally, it hadn't taken Gary long to realise that the government-issued computers came with special limiting software built in. Cracking the codes that allowed him unfettered access to the planetary datanet had been surprisingly simple, once he'd learned how to break into the computer codes. And it really was astonishing just how much was buried in the system, hidden from casual view.

Turning the computer on, he opened the game he'd been playing with hundreds of other players – all online. It was a relatively simple combat game, but with human players it rapidly became more complicated. And Gary knew, without false modesty, that he was damn good at it. There, online, he was a hero, he was respected. It almost made up for the time he had to endure Barry and Moe – and what they considered funny.

Bastards, he thought. Thankfully, neither of them played computer and datanet games, at least as far as he knew. He often fantasized that they were the players he slaughtered, one by one, in the computer network. Or that the maidens he had to rescue wore the faces of his female classmates. *An hour of playing and then I will get on with my homework.*

Three hours later, he was still playing. It was so easy to lose himself in the fantasy world, where he was far more than a helpless nerd picked on by everyone and his brother. There, he was big and strong – and no one dared to mess with him. He could do whatever he liked, free of worries.

It was so much better than the real world.

———

Darrin slipped into his apartment carefully, keeping a wary eye out for Fitz. His stepfather's work – whatever it was – gave him variable hours, something that made it difficult for Darrin to be sure of when he would be in or out of the apartment. He scowled as he caught sight of the empty bottles on one of the tables, knowing that meant that Fitz was home...and probably halfway to drunkenness by now. There was no sign of his mother.

He stepped into the kitchen and saw a bottle of processed milk, just waiting for him. Darrin poured himself a glass, then stepped back into the living room. The bottles looked to have been recently emptied, he decided, as he sat down on the sofa. A moment later, Fitz lurched into the room and stumbled to a halt in front of Darrin, who backed away carefully. The last thing he wanted was another fight with the older man. His mother would suffer for it.

"So you're home, boy," Fitz slurred. "What are you doing here?"

"I just got back from school," Darrin said. It was impossible to tell what would set his stepfather off. There were days when he was almost tolerable and days when Darrin had to fight down the urge to take one of his damn bottles and bust his head with it. "I'm having a rest."

"Well, you can fuck off and have your rest somewhere else," Fitz told him, turning and sitting down so close to him that Darrin leapt up at once. A centimetre to the left and Darrin would have been squashed under his bulk. "I'm busy here."

Darrin watched as Fitz picked up the remote control, then hurried out of the room as soon as he saw the channel Fitz was planning to watch. It showed sexual scenes that would have disgusted even Barry and Moe, scenes that made Darrin sick to even contemplate. He hesitated as soon as he had closed the door, then stepped into the bedroom his mother shared with Fitz. His mother lay on the bed, drunk out of her mind. Darrin winced in sympathy, then closed the door and walked down to his own bedroom. Inside, he locked the door – it was a right for every child to have a lockable room – and lay down on the bed. There was nothing he could do, he knew, for his mother. Even if he had been strong enough to beat hell out of Fitz – and Fitz had thrashed him once or twice, just to show him who was boss – Fitz would still make their lives hell. All he could do was wait, get an apartment of his own as soon as he was seventeen...

... And then what?

There was college, of course, and a bigger Student Living Allowance from the government, but what would he do after that? Of course, he could join the gangs. He could fight, if he had to, and he could run gambling games...and yet, he knew that joining the gangs was a ticket to a violent death. Most gangsters didn't last past their thirtieth year, if they were lucky.

And there were jobs...but the truth was that nothing really interested him enough to try to turn it into a career. He didn't have the skills or connections to become a sports star, he didn't have the intelligence or patience to operate a computer all day and everyone knew that the military was a pool for losers. There were some advantages, he knew, to joining the Civil Guard – he knew how much fun they had, harassing people – but it might not last very long. And there was no guarantee that he would be stationed on Earth...

He leaned back on his bed and closed his eyes. If nothing else, he could get a few hours of sleep before he slipped out to join the illegal basketball games. He could work off some steam there, then try to talk one of the girls into bed. It might help him forget his problems for a while, if she was good enough. Kailee might have rejected him, but there were plenty of other fish in the sea.

Judy puts out, he thought. He knew that from personal experience. *So does Karen and Rose and Sharon. All I have to do is get to them before someone else takes them away.*

———

Kailee walked with the other girls through the overpass, trying to sound brash and completely fearless as they made their way into the apartment block. No girl with a lick of common sense would go anywhere alone, certainly in the giant CityBlocks. Everyone knew that robbery, rape and murder was constantly on the rise, no matter how much the news broadcasts tried to downplay it. There was no shortage of people who had lost a daughter, girlfriend, wife or relative to a rapist who killed after he had had his fun. Safety in numbers was the only way to get around, at least outside the apartment themselves.

She didn't relax as they walked into the apartment block, for the gangsters were waiting. The bribes they had been paid kept them from *touching* the girls, but they didn't stop the gangsters from watching, whistling or calling out crude invitations. Many of the invitations even sounded good, yet Kailee had heard the stories. A gangster boyfriend would be kind and loving for a month, then start gently pushing the girl into prostitution and eventually abandon her to one of the cheap and nasty brothels at the very lowest level of the CityBlock. If, of course, she lasted that long. There were occasional skirmishes between the gangs that ended in girls being kidnapped and put to work elsewhere, without even a fig-leaf of justification.

"Hey, baby," one of the gangsters called, thrusting his pelvis forward. "Light my fire?"

Kailee ignored him, keeping her eyes fixed firmly on the floor until they were past the checkpoint and heading into the residential area. Even simple eye contact could be interpreted badly – and she knew better than to think that anyone would come to her rescue, if the gangster snatched her. It was a relief when she finally reached her apartment and pressed her fingertips against the sensor, allowing her to step inside.

Her family must have annoyed someone in the bureaucracy, she knew, for the twenty-seven of them were crammed into one relatively small apartment. Kailee's father had two sisters and a brother, all of whom had a partner of their own and several children. She had to share her bedroom – despite the law – with four other girls, all younger than her and terribly irritating. No matter how much she begged and pleaded, her father had refused to emancipate her ahead of schedule, pointing out that she was really too young to apply for her own apartment. It wouldn't be safe.

"Kailee," her aunt said. As always with Aunt Lillian, there was no break, nothing but demands, demands and demands. At least her parents left her alone most of the time, although in such a cramped apartment it was hard to be really *alone*. "Come help with the washing."

Kailee shook her head, muttered something about needing to rest and then fled into her bedroom, closing the door behind her. She dropped her bag on the bed and scowled at the mess. The little monsters had been in her makeup kit again, applying the expensive products – she'd saved for months to buy them – to their faces in hopes of making themselves look better. Swearing out loud, she picked up what remained and stuffed them under her bed, knowing that it would only delay them the next time around. There was no point in complaining to her father and his siblings, not when they didn't have the money to replace what their kids had damaged, nor the nerve to actually punish them. But then, a kid's complaint against his or her parents might easily be upheld.

Unless it comes from me, she thought, sourly. She was almost sure that her uncle had peeked at her two weeks ago, when she'd been in the shower. But she didn't know...

Bitterly, she lay down on the bed and forced herself to concentrate, plotting the email she planned to send to the agents as soon as she turned seventeen. The sooner she was out of the apartment, the better. Her success would leave her roots so far behind that no one would ever connect her to Rowdy Yates CityBlock or a cramped apartment, filled with too many people for any privacy.

Because she knew if she stayed, she was going to go mad...or worse.

There was an angry rap on the door. "Kailee," Aunt Lillian snapped. "Come here!"

Kailee sighed, knowing that her aunt wouldn't hesitate to open the door. "Coming," she said, swinging her legs over the side of the bed and standing up. Couldn't her aunt take a break, just once in a while? "I'm on my way."

CHAPTER

FIVE

However, creating a flexible mind requires flexibility. A person who can reason can move from skill to skill, a person who cannot understand the background can only learn by rote. Memorising and understanding, put bluntly, are not the same.

- Professor Leo Caesius, Education and the Decline and Fall of the Galactic Empire

Seven days later, Darrin had almost forgotten about the essay – and the whole competition. It was just another piece of pointless schoolwork that would lead to nothing, he knew, and thus was barely worth worrying about, not when he could try to lure girls into bed or play games outside school, where they could actually keep score. He was surprised when, after lunch, they were told to assemble in the main hall for an important announcement. Tired and bored, he followed the other boys into their section of the giant room. It looked as though almost all of the students had gathered for the announcement.

He rolled his eyes as he took his seat. The last 'important' announcement had consisted of a statement that the nutrient value of school lunches had been improved, thanks to the enlightened polices of the Grand Senate. None of them had tasted any improvement, Darrin remembered; if anything, the food had managed the impossible and gone further downhill. It was not surprising that students tried to smuggle in food from outside the school, he knew; the only real surprise was that the teachers ate with the students. In their place, Darrin would have brought in food from their homes and eaten it in private. But there was very little privacy for anyone in the school.

The sound of chatter grew louder as the students relaxed. Few of them would actually pay attention, Darrin knew; there was little point. The only assembly he could remember looking forward to was the annual prize-giving – and he'd changed his mind after realising that the prizes were not allocated on any basis that actually made sense. And besides, no awards were given out for either academic or sporting achievement. The whole system seemed thoroughly absurd to him.

Judy sat down next to him, her hand reaching for his. Darrin hesitated – he wasn't sure that he wanted people to think she was his girlfriend – and then took her hand, feeling her shifting until she was actually leaning against him. She felt warm to the touch, so warm that he had to fight down the urge to kiss and cuddle her in public. All around them, other couples were doing the same. If nothing else, the assembly could serve as make-out time. He kissed her gently, then stopped as he saw someone come to the stand. It wasn't the principal; it was someone in a dark suit, someone he didn't know. And that meant that he might be powerful...

"Greetings, students," the man said. He was tall and thin, his face twisted in a sneer that suggested he knew he was far more powerful than the students. The condescending tone in his voice made it very clear. "Last week, you all submitted essays on why you would like to visit a colony world. It is my pleasure to announce that four winners have come from this school."

Darrin blinked in surprise. He knew how to play the numbers – gambling was the sole skill Fitz had taught him – and the odds were staggeringly *against* four winners coming from the same school. Unless, of course, there was only one school...or hundreds of possible winners. He'd only glanced at the instructions, but he was sure that they'd said that the competition was taking place all over the world. Or maybe the whole system was fixed. The school board might have determined the winners in advance, granting four slots to Rowdy Yates Centre of Educational Excellence.

There are ten thousand pupils in this school, he thought. *The odds of any given person being the winner are one in two thousand, five hundred.*

"Those lucky winners entered well-written essays," the man continued, gathering steam. "It was my pleasure to read such pieces of work. The school has good reason to be proud of those who have entered the competition."

Darrin snorted to himself and hugged Judy as the man droned on. He doubted that more than a thousand students, if that, had entered the competition. Darrin himself had only entered a handful of sentences, more to ensure that he wasn't nagged than anything else. It wasn't as if he had much of a hope of winning...

Besides, even if there were *no* entries from outside the school, the judges would still have to read through over a thousand different essays. It was probably fixed.

"I will now read the names of those four lucky winners," the man concluded. "Once I have read out the names, those winners will come up on stage and receive their congratulations from me personally."

And get jeered at by the rest of the school, Darrin thought. No doubt all four slots had gone to the swots, the ones who had actually bothered to write a proper essay. *Who is this asshole?*

"The names are as follows," the man said, dragging the whole affair out as much as possible. "Gary Seaman..."

A dull chuckle ran through the class. Darrin wasn't too surprised; Gary *was* a swot, someone who wouldn't hesitate to complete the essay even though he knew it was probably pointless. Gary looked terrified; the teacher standing near him urged the young man to his feet, even though he clearly wanted to run and hide.

"Come on," the man said, his voice echoing around the hall. "Don't be shy."

Darrin joined in the laughter as Gary somehow walked towards the stage. A number of students, seeing weakness, jeered and catcalled as Gary passed them, the back of his neck glowing red. Luckily for him, he didn't have to pick his way out of the rows of seats or he would probably have been kicked a hundred times before he even reached the aisle. The hall settled down, slightly, as Gary took a seat on the stage and waited, his head in his hands.

"The second lucky winner," the man said, "is Kailee Singh."

The hall erupted into wolf-whistles as Kailee was pushed to her feet. Darrin saw the shocked expression on her face and knew, beyond a shadow of a doubt, that she hadn't even *entered* the competition. Whatever her goals in life happened to be – and he was sure that she had goals, or she would have put out for him – they probably didn't include a trip away from Earth. Kailee's long dark hair fell around her ass as she walked up to the stage, drawing the attention of every boy and not a few of the girls in the room. But she didn't look happy as she sat down next to Gary.

"The third lucky winner," the man announced, "is Darrin Person."

Darrin stared at him in absolute shock. For a moment, he didn't even believe his ears. How the hell had he won? His essay had been nothing more than a handful of sentences! The whole system was fixed, but why had it been fixed in his favour? It wasn't as if he was a prize student or even someone the teachers wanted to get rid of for a few months...no, he just tried to get through the day with a minimal amount of actual work, then play sports until he was sent home.

Judy untangled herself from him, her face a strange mixture of awe and shock. She seemed to have decided to make him her boyfriend – and protector. Having him go away for several months would put a crimp in *that* plan. But, at the same time, if he had been so lucky...Darrin had to force his legs into cooperating as he stood and started to move towards the stage. The entire school seemed to be staring at him, some cat-calling from the safety of the crowds, others cheering loudly. After all, he wasn't as unpopular as some other students...

Kailee gave him a weak smile as he sat down on the other side of her, but her face was pinched and wan. She hadn't wanted to go, Darrin saw; Gary, sitting next to her, hardly looked any more enthusiastic. Now the shock was fading away, Darrin could see some advantages in spending a few months away from Fitz. It wasn't as if he could do anything to help his mother...and, by the time he returned, he might be old enough to apply for premature emancipation and get his own apartment.

And at least it isn't school, he thought, although he had no idea what a trip to the colonies actually entailed. He made a mental note to read the essay instructions more carefully; somehow, he doubted they were going however many light years just to sit behind desks in a colonial school. What did a colonial school even *look* like? He honestly didn't know.

"The fourth lucky winner is Barry Sycamore," the man concluded. "Come up here, young man, and join us on the stage."

Yep, Darrin decided, it was definitely a fix. If Barry had entered the competition at all, Darrin would be very surprised. He heard Gary let out a groan as the oversized student made his way up to the stage and sat down next to Darrin, grinning inanely at the students in the audience. In all honestly, Darrin tended to agree. Being close to Barry was like being close to a savage dog, with the added disadvantage that the dog had a certain animal cunning.

He scowled as the man droned on, extolling their virtues to the skies. Agreeing with Gary was painful – he didn't want to agree with a nerd on anything – but he had to agree that while the trip might have been tolerable without Barry, it would be a nightmare with him.

But at least Fitz won't be there, he thought. *Look on the bright side.*

———

Gary felt too stunned to move – or to listen to the stranger telling the entire school just how wonderful he was, even though he knew it would just make him more of a target. How the hell had he won? The essay hadn't been that good, had it? But then, the instructions had claimed that the competition was global; it was unlikely that someone had even bothered to read the essays. It was much more likely that they'd picked at random and he'd simply been unlucky. And Barry...Gary tried not to look at the hulking student sitting next to Darrin and grinning like a loon. If there was one thing guaranteed to ruin the trip, it was having to share it with one of his worst tormentors.

He *couldn't* take nine months away from Earth, not with the really important exams coming up. If he missed them, he would have to retake the entire year, forcing him to spend more time in the goddamned school. And he hadn't even *wanted* to go! Somewhere in the school, he was *sure* that there were students who wanted to spend some time on a colony world. Why couldn't they go and not him?

Beside him, Kailee looked as irked as Gary felt. For once, he was sitting next to a truly hot girl and he couldn't even *enjoy* it. He wondered, absently, what she'd written on her essay, before deciding that it didn't matter. Barry had probably submitted a blank sheet of paper, if he'd bothered to submit anything at all. Maybe one of the teachers had entered him in the hopes of getting the bastard out of their hair for a few months. If so, Gary decided, they'd done very well indeed.

The man finally stopped droning and the principal dismissed the students back to their classes, then told Gary and the other winners to remain behind where they were. Gary sighed, inwardly; he would have to speak to the principal in private to ask if he could decline the honour. Perhaps he could give his slot to Moe and the two bullies could spend six months away from the school...he tried to form a mental image of their starship being boarded by pirates and the assholes being sold into slavery, but it refused to form properly. It was much more likely that the pirates would recruit Barry and Moe into their ranks.

"The departure date is one week from today," the man informed them. They still didn't know his name. "Instead of your standard afterschool classes, you will be expected to attend lectures on Meridian, your destination. I strongly suggest that you listen carefully, read about the subject and remember everything. It could come in handy when you're on the planet's surface."

Gary snorted to himself. *He* could read, but he doubted that Barry or even Darrin could read very well. Could Kailee read? He had no idea. But it hardly mattered; the readers could read the textbooks out to the students, if necessary. They even provided explanations for the most difficult words. Sighing inwardly, Gary stood when dismissed and headed directly towards the principal's office. He could wait there for the man all day, even though it was a technical breach of school rules.

And then, if he were lucky, he could get out of the whole trip.

———

Kailee knew that she should be used to attention. After all, when she became an actress, she would have to perform on stage in front of gawking crowds. But facing the entire school was difficult – and not just because of the wolf-whistles and other harassment. She hadn't expected to win the contest, not really. How the hell had she won?

She walked through the deserted corridors in a daze, barely aware of her surroundings until she reached the classroom door. Kailee hesitated for a long moment, then opened the door and stepped into the classroom. The girls looked up at her as she sat down next to them, the teacher saying nothing about her lateness. But then, he would have been at the assembly too; he *knew* that she'd won the competition. He wouldn't penalise her for that, would he?

But there were always rumours, stories of teachers who had abused their charges – or taken advantage of them. Kailee knew that she was relatively immune – it wasn't as if she cared about her grades – but she knew better than to lower her guard. And yet, she'd walked alone through the school's corridors...she shook her head, then pulled the reader from her pocket and placed it on the desk.

"You won," Sally muttered to her, as soon as the teacher's back was turned. He was droning on about something called the verb-noun infinity. "Well done!"

"Thank you," Kailee said, sourly.

She gritted her teeth. A few months on a colony world would completely ruin her looks. Someone had heard that she planned to enter the acting world and deliberately set out to ruin her chances. There could be no other explanation. Gary might have won the competition fairly – the little nerd was smart – but Kailee had entered a blank sheet of paper, satisfying the basic requirements.

"You'll get to spend time with hunks, like in *Farmer's World: This Time We're Sowing*," Gayle put in, from the other side of the desk. "I think it would be great fun."

Kailee scowled at her. *Farmer's World* was a pornographic flick, shared on the datanet and watched by countless students. It was set on a farm; Kailee knew nothing about farming, but surely the farmers didn't spend all their time making love. Besides, the scene where the heroine had been taken by four men in the middle of the pigpen had been thoroughly disconcerting.

"It's going to be boring," she predicted, crossly. "And I don't want to go."

"But you'd be able to introduce them to Earth's fashions," Sally pointed out. "Get a set of new outfits before you leave, take them with you and wear them on the farm."

"If there is a farm," Gayle said. "It might be more like *Rumble In The Jungle*..."

"Oh, shut up," Kailee said. She couldn't afford even one new outfit. There were ways to get loans from the gangs, but she knew she couldn't meet their payment schedules. She'd end up indentured and working in a brothel, if she was lucky. "I don't think it's going to be like a movie at all."

"*Crabby Bitch III*," Gayle offered. "Or *Break the Cutie*."

"Shut up," Kailee snapped. Gayle's porn addiction was an open secret, as was her desire to sleep with as many boys and girls as possible. "Please!"

Dismissing the thought of actually trying to catch up with whatever the teacher was saying, she activated her reader and downloaded the instructions, reading through them quickly. It wasn't too clear on just how long the lucky winners would spend away from Earth; the figure given was six months, but there were plenty of weasel words written into the instructions to make her think that it might be longer. She had to admit that the thought of spending time away from the cramped apartment was a good one, but what would happen to her career?

The average actress started work at seventeen, she'd discovered, unless they had a special permit to act at a younger age. Assuming she returned before her seventeenth birthday, she should still have a chance...but if she returned later, she would already have burnt up some of her time. If she failed to get in at seventeen, it wasn't too likely that she would get in when she was older. Youth was *in* at the moment too.

But her family would be pleased...

Of course they will be pleased, she thought, bitterly. The thought was not a pleasant one. *They'd get the bedroom for themselves while I am gone.*

CHAPTER
SIX

On a wider scale, the educational process also trains and equips the next generation to take their place in society as adults. Even the basic skills of reading and writing are almost mandatory in jobs, while additional skills like operating a computer and suchlike are strongly preferable.

- Professor Leo Caesius, *Education and the Decline and Fall of the Galactic Empire*

Gary didn't really like Principal Rico and he suspected that the feeling was mutual. Rico was short, stout and smiled too much – and he was a completely ineffective disciplinarian. Gary had gone to his office once before, after he'd been advised to report bullying behaviour to the principal, only to discover that the principal could do nothing more than ask him to stop whatever he was doing to incite them. The fact that Barry and Moe and their ilk would have picked on Gary whatever he was doing seemed to have passed him by.

"I can't go on the trip," he said, as soon as the door was closed. "Please can you give my slot to someone else?"

"I'm afraid not," Principal Rico said. He didn't sound as though he cared. "The selections were made well above my station, Mr. Seaman. I cannot change them at a whim."

"But I didn't mean to win," Gary pleaded. "I cannot go."

Principal Rico eyed him, suspiciously. "And why, if you didn't want to win, did you even enter the competition?"

Gary stared at him, fighting the urge to burst into tears. He'd entered the competition because he'd believed that *not* entering the competition would blight his academic career. And then he'd won...and winning the competition would *also* blight his career. Having to retake a year of schooling would automatically downgrade him when it came to entering Imperial University. He might not even make it in at all. The thought was so horrifying that he refused to face it. Where else could he go?

"This is an important initiative that was mandated by senior authority," Principal Rico said. His eyes met Gary's, as if he were trying to say something important without being able to come right out and say it. "I do not believe that anyone in this school has the authority to change the winner, no matter how...unhappy the winner has become."

His eyes hardened. "And there *will* be consequences for not going."

Gary closed his eyes, trying to recall some of the courage he felt online. "There are students who have done nothing in class and do not face consequences..."

Principal Rico looked, for a long moment, bitter and helpless. "You do not understand," he said. "Who do you think is in charge of the school system?"

Gary blinked in surprise. Principal Rico had never talked to him as though he were an adult before, not ever. He'd normally talked down to all of his students, no matter how old they were.

"You," he said, finally. "You're the boss..."

"I wish that were true," Principal Rico said. His gaze never left Gary's eyes. "Do you realise just how little authority I actually have? Of course you don't. I have to follow orders issued by someone much higher in the hierarchy than myself. Those people are the ones who set the exam question, who set up the entire competition. And it was those people, those truly powerful people, who picked the winners."

Gary hesitated. "But..."

"But nothing," Principal Rico interrupted. "Those people don't care about your concerns, young man, or about why you entered the competition. All they care about is making sure the entire process runs smoothly – or as smoothly as possible. And if you anger them, you can be sure that they will definitely take it out on you."

His voice hardened. "Do you understand me?"

Gary shuddered. He'd heard stories – they'd all heard stories – of what happened to those who pissed off the bureaucrats. Their support allowances were delayed or cut completely, their requests for new apartments were ignored, they were put at the bottom of the list for receiving medical aid...and that was just the tip of the iceberg. If he angered someone much higher up the food chain, his life – and that of his family – would not be worth living.

"Yes, sir," he said, reluctantly. Damned if he did, damned if he didn't. "I understand."

"Good," Principal Rico said. "I'll expect you to attend all of the orientation classes, Mr. Seaman. You are going to need them."

With that, he motioned for Gary to walk out the door.

———

Darrin had spent the day in a daze, despite the vast number of students who wanted to congratulate him or try to pick a fight. It didn't seem possible that he'd won; it just didn't seem *real*. And he honestly couldn't decide if he wanted to go or not. But he knew that there was no point in trying to argue with the system. If it said he'd won, he'd won. By the end of the formal hours of schooling, he couldn't wait to tell Fitz that he was going to be away for several months.

He was still contemplating it when he entered the classroom that had been put aside for orientation lessons. A man was standing at the head of the room, wearing a uniform that seemed strikingly military and a cloth hat that cast a shadow over his eyes. He was tall, muscular and wore a neatly-clipped beard that gave him an untidy air. But his sharp blue eyes followed Darrin as he sat down and looked back at the newcomer. Moments later, Barry swaggered in and took the seat at the end of the room.

"Sit at the front," the newcomer ordered. There was something in his tone that suggested that disobedience would be a very bad idea. "Now."

Barry stood up and reluctantly moved to sit beside Darrin. The newcomer eyed him, then lifted an eyebrow as Kailee slipped into the room, followed by a reluctant-looking Gary. Darrin concealed a smile; the nerd was behind one of the best asses in the school, yet he wasn't even *looking* at her. But then, Gary would have been targeted too...and everyone knew that he couldn't defend himself. He'd probably spent the day trying to hide.

"Close that door," the newcomer ordered. Gary obeyed, then sat down next to Kailee, as far from Barry as he could. "My name is Yates, Mathew Yates. And no, I am not related to Rowdy Yates. For my sins, I have been charged with serving as your guide, supervisor and teacher while you are on Meridian. This is not a task I welcome, so I suggest – very strongly – that you listen carefully to me, because I hate having to repeat myself."

Darrin blinked in surprise. Teachers were rarely firm with their students, if only because they knew they could do nothing to back it up. But Yates looked tough, tougher than Mr. Howarth...and used to obedience. Even Barry, who looked muscled enough to pass for a primate in the holographic zoo, said nothing. He just stared at the newcomer.

"I have been told to assume that you know absolutely nothing about Meridian," Yates said, when that had sunk in. "This strikes me as a very reasonable statement, given the general quality of information available on Earth about the outermost worlds. We shall start, therefore, with a video presentation prepared by the Meridian Development Consortium, which began settling the planet ninety years ago."

He picked up a remote and pushed a switch, then moved over to sit next to Barry. The lights dimmed, then the screen activated, displaying a logo that looked like a planet surrounded by a golden ring. Words, too small for Darrin to read, appeared beneath the logo and hung there for a long moment, before fading away into the darkness.

"Welcome to Meridian," a soft female voice said. "Where a new world is waiting for you."

The screen glowed with light, showing a montage of images; the planet from orbit, shuttles landing at the spaceport, small homes built out of wood, giant boats making their way up the river into the hinterlands... Darrin found himself fascinated by the people, particularly the young women. They all looked bright, enthusiastic and healthy, very different from the pallid women he knew on Earth. Several of them rode large four-legged animals; horses, if he recalled correctly. He'd never seen any of them on Earth.

"Meridian," the voice said, as the images started to repeat themselves. "A place to live, a place to spread out, a place to grow, a place to..."

Darrin found himself tuning the woman out as she kept talking, extolling Meridian and his virtues in glowing terms. If there was anything bad about the colony world, she didn't say anything about it. Instead, she talked about how new settlers would have first pick of the land, guaranteed loans from the development consortium and free access to indentured labour. There were special discounts for families, particularly ones who intended to have more children; in short, Meridian was a pretty good place to live. Darrin wasn't sure that he believed a word of it.

The presentation came to an end and Yates turned it off. "Any questions?"

"Yeah," Darrin said, before he could stop himself. "How much of that is true?"

Yates might have smiled. It was hard to tell under the beard. "I would say that it is true, but incomplete," he said, after a moment. "The images they showed you are those farms and settlements that were developed over the past ninety years, the ones that were the most successful. It will take years of work, even with the assistance of indentured labour, to produce a properly functioning farm. But many settlers have succeeded."

He stood and walked to the front of the room. "Meridian is not Earth. You know, I believe, most of the dangers on Earth's surface. Meridian, however, has other dangers. Like every other settled world, the ecosystem throws up its own set of surprises as it reacts to the terraforming packages. There are poisonous plants, dangerous animals and other nasty problems for the settlers to encounter. You have to be prepared to encounter them too."

Darrin shivered. Dangerous *animals*? He'd heard the rumours about creatures that had escaped from the Arena and were hiding out in the Undercity, but he'd never actually seen anything larger than a cockroach. He *had* seen images, of course, in the holographic zoo, yet apparently that wasn't quite the same.

And dangerous plants?

Kailee leaned forward. "Are you saying that the settlers...actually grow their own crops? In the wild?"

"Of course," Yates said. "There are no algae farms on the colony worlds, just crops and animals they raise themselves for the table."

Darrin concealed a smile at Kailee's expression. They'd been told, ever since they were old enough to understand, that algae-farms and vat-grown foodstuffs were far healthier than anything grown naturally. Indeed, they'd been told it so often that most people had a phobia about eating naturally-produced food and drinking unprocessed water. Darrin himself wasn't so sure – it struck him that nothing could taste worse than school food – but it hardly mattered. Fitz was hardly going to waste money on expensive food from off-world when he could spend it on alcohol instead.

"The first problem, however, is the starship you will take to the colonies," Yates said. "Normally, you would be placed in a stasis tube and the journey would seem to take no time at all. Unfortunately, there is a new requirement for those tubes, which means that you will be expected to spend the journey awake and aware. You may well enjoy it."

Barry snorted, rudely. "What's there to do on the ship?"

"Education and games, mainly," Yates said. "I suggest that you spend some time reading the ship's database. Quite apart from useful information on Meridian, it will tell you more about the state of the galaxy than you might find in any database on Earth."

He paused, then launched into a long lecture on safety. Darrin found himself struggling to take in all the details; wear a shipsuit at all times, stay in the civilian parts of the ship and don't touch anything unless they knew what it did. He had no idea how they were meant to keep all those rules straight in their head, unless they were meant to write them all down and memorise them later. Gary, the little swot, had set his reader to record the entire lecture for later replaying. Darrin made a mental note to get a copy off him and listen to it again himself.

"We will be going over the planet's history in greater detail on the ship," Yates said. He produced a set of datachips, dropping one in front of each of them. "However, I expect you to read this before you come back tomorrow. These are copies of the standard ecological assessment, safety reports and several other documents you need to read. In particular, I suggest that you pay close attention to what is edible and what isn't."

Gary stuck up a nervous hand. "Are we going to have to pick crops?"

"Maybe," Yates said. He gave Gary a toothy grin. "But quite a few settlers have landed on the planet, bitten into a leaf...and ended up in the hospital, if they were lucky. They watched the wrong videos on Earth and concluded that anything could be eaten, as long as it looked green. And I would prefer not to have to tell your parents that you died because you ate the wrong thing."

Kailee's head jerked up. "This place isn't *safe*? Don't the settlers sue?"

Yates chuckled, unpleasantly. "Sue who?"

He tapped the datachip on Kailee's desk. "That chip lists every edible plant on the planet's surface," he said. "You can eat one of the ones not listed if you like...and you might get lucky...but if you got ill, it would be your own stupid fault. You could sue the consortium, I suppose, if you found a lawyer willing to take your case."

"It wouldn't work," Gary said. "Would it?"

Yates shook his head, wordlessly.

"But why?" Kailee asked. "Why wouldn't it work?"

"Because you were told, quite clearly, what plants are safe to eat," Yates said. He reached out, picked up the datachip and held it in front of her eyes. "The consortium has done its best to prepare the settlers – and you – for Meridian, but if you're stupid enough to ignore what you're told...well, it's your own stupid fault."

His voice hardened as he looked around the room, his eyes moving from face to face. "You have been spoiled on Earth," he explained. "The tasteless slop they feed you *is* safe, the water they pump into the pipes is processed so thoroughly that there isn't any risk of infection...and there is always someone to blame if something goes wrong. But on the colonies... well, if you fuck up, you take the blame yourself. There isn't anyone willing to hold your hand, clean up after you or do anything else that you can do for yourself. I suggest you bear that in mind at all times."

"No one to help?" Kailee asked, bleakly. "No one at all."

"There are more people in this CityBlock," Yates said, "than there are on the entire surface of Meridian. The settlers, particularly those living away from the towns, are often miles away from anyone who might be able to help them. They have to learn to rely on themselves, not on the government and not on their neighbours. Often, neither the government nor their neighbours *can* help them."

Yates stepped backwards, then smiled openly. "This trip is the opportunity of a lifetime," he concluded. "But you have to bear in mind that you're not going to a carbon copy of Earth."

Darrin swallowed – and saw Gary swallow too. Kailee still seemed stunned, while Barry was merely grinning inanely. It looked as though he hadn't listened to a word Yates had said.

"As a special treat," Yates said, "the four of you can go home early and tell your families. I'll see you again tomorrow."

Gary hastened out the room, followed rapidly by Barry. Kailee eyed Darrin for a moment – he wondered if she were going to ask him to escort her home – before she left the classroom and headed down towards the common room. She could wait there for the other girls, Darrin knew; she wouldn't want to walk home with him, even if he hadn't asked her out earlier. He wondered, briefly, what Judy was doing – and if she'd already started looking for another boyfriend. She would need a protector while he was gone.

"Good luck," Yates said, as he walked towards the door. Darrin watched him go – and was surprised to note that Yates was walking with a faint limp. Yates stopped at the door and turned around. "Or is there something else you wished to ask me?"

"No, sir," Darrin said. There was something about the older man that brought out the respect, respect Darrin rarely showed to anyone else. "But..."

He shook his head. His half-formed thoughts were unlikely to be of interest to anyone – and, somehow, he didn't want to disappoint Yates. Instead, he walked down towards the security gates and left the school, then walked towards his apartment block. Fitz would be pleased at the thought of never seeing him again, he was sure. And his mother...

Maybe I could stay on the world, he thought. The video had made it look like an enticing possibility, very different from the information they'd been given at school. *No one would miss me.*

But he knew, deep in his heart, that wasn't a possibility. If the system was prepared to ensure that he went to school and attended his classes, it would never let him go. There was no point in daydreaming of a future that would never be, no point at all.

CHAPTER

SEVEN

And education can provide a way to monitor and qualify a child's progress. If one must prove competence in a certain field, one can point to a degree handed out after a test or an exam. It saves employers from having to run tests of their own – although, as most employers rapidly learn, experience on paper is not the same as experience in the field.

- Professor Leo Caesius, Education and the
Decline and Fall of the Galactic Empire

"So," Aunt Lillian said, "is that all you're taking?"

Kailee bit her lip to keep her face from scowling. Her packing would have been done by now if Aunt Lillian hadn't kept sticking her long nose into the room and insisting on inspecting Kailee's bag. Did she really think that Kailee was going to walk off with the family jewels, such as they were, or did she intend to insist that Kailee leave behind some of her makeup for her younger relatives? Either way, it was just a nuisance, one Kailee would happily have foregone.

"Yes," she said, crossly. Yates had provided them with a list of recommended items, starting with clothes and ending with any medical supplies they might need. She'd packed enough to last her for a week or two without washing, she hoped. And then she'd put her handful of truly expensive clothes and cosmetics into the bag too. "That's everything."

Her aunt picked up the bag, opened it up and tipped the contents onto the floor. Kailee swallowed a word that would probably have earned her a slap as her aunt picked though the clothes, then started to pack properly.

By the time she'd finished, the clothes all fitted neatly, the cosmetics were wrapped up in plastic and there was some space left at the top, enough room for some additional clothes. Her aunt had actually been helpful.

"I'd suggest you take Jake's reader, if he will let you," Aunt Lillian said. "Load it up with enough videos and textbooks to keep you going, when you're hundreds of light years from Earth."

This time, Kailee couldn't keep herself from glaring at her aunt. She'd taken Kailee's enforced departure in her stride, barely even bothering to conceal her relief at having one less mouth to feed for a few months. Her children had even gloated over having the bedroom to themselves; by the time she got back, she suspected that everything she left behind would have been thoroughly ruined.

"They promised a reader on the ship," she said, tightly. She didn't want to ask Uncle Jake for anything, not when he'd been the one to take a peek at her while she was in the shower. "I should be fine."

"Make sure you are," her aunt grated. She hesitated, then reached into her pocket and produced a credit coin. "Press your thumb against the reader."

Kailee obeyed. There was a faint bleep as the coin registered her fingerprint, locking itself to her. The tiny screen on the top displayed a balance of seven thousand credits, more money than she'd had in her entire life. She stared at it, then looked up at her aunt. For once, Aunt Lillian's face had softened into something resembling a smile.

"You may run into trouble," she said, softly. "If you do...that may help you get out of it."

"Oh," Kailee said. She didn't want to ask, but she knew she had to. "Where...where did you get the money?"

"Never you mind," her aunt snapped, returning to her normal form of communication. "If you bring it all back to me, I won't mind at all. But if you need to use it, use it."

"I will," Kailee said, genuinely touched. Her parents had never done anything like it for her, nor had anyone else. "And thank you."

Her aunt leaned forward and gave her a hug. "Think of this whole trip as a story you can tell your grandkids," she said, dryly. "And enjoy yourself."

Kailee shook her head, wearily. Her plans might have been slightly derailed – although Yates had informed her that they would be away for nine months at most, which would still give her time to try to catch an agent's attention – but she still had no intention of remaining in the CityBlock for the rest of her life. She didn't want to be trapped there indefinitely, just like her aunt and uncle. Or the rest of her classmates, for that matter.

"I'll do my best," she promised. "And thanks again."

"Thank me when you get home," Aunt Lillian said. "I have no idea what that chip is going to be worth on the outer planets."

Kailee's puzzlement must have shown on her face, for her aunt explained.

"The value of money is going down, even as our income is going up," she admitted. It made no sense to Kailee, but she knew that her aunt was generally right about everything, no matter how irritating. "I honestly don't know when it will end."

―――――

Judy tasted of strawberries and cream, Darrin decided, as he kissed her on the lips. They'd gone out dancing on the final night, then moved to a tiny room that young couples could hire for the hour. Darrin knew that Fitz would be annoyed at how much of his Student Living Allowance he'd spent over the last two days, but for once he didn't care. If he was going to be forced to go to a colony world for nine months, he was going to have some fun first, even if he *was* saving up trouble for later.

She kissed him back for a long moment, then broke contact and looked him in the eye. "Are you going to come back?"

Darrin hesitated. Part of him just wanted to finish undoing her shirt and allow her tantalisingly large breasts to bob free, part of him wanted to try to reassure her. But reassure her about what? He was going to be away for at least six months, six months during which time Judy would be horrendously vulnerable. She was going to look for another protector, he knew. The thought gnawed at him, even as he knew she had no choice. He wasn't going to be around to look after her.

"I think so," he said. He reached for her shirt and undid the remaining buttons, then unclipped her bra. Her breasts caught his attention and held it firmly. "But let's make the most of this night."

Judy shifted, allowing him to push her down and lift up her skirt. She wasn't wearing any panties. Darrin felt his cock stiffen as he mounted her and pushed his way into her. His hands caught her breasts, kneading them against her skin. Judy grunted and clutched at him as he started to move inside her. Moments later, it was all over.

Afterwards, they cleaned themselves up and dressed quickly. It was funny, Darrin had often wondered, how he loved looking at her before sex, but afterwards he found himself largely indifferent to her. He watched, dispassionately, as she buttoned up her shirt, hiding her breasts once again. It was hard to believe that, five minutes ago, he'd been licking and sucking at those very breasts.

"Thank you," Judy said. "Will...will you walk me home?"

"Of course," Darrin said. The gangs might have taken their bribes, but it was late at night and there were plenty of drunkards and druggies wandering the lower levels. "I'll be glad to take you home."

Outside, he could hear music drifting down the corridors as they walked back towards the stairs. A handful of revellers ran past them, singing the words of a bawdy song loudly enough to make Darrin's ears hurt, and vanished into the distance. Half of them were naked, he saw, their bare buttocks winking at him. Judging by the faint scent in the air, they'd overdosed on Sparkle Dust and would be highly suggestible for the next few hours. He shook his head, wondering at their idiocy. He'd experimented with drugs before – everyone had – but he knew better than to mess with Sparkle Dust. It was too dangerous even for him.

Judy clung to his arm as they reached the stairs and began to make their way up to the apartment block, trying to remain in the shadows. The precise lines between the different gangs grew blurred down in the lower levels, where thousands of youngsters came to drink, dance and forget that they were trapped in the towering CityBlocks. He heard someone shouting and half-turned, peering into the darkened corridor. Someone bigger and nastier than Barry had shoved someone small into the wall and was busy tearing at their victim's clothes. Darrin couldn't tell if the victim was male or female.

He winced, then pulled Judy further up the stairs. There was no point in trying to intervene, no matter what he thought was going on. The victim wouldn't thank him, while the gangs – if the victimiser was a gang member – might take it out on his family. He took Judy the rest of the way without incident, then paused outside her door for a quick kissing session. His cock stiffened, urging him to try to talk her into bed for a second round, but he knew it would be futile. Judy's parents were stricter than his own, with good reason.

"Goodbye," he muttered.

He strode away before she could say anything, if she had anything to say. Behind him, he heard her door opening and the voice of Judy's mother demanding to know where she'd been all night. The woman had a voice like a fucking cat, Darrin had decided when he'd first met the bitch, one of the women who liked keeping up appearances even in the CityBlock. And, sure as his name was Darrin, she had a whole series of embarrassing secrets in her past. It explained why she was so damn strident.

Fitz was staggering against the wall when Darrin reached his own apartment, his fingers jabbing at the concrete as if he expected it to magically become a door. Darrin smirked, realising that his stepfather was so drunk he couldn't see the fingerprint sensor clearly, then slipped past him and opened the door. He half-hoped it would close before Fitz managed to bumble in, but no such luck. The bastard lurched in, collapsed on the floor, then staggered back to his feet and advanced on Darrin.

"You bastard," he said, his words slurred together. "You should have told me."

It took Darrin a moment to realise what Fitz meant. The results of the competition hadn't been announced publically until a day after Darrin and the other winners had been told, leaving the gamblers in the CityBlock a chance to lay their bets on the sure thing. Darrin could have told Fitz, but he'd kept it to himself. For someone who spent most of his days drunk off his ass, Fitz had realised that he'd missed the opportunity to make some easy money very quickly.

"You should have told me that people were gambling on it," Darrin countered, quickly. He honestly hadn't known, although if he had he might have placed a bet on Gary. The nerd had had the best chance of winning fairly...but then, the competition wasn't fair. How else did one explain Barry and Darrin winning too? "I didn't know."

"Of course you did, you little bastard," Fitz slurred. He pointed towards the sofa. "Get bent over, now! And get your trousers down!"

Darrin shook his head, taking a step backwards. He'd been thrashed bent over the sofa once and the bruises had lasted for days afterwards. And besides, he was younger and weaker then, without the strength that came from exercising regularly. He told himself, desperately, that Fitz didn't have the right to touch him, even as his stepfather ambled towards him, murder in his eye. His fists suddenly looked as big as planets...

Fitz took a drunken swing at him. Darrin moved to one side, then threw a punch back, right into his stepfather's nose. There was a satisfying crunching sound as the nose broke under the blow, but – drunk as he was – Fitz barely seemed to notice. Instead, blood dripping from his smashed nose, he took another swing at Darrin. Darrin jumped backwards.... and crashed into the wall. He'd been backed right up against it.

"Gotcha, you little bastard," Fitz said. "I bring you up, I pay for your schooling, I put food on the table..."

"That's a damn lie," Darrin snapped, anger overriding fear. "You take the SLA from me and use it for yourself..."

Fitz threw a punch. Darrin managed to dodge it and Fitz's fist hit the wall. He let out a howl – that had to have hurt, even though the drink – and Darrin brought up his knee, hitting him in the groin. Fitz bent double, screaming in agony; Darrin kicked him in the head as hard as he could. The drunkard fell to the ground, stunned.

For an awful moment, Darrin thought he'd killed his stepfather. The man had been a bastard – and it wasn't as if getting away with it would be hard – but losing him would affect his mother quite badly. And yet, when he checked, Fitz was still breathing...Darrin hesitated, utterly unsure of what to do. Part of his mind suggested, quite urgently, cutting the man's throat while he was helpless. The rest of him just screamed for him to run.

Quickly, he walked back to his room, picked up his bag...then paused, outside his mother's bedroom. He peeked inside and swore, grimly. She was lying on the bed, drunk out of her mind. Darrin silently bid her farewell, then walked past Fitz's body to the door. Maybe his stepfather wouldn't recover, maybe he would...but Darrin knew that he could never go home. He might as well stay on the colony world. Yates *had* said that there was always work for those willing to work hard.

He took one last look at the apartment, realising just how little personality had been stamped into the walls over the years. And then he stepped out into the corridor, closing the door behind him.

––––––––––

It was eight in the morning.

Gary tore himself away from the computer, then activated a special program he'd traded with several online contacts to obtain. All evidence of his non-scholarly activities – the hacked computer codes, the game programs and the porn stash – were wiped within seconds, leaving the computer returned to normal. He would have to re-hack the system when he came back, if he had time to play games while studying frantically for his exams. It was irritating to know that all of his high scores were gone, but he would have to live with it. If nothing else, he could take pride in having an unbroken string of victories.

I'm the most popular person in the gaming network, he thought, recalling a joke that was so old no one had any idea where it actually came from. *That makes me number billion on the datanet as a whole, behind all the porn stars.*

He checked his bag carefully, making sure that his reader and small computer terminal were carefully stowed away. Yates had advised them to be careful what they brought, pointing out that Meridian couldn't produce everything they might want. Gary had actually looked up investment opportunities, downloading a number of flicks and musical tracks that might not have reached Meridian yet, but there wasn't much they could actually carry. It was annoying to realise that the starship they were taking was huge, yet relatively small when it came to cargo capacity. But then, most of its hold carried colony gear.

Undressing, he inspected the bruise on his chest where Moe had hit him. Barry had been keeping his distance over the last few days, much to his surprise, but Moe seemed to be under no obligation to leave him in peace. Nor was anyone else; the last two days had been hellish, with almost everyone playing jokes and pranks on him. But he'd soon be gone. If Barry hadn't been coming along, he might almost have welcomed the trip...

There was a tap on the door. "One moment," he called, reaching for his dressing gown and buckling it on. "Come in."

The door opened, revealing Sammie. She looked wide-eyed and innocent, only slightly marred by the mark on her face. Gary knew what that meant; someone had hit her, deliberately. But she was only nine...

He shook his head. What did age matter? They'd started getting at *him* as soon as he'd entered school for the first time.

"I wish I could come with you," Sammie said. "I'm going to miss you."

"I'll miss you too," Gary said, although he knew that he could do nothing to protect his sister. What good was he when he couldn't even stand up to a pack of nine-year-olds? But then, those nine-year-old brats had older siblings, siblings who shared his classes at school. They would get at him if he got at them. "Take care of mum and dad, ok?"

Sammie nodded. Gary picked up his bag, checked it one last time, then slung it over his back. Yates had told them that they wouldn't be going to school, but the aircar pad on top of the CityBlock. He gave his sister a tight hug, then walked out of his bedroom and said goodbye to his parents. Both of them muttered something, then turned their attention back to the big screen in front of the sofa. They preferred fantasy worlds to reality.

Gary's lips twitched. How could he complain? He spent most of his time playing in VR environments as it was.

Waving goodbye to Sammie, he stepped out of the door and headed for the lifts.

CHAPTER
EIGHT

In short, the educational ideal is to fill young children with knowledge and awaken their intelligence, making them fit to discharge the duties of citizenship in an enlightened and independent manner.

- Professor Leo Caesius, *Education and the Decline and Fall of the Galactic Empire*

There was a bleep as someone tapped the buzzer on the far side of the door.

Kailee opened it, then smiled in relief as she saw Yates. He'd offered to escort her to the aircar pad – the rest of the girls wouldn't be going, naturally – but she hadn't been sure he would keep his word. It was hard to get any sense of personality out of him; there were times when she thought he approved of her and times when she had the impression that he hated all four of his charges. And she had never caught him looking at her breasts when he had the chance.

"Thank you," she said, picking up her bag and slinging it over her shoulder. Yates moved to take it, but she shook her head. Boys had a habit of assuming that doing favours for a girl automatically gave them rights over the girl or access to her body – and it was easier to refuse the offer than tell them otherwise, after the fact. "Are we going now?"

Yates nodded, gravely. Kailee flushed, then turned to say goodbye to her family. Her mother and father made a brief appearance to wish her well, then returned to sit in front of the display scene and lose themselves in the latest soap opera. One day, Kailee promised herself, they would watch in awe as their daughter took the starring role. Aunt Lillian gave her a hug, inspected Yates with a thoughtful expression, then stepped backwards. The kids were already invading Kailee's room and exploring what she'd left behind.

"Goodbye," Kailee said. She felt conflicted; it was good to get out of the apartment, but she really didn't want to go millions of light years from Earth. "Let's go."

Yates smiled. She followed him out of the apartment, then down a long corridor towards the central elevators. The gangsters seemed to keep their distance from the two of them, although she couldn't decide if they found Yates intimidating or if someone had bought them off beforehand. Once they reached the elevators   the block was slowly coming to life around them, now the teenagers were in school – Yates tapped a code into the control panel and called the emergency elevator. Kailee lifted her eyebrows; the only people who were permitted to use the emergency elevator were the emergency services and the bureaucrats. But when the elevator arrived and opened its doors, it was clear that it was nothing special at all, merely another metal box.

"Inside," Yates said, shortly. Kailee obeyed, then watched as he keyed another set of commands into the panel inside the elevator. The doors hissed closed; the elevator lurched into life, heading upwards. "This may take some time."

Kailee scowled in understanding. The CityBlock had a thousand levels, divided between residential, shopping, entertainment and storage blocks. She had never left the CityBlock; as far as she knew, only a handful of her fellow students had ever gone to the uppermost levels and seen the sky overhead. Hundreds of thousands of millions of people were born, lived and died in the CityBlocks without ever leaving. Their CityBlock was their home.

And she was leaving. The thought made her feel strange, even though she'd planned to leave ever since she'd decided that acting offered her the best chance of escape. If there was one advantage to living in a CityBlock, it was that she knew most of the people near her apartment – although she knew that only went so far. People might be friendly, but they wouldn't help her if she got into trouble. No one wanted to help for fear it would splash over them.

It took nearly thirty minutes for the elevator to reach its destination. Kailee half-expected Yates to try something – he was a man, wasn't he? – but he seemed inclined to just lean against the wall and relax. Kailee watched him, puzzled; he seemed very different from most of the boys she knew, even the ones who played sports almost constantly. There was something about him she found dangerous...but at the same time, she found it reassuring. It made no sense to her. What sort of man *was* he?

When the elevator doors hissed open, she found herself looking out through a large set of windows at a darkening sky. She checked her watch automatically; surely it wasn't still dark outside? But when she stepped closer, she saw ominous dark clouds hovering around the towering CityBlocks. Strange flickers of light seemed to dance among the clouds, making her take a step backwards in shock. She knew about the weather, of course, but she'd never seen it for herself. There was no weather deep inside the CityBlocks.

"Now, we wait," Yates said. He sounded irritated. The others were late. Kailee wasn't too surprised; if they were coming on their own, they would have to convince the security guards that they were allowed up to the uppermost levels. And besides, being on time for anything *official* just wasn't cool. "Have you reviewed the files I gave you?"

"Yes," Kailee said, feeling everything she'd learnt drain out of her mind. She hoped he wasn't planning a pop quiz. There were teachers who questioned their pupils from time to time. They rarely lasted long – someone would issue a complaint after the first day – but they were always irritating. "I reviewed them all."

Yates gave her a faint smile that suggested he knew what she really meant. "You'll be tested, all right," he warned. "And if you fail, you won't get a second chance."

Kailee bit her lip. "What...what does that mean?"

"Wait and see," Yates said. His smile grew wider. "Just you wait and see."

Darrin had spent an uncomfortable night in one of the entertainment compartments, watching a couple of flicks and trying to forget the last sight he'd had of Fitz, crumpled on the floor. It bothered him badly that he'd left his stepfather in such a place, no matter how badly the bastard had deserved a beating. Part of him wanted to go back to the apartment and make sure that Fitz was alright, part of him knew perfectly well that Fitz would never show him the same consideration. By the time morning rolled around, Darrin was tired, irritable and headachy. He drew a pain-killer from the compartment's stores – headaches were a frequent side-effect of VR simulations – and started to walk towards the stairs.

Fitz will just have to take care of himself, he thought. It still gnawed at him. *And damn the bastard.*

He kept his expression carefully blank as he stepped aside to allow a pair of Civil Guardsmen to walk past him. They paid him no special attention, but he couldn't help worrying that they'd been sent to arrest him. Maybe Fitz had lodged an official complaint...no, somehow Darrin doubted that was true. The man might have bragged endlessly of his connections, but if he'd had *real* connections he wouldn't be living with Darrin's mother. And if the authorities didn't care about the gangs or the prostitution, rape or murder that took place in the CityBlock on a daily basis, they were unlikely to care about Fitz either. Seeing the Guardsmen still unnerved him, though.

There was no point in trying to talk his way past the security guards at the elevators. They were unlikely to believe him, whatever he said; few people from his level were ever given permission to travel freely to the higher levels. Instead, he found the stairwell and started to walk upwards. It took nearly an hour, but he finally reached the top, sweating like a pig. Yates tossed him a sardonic look as he staggered out of the door; Kailee merely looked amused...and disgustingly sweat-free. No doubt she'd talked the guards into letting her ride the elevator.

The nearest pair of doors opened, revealing Gary. Darrin glared at the nerd, who stopped and took a step backwards. How had *he* managed to get on the elevators? Gary gave him a nervous look, then walked towards the windows and stared outside. Darrin was too busy catching his breath to care about what was going on outside the CityBlock.

"Take some water from the dispenser," Yates advised, dryly. "And next time, just show the guards your papers."

Darrin flushed, angry at himself. They could have *told* him that their papers included permits to use the elevators! But clearly they'd assumed that the lucky winners could work it out for themselves. Gary certainly had...it gave Darrin no pleasure when Barry stumbled out of the stairwell, clearly the worse for drink. Darrin gulped as much water as he could, then stepped aside to allow Barry a chance at the dispenser. Yates watched them with a sardonic eye, then cleared his throat loudly.

"Now that we are *finally* all here," he said, "you can follow me."

Kailee and Gary trotted after him at once. Darrin and Barry followed, a little more reluctantly. It helped that Kailee was wearing something tight enough to show the shape of her ass. If she knew she was encouraging them, she didn't show any sign of it – but then, she had always been an ice princess. There were stories shared among the guys of each and every girl in the school, yet none of the ones about Kailee had ever been verified. As far as Darrin knew, she was still a virgin. That made her almost unique in their class.

They reached the end of the corridor and looked out into a small hanger. An aircar sat on its landing struts, waiting for them. It was smaller than Darrin had expected – most of the flicks he'd seen had made aircars out to be big bulky things – but it was large enough to take all five of them. Yates pulled a small device out of his pocket and clicked it, opening the doors, then motioned for Kailee to take the front seat. Darrin, who had been hoping to sit next to her, rolled his eyes. Clearly, Yates was interested in her too. She wasn't *that* much younger than him.

Gary sat at one of the window seats, Darrin sat in the middle, separating Gary and Barry. It was practical, he told himself; he didn't want to be disturbed by Barry picking on Gary – and he would, he knew. Barry delighted in picking on everyone, even if the hangover he was clearly nursing seemed to have sapped his energy. The doors hissed closed a moment later, then locked. A faint hum echoed through the aircar as the hatch ahead of the vehicle opened, then the craft lurched into the air and raced forward. Darrin barely had time to draw in a breath before they were in the open air and heading out, away from the CityBlock.

The aircar shuddered and bounced like it was a living thing. Something – gusts of wind, perhaps – seemed to be battering at its hull, shaking the entire vehicle. He heard Gary let out a yelp as the vehicle tilted, as if it were on the verge of flipping over completely, then stabilised. Craning his head behind them, he beheld the CityBlock in all its glory.

He'd seen pictures, of course, but they didn't compare to the real thing. Rowdy Yates was a towering structure, growing out of the Undercity and clawing upwards towards the sky. It was staggeringly ugly, utterly solid. He couldn't imagine anything that would damage the giant building, let alone destroy it. The ominous clouds around the very highest levels seemed harmless, compared to the towering CityBlock.

And it wasn't alone. As the aircar rose higher, he saw hundreds – no, thousands – of similar structures, reaching towards the sky. If Rowdy Yates held upwards of a million inhabitants – they'd never been given any precise figures, if they existed – he couldn't imagine just how many people lived in the surrounding blocks. He'd certainly never left his CityBlock in his entire life, even the handful of field trips had been done through VR simulations. Who knew what it would be like in the next CityBlock?

It would be just the same, he thought. Block residents had a tendency to focus on their own block, completely disregarding the rest of the planet. There was near-constant warfare between the gangs over access routes and tolls, but most of them remained locked in their separate blocks. Nothing he'd seen, however, had suggested that there were real differences between the blocks, at least those close to one another. *They'd be just like us.*

He looked towards Yates and blinked in surprise as he realised the older man was actually flying the aircar personally. Darrin had never been on an aircar before, but he'd had endless lectures on how safe the automatic command and control network actually was...and how fallible humans weren't allowed to fly their own vehicles. Now, he couldn't help wondering why they'd been taught that in the first place. It wasn't as if it was any use to them.

But what have we been taught that is useful?

The thought nagged at his mind. He'd learned more about playing the numbers from Fitz than he'd learned at school. His mother had taught him more about taking care of himself than school, largely through having as little to do with her son as possible. But school...what good was everything they'd learned, really? All it seemed to do was keep the kids busy eight till six, including the time necessary to pass through the security gates. Maybe that was all the teachers wanted...

He shook his head. If they'd been shown the towering CityBlocks, what would they have made of them? But that had never been an option.

———

Gary had never expected to feel pathetically grateful to Darrin, but in taking the middle seat – and sparing him from Barry – he had good reason to be thankful for the other boy. It was hard enough being on the aircar; every time the vehicle lurched or shuddered, Gary had to fight down a rising tide of panic. He'd flown in vehicles before, in the VR worlds he'd fought in online, but it wasn't quite the same. Here, he could die if the vehicle fell out of the sky. The black clouds, seemingly bare metres above their heads, looked solid. He knew that was an illusion, that they would just pass through the clouds if they rose higher, but he couldn't escape the conviction that they were all going to die.

He fixed his gaze on the back of Kailee's neck, trying to keep his mind occupied with something else. Fantasizing about the girls in his class had always seemed pointless – besides, he could download enough porn to keep himself occupied for hours – but there was little else to distract him. He was just grateful that he wasn't sitting next to Barry. The bastard would probably have pushed him towards the window, threatening to break through the glass – or whatever it was – and send him falling down towards the ground. Cold logic suggested that it would be impossible, but cold logic had little to do with his life.

Somehow, he managed to look down. The endless waves of CityBlocks had come to a brief halt. Instead, there was a black liquid; it took him a moment to realise that he was staring down at the dangerously-polluted ocean, the same ocean that served as an excuse for the endless recycling and other government initiatives to save what remained of the planet's environment. Looking down at the heaving mass, Gary couldn't help thinking that it was far too late – and besides, no one bothered to recycle anything anyway. There was just too much nagging and too little positive reinforcement. They didn't even bother with negative reinforcement.

If there are fish down there, they're all dead, he thought. According to their one trip to the holographic zoo, millions of different animals now only existed off-world – or in zoos. *That liquid is poisonous.*

In the distance, he caught sight of...*something* reaching up towards the sky. It looked like a needle, thin and barely strong enough to survive, but as they flew closer it grew larger and larger until it dominated the horizon. The building was larger – far larger – than any of the CityBlocks they'd passed over; unlike them, it punched right through the clouds as if they weren't there. And it was still growing larger...just how big *was* it?

"That's Orbital Tower One," Yates said, when Kailee asked. "It's base is massive, over a hundred kilometres wide, set firmly in the planet's crust. They say it took decades to build the tower and the other three, but once they were built humanity could *really* start expanding across the universe. Those towers are the gateway to the stars."

The aircar dropped down towards the lower levels, finally coming into land on a small pad that dropped into the ground as soon as they touched down. Overhead, a hatch slid closed, blocking out the dark sky – and the first drops of rain. The lights came on, revealing a large hanger. All around them, there were dozens of other aircars.

"Stay inside the designated footpaths," Yates ordered, as the doors opened. "You can get seriously hurt here if you stand in the wrong place."

Gary climbed out of the aircar and hastened to stand in the safe zone. Kailee followed him a moment later, Darrin and Barry took longer. Yates ended up barking at them to hurry, then led them down the pathway as soon as they were both out of the vehicle. Gary and Kailee exchanged glances – she'd been just as scared as Gary, he realised – and followed him, allowing the other two to bring up the rear.

Despite himself, he felt a twinge of excitement. No one in his school had ever been to the orbital towers. The four of them would have a real story to tell when they got home...

Not that it would help his social position, he knew. He would always be on the very lowest level of the social order. And there was nothing he could do about that.

CHAPTER
NINE

Needless to say, public education within the Empire did not live up to these lofty goals. It did not even come close to living up to those goals. And the fact that each successive generation of children were worse-educated than the last played a large role in the eventual collapse of the Empire. As I have noted in my prior textbooks, towards the end the Empire was not even able to maintain – let alone expand – the society it had developed.

- Professor Leo Caesius, *Education and the Decline and Fall of the Galactic Empire*

"These are your ID bracelets," Yates said, once they had passed through an airlock into a thoroughfare. "Put them on, do not remove them until I tell you to take them off. At best, there's a stiff fine for replacing them."

Kailee took hers and examined it briefly. It didn't look any different to the bracelet she had to wear every day at school, at least on the outside. They were specifically forbidden to try to open them and, as far as she knew, no one had ever actually succeeded. Hell, none of the kids had ever even been able to take them off while they were in school. She wrapped it around her wrist, then followed Yates as he led them down towards a large crowd forming in front of a pair of gates.

She couldn't help glancing around with interest as she saw the thousands of people milling through the hall. Some of them were dressed just like her parents, others wore colourful costumes or uniforms she hadn't seen outside the entertainment flicks. One woman, wearing the navy blue uniform of the Imperial Navy, caught and held her attention for a long moment, before she walked away arm-in-arm with another uniformed man. Kailee couldn't help noticing that her uniform was carefully tailored to show off her curves to best advantage; absently, she wondered if that was a regulation uniform or if the woman was sleeping her way to the top. Stellar Star had never shared her body in exchange for promotion, but given her sheer number of conquests it was easy to believe that she might have benefited from the goodwill of her sexual partners.

A handful of men and women wearing long black robes that covered every inch of their bodies walked past them, even their faces hidden from prying eyes. Kailee had heard of the Faceless Ones, a religious sect that believed in hiding themselves, but she'd never met one before. In fact, looking at them, it was hard to tell which of them were male and which were female. If they weren't allowed to undress in public, even amongst their own kind, how would they know how to tell the difference? Coming to think of it, how did they even procreate?

They reached the front of the line and stopped outside a counter. The bored looking woman at the desk scanned their bracelets, then fired off a series of increasingly stupid and inane questions. No, they hadn't been off-Earth before; no, they didn't have any infectious diseases; no, they already had clearance to leave the planet...by the time the woman was finished, Kailee was wondering if this was the sort of job most of her classmates could expect when they graduated. It didn't seem to require any skills apart from a high tolerance for boredom, which was the one useful skill taught in school.

"Give her your bags," Yates ordered. "They will be shipped to the starship separately."

Kailee scowled – if there was one thing she'd learned living in a CityBlock, it was that one should never leave one's property unattended – but obeyed, handing over her bag. The woman took it, attached a bracelet to the straps, then dumped it on a moving line that whisked it away into the bowels of the tower. Gary looked ready to protest as his bag was dropped down hard enough to break anything fragile, but a warning look from Yates told him to keep his mouth shut. Once the final two bags were handed over, the gate hissed open, allowing them to proceed.

"Just to remind you that you are responsible for the content of your bags," Yates said, once they were through the gates and heading towards the next checkpoint. "Should you happen to be carrying anything forbidden, they'll ship you over to the holding pens and add you to the next batch of indents."

You could have told us that earlier, Kailee thought, sourly. She'd actually read the instructions – there were a long list of things that they were forbidden to bring, starting with any form of weapon or explosives – but she doubted that either Darrin or Barry had bothered to read the list or have it read to them. Makeshift weapons were common in the lower levels of the CityBlock, despite endless laws against possession. Kailee honestly didn't know why the authorities bothered.

Gary had a different question. "What's an indent?"

"An indentured colonist," Yates explained. "They're generally petty criminals from Earth, snatched up by the Civil Guard and sentenced to exile. Most of them spend five to twenty years on the outermost colony worlds, helping to prepare them for settlement."

"That sounds bad," Kailee said.

"It can be," Yates agreed. "But a surprising number of indents have made something of themselves in the colonies. I knew a successful businessman who was shipped to his new homeworld after being caught purse-snatching in East-Meg One. He started as grunt labour in a farm, but soon realised how he could make a profit for himself."

Gary looked appalled. "The criminal became an important man?"

"The colonies generally don't care what someone did on Earth, as long as they are willing to work," Yates said. "There are some who never learn, who spend the rest of their days in chains, but the ones who work hard can make something of themselves. And their children are considered proper colonists."

He paused as they reached the second set of gates. "I suggest that you cooperate with the guards here, no matter what happens," he added. "There was an...incident two days ago and security has been tightened extensively."

Kailee saw what he meant as soon as they stepped through the gates. Grim-faced Civil Guardsmen, carrying stunners and plastic ties on their belts, were watching the lines of people as they made their way through the security gates. She gritted her teeth as she realised that each and every person had to pass through the check alone. It was just like being at school, apart from the weapons and the clear aroma of fear in the air. Whatever had happened two days ago, it had been bad.

But I heard nothing on the news about it, she thought. She rarely watched the news, but Aunt Lillian watched it whenever she had a spare moment. Surely, her aunt would have told her if something had gone wrong. *What happened?*

Yates motioned for Barry to go first when they reached the second set of gates. The gate opened, then closed behind him with an air of stunning finality. Kailee discovered that her mouth was dry, even though she'd passed through similar gates every day she'd gone to school. When her time came around, Yates had to push her through the gate and into the small compartment. It was barely large enough for her to swing a cat.

"Hold out your arms," a toneless voice ordered. "Spread your legs as far as they will go."

Kailee hesitated, then obeyed. A dull buzzing sound echoed through the compartment, then nothing. She started to straighten up, then stopped when the voice spoke again, ordering her to turn around and bend over. Irritated, Kailee did as she was told. There was another buzzing sound, then the other door opened up. Kailee straightened up, stepped through and came face-to-face with a Civil Guardsman who leered at her. Had he been watching through a hidden sensor? How much could the sensors see?

"Show me your bracelet," he ordered, holding a scanner in one hand. He pressed it against the bracelet when she held it up for him, then nodded down at the result. "You have a slot on Elevator Seventeen, departing in one hour. Do not be late or you will have to go through the whole procedure again."

He nodded towards a door at the far end of the compartment, which opened. Kailee started to step through, then jumped forward as he aimed a slap at her buttocks. She heard him snickering behind her as she practically ran through the door; there was no point, she knew, in complaining about that sort of harassment. Civil Guardsmen were immune to lawsuits, even assuming that she had been able to put together the money to file suit. Outside, she saw Barry and Darrin sitting on comfortable chairs, waiting for her. The atmosphere seemed a great deal more relaxed now that they were through the security precautions. There were even readers placed on the tables, waiting for users.

"This is your one chance to explore the departure lounge, but we cannot miss the elevator," Yates informed them. Kailee jumped; she hadn't heard him coming through the gates. "I want you to meet me over there" – he pointed to a large painting of the Childe Roland – "in forty minutes. Do *not* be late."

Kailee nodded. Darrin and Barry took off at once. Gary hesitated, then sat down next to Yates and picked up one of the readers. After a moment, Kailee joined him. Despite the safety precautions, she didn't feel safe at all.

She looked over at Yates, who had found a reader of his own. "What happened two days ago?"

"The Nihilists attacked Enid Blyton CityBlock and took thousands of hostages," Yates said, grimly. "You won't have heard anything about it because the news was largely blacked out by the Government. The Civil Guard proved unable to quell the uprising and the Marines had to be sent in. You won't have heard anything about that either."

Kailee blinked in surprise. She'd heard of the Nihilists, of course; they believed that life was completely worthless, encouraging their followers to commit suicide. But she'd never realised that they would attack others...

"They don't care about anything, apart from their beliefs," Yates explained. "And that makes them deadly dangerous. I shudder to think about what might happen if one of them got onto the orbital tower with enough explosive to do real damage. Billions of people might be killed."

———

Darrin had mixed feelings about spending time with Barry. One on hand, Barry could actually be fun; on the other hand, spending time with him was like living next to one of the man-eating monsters from the Arena. One never knew when the monster might turn on him when it next needed some amusement. But for the moment, walking through the departure lounge was a strange experience. Many of the people he saw, he realised, were actually leaving Earth permanently.

He looked at the stalls and smiled as he realised that the prices were actually cheaper than the prices in the CityBlock. There were even fresh fruits and vegetables, as well as the more common algae-based ration bars. The smell of freshly cooked meat drew him forwards and he found himself staring at a burger bar, before he remembered that he didn't have any money to buy anything. He considered, briefly, asking Yates for money, before dismissing the thought. They'd be fed on the elevator, they'd been told.

They walked back to the meeting point, then followed Yates through another set of gates and into a large room, crammed with comfortable chairs. A large display screen dominated one wall, another held a handful of automated food stalls. Yates motioned for them to find seats and sit down, leaving Darrin puzzled. Where *was* the elevator? The doors hissed closed and the entire room lurched, then there was a faint feeling of acceleration. Darrin shook his head in disbelief as the screen came to life; the entire room *was* the elevator. Outside, he saw the endless cities of Earth falling away as the elevator rose up into the air.

"It isn't real," Yates commented, quietly. "The elevator isn't on the outside of the tower at all."

Darrin nodded, feeling a strange sense of disappointment as he saw the other problems with the image. The weather had been dark and overcast when they'd landed – the orbital tower seemed to attract clouds – but the screen was showing a bright sunny day. There was no hint of the pollution they'd seen as they flew over towards the orbital tower. As they moved higher, the curve of the Earth's surface started to appear and the CityBlocks started to merge into an omnipresent greyness.

Kailee, who had been scanning the crowd, let out a gasp. Darrin turned, just in time to see her pointing towards a handful of young men. "Who...who are they?"

"Soldiers from the Imperial Army," Yates said. He sounded oddly irked by her question, although Darrin couldn't see why. "I think they're from the First Horse Regiment, judging by their uniform badges. One of the better regiments out there."

Darrin studied the soldiers with undisguised fascination. They wore green uniforms and looked...tough. He couldn't tell which of them was in charge; the golden stripes on their uniforms made no sense to him. And they kept their distance from the civilians, sometimes throwing them glances of barely considered disdain. The civilians seemed eager to return the favour.

"They shouldn't be here," Kailee said. "It isn't safe."

Yates gave her a look that made her shut up, sharply. "They're better men than you or I," he snapped. "And they put their lives on the line, daily, so you can enjoy the lives you do. Be grateful."

Darrin wondered, absently, if Yates had been a soldier himself. He certainly had the right attitude. Dismissing the thought, he turned away to look at the screen. They were passing through the clouds now; the atmosphere had become a hazy wisp surrounding the orbital tower, clinging to it as if the tower had its own gravity field. There was no way to know if the representation was accurate; right now, it looked as though Earth was growing smaller and smaller, while the tower was growing larger. It made his head hurt to think about the possible implications.

One by one, the pieces of Earth's giant network of orbital settlements and industrial nodes came into view. Darrin had learned about them in school, but seeing them now – so close to him – was something else. Earth had the largest industrial sector in the galaxy, he'd been taught, as befitted the planet's role as the font of all civilisation. Each day, the planet produced enough goods to keep the entire galaxy going. Or so they had been taught. It was evident that some of what they had been taught was far from accurate.

"There's nothing permitted anywhere near the orbital towers," Yates said, dryly. "Most of the orbital settlements are actually higher than the uppermost edge of the tower. You don't have to worry about an asteroid slamming into the building."

Gary looked disappointed. "So it's all fiction?"

"Not...*fiction*," Yates said, "just a misrepresentation."

Darrin nodded as the first starships came into view. Most of them were bulky, surprisingly crude; dull boxy shapes that suggested that their designers had focused on practicalities over aesthetics. A handful looked thoroughly nasty, bristling with weapons and sensor nodes; he recognised one design of battleship from watching Stellar Star strutting her stuff over the datanet. Somehow, he doubted that they would be travelling on one of *those*.

He looked down, towards Earth. The planet was a blue-green sphere, hanging in the darkness of interplanetary space. It seemed suddenly small and fragile to him; he couldn't make out the towering CityBlocks at all. But surely he should have been able to see the megacities...something tore at his heart as he realised that the entire planet was nothing more than an idealised depiction of what Earth should have been. Now, the planet was so badly polluted that it was dying.

The elevator jerked slightly, then slowed to a halt. There was a long pause – the floor shuddered slightly under their feet – then the doors opened, revealing another lounge. This one was barren, with chairs and little else; there was no form of entertainment apart from a single display screen showing what looked like a series of cartoons. Darrin hesitated as he caught sight of a group of men and women wearing bright orange overalls sitting in one corner, their hands and legs chained to make it hard for them to walk or escape. They had to be indents.

"We have to wait again," Yates said, after exchanging a few words with a uniformed man. "Sit down and be patient."

Sighing, Darrin obeyed. He took his seat, then looked around. The soldiers marched past them and headed into a door, which closed behind them as soon as the last one was through the gap. A handful of young children were running around, chasing one another with seemingly limitless energy; an older girl, around the same age as Kailee, seemed depressed as she sat beside her parents. Darrin guessed that she didn't want to leave Earth either.

Surprisingly, Barry was quiet as he sat down next to Darrin. He seemed to be staring at the indents, perhaps wondering just how close he'd come to joining them. Darrin wondered the same thing himself; he'd never seen anyone punished for anything in the lower levels, but people *did* vanish all the time. What if they'd been arrested, sentenced and evicted from Earth, leaving their families behind to come up with a story to explain their departure? But surely the authorities would want to tell everyone that there *was* punishment...?

He shook his head. There was no telling what seemed logical to the authorities. After all, if they could fix a competition and give seats on a starship to four teenagers who didn't really *want* to go, surely keeping quiet would seem logical to them too. Or maybe they were just insane.

It seemed as good a theory as anything else.

CHAPTER
TEN

Unfortunately, when operated on a large scale, education tends to put other matters before educating children. This becomes all the more apparent when the decision-makers are separated from the actual educational process. Lacking any real understanding of what is going on in the classrooms, educational bureaucrats found themselves looking for ways to measure progress that could actually be quantified.

- Professor Leo Caesius, *Education and the Decline and Fall of the Galactic Empire*

Gary had seen enough flicks, he thought, to know what it was like when someone left Earth. There was a walk through a near-transparent tube, where the starship could be seen in all its glory, then a jump through an airlock into the ship. It was a disappointment, when the time finally came to board the starship, to discover that it was nothing more than walking down a corridor, passing their bracelets to a pair of uniformed guards, then stepping through an airlock into the ship. The only sign that they had actually boarded a *real* starship was a faint quiver in the gravity field, where the tower's gravity had been replaced by the starship's artificial gravity.

Inside, the starship made him feel almost claustrophobic. The passageways were smaller than the corridors back home, making Yates and Barry bow their heads as they stepped through a series of passageways. Some of them were lined with enigmatic pipes, others were cold and completely sterile. The handful of crewmen they met cast distrustful glances at them, then ignored the newcomers completely. By the time they reached their compartment, Gary was wishing that he could go home. The environment was just familiar enough to be disconcerting. It was certainly nothing like Stellar Star's starships, which had been bright, roomy and utterly unbeatable.

He followed Yates into the compartment and stopped in surprise as he saw eight other teenagers and a grim-faced woman waiting for them. He'd known that the four of them weren't the only winners, but it was still a surprise to meet someone from another CityBlock. The woman rapidly introduced herself as Janet Livingston, their other escort; she looked friendlier than Yates, although there was a hardness in her voice that bothered Gary more than he cared to admit. She intimidated him.

"There are six boys and six girls," Janet said. "One compartment" – she pointed a long finger towards a hatch – "has been put aside for the girls, the other is for the boys. Boys will not go into the girls compartment and vice versa. Does anyone wish to argue about that?"

Gary kept his mouth firmly closed. He would have preferred a compartment he didn't have to share with Barry, let alone four other teenage boys, but he knew he wasn't going to be that lucky. Quietly, he resigned himself to a month or two of hell. Maybe he could find a friend among the ship's crew and explore her hull, keeping his distance from Barry and the others.

"We have been told to remain in this compartment until the ship is underway, which is expected to be in four hours," Janet continued, when no one spoke up. "Once we are underway, there *will* be tours of the ship and plenty of opportunity for you to keep up with your studies and learn from the crew. However, there are a number of safety precautions you are expected to bear in mind at all times. I have been informed by the XO that the Captain will not hesitate to lock up any of you who cause trouble or put lives in danger."

I'll bet, Gary thought, sarcastically. In his experience, no authority figure had been able to control Barry – and there was no reason to assume that the ship's Captain would be any different. Barry would do what came naturally – and that was picking on anyone weaker than himself. He found himself looking at the other winners and wondering which of them could stand up to Barry. None of them looked very impressive, although the girls looked quite pretty. Darrin and Barry had to be in heaven.

"For the moment, you are not to leave this section of the ship without an escort," Janet informed them. Gary groaned inwardly. "You are to be extremely careful not to damage any part of the ship, no matter how insignificant it appears. You are not permitted to enter the bridge, the engineering compartment or any exterior airlocks without permission. Anyone caught trying to enter the restricted sections will be in deep trouble."

Gary listened as she spoke on and on, outlining a list of precautions they were expected to take at all times. Shipsuits were to be worn; if they heard alarms, they were to don their masks and scramble into the nearest safe compartment. Water was not to be wasted; their showers would last two minutes precisely, then shut off. Gary silently prayed that nothing would go wrong. Knowing Barry, he would probably push Gary out of the safe compartment and leave him to die as the air exploded out of the ship.

"Interstellar travel is fairly safe," Janet concluded. "But bear this in mind at all times. Space does not suffer fools gladly. Something that would result in minor injury on Earth could get you and others killed in space. And believe me, you cannot come back from the dead."

She glanced down at her watch. "Your bags should have already been placed within the compartments. You may go and inspect them now, if you wish."

Reluctantly, Gary followed Darrin and the other boys into their compartment. It looked like a military barracks, with bunk beds and small cabinets; he hoped and prayed that Yates would be sleeping in the same room, even though he knew it was unlikely. There were twelve beds in all, as if they'd believed that there would be other winners. Or as if they didn't normally bother to separate the sexes.

"You take that bed," Barry ordered, pushing Gary towards the bed that was furthest from the hatch. Gary winced inwardly, then obeyed. There was no point in trying to fight, not when all it would get him was a beating. Barry just seemed to get off on hurting people; Gary had seen him pick fights with other boys, boys who were almost as big as Barry himself. "I'll take this one."

Darrin took another top bunk; the others chose their own beds in silence. They looked as unsure as Gary felt; they hadn't even bothered to introduce themselves. Quietly, Gary opened his bag and inspected it, quickly. Someone had gone through it, inspected the reader and the small computer, then placed them back in the bag. As far as he could tell, nothing was actually missing...

He looked up to see Barry leering at him. Gary shuddered, silently cursing whoever had rigged the competition. There was no way Barry should have won – and he had his doubts about both Darrin and Kailee. But whoever had rigged it had put him in the same compartment as a monster. Gary didn't even have the nerve to stand up and walk past Barry to get to the hatch. He was trapped.

Damn you, he thought, unsure of who he was cursing. Barry, the person who had designed the competition...or himself? *Damn you to hell.*

Someone had pawed through her stuff, Kailee realised, as soon as she opened her bag. Aunt Lillian had packed everything neatly, then placed the reader right at the top. Now, the reader was at the bottom and all of her underwear had been pushed out of shape. The searcher seemed to have paid more attention to her lingerie than anything that might be actually *dangerous*...Kailee scowled, barely able to repress her disgust, as she inspected the underwear piece by piece. The boys at school sometimes stole underwear from the laundry and did unspeakable things with it. She had to make sure it was clean.

"They did it to me too," a new voice said. "Bastards."

Kailee looked up. The speaker had dark skin, dark hair and darker eyes. Kailee felt a flash of envy; she looked exotic, compared to the girl-next-door image Kailee had tried hard to perfect. But there was something shy about the newcomer that reassured Kailee that she wouldn't be real competition. If, of course, there was something worth competing *for*.

"I think they thought we wouldn't be returning to Earth," Kailee said, crossly. Did the security guards really think that one bag of clothing was enough for someone who was leaving Earth permanently? But if the corporate-sponsored flick about Meridian was accurate, the corporation would provide everything the settlers needed. It wasn't a good idea to get too attached to anything on Earth. "But you're right. Bastards."

The girl smiled, rather shyly. "I'm India," she said, holding out a hand. "I come from Calcutta-Meg."

"Kailee," Kailee said. Maybe she could try to be nice. "Pleased to meet you."

As if that were an opening, the other girls tossed in their names too. There was Samantha from Erie City, Honey from Mega Lumpur, Yuki from Edo and Li from Sino-Cit. They were astonished to hear that four winners had come from the same block; the remaining winners were apparently strangers to one another. Kailee wondered absently if Principal Rico had called in favours to ensure that four of his students were declared winners or if it had been random chance. But that didn't seem too likely.

India seemed rather shy, she decided after ten minutes, even though she had taken the lead in opening conversation. Samantha and Honey, on the other hand, were as friendly and outgoing as most of the girls Kailee knew from back home, while Yuki and Li seemed more reserved. Li admitted that her family hadn't been pleased about her going at all; Yuki confessed that *her* family had asked her to scout Meridian, just to see if it was worth settling there. Kailee was surprised to hear that it was possible to leave without winning a competition, even though she should have known better. Yates had told her that the information for finding a colony development consortium and signing up as new settlers was available freely on the datanet. It just wasn't presented to them at school.

"We have to stick together," Samantha insisted, once they'd finished swapping stories. "Who knows what the crew will be like?"

"Good thought," Kailee agreed. And even if there wasn't the crew, she knew that Barry would cause trouble. She didn't know the other boys well enough to judge, but somehow she doubted that they were harmless. Few boys their age were harmless when confronted with something young, female and apparently defenceless. "We should ask Janet to stay in the same compartment."

She stood and looked into the washroom. It was tiny, but cleaner than anything back at school, where even the toilets reserved for the teachers stank terribly. The toilet itself seemed small, yet it was clearly functional. There was a tiny showerhead, just high enough to scatter water over her hair. Below it, there was a sign written in Imperial Standard. Kailee recognised some of the letters, but her attempts at sounding the words out ended in failure.

"It says that there will be a buzzer thirty seconds before the water stops," Yuki said. "I think we may have to cut our hair."

Kailee muttered a vile word under her breath. Long hair was *in* at the moment too – and she'd grown her hair out until it reached down to her ass. Taking care of it was a pain, but it was her crowning glory. But Yuki was right. If she kept her hair long, washing it while they were on the starship would be a major problem.

She weighed it in her mind as she stepped back, allowing the other girls to inspect the washroom. Aunt Lillian had packed a small selection of pills in her bag, she discovered as she pulled out her clothes and shoved them into the cabinet. That was technically illegal but the searchers had concentrated on her underwear and ignored the pills. There were painkillers, a handful of broad-spectrum antibiotics and a number of menstruation pills. It was easy to forget them when schools normally provided blanket doses for girls every month.

"At least your mother cared," Honey said. "Mine just wished me good luck and let me go."

"My aunt cared," Kailee said. It was strange to realise just how much her aunt had cared, now that she was hundreds of kilometres from the CityBlock and about to travel much further away. Tears stung her eyes as she carefully placed the pills in the cabinet, then buried them behind her underwear. "I never really realised until it was too late."

"Send her a message," Honey advised. "There's a communications console in the main room."

Kailee nodded and stepped out of the compartment. Yates and Janet were sitting on the sofa, talking in low voices. Kailee guessed that they were comparing notes on their charges, although as Janet hadn't met any of hers before they'd been picked up, it was hard to see what they might know about them. Schools were legally forbidden from keeping any records, apart from grades; employers, according to the Your Rights

Class, weren't even permitted to ask about a prospective employee's conduct while they were at school. But Yates might have been with them long enough to pick up an idea about their personalities...

"I need to send a message back home," she said, when Yates looked up at her. "How do I do it?"

Yates lifted his eyebrows in an exaggerated gesture of curiosity. "If you've forgotten something," he said, "there is no way they can get it to you before departure."

Kailee found herself flushing under his gaze. "No, sir," she said. "I just want to thank my aunt for packing for me."

Yates stood, then motioned for her to walk over to the corner. "Have you ever used one of these before?"

"No," Kailee admitted. She'd used the wristcom she'd been given at school, but it had had a number of addresses preloaded and no way to add or erase them. Her teachers had been able to harass her, her friends had not been allowed to add their codes to the system. "How do they work?"

Yates gave her a long look. "Do you know your family's code?"

Kailee shook her head, helplessly.

"Then you can't send them a message," Yates said, dryly. "Why didn't you memorise it when you were a child?"

"You should have my code," Kailee protested, finding her voice. "Surely it's in my file..."

"It could be," Yates offered. "But what would you do if your file was elsewhere?"

Janet tapped a datapad, then passed it to Yates. Yates took it, keyed a code into the console and nodded at Kailee. Kailee swallowed and began to speak, thanking her aunt for everything she'd done for her. Once she'd finished, Yates tapped a switch and sent the recorded message into the communications network.

"I'd suggest that you memorise such information in future," Yates commented, as Kailee turned to walk back to her compartment. "There won't always be someone around to help you."

Darrin sat upright as a dull throbbing suddenly ran through the ship. The bunk was quivering slightly, strange vibrations echoing through the bulkhead and his fingers, when he touched the edge of the compartment. A series of loud *clunks* echoed through the ship, then the dull throbbing grew louder. Moments later, the intercom activated and a voice spoke throughout the ship.

"Attention all hands, attention all hands," it said. "Assume departure stations; I say again, assume departure stations."

The hatch opened, revealing Yates. "Remain in this section," Yates ordered. "You have no departure stations."

Gary stood, snatched up his reader and walked outside. Darrin smiled to himself. He wasn't unaware of Barry's bullying games, but better Gary than himself or one of the other boys. It was quite possible that one of the other boys – he still didn't know their names – was secretly a good fighter, or mad enough to try to hurt Barry even if he was hurt badly himself. There were a handful of such boys at school, boys everyone avoided as much as possible. They were just crazy.

The starship seemed to shudder for a long moment, then smoothed out. Darrin guessed that they were heading away from the tower now, but compared to the starships in the entertainment flicks it was almost disappointing. There was no giant roar as the engines came to life...and nothing to see, apart from their compartment's bulkheads. He wondered, briefly, if it looked any different on the bridge. Or had the movies simply taken a few liberties with the truth just to make everything seem more dramatic?

"You should all get some rest," Yates said. "If you look inside your drawers, you'll find a starship-issue wristcom, linked into the ship's communications network. I'll wake you all up at 0800 tomorrow, precisely. We have a great deal of ground to cover."

Darrin nodded, wondering if Gary would come back or if he would try to sleep outside. They still didn't know where Yates and Janet were going to sleep. On impulse, Darrin asked.

"I'll be sleeping in here to make sure you behave yourselves," Yates said, sternly. He looked over at Barry, silently daring him to say anything. For once, Barry had the wit to keep his mouth shut. "And I would *advise* you to behave yourselves. The Captain has near-absolute authority over his vessel. He could put you out of the airlock and no one would bat an eyelid."

He turned and left the compartment. Barry let out an exaggerated sigh, then winked at Darrin.

Darrin sighed. That meant trouble, he was sure of it.

But as long as it was trouble for someone else, he didn't really care.

CHAPTER
ELEVEN

One simple example might be exams. Put crudely, the bureaucrats reasoned that the more students who passed the exams, the better the educational system was working. On the face of it, this didn't seem a bad idea. Teachers – those who actually worked with children – often knew better. When attempting to pass an exam, students would cram and review in the weeks prior to the test – and then forget everything once the exam was over.

- Professor Leo Caesius, *Education and the Decline and Fall of the Galactic Empire*

Gary had to admit, reluctantly, that he'd been spoiled by the entertainment flicks he'd watched. They showed deadly weapons, half-naked crewwomen in miniskirts and exploding consoles, but they didn't show the deadly boredom of moving from star to star. Five days after *Hawkins* had crossed the Phase Limit, they had largely explored the entire ship and were starting to feel confined. Yates had pointed out, rather sarcastically, that they'd been confined in the CityBlock too, but somehow it wasn't quite the same.

But the starship did have some unusual pieces of equipment to help pass the time. There was a gaming system that was actually far in advance of anything Gary had seen on Earth, a VR lounge that was largely configured for porn and a set of teaching machines that the crew claimed were far more effective than human teachers. Gary had had his doubts until he'd actually *tried* one of them, hoping to keep his studies going. The teaching machines were definitely far more interesting than the human teachers, if only because everything was cross-referenced and carefully explained. A human teacher wouldn't bother to explain something if it wasn't in the lesson plan.

"This system is designed to help overcome the effects of teaching on Earth," Lieutenant Royce said. He seemed to have been assigned to work with the lucky winners, which Gary suspected meant keeping an eye on them. They'd only met the Captain once, but he hadn't looked too pleased at having twelve teenage children on his ship. "Most of the new recruits we get can't even add five and six without taking off their socks."

Gary nodded. He considered himself one of the brightest students in his class, but the teaching machine constantly pushed him right to the limits. There were entire fields of study, it seemed, where he was completely ignorant, while there were others where he was nowhere near as knowledgeable or as smart as he had believed. The first exam he'd taken on the starship had been a dismal failure, even though the teaching machine had explained with inhuman patience precisely where he'd gone wrong. It had been humiliating, but it had also been reassuring. That level of feedback was never available on Earth,

"There have to be jobs for the teachers," Royce explained, when Gary said that out loud. "So your classmates will be denied the use of such machines, just to keep the teachers employed."

"...Oh," Gary said. He wasn't sure he believed Royce. The teachers he'd met had never seemed very happy about their jobs, apart from the PE teacher. But then, the PE teacher was actually respected by the students. Surely, if they could be replaced by machines, why wouldn't they *want* to be replaced by machines? "That isn't fair."

Royce laughed. "Of course it isn't fair," he said, as he stood. "It's just the way the system works."

He tapped a command into the console, then smiled. "Why don't you try following this course?"

Gary read through the précis as Royce left the compartment, leaving him alone. The course covered starship operations and navigation, everything from life support to interstellar shipping. Curious, he opened it up and discovered that it was organised neatly into a set of sub-modules, each one with their own certificate. Some seemed relatively simple, particularly when explained by the teaching machine, others seemed remarkably complicated and beyond his comprehension. What did the size of a star matter when it came to calculating the Phase Limit?

Two hours later, he took a break, poured himself a cup of coffee and pulled a random article from the database to read. He'd read plenty of semi-forbidden knowledge on Earth, once he'd by-passed the security codes on his government-issue computer, but some of the information on the starship's database was fascinating...and some made absolutely no sense at all. He simply didn't have the context to understand it.

When looking at the Stellar Star series of entertainment flicks, the first word that comes to mind is plagiarism. The producers claim that Stellar Star's adventures are as original as her good looks. In reality, almost all of the flicks draw their plots from far older stories, which have often been oddly bowdlerised to suit the Empire. For example, Stellar Star XXVI takes its plot almost completely from Cosmic Wars V, which itself was drawn from a pre-space entertainment flick on Old Earth. The scene where she comes face to face with her real father for the first time is almost precisely the same as the original.

The only real difference lies in the background situation. Where the heroes of Cosmic Wars fought against the Galactic Empire, Stellar Star fights to uphold the Empire – and the rebels are presented as wreckers, degenerates and outright monsters, people who have to be killed. This none-too-subtle piece of propaganda is part of a long-term effort to uphold the ideal of the Empire in the minds of its citizens.

Gary shook his head. He'd watched the latest Stellar Star – although, like most of his classmates, he'd been more interested in the actress herself than the plot, which had been rather bland. But looking back at it, it was easy to see that the writer was right; Stellar Star's enemies were the same as the enemies of the *real* Empire, painted as monsters. The underlying message was that the good guys always supported the Empire.

He'd never really considered it before, not so clearly. How much else had they been exposed to in school, without even *noticing*? They'd been told all sorts of things about how wonderful the Empire was and how it took care of each and every one of its citizens...how much of that, he asked himself, had been a lie? And then there were the exams where one had to work out what answer was actually *wanted*, instead of what answer was actually correct...

There was a tap at the hatch. He blanked the screen hastily – pornography would have been understandable, but he had his doubts about forbidden knowledge – and looked up as the hatch hissed open, revealing Yates. Gary sighed in relief; he wasn't sure if he liked the older man or not, but his presence in the sleeping compartment had probably saved Gary from all sorts of humiliations. Even Barry seemed reluctant to challenge him.

"Good afternoon," Yates said. "How are you doing?"

Gary looked down at the screen. "I was studying starship operations," he said. It was something that had never been presented to them on Earth. "It seemed tricky at first, but as I got the hang of it..."

Yates snorted. "There's a difference between schooling and actual experience," he said, sardonically. "I've never seen a starship that was precisely as the specifications demanded – or a CityBlock, for that matter."

Gary nodded. One of his uncles had been a maintenance engineer before he'd vanished, somewhere down in the bowels of the CityBlock. He'd often complained that half his problems were caused by idiot residents overstressing the system or trying to use it to dispose of something the system wasn't designed to handle. And then he'd gone out one day and never come home. Gary sometimes wondered if he hadn't simply deserted his post. Apparently, people like him were never permitted to leave...

"Still, if you impress the crew, you might be able to actually try to get some actual experience," Yates added. "I rather doubt they'll let you work on the drive, but if you don't mind getting your hands dirty they might have something for you to do."

"I don't know," Gary admitted. He had to get ready for his exams...but the more he worked with the teaching machine, the more he suspected that the exams were actually worthless, even the ones that should get him into Imperial University. "Is it worth it?"

Yates looked him in the eye. "What do you plan to do with your life?"

Gary hesitated, trying to think. In truth, he'd been so focused on getting away from the CityBlock that he hadn't thought much further ahead. Imperial University offered courses on just about everything, from law to economics. He'd even go for remedial basket-weaving if it got him out of Rowdy Yates.

"You could spend three more years in schooling if you tried," Yates said, softly. "You're certainly capable of passing the exams to enter university, although you should have realised by now that exams aren't the only way of determining who gets into the system. Or you could go to college..."

"No," Gary said. He'd heard enough about the college nearest his apartment block to know that he didn't want to go there. He might as well claim his BLA and remain in the apartment for the rest of his life, spending all of his time on the datanet. "I am *not* going there."

Yates seemed oddly pleased by the response. "And what will you do after university?"

"I don't know," Gary admitted. "What *could* I do?"

"Well, that depends," Yates said. "What do you *want* to do with your life?"

Gary took a breath. "A life somewhere safe, a life I can enjoy..."

"Not a bad answer," Yates interrupted. "What do you enjoy doing?"

"Computing," Gary said, immediately. "I'm *good* with computers."

"Quite a few people have claimed to be good with computers," Yates pointed out. "How good are you?"

"I bypassed the security codes on my computer," Gary said, stung. It struck him, a moment later, that confessing that might not have been a good idea. But it was too late. "I did it all on my own."

"Slightly more impressive," Yates commented. "Why don't you build on that?"

He tapped the teaching machine with one long finger. "There are educational courses loaded into this machine that would help you to develop your skills," he added. "And there is always work for proper computer experts."

Gary stared at him. "Why...why wasn't I told this on Earth?"

Yates gave him a droll look. "Why do you think that your teachers give a shit about you personally?"

"I *know* they don't care about me," Gary protested. If he'd doubted that, the absolute lack of concern the teachers had shown about the rampant bullying in the school would have shattered the delusion. Kids had been *crippled* in the school, even *raped* in the school...and the teachers hadn't really cared. "But they should have told me..."

"The irony is that the information is probably available, if you look for it," Yates said, ignoring Gary's tone. "But you'd need to guess at its existence before you go look for it, wouldn't you? Tell me...did you have any career in mind at all when you plotted your escape?"

Gary shook his head, not trusting himself to speak.

"I'd suggest, very strongly, that you complete as many of the modules as possible, then ask the Captain to consider recruiting you as an apprentice spacer and computer expert," Yates offered. "The consortium that operates these starships is always looking for qualified manpower; if you showed talent and willingness, they'd certainly offer to help you meet the remaining requirements. You're underage, technically, but the recruiters probably won't care."

"But..."

Gary swallowed, unsure of how Yates would react to blatant contradiction, then pressed onwards. "But there were kids who tried to apply for jobs in my apartment block and they were refused..."

"Only for the legal ones, I'd guess," Yates said, dryly.

Gary nodded. It was illegal to hire anyone younger than seventeen – and only then if they'd completed their schooling. The handful of small businesses operating in the upper levels of the CityBlock might have been desperate for manpower, but they hadn't taken anyone who was too young, even if they could have worked while they weren't in school.

"No," he said. The gangs had hired children as runners – and worse – but the gangs weren't remotely legal anyway. "Why would the Captain take me...?"

"The rules are different when a big consortium is involved," Yates said. His tone hadn't changed, but Gary thought he saw sardonic amusement in his eyes. "A few bribes to the right person and you will have a record that says you're old enough to do whatever the hell you like."

"But..."

Gary stopped. For all of his life, he had been told that the government would look after him and his fellows, no matter how well they did in school. There was the SLA, then the BLA...and free food, served up in CityBlock canteens. Everyone was registered, the teachers had said; no one was allowed to fall through the cracks and vanish. But the more he thought about it, the more he realised that their claims were nonsense. There was no shortage of unregistered people living in the lower levels – or in the Undercity itself.

And then his father and uncle had grumbled about having to pay bribes...

"But you will have to *work*," Yates warned. He stood and beckoned Gary to follow him. "And I would suggest something else as well."

Gary rose to his feet and followed Yates through the hatch and down a long passageway, towards the prow of the ship. It was hard, sometimes, to keep track of the ship's interior, even though it didn't change. He'd been told that he would get used to it, but for the moment he kept getting lost every so often. It didn't help that at least half the crewmen he'd asked for help had pointed him in the wrong direction.

Yates led him through a large hatch and stopped, inviting Gary to look around. The room was crammed with strange-looking devices. One looked like the bicycles he'd seen on the flicks, the others were completely new to him. He heard the hatch hiss closed behind them as Yates pointed to the devices and named them, one by one.

"Leg-breaker, jaw-smasher, muscle-puller, chest-thumper..."

He turned back to grin toothily at Gary. "Just kidding."

Gary swallowed, hard.

"I read your medical report," Yates said. "It made interesting reading."

He went on before Gary could point out that reading medical reports without the permission of the patient was illegal. The whole process had pushed the legal limits, Gary was sure; the ship's doctor had poked and prodded him in crevices he hadn't even known he had, before brusquely confirming that he was as fit as could be expected. Gary had been so unnerved by the procedure that he hadn't waited around as soon as he'd been told he could go.

"You are *not* particularly healthy," Yates continued. "A steady diet of algae-based food is not good for long-term health, although you *can* survive on it. And they didn't give you any gene-spliced treatments to help you cope either, which isn't too surprising. Earth has always been reluctant to provide such treatments without a very valid reason.

"Most importantly" – he turned to face Gary, his expression dark enough to send Gary inching backwards – "you are physically weak."

"I *know*," Gary said, numbly. He *knew* he was weak. His face was rubbed in that simple fact every time Barry – or one of the others – picked on him. There was no point in fighting, not against someone far bigger and stronger than himself. Even the girls were stronger than him. "But I can't do anything about it."

Yates placed his hand on Gary's shoulder and squeezed, gently. "Why not?"

"Because...because I *can't*," Gary said, desperately. "I just can't fight."

"That's an attitude you need to lose," Yates said. He nodded to the machines. "These machines are designed to help spacers maintain their physical fitness. Given a proper exercise program, you could start building up muscles within a month or two. It wouldn't be *easy*, not with your body as badly degraded as it is, but it would be doable."

He met Gary's eyes. "If, of course, you are willing to make the effort," he added. "Or you could just stay a victim for the rest of your life.

"Your teachers will have told you that fighting is morally wrong, of course. That's the message they've been told to give you and they *will* give it to you, even though common sense should tell them otherwise. And you haven't been given much physical exercise at all..."

Gary winced. The handful of mandatory PE classes had been hellish. It had been a relief to be allowed to go study instead, knowing that Barry and Moe wouldn't drop their chance to play just to come torment him. How could he enjoy himself when half the class had thought that slamming the ball into his face was *funny*?

"They should have made it compulsory," Yates told him. "Maybe separated out the weaker students and helped them to develop muscles. But that would have forced them to acknowledge the simple fact that some people *are* violent. And that, no matter what they told you, the violent are rarely punished."

"I don't know if I can do it," Gary confessed. "I..."

"It won't be easy," Yates said, again. "Your body will hurt and you'll curse my name. But if you make the effort, it will be worthwhile. And, one day, you will be able to fight."

It seemed impossible, Gary knew. How could *he* fight? But if Yates was right...

"I'll try," he promised. He looked at the machines, doubtfully. "Where do I begin?"

CHAPTER
TWELVE

This also warped the incentives faced by the teachers. Failing to get their children through the exams would make it seem that they were poor teachers (and thus risk them being sacked). Naturally, they taught to the test, rather than teaching the children to develop their own minds. There was also a strong incentive to cheat, particularly when they knew the tests were largely worthless.

- Professor Leo Caesius, *Education and the Decline and Fall of the Galactic Empire*

Kailee looked around nervously as Janet led all six of the girls into a large compartment and closed the hatch behind them. The trip had been boring so far – none of the other girls shared her interests – but she couldn't help feeling worried. Janet had watched all of them so closely that Kailee had become convinced that she was being *assessed* for something. But what?

She'd certainly learned more than she'd ever wanted to know about Meridian. Yates and Janet were good teachers; every day, they'd spent the morning lecturing their charges, then giving them material to read that tied in with the lectures. And they were tested, not just on what they'd memorised, but on its implications. Kailee had never felt quite so tested in her life. Even the endless exams at school hadn't been so bad – but then, she'd been able to refuse to actually do the work. Here, she had the feeling that not trying her best would have unpleasant consequences.

Janet motioned for them to sit on the deck. Kailee sat, silently cursing her shipsuit under her breath. It covered everything below the neck – taking it off to go to the toilet was a major hassle – but it was tight enough to leave nothing to the imagination. The boys gawked and stared at the girls, not even trying to hide their reactions.

"I shall be blunt," Janet said. "You are all vulnerable."

Kailee couldn't disagree. The one lesson hammered into the head of every girl born within the CityBlock was pretty much the same. Girls were vulnerable, more vulnerable than their fathers, brothers and sons. If Kailee had been inclined to doubt it, there were no shortage of real-life horror stories shared in whispers, ranging from rape to slow torture and murder. She *knew* a dozen girls who had been raped outright – and others, who hadn't been openly raped, but hadn't really given their consent. The schools taught that consent was important, yet the authorities did nothing to ensure that rapists were punished.

If you go somewhere, Aunt Lillian had said, *go with friends or your brothers, people you can trust to look after you. But don't trust anyone completely.*

She'd been right, Kailee knew. There were stories of girls sold into prostitution by their families, often to pay debts to the gangs. No one could be trusted completely, no one at all.

"You have also been denied any form of self-defence training," Janet continued. "In their infinite wisdom" – the words were sneered, rudely – "the authorities on Earth frown on teaching anyone how to fight. To add to this problem, most of you are actually quite puny by my standards. In short, you are largely incapable of protecting yourselves. Tell me...what would you actually do if rapists attacked your group?"

Kailee swallowed, feeling a chill spreading through her body. The girls had told themselves that they would fight, but they'd never really been tested. What would they have done if the boys had launched a mass charge, instead of merely wolf-whistling from a safe distance? It was hard to imagine herself actually *fighting*.

"We would have tried to fight," Li said. She sounded worried, as if she didn't quite believe her own words. "And we might have won."

"*Might* being the operative word," Janet sneered. She pulled back her shipsuit sleeve, exposing a muscled arm. "None of you are strong enough or practiced enough to defend yourselves – and believe me, there *will* be dangers wherever you go."

Kailee looked at Janet, then asked the question that had been bothering her since Janet had begun the lecture. "Are there rapists on Meridian?"

Janet gave her a droll look. "Do you think they need to import them?"

She pressed on before Kailee could say a word. "The first step towards true independence is learning to take care of yourselves. You're from Earth; you *know* how savage life can become, even in a so-called civilised CityBlock. And believe me, having your rapist hanged afterwards doesn't really take away the pain."

The girls gasped. If they'd grown up in CityBlocks too they'd probably run the risk of being raped every day, just like Kailee herself. Some of the girls she knew who had been raped had seemed to take it in their stride, others had killed themselves soon afterwards. Maybe the attitude some of them had to 'surprise sex' was a mental defence against the realisation that one had been forced into it against one's will. But it was still rape and it was still sickening.

"So," Janet said, into the silence. "There is a truth that your teachers never taught you, probably because they never knew it themselves. You can choose if you are going to be a victim or someone who will stand up for herself. If the former, you might as well roll over and spread your legs for the first tough-looking guy who comes along. If the latter, you might still die...but you will have clawed the bastard nice and proper in the meantime.

"I don't promise that I can turn you into Stellar Star," she added. "You won't have the benefit of a scriptwriter, cosmetic body-shops, a stunt double or a set of enemy goons who know that they have to stick to the script. What you will have, if you work with me, is the confidence to stand up for yourself and a chance to hurt someone who might hurt you."

Kailee hesitated. She had never really thought of actually learning to fight – in hindsight, it was clear that the whole idea had never been suggested to any of them. But...did she have the determination to fight? She knew that there were girls who had tried to fight, when confronted by a mugger or a rapist; those girls had invariably come off worst. If any of their attackers had been hurt, no one had ever said anything about it.

She stuck up her hand. "Can you *really* teach us how to fight?"

"You have to be willing to learn," Janet said, bluntly. "And you have to develop the attitude that will allow you to fight. Because, right now, the impression I get from each of you is that you will surrender to the slightest challenge. If you feel, deep inside, that submitting yourself to the whims of a random man is the only way to survive, you may as well do just that. But if you want some *control* over your own lives...well, this is the only way to get it."

Kailee remembered the moment when Darrin had tried to ask her out. They'd been alone...and she had feared that he would hurt her, or worse, if she turned him down. Darrin hadn't...but she knew that there were others who thought that they could just force themselves on the girl and she would submit to them. Maybe, just maybe, they thought it because they knew that the girl wouldn't fight and there would be no real risk of injury. Would the rapists stop if they believed that their targets would fight back?

"You will have been told, no doubt, to stay with your friends and families," Janet continued, breaking into Kailee's thoughts. "But relying on someone else for protection is always a bad idea. What if they let you down? Or what if they turn on you?"

She was right, Kailee knew. A protector could turn into an enemy very quickly. She knew women whose husbands had become monsters after they married, yet they didn't dare leave for fear of what might be lurking outside their apartments. And there were girls in her school who had found themselves pushed into becoming more and more...accommodating to their boyfriends, or eventually sold into slavery with the gangs. It was horrific...and yet it happened. No one in authority seemed to bat an eyelid.

Kailee leaned forward. "Can we actually win?"

Janet snorted, rudely. "There is no guarantee of *anything*," she said. "Your teachers won't have told you this either, but I think you already know it. On average, a man is thirty percent stronger and faster than a woman. That's a fact of life, at least on Earth. There are planets where men and women have been engineered to be equal, or women have been designed to be stronger than men, but you don't happen to live there.

"Training can make the difference," she added. "If you know what you're doing and the man doesn't, you can kick his ass from one end of the planet to the other. There are women in the military, even in the Marines, who would have no difficulty breaking your male compatriots, one by one or all together. But those women...even the least of them spent *years* learning their trade.

"I don't propose to turn you all into soldiers," she concluded. "But I swear to you that if you learn from me, you will develop the attitude that will allow you to kick a rapist so hard that his balls end up in his eye sockets."

Honey frowned. "What happens if we run into a trained man?"

"Then you lose," Janet said, flatly. "But if you believe that you're always going to fail, you *will* fail."

Kailee hesitated, looking from face to face. She hadn't discussed anything sensitive with them, she had no idea if any of them had been raped or not. But some of them looked eager to learn and others seemed to have their doubts. Kailee herself was unsure. She'd put a great deal of effort into maintaining her body and she didn't really want to risk damaging it. A muscled woman might not get the best roles, at least outside pornographic material.

But what did she actually *want*? She asked herself the question, time and time again. It was easy to say that she wanted to become an actress, but what *else* did she want? What if Janet was right and learning to look after herself might actually help in the future? After all, what would she do when she was kicked out of her family's apartment? There just wasn't enough room for all of them, certainly not once Kailee was of age.

She found herself torn in two. Part of her wanted the lessons, wanted Janet's easy confidence – she hadn't seen Janet show any doubt or hesitation around the boys – but part of her was scared. What if she damaged her own body? Or what if she looked *too* confident? There were stories of boys deciding that certain girls were too uppity and 'teaching them a lesson...'

"I will be talking to each of you, individually, over the next few days," Janet said, breaking into Kailee's thoughts. "But, for the moment, you can take some time to think about what you actually *want* from life. Come back here in an hour."

The other girls stood and headed for the hatch. Kailee saw, suddenly, just how strange the dynamic actually was. She'd known the girls in Rowdy Yates; they'd been her allies, even if they hadn't all been her friends. But the girls here were strangers, not just to her but to each other as well. There was no strength in numbers, she decided, when the numbers didn't really add up properly. Or was she merely imagining it?

A hand fell on her shoulder and she jumped, then turned to look at Janet.

"Staying here?" Janet asked. "Or do you want to talk?"

"I want to talk," Kailee said. "I don't know what to do."

"A common problem," Janet agreed. "You were never taught how to be decisive, were you?"

The blunt contempt in her voice *stung*. "I did the best I could," Kailee said. "I'm going to leave, if this hadn't happened..."

"Leave?" Janet asked. "Leave where?"

Kailee hadn't meant to tell anyone, but there was something in Janet's voice that made her spill the beans. She told her about her plans to become an actress, how she planned to leave the CityBlock at the earliest opportunity and make herself famous and successful. And then she confessed how she'd always underestimated Aunt Lillian and never really realised that her aunt was trying to take care of her. Janet listened, her face expressionless, as Kailee finished, then smiled.

"At least you have ambition," she said. "I've noticed that very few of your friends have *any* ambition, any desire to better themselves."

"Thank you," Kailee said. Was that a hint of approval in Janet's voice? She couldn't say for sure. "I don't really want to waste time..."

Janet caught her arm, preventing her from continuing. "If you never listen to anything else I tell you," Janet snapped. "listen to this. This trip is the best thing that has happened to you – and will ever happen to you. You may not believe it, but you will have opportunities aplenty to grow and better yourself over the coming months. I *strongly* advise you to take advantage of them!"

Kailee tried to step backwards, but Janet held her arm too tightly. "You cannot afford to assume that you can coast along for a few months, then return to Earth and the fame you feel you deserve," Janet added. "This trip will give you opportunities, if you use them. Use them!"

She smiled and let go of Kailee's arm. "If nothing else, you will have something to brag about on the talk show circuit."

Kailee rubbed at her arm. Janet really was quite strong, stronger than any other woman Kailee had met. She found herself studying the older woman, trying to determine if she had worked hard to build her muscles – or if she had gone to the body-shops and had her body reshaped into something more suitable for her. Kailee had never been able to go herself, save for a handful of minor treatments. The idea of completely revamping her entire body was a dream she knew would never be realised, at least until she was rich and famous.

"I don't know," she confessed. "Will anyone really care?"

"It's always hard to know what Earth will care about," Janet said. "It's a strange place."

Understanding clicked in Kailee's mind. "You're not from Earth, are you?"

Janet shook her head. "I was born on Hamish's World," she said. "You probably wouldn't like it very much. Marshal Hamish believed, very strongly, that technology had to be tightly restricted for the betterment of the human soul. My parents were farmers; I practically grew up staring at the back end of a mule. We had nothing like the readers and wristcoms and other junk you're so used to on Earth. Our nights were spent playing board games or reading the bible.

"When I was fifteen, the local squire decided to have some fun with me," she added. "The entire community thought he was a noble man – quite literally. I didn't see trouble coming as he rode up on his horse and jumped down beside me; by the time he had grabbed me, it was too late. I fought, as desperately as I could, but he held me down and..."

Kailee nodded. She could guess.

"He left me there, afterwards," Janet added. "Broken, bleeding...and angry. I didn't tell anyone what had happened; I thought they wouldn't believe me. Instead, I took my hunting bow and put an arrow through his head the next time he went riding. And then I fled to the local recruiting office and joined the Imperial Army. They took me off Hamish's World and I never looked back.

"Earth is a nightmare. I don't understand how you and your friends can *live* there. You get fed crap to eat and crap to believe, yet you think that the government takes care of you. It is manifestly obvious that the government *doesn't* take care of you, yet you believe it. And there isn't even a *hint* of safety anywhere. How can you *stand* it?"

"You were raped on your homeworld," Kailee pointed out, before she could stop herself. "I..."

"I was the unlucky exception," Janet snapped. "Rape is *rare* on Hamish's World. On Earth, a girl like you is lucky to live to her twenties without being forced into sex at least once. The figures for men aren't much better. Hell, chances are that half of your classmates will be dead of something violent before they reach their thirties! You don't even try to punish the offenders, which only encourages them."

She shook her head, visibly forcing herself to calm down. "You might make your dream come true," she added. "But my honest advice to anyone would be to try to find something that took them away from Earth before it was too late. And *you* have been handed such an opportunity on a silver platter. You could just stay on Meridian if you wished."

"The government would know," Kailee said, dully. "I..."

Janet surprised her by laughing. "You don't get it," she said. "The government doesn't give a *shit* about you – or anyone else. You have this myth of government super-competence burned into your head, even when you should be able to see that the government is far from perfect and doesn't really care about anyone. It cannot even *begin* to provide all the services you think you're entitled to claim."

She lowered her voice. "If you chose to stay," she added, "no one would care in the slightest. Why would they bother to hunt you down?"

Unsure, Kailee shook her head in disbelief. Or denial.

She honestly wasn't sure which.

CHAPTER

THIRTEEN

As strange and absurd as this seems, the bureaucrats had a rational goal in creating the examination system (and other such ideas). Better results meant more funding, which allowed them to build up their bureaucratic empires – and gave them something to fight for. The fact that this actually ignored the whole concept of what was best for the kids was immaterial. Indeed, the overall goal – of educating children – was replaced by the goal of obtaining as much funding as possible.

- Professor Leo Caesius, Education and the
Decline and Fall of the Galactic Empire

"I am bored," Barry said.

Darrin nodded in agreement. Neither of them were particularly interested in their studies, while Steve, Abdul and Harold had formed their own study group and Gary was off on his own somewhere. All *they* had to do was play endless games; the simple ones were boring, while neither of them had the patience to learn how to play the more complex ones. There was no shortage of flicks and other entertainments in the starship's datanet, but – for some reason – there were restrictions on how long they could just sit in front of the screen and watch.

It wasn't as if the starship was very exciting. The bridge, engineering and a handful of other sections were completely sealed off, while the remainder of the ship was just...boring. They had found some entertainment while sneaking into the stasis compartments and admiring girls trapped in the fields like flies in amber, but after they'd been caught by a crewman the doors had been locked and they'd received a stern lecture from Lieutenant Royce. Darrin hadn't taken the lecture too seriously, yet there had been no way to get back into the compartment.

He looked down at the game board and rolled his eyes. The only way to make Starships and Wormholes more exciting was to have imaginative forfeits – and to do that properly they would need girls. Most of the other games weren't any more interesting, particularly the ones where Barry could be outthought. He took it badly.

Barry stood up and started to pace around the living compartment. They were alone – Janet had taken the girls somewhere, Yates was away doing something of his own – without anything to do to keep themselves occupied. Darrin watched Barry uneasily, unsure quite what the tougher boy had in mind. They'd been pushed together by circumstance, but he neither liked nor trusted Barry. He might turn on Darrin at any moment.

"There has to be something we can do," Barry said. "I wonder..."

He pushed at the hatch leading into the female sleeping compartment. It clicked open; Darrin looked up in shock. The hatch was supposed to be locked at all times, only accessible through the wristcoms handed out to the girls. He didn't even know if *Yates* had access, although he would have bet against it. The male teachers back home were barred from entering the female toilets, even in case of emergency. It would mean instant dismissal.

Fascinated, he stood up and followed Barry into their sleeping compartment. It was disappointingly similar to the male compartment, although it was definitely neater; a handful of pieces of clothing hung from one of the unoccupied beds, drawing Barry towards them like a moth to a flame. He pulled a bra from the bed and held it up, a strange leer on his face. It was such an odd expression that Darrin found himself bursting into laughter.

"So tell me," Barry said, "who do you think *this* belongs to?"

Darrin considered it. Thanks to the shipsuits, they knew that Samantha and Yuki were the only two girls with large enough breasts to wear the bra properly. Yuki had always struck him as shy, while the bra definitely was not designed for a shy girl. It had to be Samantha's, by process of elimination. Who else could it belong to?

"Samantha," he said.

Barry grinned, then pulled open one of the cabinets. Unlike the lockers at school, the cabinets didn't seem lockable. Inside, there were pieces of underwear ranging from boringly practical to outrageously sexy. Barry pulled them out, examined them and then stuffed a couple in his pocket. Darrin considered taking a pair of panties for himself, then dismissed the thought. Nice as it would be, he had a feeling that the girls would notice. His plans to talk one or more of them into bed would take a blow.

He swore as he heard the main hatch opening, then tried to press himself against the bulkhead even though he knew it would be futile. Who knew *what* would happen if they were caught inside the female compartment. Barry, the dunderhead, strode up to the hatch as if he didn't have a care in the world, still carrying one of the bras in his hands. And then Darrin heard him laugh.

"Gary," he sneered. "Come and have a look at *this*!"

———

Yates hadn't been kidding, Gary decided, when he'd said that exercise machines were really redesigned torture devices. His body had started to ache after two minutes of riding the bike-like machine and he'd only managed to stay on for another minute before he'd given up and climbed off. One of the other machines had been taken by a starship crewman and he'd watched in disbelief as the burly man lifted weights into the air, each one heavier than anything Gary could lift with his bare hands.

He'd left the compartment soon afterwards and walked back to their sleeping quarters, hoping that Yates or Janet would be there. Instead, he'd walked inside...and come face-to-face with Barry, who seemed to have managed to get into the female compartment. The bully caught Gary's arm before Gary could retreat, pulling him forward into the forbidden compartment and pushing him into the wall. No matter what Yates had said, Gary didn't dare resist.

"Look around you," Barry said, waving a pair of frilly panties under Gary's nose. "Doesn't this place excite you?"

Gary told himself he could endure, as he had endured so much before. He'd always been at Barry's mercy; that had been a fact of life, ever since the oversized boy had first taken a dislike to him. Part of him might have been interested in seeing where the girls slept, but having Barry there too was a distraction. He blinked in surprise as he saw Darrin, then wondered why he was bothering to be surprised. He'd learned the simple fact that everyone ganged up on him long ago.

Barry half-pulled him into the tiny washroom and snickered. "Just think," he said, in a genial voice that didn't fool Gary for a second. "Here, those pretty girls are naked, washing the dirt and sweat and whatever off their bodies. Aren't you lucky to be here?"

Gary glared at him, but he didn't dare struggle. Few girls showered at school, if only because they knew that the boys might sneak in at any moment. There were even hundreds of pictures of girls making their way around the school, some of them very compromising indeed. Even *Gary* had seen them.

Barry pulled something from his pockets, then pushed Gary's hands against the railing. A moment later, Gary found himself firmly tied in place. Barry tied his feet together too, then stood back and laughed. Gary had to stand on his toes just to be even remotely comfortable.

"Quite a picture," Barry said. He motioned for Darrin to look, then tugged down the lower half of Gary's shipsuit, revealing his groin. "And just *think* what the girls will say."

He banged the door closed before Gary could say anything, leaving him hanging there helplessly. The light clicked off a moment later. Gary struggled in the darkness, but whatever Barry had used to bind his hands was strong enough to resist his best efforts, no matter how hard he struggled. Desperately, he tried putting all of his weight on the railing, but it refused to break...

How long had it been? He couldn't see his wristcom, but it already felt like hours. God knew Barry had locked him in the lockers or storage compartments at school, yet sooner or later someone had come along and let him out. Here...he had a sudden awful image of a girl opening the door and staring at his exposed penis. The thought terrified him; even if Yates and Janet believed him when he told them what happened, everyone would laugh. Shame boiled through his soul, mocking him. Yates was wrong. He didn't have the potential to be strong and brave and look after himself.

You're always going to be a victim, the voice said. *Everyone will taunt you for the rest of your life, until the day you die.*

Yates had taunted him too, he thought. He'd held out a promise that things could get better, that he would find a meaningful job away from Earth, that he would be able to stand up for himself...but the promise was a lie. How could someone as weak as Gary become strong enough to stand up to Barry? He hadn't even dared to cry out when he'd been tied to the railing and forced to stand in the girls washroom, waiting helplessly for discovery. What could he do?

There was a sound from outside. It was impossible to tell what it was; the CityBlock was almost completely soundproofed, but odd sounds sometimes echoed through the starship's hull at random intervals, quite apart from the ever-present hum of the drives. The sounds had made it harder to sleep, although that might also have been something to do with sleeping near Barry and fearing that Yates might leave at any moment. Was that one of the girls or was Barry just messing with his mind? Or was it something altogether different?

He heard an outraged yell and felt his blood run cold. Barry probably hadn't bothered to clean up the mess, not after emptying so many cabinets out onto the deck. His desperate search for underwear...Gary felt sick at the very thought. Some of the boys at school had prided themselves on stealing underwear after having sex with the girls, or even simply pinching it from a locker while the girls were at PE, but *he* had never indulged himself like that. What was the point?

There was a crashing sound, then someone pulled the door open. The light clicked on at the same moment; Gary closed his eyes against the light, a moment before he heard a loud scream. The girl had come face to face with his naked penis. He opened his eyes, just in time to see the girl spin around and run for her life. She clearly hadn't noticed that his hands were tied firmly to the railing.

Gary would have collapsed if he could have moved. The girl would be making fun of him by now, probably mocking his size to the other girls. There were boys who would have beaten any girl who dared to suggest that their penises were not giant-sized, but everyone knew that Gary couldn't fight to save his life. They'd have more proof now...

A moment later, the hatch opened and Janet stalked in. Her gaze flickered disapprovingly over the mess, then fixed on Gary's face. Gary cringed backwards, expecting a blow – or worse – at any moment. No authority figure had ever taken his side. It was easier to blame the victim than try to stand up to Barry and his cronies.

"Hold still," Janet ordered. She reached out and pulled the cloth wrapped around Gary's hands free. A moment later, he pulled his pants up and covered himself, then started to pick at the cloth around his ankles. Janet's next question surprised him. "Who did this to you?"

Gary stared at her, helplessly. He could tell her...and yet, he knew that nothing would be done. Barry would merely take it out on him later, as if being a sneak was something contemptible while humiliating someone else was acceptable behaviour. But might made right, Gary knew. Barry's might ensured that no one would dare to mess with him.

Janet studied him for a long moment. "Stay here," she ordered, quietly. "I'll be back soon."

She left, closing the hatch behind her. Gary looked at it for a long moment, then started to cry.

———

Barry giggled like a little girl as they heard the yell from the female compartment. Darrin was much less amused, although the sight of Yuki running out of the hatch screaming was actually quite funny. Barry had given him a sip from a flask he'd borrowed from a crewman and his teeth had started to hurt immediately afterwards. But Barry seemed to have no trouble drinking it.

They closed the door to the male compartment as Janet came into the main compartment and marched into the female section. Barry's sniggers grew louder; Gary was going to be in real trouble, he gloated, for stealing all the underwear *and* for exposing himself to Yuki. No one would believe Gary, Barry insisted, if Gary told them what had really happened. Darrin frowned, then gulped as the hatch opened, revealing Yates. An extremely-cross looking Yates.

"Perhaps you would like to explain," Yates said, before either of them could say a word, "just what you were thinking?"

"We weren't thinking anything," Barry said. "The little idiot got himself tied up..."

His voice trailed off as Yates glared at him. "I would be really impressed," he said, with a mildness that didn't fool Darrin for a moment, "if Gary *had* managed to tie himself up so effectively. Dear me! It would be *quite* a feat. And I wonder, if he did it himself, just how you knew what had happened to him?"

Darrin winced. Yates wasn't looking directly at him, but he was somehow certain that Yates had caught his movement. The man was uncanny. And he was directly challenging them...most teachers wouldn't have said a word to Barry or even Darrin, no matter how much evidence there was of their guilt. It was much easier to blame the pupils like Gary, the ones who couldn't fight back.

"I heard him gloating," Barry said, unconvincingly. "We tried to talk him out of it."

Yates snorted. "Do you really think that I am foolish enough to *believe* you?"

Barry swung his legs over the side of his bunk and stood. "Are you suggesting that I am a liar?"

Shut up, Darrin thought, desperately. *Yates isn't like any of our teachers, even Mr. Howarth...*

"I *know* you're lying," Yates snapped. He pointed his finger towards the pair of panties lying on the bed. "And I know you took something from their compartment..."

Barry let out a roar and lunged at Yates. Yates seemed unmoved; he moved to one side, cocked his fist and threw a punch into Barry's jaw. Barry's entire body seemed to vibrate, as if he was on the verge of falling over backwards, then he collapsed and hit the deck. A nasty mark appeared on his jaw, but there was no blood.

Darrin gulped as Yates looked up at him. He'd thought himself used to violence – he'd had to fight himself, even before he'd knocked out

Fitz – but he'd never seen anything like *that*. One moment, Barry had been as tough and intimidating as always, the next...he was lying in a heap on the deck, having failed to land even a single blow. Darrin wished, suddenly, that there had been more witnesses. No one would be so scared of Barry after he had been taken down so quickly.

"I trust," Yates said, in a deceptively casual voice, "that you are not going to be as foolish?"

"No, sir," Darrin said, quickly. He couldn't keep his eyes off Yates. Any teacher back home on Earth who had laid hands on a student would be dismissed, no matter how much the student had deserved it. Yates...had just knocked Barry out with a single punch. "I..."

Yates picked up the flask and sniffed it. "It is not a good idea to drink ship-brewed alcohol," he said, as casually as if he were ordering dinner. "Most of it is dangerously strong – spacers tend to have a higher alcohol tolerance engineered into their bodies, allowing them to consume it safely. You could have seriously injured yourself if you had drunk too much."

He picked up Barry and slung him over his shoulder. "Once he recovers, you and he will be scrubbing decks for the rest of the trip, I think," he added. "And I suggest that you don't spend too long complaining about how *unfair* this punishment is. Believe me, it could be a great deal worse.

"In fact, you might want to think carefully about associating with your friend here at all."

Darrin watched, unable to quite believe his eyes, as Yates carried Barry effortlessly through the hatch. Once he was gone, Darrin stood, scooped up the underwear Barry had stolen and carried it back into the main compartment. Janet stared at him coldly as he passed her the underwear, the look in her eye making him feel as though he was a slug – or something worse. But she took the underwear without a word.

Returning to the male compartment, he sat down on the bunk and stared at where Barry had fallen. He'd been afraid of Barry; he hated to admit it, but it was true. And now...Barry was no longer invincible. And yet...he was the only person Darrin really knew. Maybe the experience of being knocked down so easily would be good for Barry. Fitz had told him that some people improved after a beating...

He said that about you, his thoughts reminded him. *And you might well have killed him.*

It was a long time before Darrin managed to drift off to sleep.

CHAPTER

FOURTEEN

Unsurprisingly, the bureaucrats – constantly looking for new ways to obtain funds – fell victim to educational fads that ranged from the idealistic to the absurd. These invariably sounded good, but rarely worked in practice – and even when they did, they were not kept around long enough to do any good.

- Professor Leo Caesius, *Education and the Decline and Fall of the Galactic Empire*

Gary rubbed at his wrists, pathetically. The ship's doctor had given him something for the pain, but very little else – and certainly no sympathy. Rumours seemed to have already spread through the entire ship, rumours that bore little relationship to reality. Apparently, he'd hidden himself in the washroom deliberately, hoping to surprise the girls.

He shook his head wearily, silently cursing whoever had picked Barry as a contest winner – and Darrin too, for that matter. Gary would have bet his meagre fortune that neither of them had actually entered the competition, or that they'd only handed in blank sheets of paper. But someone had designated them the winners...Gary sighed, looking down at his wrists. He might have been able to use the resources onboard the ship to make himself successful and leave the CityBlock behind forever, but with those two around it was hopeless. They'd ruin everything he tried to do.

The doctor had told him to wait in the small compartment, then pulled the curtain around him to provide some privacy. Gary sat on the bed and waited, wondering what would happen; if Yates genuinely believed that Gary was responsible for the whole affair...the thought made him sick.

Every other teacher had always chosen to side against Gary, either because they'd believed the united front the other children presented or because it was easier to deal with Gary than the others. Why should Yates be any different?

Outside, he heard someone talking. He closed his eyes and tried to listen.

"Minor damage to the jaw," the doctor was saying. "He should recover within a day or so with proper treatment."

"Good," Yates said. He didn't sound happy. "Make sure you call me when he awakens so I can lay down the law."

Gary blinked in surprise, opening his eyes. Lay down the law to who? There was no damage to *Gary's* jaw, not as far as he knew. He rubbed it experimentally and found nothing, apart from a few hints of stubble. His failure to grow proper sideburns had been yet another source of mockery from Barry and Moe, both of whom claimed to have been shaving when they first came to school. Gary was sure that was nonsense, but their words still stung.

He looked up sharply as Yates pulled back the curtain, then stepped into the compartment and sat down on the bed. Their escort looked... *annoyed*, but unlike all the other teachers Gary had known, *he* didn't seem to be the target. Yates studied him for a long moment, then reached for Gary's left wrist and took it in a surprisingly gentle grip. Gary winced slightly as the man's fingers prodded at the marks, then let go of him.

"So tell me," Yates said. "What actually happened?"

Gary shook his head, mutely. It wouldn't make any difference, he knew from bitter experience, if he told Yates the truth. He'd told teachers and tutors back when Barry and Moe had started to pick on him, but they'd done nothing. Barry had even harassed him right in front of teachers and they'd merely ignored the whole affair. What possible good would it do, he asked himself, to tell the truth? Ashamed of his own weakness, feeling a deep sensation of absolute hopelessness, he started to wonder if he shouldn't just kill himself and end it all. He knew that other victims had been *killed* by their tormentors over the years...

"Let me tell you, then," Yates said. His tone was soft, patient. "Barry and Darrin tied you to the railing, exposed you and left you there. Right?"

Gary stared at him. Had the two boasted, knowing that Yates couldn't touch them? Or had something else happened?

"I need to show you something," Yates said, abruptly. He stood. "Come with me."

He pushed the curtain aside and walked outside. Gary hesitated, then followed him as he walked towards another set of curtains. Yates glanced from left to right – looking for the doctor, Gary guessed – and then pulled back the curtains. Inside, Barry was lying on the bed, a nasty bruise covering his lower jaw. He was asleep. No, Gary realised with a sudden thrill of excitement; he'd been knocked out.

"I came very close to breaking his jaw," Yates said. There was no hint of regret in his tone, merely a droll amusement. "For all of his immense bulk, Barry has little actual skill. I know people your size who could have taken him apart without breaking a sweat."

Gary stared at Barry, then looked at Yates, concerned. No teacher was ever allowed to raise a hand to his pupils, no matter how badly they behaved. It was a cause for immediate dismissal, if not for criminal charges. The one teacher he'd known who had struck out at a pupil had been sent to jail, according to rumour. But maybe he'd simply been turned into an indent instead. The hell of it, Gary realised suddenly, was that indenture might seem preferable to teaching in a CityBlock school.

But if Yates had hit Barry...

Gary shuddered, inwardly. Yates was doomed. There was no doubt about it. Barry would file a complaint and the authorities would come down against Yates like the hammer of God. He would lose his job, at the very least; he might even lose his freedom. No, he *would* lose his freedom. Natural law was on the side of jerks like Barry, not those who might hit them and actually *beat* them. And if they looked like losing, the laws would simply be changed to allow them to win. Gary had seen it happen before; no doubt it would happen again.

"I'm sorry," he said, and meant it. Yates was scary, but he'd never been pointlessly cruel; he'd certainly never acted like Barry. "I..."

Yates caught his arm and swung him around so that Gary was facing the older man. "Why?"

"Because you'll lose your job," Gary said. He fought down the urge to cry. It just wasn't *right*! It just wasn't *fair*! "I didn't mean to be a problem..."

Yates laughed. "And why do you think I'll lose my job?"

"You hit him," Gary said. Something was wrong. Yates wasn't trying desperately to cover the whole affair up – or make nice with Barry, in the hopes it would stop him filing a complaint. He'd seen both forms of reaction in school. Instead, he seemed almost amused at Gary's concern. "He won't let it go..."

"He can whistle, if he wishes to complain," Yates said, tiring of his game. He pulled the curtains shut, then led Gary towards the hatch leading out of sickbay. "This is a starship under corporate discipline, not one of the schools on Earth. Given how lightly he and his friend got off, my superiors are more likely to ask me why I didn't break bones than insist on immediate punishment."

Gary blinked in shock, trying to wrap his head around a totally new concept. Had Barry...actually been *punished* for his crimes? It had never happened before, even when they'd all been children. Barry had always been feted and rewarded by the teachers, allowed to kiss and caress and girls...he'd been the first to go all the way, if rumour was to be believed. But then, if rumour was true, Barry would be so busy fucking the girls that he would have no time to make Gary's life a misery.

"And he is going to spend the rest of the trip scrubbing floors and cleaning out pipes," Yates continued, as they stepped out into the corridor. "And the salary he would have earned from doing that will go to replace the damaged underwear."

Gary hesitated, then took the plunge. "And what will you do when he refuses to work?"

"I will make him work," Yates said, simply.

"Oh," Gary said. It sounded unbelievable. And yet, when he looked up at Yates, he saw a solid confidence that outshone Barry's constant aggression. Somehow, he found himself hoping that Yates would have to force Barry to work. "What do I do now?"

"Well, I have explained to the girls that it wasn't your fault that you were trapped and exposed," Yates said, shortly. "They understand. So does Janet. But you really do need to work on your exercises."

They turned and passed through a hatch into the exercise compartment. Gary eyed the devices warily, remembering how he'd ached after a few brief minutes riding the simplest machine. Yates tapped a switch on a console, then frowned. Gary shivered at the expression, realising what it meant. Yates was not impressed by his exercises.

"It does hurt, at first," Yates said, before Gary could say a word. "That's a sign its working, that long-disused muscles are being forced to work. But you have to keep pushing it forward."

Gary sighed. "I froze," he confessed. "I didn't even *try* to fight when..."

Yates nodded. "I thought as much," he said. His voice had gone absolutely toneless. "You need to build up confidence as well as muscles. But the former generally does come with the latter."

He nodded to one of the machines. "You'll do a solid hour on that machine, every day," he added. "I'll ask for one of the crew to work with you, when I'm not available. And, when you're not exercising, you can work on your studies. That too will give you options you would never have had on Earth."

———

Kailee looked down at the piece of cloth in her hands. Panties from Lourdes had been all the rage six months ago; she'd saved her meagre allowance to buy them, even though she had no intention of wearing them for anyone else. They were really nothing more than frilly lace, but they'd looked nice on her body. Now, they were ruined. The thought of a boy *touching* them – and she knew what some boys were reputed to do with clothes they'd stolen from the changing rooms – was disgusting. Even if they hadn't been ruined, she would have had to throw them out.

The other girls sat in silence, each one cataloguing what they'd lost to Barry and Darrin. At least twelve pairs of underwear had been stolen or ruined, including a bra that had been turned into a makeshift pair of restraints. Kailee still didn't know who'd left the hatch open, assuming the boys hadn't managed to hack into the system, but she did know that it had cost them their sense of security. But then, it had been rare for her to feel safe outside the apartment.

And that was an illusion, she thought. Their safety had depended on gangs, gangs crammed with volatile and often stupid young men. There were rumours, passed from apartment block to apartment block, that the gangs often lost control. When they did, apartments were looted, girls were raped and property was stolen...and nothing was ever done about it. There was no one the inhabitants could complain to if the gangs just decided to forget their protection rackets and attack. *We were always vulnerable.*

She couldn't help wondering if their lives were always going to be unsafe, no matter what Janet said about training to rely only on themselves. Was that all she had to look forward to in her life, if her ambitions were never realised? The oldest person she knew was seventy years old. Assuming she lived so long, would she be able to endure...she stumbled over the calculation, unsure of the answer. Would she be able to endure seventy years of fear? Aunt Lillian had turned gray early, according to her mother; her parents had just zoned out completely, drowning themselves in the endless tide of entertainment on the datanet. But were they reacting to living in constant fear?

"We shun those boys," Honey said, breaking the silence. Kailee put down the panties and looked at her. "We don't talk to them, we don't do anything for them, we certainly don't *sleep* with them. Are we all agreed?"

Kailee wondered, cynically, just how long that would last. It had been tried at her school, with several of the girls organising a sexual boycott of the worst boys. But it hadn't worked; someone had always broken ranks, seeking protection in exchange for sexual favours. And yet...there were only six girls in the compartment. Surely they could all stick together...

"We can try," she said, when Honey looked at her. None of the girls had started to blame her just for sharing a school with Barry and Darrin – and Gary, for that matter – but she knew that it was only a matter of time. "We can try, definitely."

She looked up as Janet entered the compartment. "Put your damaged and otherwise useless items in this basket," Janet ordered, without preamble. "And make sure you have a nametag on them. They're going to pay to replace them."

Kailee snorted in disbelief. *No one* at school was ever forced to replace *anything*, no matter how expensive. Clothes weren't the only items that were stolen regularly; smart children rapidly learnt never to bring anything they couldn't replace easily to school. The only ones who openly carried expensive goods were the ones strong enough to defend themselves... and even they would never leave their items unattended. No one had any real faith in the lockers to keep out thieves.

"Aye, right," Samantha said. "And how will they be forced to pay?"

"They are going to be doing mandatory work," Janet said, simply. "The salary they would normally earn from doing the work will be redirected to you."

She put the basket down on the deck and glanced from girl to girl, her eyes lingering on Kailee's face a moment longer than strictly necessary. "You have to learn from this," she warned, coldly. "What happened today could have been a great deal worse."

Kailee nodded. She knew that Janet was right.

———

It was three days before Barry was discharged from sickbay, three days during which Darrin was ignored by Gary and harassed by the other three boys. Apparently, a couple of the girls had offered sexual favours in exchange for the boys picking on Darrin. Darrin had no idea if that was actually true, but he had taken to hiding himself and trying to ignore the rest of them as much as possible. By the time Barry was released, Darrin was almost relieved.

The feeling slowly slid away as Yates led them through the corridors and down into a long passageway. There were faint marks on the deck, some clearly footprints; others looked to have been left behind by trolleys. Barry eyed the deck unpleasantly, then met Darrin's eyes and winked at him. Clearly, being in sickbay for a few days hadn't had any real effect on him.

"You will be scrubbing the decks for the next few weeks," Yates informed them. He opened a compartment, revealing brushes, buckets and small bottles of funny-smelling liquid. "Each day, after your basic lessons, you will come here and scrub until I can actually see my own face reflected back at me. When this section is done, you will move onto the next section and next. You will continue to do this until you have earned enough money to pay for the clothes you damaged."

"I refuse," Barry said, at once. "You can't make me do anything."

Yates smiled at him, unpleasantly. "Do you want to test that, really?"

Darrin winced, unable to tear his eyes away from them. Did Barry *know* what had happened to him? Yates had moved so quickly that Darrin hadn't quite realised what had happened until it was far too late. Did Barry think that he'd been in his compartment one moment and sickbay the next, without anything in-between? Or was the experience of actually been knocked out by someone so far outside his comprehension that he'd decided it simply hadn't happened at all?

Barry glared at him, then backed down. "And what," he demanded sullenly, "will you do while we're here?"

"I have better things to do than watch you, of course," Yates said. He gave them a brilliant smile. "Oh, lest I forget to mention it, you *will* be supervised by the starship's internal datanet at all times. You might think that you can slack off, or even sneak away for an hour or so, but you will be caught and you will be punished. You'd really be quite surprised, I think, to know how much authority I have over you."

Darrin nodded. He'd looked it up, ever since it had become clear that no one seemed interested in punishing Yates for punching Barry and knocking him out. Yates had vast authority – and the starship's commander had a great deal more. If worst came to worst, he could declare them both to be mutineers and put them out the airlock. And, given the crew's attitude to him after the whole underwear affair, it was clear that none of them would defy their commander over him.

Sighing, he picked up the brushes, filled one of the buckets with water and carried it over to the deck.

"Good luck," Yates said, nastily. "Oh, one other thing..."

The two boys looked up at him, expectantly.

"If you clean well, you may be offered a chance to train as something more useful," Yates said. "But you really have to develop self-discipline first. And *that* is one thing that has never been taught at your school."

CHAPTER
FIFTEEN

Not all of these fads had much (if anything) to do with education. One fad embraced by the Empire, certainly on Earth, was to teach the children their rights by law, as opposed to their responsibilities. Another was to encourage them to look towards the government as the true provider of everything, from food to jobs after they graduated.

- Professor Leo Caesius, *Education and the Decline and Fall of the Galactic Empire*

"Welcome to the bridge," Captain Yang said. "I understand that you did very well on your exams?"

Gary nodded, not trusting himself to speak. He wasn't quite sure what to make of Captain Yang. On one hand, the Captain was no larger than Gary's sister, with a body that appeared physically immature. On the other hand, he clearly commanded the respect of his officers and crew, despite his size. There was a clear assumption of authority in his voice that Gary both admired and distrusted. He wasn't sure why.

The bridge itself was something of a disappointment. Stellar Star commanded from a bridge that had been designed by the finest artisans in known space, but *Hawkins* was commanded from a large compartment that had a handful of consoles, a command chair, a holographic display and very little else. Apparently, consoles didn't explode unless the ship was about to be blown apart – and when that happened, the crews generally had worse things to worry about. Lieutenant Royce had laughed when

Gary had asked and told him, in great detail, just how many details the entertainment flick writers had managed to get wrong.

"He did, sir," Lieutenant Royce said. He looked like a giant compared to the diminutive commander. "Still lacking on the practical work, but getting there."

Gary sucked in a breath. Six weeks of hard work had left him convinced that his schooling had included almost nothing of practical value. None of the maths puzzles he'd solved in school had been any help when it came to plotting out navigational courses for starships, or even working out the correct ratios of gases in the life support. The only experience he had that was actually helpful came from playing with computers – and *that* hadn't been taught at school. If he'd relied on what he'd been taught in first grade, he would barely have been able to manipulate a reader and he certainly wouldn't have understood how it worked.

"Good enough for someone from Earth," the Captain said. "And good enough to merit a reward."

He turned and led the way towards the holographic display. Gary wondered, rather spitefully, just where the Captain came from if he was so dismissive of Earth. There were quite a few planets where people had been engineered to exceed standard human norms, although he had no idea why anyone would choose to remain physically a child. But surely the Captain's homeworld would want women to have babies...he made a mental note to look it up, then followed the Captain towards the display. At the moment, all it was showing was the starship itself.

Hawkins was crude and, if Gary was being honest, rather ugly. She was a blocky mass, studded with a handful of sensor blisters; there was nothing elegant about her at all. But that seemed to be true of most starships, apart from a handful of specialised designs. The really elegant designs, according to the computer database, were completely impractical for anything other than luxury liners and personal transports. And the people who owned them were so staggeringly wealthy that they could afford the inefficiency.

"We will hit the outermost edge of the Phase Limit in two minutes," the Captain said, taking his seat. "Before then, we will drop out of Phase

Space and head into the system in normal space. You will, I think, enjoy the experience."

Gary frowned, but said nothing as the final seconds counted down to zero. A strange queasy feeling surged through him, then faded away into nothingness. From what he'd read, some people reacted quite badly to transits in and out of Phase Space; he was silently relieved that he wasn't one of them. Perhaps he did have a chance to get the Captain to write him a letter of recommendation after all. Yates had told him that such a letter would go a very long way.

"Transit complete, Captain," the woman at the helm said. "Drive cycling down now."

Gary studied her with genuine interest. Like her commander, she was another oddity; her face was pale, so pale that he could see blood vessels under her skin, while her hair was completely white. But she also seemed young enough to be in Gary's class at school. From some of the snide comments dropped by Royce, spacers considered going to school on Earth a fate worse than death. Gary rather suspected that they had a point.

"Confirm local space clear of encroachments," another officer said. "No starships detected; I say again, no starships detected."

Good, Gary thought. He'd thought that space pirates were the stuff of legends until he'd discovered that they were actually real. It was apparently rare for pirates to pick on colonist-carriers, but it did happen; Royce had told him that the pirates would probably throw him and the rest of the males onboard ship into space if they were captured. The women would be taken prisoner and used as sex slaves, if they weren't sold to black colonies in desperate need of more breeding stock. A great deal happened on the Rim, apparently, that was never reported on Earth. Starships were hijacked, planets were raided...there were even reports of contact with non-human life forms.

It was a fascinating thought. But such reports had never been verified.

"Take us in," the Captain ordered. A faint hum echoed through the ship as the normal space drives came online. "ETA Meridian?"

"Seven hours," the helmswoman said.

The Captain turned to face Gary. "I shall provide you with a contact code for a friend of mine on Orbit Station," he said. "Should you wish to remain in space, merely contact him once your time on the planet is up. I dare say Mr. Yates will not stand in your way."

Gary nodded. "Thank you, Captain," he said. "And thank you for letting me see this."

"Not much to see," the Captain said. "Just you wait until you see a gas giant."

———

"Make damn sure that you pack everything," Janet said, shortly. "Anything you leave behind may be impossible to recover. And don't steal anything from the ship."

Kailee nodded as she slowly emptied her cabinet onto her bed, then started to pack her bag. Aunt Lillian had made it look easy; now, even with the lost clothing, it was still hard to stuff everything inside and secure the straps. Beside her, the other girls appeared to be having similar problems, apart from Li. *She'd* managed to fill her bag neatly then tie the zips without problems.

"You'll be carrying the bags, so there shouldn't be any attempt at stealing them," Janet said. "But make sure you keep them with you or ask a friend to guard them, should you need to leave them somewhere. There are people on the planet who might steal from you."

"Just like Earth," Kailee commented.

"But hotter, muddier and more civilised," Janet countered. She smiled at Kailee, then moved to the next girl. "Clothes are probably fine, but readers and money – if you have money – should be watched carefully. If you were permanent settlers, I'd tell you to assign guards to your supplies. Quite a few people are desperate down there."

Kailee finally managed to fill her bag, then – as an afterthought – she took the credit coin and concealed it in her pocket. As far as she knew, none of the other girls knew she had it and she had no intention of telling them. Nothing had been stolen, apart from pieces of underwear, but she didn't know how far she could trust them. Down on the surface, it would be a great deal easier to get away with stealing something.

Outside, she saw the boys with their own bags. They all seemed more excited than Kailee felt, but then they'd spent weeks learning about the planet. Some of them even viewed the whole affair as a great adventure. Kailee was much less sure; the more she learned about the planet, the more she wished that the whole trip was already over. She didn't want to spend the rest of her life working on a farm or churning out babies or whatever other jobs there were for women on the surface.

She started as another dull rumble echoed through the ship, followed by a thump that made two of the girls jump. Janet smiled at them, then proceeded to explain; the giant starship had just docked at the orbital station. It was, rather unimaginatively, called Orbit Station.

"There's at least one such station in orbit around every stage-one colony world," Janet said. "Or at least there *should* be. Some planets have problems paying for the station or simply choose not to have one, for one reason or another. There should also be a complete network of satellites in orbit too, but Meridian is short on them. The planet's budget wouldn't cover the satellites and additional heavy-lift shuttles."

Abdul lifted a hand. He was a dark-skinned youth from Istanbul-Cit; Kailee didn't know him that well, apart from the few times they'd played board games in the cabin. In some ways, he reminded her of Gary, who seemed reluctant to ever look a girl in the eye. But they were very different in other ways.

"What happens when someone is referring to several stations?" He asked. "Like the station here and the station in the next system over?"

Janet smiled. "They'd just call the station Meridian Station," she said, simply. "It's actually quite simple."

She clapped her hands together before anyone else could ask a silly question. "We're booked into the first set of shuttles down to the surface," she said. "The precise shuttle has yet to be determined, but we will be moving to the station as soon as the airlocks are mated and opened. Take a moment to make sure that you have *everything* with you. Once we're on the station, we may have to wait again."

Kailee sighed. The girls nipped back to their compartment and checked, one final time, for anything left behind, but saw nothing. Kailee inspected her bed – Aunt Lillian had thrown a fit every time she didn't make the bed in the morning before school – and then returned to the main compartment. She was just in time to see Darrin and Barry shoved into the compartment, both wearing the dingy overalls they'd been given after the second day of cleaning the decks. Both of them smelt thoroughly unpleasant.

She concealed her amusement with an effort. Barry had been in an increasingly foul mood as he'd learned, very slowly, that Yates hadn't been joking about forcing them to work. Kailee had heard, from a crewman who had tried to chat her up, that Yates had told them that they would also have to cover the wages of whatever crewman was assigned to watch them, if they couldn't be trusted to stay where they were and actually work. It was impossible to be sure, but she was fairly certain that they'd still be in debt by the time they reached the planet. Who knew what would happen then?

"We will be leaving in five minutes," Yates said. "I would *suggest*" – he eyed Barry and Darrin coldly – "that you get changed, then packed. And that you hurry."

––––––––

Darrin flushed. His entire body was aching after weeks of scrubbing the decks, one after the other. He'd never really comprehended just how *large* the starship actually was, or just how many decks it actually had, not until he'd scrubbed most of them until they were clean and shining. Yates had left them alone for the first two days, then – after Barry had convinced Darrin to sneak off to the games room – told them that they would *also* have to pay the wages of the crewmen who supervised them. Darrin couldn't even begin to do the maths, but if Fitz's grumbles about endless debt were accurate, they would still be in debt if they worked for years.

"There's no such thing as a free lunch," Yates had said, when he'd protested. "Why should the Captain have to pay for the crewman's wages?"

He scrambled into the compartment and tore off the overalls, dumping them into the laundry basket, then removed the shipsuit with a sigh of relief. His normal clothes were lying where he'd left them, so he pulled them on and then started to frantically pack his bag. At least the other boys hadn't messed around with his stuff, not after Barry had made it clear that anyone who did would be eating through a straw for the rest of the week. The girls might have tried to pressure them, but what was the possibility of sexual favours compared to the certainty of violence?

"Hurry up in there," Yates bellowed. "You have two minutes left."

Darrin swore and finished packing, then moved past Barry and out into the main compartment. He felt dirty; he wanted – needed – a shower, but there was no time. Besides, he knew from bitter experience that the smell of cleaning fluid would remain with him for days to come, no matter what he did. He had no idea what had marred the starship's decks, but it was awfully difficult to remove.

"Good," Yates said, crossly. He'd watched them for the last few days, his eyes cold and disapproving. "All of you, follow me."

Darrin and Barry lagged behind as they walked out the cabin and down towards the main airlocks. The whole compartment had been sealed while the ship was in transit, but now it was open and a pair of officers were guarding the hatch. They exchanged a few words with Yates, then permitted him to lead his charges through the airlock and out into the station. It was surprisingly simple, compared to Earth's exaggerated security precautions. But anyone who managed to stow away on a colonist-carrier would simply be added to the indents and put to work at the far end.

The station seemed crude, yet fully functional. Great trolley-loads of goods and supplies moved through the passageways, supervised by crewmen and women wearing very light clothes. The station was cold, but they were sweating like animals. Darrin didn't understand it until he realised that they were working frantically to unload the ship. The longer it stayed in orbit, the more money its owners would be losing. They stepped through a set of airlocks, had a brief pause in front of another airlock, then stepped through into a stairwell that led down into the bowels of the station.

"Through the airlock," Yates instructed. He waited at the hatch, counting heads. "Take a seat and strap yourself down."

Darrin stopped and stared as he stepped into the shuttle. It was nothing like the aircar; it was larger, with nearly a hundred seats lined up in the passenger compartment. There seemed to be no way to step into the cockpit, at least as far as he could tell. He hastened towards a window seat and looked outside. There was nothing, but the inky darkness of space – and the glimmer of a thousand stars.

"All passengers are ordered to make sure that they are secured to their seats," a voice said, coldly. "Meridian Development Consortium takes no responsibility for injury or death caused by stupidity. You have been warned."

Yates moved from seat to seat, checking the straps and altering them where necessary. Darrin scowled inwardly as Yates corrected his straps, then ordered Barry to move to the other side of the shuttle. Janet sat down next to Darrin a moment later, without saying a word. Darrin wasn't sure if he should be relieved or fearful. There was something about Janet that bothered him, a coldness that suggested she would think nothing of doing him great harm, if she decided it had to be done. But she'd barely said anything to any of the boys.

A dull thump ran through the shuttle, then there was a faint sense of acceleration as the shuttle turned and headed towards the planet. Darrin caught a glimpse of a blue-green orb, hanging in the sky, then all he could see were moving stars. Moments later, the shuttle jerked violently as it entered the planet's atmosphere and dropped down towards the ground. Darrin gritted his teeth as the shaking grew worse, but refused to take his eyes away from the viewport. His head spun as the planet moved from being an orb to something vast, then they were over the ocean and heading downwards. Gary let out a yelp as the shuttle shook again and again, then stabilised. Darrin tried his best to ignore the nerd.

Slowly, the main continent came into view. He'd seen holographic images of forests and rivers in presentations at school, but he'd never seen *real* trees, let alone a forest. Now...it was strange to see something other than endless dark passageways, broken only by entertainment complexes and gang hideouts. He felt his head spin again as he caught sight of boats on the water's surface. On Earth, no one in their right mind would sail on the oceans.

"That's Sabre City to the north," Yates said. In the distance, Darrin could see smoke rising up to the sky. "The river flowing down to the sea is the Jordan. It's actually how most people move around the continent, as it links into a natural network of rivers boats can navigate fairly easily. We will travel on one of those boats later."

Darrin sucked in his breath as the shuttle rocked again, then headed towards the spaceport so it could land. The flight had been thoroughly unnerving. No wonder Earth had built the orbital towers as quickly as possible.

Five minutes later, they were down on the ground.

CHAPTER
SIXTEEN

This was linked to the Empire's huge level of intrusion into the private lives of its citizens. They were nagged constantly, all for their own good (and for the maintenance of the power structure). Children were not taught to think logically about the bureaucratic intrusion because this would have raised uncomfortable questions about the sanity of the whole system. For example, why was baby food strictly rationed and yet there was no attempt to discourage couples from having more than one child?

- Professor Leo Caesius, *Education and the Decline and Fall of the Galactic Empire*

Austin Livingston couldn't help a flicker of excitement as he watched the shuttle come to a hover over the spaceport, then slowly lower itself down to the tarmac. He'd been excited ever since he'd been told that *he* would be serving as native guide to twelve students from Earth. The chance to show people round Sabre City – and the entire settled region of the planet – wasn't one that came very often. Most immigrants tended to make their way to their settlements at once, then learn more about the planet later.

He grinned, nervously, as the shuttle came to a halt. These were teenagers from *Earth*, the legendary homeworld of the human race! What would they be like? He'd seen a handful of images of the planet while he'd been in the schoolroom, but nothing really important or detailed. His father had left Earth as a child and barely remembered it; Grandfather Rupert muttered curses and spat every time someone asked him about his past. But then, Grandfather had been an indent, exiled for a minor crime.

It was understandable that he would be a little bitter about the world that had kicked him out.

"Relax, son," the spaceport manager told him. "You don't want to seem *too* eager."

Austin smiled. The spaceport was only fully staffed when a starship entered orbit; at all other times there was just a skeleton crew, including a pair of shuttle pilots. Austin had actually spent two months working at the spaceport, back when he'd been half-considering trying to sign up for a hitch in outer space, but he'd discovered that it wasn't as fun as working on the farm or patrolling in the bush. Indeed, he'd been told that if he did well with the newcomers from Earth, his application to become a Bush Ranger would be fast-tracked. He'd still have to complete his apprenticeship, but he knew he could do that.

He glanced up as two more heavy-lift shuttles took off, clawing for the sky. They'd dock with Orbit Station and start bringing down the supplies, then the settlers would be removed from their stasis pods and transhipped down to the planet. Every time, according to the manager, half of them would bitch and moan about not being kept in stasis until they reached the surface. Didn't they realise that the stasis pods were firmly secured within the starships?

There was a dull click as the shuttle's hatch opened, allowing the newcomers to exit the craft one by one. Austin found himself staring as the first of them – a girl – emerged from the craft. Didn't she know where she was going? Her outfit was striking, but completely impractical for the weather. Behind her, there was a dark-skinned boy who looked slightly better dressed, yet Austin doubted that his clothes would last long either. He wiped his astonishment off his face with an effort as the final newcomers disembarked, staring around in wonder – and not a little disgust. One of the girls seemed to have doubts about what she was standing on – and her shoes, just like the rest of her outfit, were completely impractical.

Austin hesitated, for once unsure of what to do. He'd been told that escorting them would be hard, but he hadn't really understood. Up close, they were dirty and smelly and either stupid or ignorant. And they looked faintly unhealthy. Even the strongest of them, a boy who looked like his mother had been a gorilla-analogue, looked oddly misshapen.

But his father had taught him never to give up.

He took a step forward and held out his hand. "I'm Austin," he said, in the friendliest voice he could muster. "Welcome to Meridian."

———

The stench had struck Darrin the moment he stepped up to the shuttle's hatch. It was strange, a mixture of smells he simply didn't recognise – and yet there was something in it that called to him. Yates had said, he recalled dimly, that every planet had its own smell, but Darrin hadn't really believed him. Earth had no smell. But Yates had been right, Darrin realised now. Meridian *stunk*.

"You'll get used to it," Janet said, as she prodded him out the hatch. "Everyone does."

It was hotter than hell outside the shuttle. Darrin wondered, inanely, if they were going to sweat to death. His clothes were poorly chosen for the heat - and for the sunlight beating remorselessly down from high overhead. He half-covered his eyes, glancing around to see a handful of small buildings, some made out of wood and brick, others made out of metal that shone brightly in the sun. At one edge of the spaceport, the forest began; at the other, the ocean looked blue and inviting. He could even see boats bobbling far out to sea.

Fishermen, he thought, recalling more of the lectures. The terraforming package had included a cross-section of fish and other water-life from Earth, all of which had promptly pushed the planet's native ecology to the brink of extinction. Even if the settlers didn't manage to grow crops, they could eat fish to keep themselves alive. Absently, he wondered what fish tasted like. He'd never eaten real fish in his life.

"I'm Austin," their greeter said. "Welcome to Meridian."

Darrin stared at him. There was something about Austin that was strange, almost alien. The clothes he wore looked tough, the hat he wore kept his face under the shade...and he didn't look *that* different, yet there was something about him that puzzled Darrin. It was impossible, no matter how much he considered it, to understand what he was seeing. And yet, it nagged at the back of his mind.

The young man was tall, what little of his hair could be seen was blond. His body was muscular, but not as muscular as Barry or Darrin...and yet he carried himself with an easy confidence that perplexed Darrin. What was he missing? Austin shook hands with each of them, taking names and welcoming them all personally, while his companion – an older man with a rather more familiar air of harassed competence – watched sardonically. Yates stepped forward and spoke to him briefly, then turned to face his charges. Austin turned too...and Darrin felt his mouth drop open. He was carrying a *gun*.

———

Austin was...odd, Gary decided, as he shook hands with the colonial boy. Gary's first impression of him had been another bully, but there was no power play in the handshake or challenge in Austin's eyes. And yet there was something about him that irritated Gary, pressing at his mind...

Austin has never been scared, Gary realised, suddenly. He'd never been subject to the all-pervading fear that ran through the CityBlock, from the highest to the lowest; he'd never been convinced that his life had no value. Gary felt a surge of envy that was so powerful that he found himself shaking in silent outrage. Austin was *free* of the demons that lurked in Gary's mind, no matter how hard he exercised on the machines. He'd lived a safe life, one where there was no bullies and no bullied.

"All right, listen up," Yates said. Gary tore his attention away from Austin with an effort, focusing on Yates. At least he knew the man. "We have to walk to the city, so we're going to pick up hats from the spaceport and then start walking. It's only a couple of kilometres from the spaceport, which is absolutely nothing. Any questions?"

Samantha stuck up her hand. "Why didn't you tell us to wear something more suitable?"

Gary had wondered the same thing himself. Their outfits were designed for the CityBlocks, not for a very different planet...hell, the more he looked around, the stranger he felt. The locals, such as they were, wore clothes that covered without being too heavy, keeping the sun off their bare skin. Yates could have warned them; hell, he could have told them to dress properly before they left the starship. But he hadn't said a word.

He knew the answer a moment before Yates spoke. "Why didn't you read the briefing notes?"

There was a pause as everyone tried to remember what they'd said. "But that isn't fair," Honey objected. "No one knew what they actually meant!"

She did have a point, part of Gary's mind insisted. The temperature in the CityBlocks rarely changed, unless something had gone wrong with the environment monitors. None of them had really comprehended what a planet's weather actually meant...but, on the other hand, the information had been right there in front of them, before they'd ever even boarded the starship. They'd just lacked the information to process it properly.

He scowled at Yates. If there was one thing he had learned about the man, while he'd been forcing Gary to exercise, it was that he preferred to let his charges learn from their own mistakes rather than correct them before it was too late. The only time he'd intervened before something went wrong had been when Gary had been on the verge of hurting himself quite badly. It was nothing like the way they'd been treated at school, but it did force them to *think*...

"Then you should have asked," Yates informed her, bluntly. "Follow me."

Gary's gaze slipped to Austin as Yates turned and started jogging towards one of the metal buildings...and he gasped in shock. Austin was carrying a *gun*! A real gun! Guns were rare on Earth, according to their teachers, no matter how often Gary had wished for a weapon and a free shot at Barry and Moe. Even the gangsters carried makeshift swords and shields rather than actual weapons, assuming they had any at all. The one thing that Gary had heard was guaranteed to draw a reaction from the Civil Guard was the possession of genuine firearms.

And Austin was carrying one *openly*.

He found himself starting to hyperventilate as he stared. Guns were dangerous, everyone knew that; the thought of Barry or Moe with a gun was terrifying. Cold logic told him that the bastards were dangerous anyway, but cold logic had never helped in the past. He'd seen too many entertainment flicks where guns made their possessors all-powerful, as if they were talismans of evil. And he'd certainly never seen or touched one in real life. From what he'd read on the datanet, even a third of the soldiers who joined the military were never allowed to touch a gun.

Somehow, he forced himself to look away and stare around the spaceport as they made their way towards the building. Compared to Earth, it was very lax indeed; there was no security...although there were guns. Austin wasn't the only person with a weapon slung over his shoulder; in fact, when he looked at the older man, it was clear that he was carrying a weapon at his belt too. A long chain of men wearing hats and orange overalls, their legs shackled, appeared out of the building, escorted by a couple of men wearing green uniforms. They were marched off towards the road and rapidly faded into the distance.

Inside, it was barely cooler than the outside, despite the presence of a handful of fans attached to the wall and whirring busily. Austin ran forward, picked up a number of hats and started to pass them round. Gary took one, placed it on his head and looked around. The hats were absurd compared to Earth's fashions, although he had a feeling that Earth's fashions weren't very practical on Meridian. Kailee and her friends were already sweating their way out of their clothes.

Yates nodded to Austin, who stepped onto a chair and peered down at them. "There are three lanes to the road," he announced, loudly enough for them all to hear. His voice shone with an easy confidence that made Gary feel a surge of hatred as well as envy. "We will be walking on the far left of the road; the other two lanes are for motor vehicles. Don't wander into those lanes unless you cannot avoid it, in which case watch for oncoming vehicles. The drivers are not always as careful as they should be.

"We've put aside some living space for you in the city itself, so you can explore for a couple of days. You might also want to buy some better clothing for yourselves, as well as any other supplies you might be missing."

He jumped down and headed towards the door. Yates motioned impatiently for his charges to follow him, which they did. Gary gritted his teeth and brought up the rear, trying to keep his distance from Darrin and Barry. He really didn't like the way they were muttering together. Or the glances they kept throwing at Austin's back...

––––––––––

Kailee had never walked so much in her life, not in the temperature-controlled CityBlock where she'd spent her entire life. Even when walking to and from school with the other girls, she had never really walked *that* far. But on Meridian, she found herself sweating like a pig within seconds of leaving the shuttle. Her makeup, she was sure, was running down her face as she walked, sweat pooling at the bottom of her shoes. It was a thoroughly unpleasant sensation.

And it would be impossible without Janet's training, she thought, as she forced herself onwards. *We owe her one.*

The sun seemed to be growing hotter and hotter, to the point where she found herself wondering why the forest hadn't burst into flames. Her world had shrunk to her view of Abdul's back and little else; she could barely even lift her head to look around. She swore inwardly as a pair of vehicles raced by the walkers, leaving a faint stench of...*something* mechanical in the air. Surely the drivers – she could see them sitting at the front of the trucks - could have given them a lift. But they might have demanded a price for their services...

She glanced down at her chest and winced at just how badly her sweat had soaked her shirt, leaving the shape of her breasts and nipples clearly visible. The other girls weren't any better, although it looked as though the boys were in no state to appreciate the view. Even Barry seemed to be having problems with the walk; he'd pulled on additional clothes rather than shoving them in his bag and it had cost him.

There was a dull rumble from overhead, followed rapidly by a shower of water. Kailee wondered, for a brief moment, if there was a leak in the water pipes before she realised the truth. It was raining! Rain on Earth could be dangerous, she knew; she heard the sounds of panic from the others before Yates started to laugh at them. On Meridian, the rain was safe to drink. The rain was surprisingly warm, but heavy; at first, she almost welcomed its touch as it washed the sweat from her body. But as her clothes became sodden, she realised that the water would damage everything in her bag. It wasn't meant to be waterproof!

Brilliant lightning flashed in the sky, then faded away into nothingness. The rain drizzled to a halt moments later, leaving her staring around at her companions. They were all drenched, although Gary and Abdul had had the bright idea of trying to shield their bags with their own bodies. She looked back down at herself and sighed, inwardly. Her clothes were stuck to her as firmly as before, while there was mud on her trousers and her shoes seemed on the verge of coming apart.

And...somehow...they were on the edge of the city.

Kailee had no inclination to look around as Austin led them to a long low building, then showed them into the female compartment. It was cooler inside than outside; this time, the air conditioning actually seemed to work. Or maybe it was the lack of windows; the only light came from a single light bulb, hanging over their heads. The female compartment wasn't lockable, she noted in some alarm, but she was too wet to care. She stripped off her clothes at Janet's command, then hung them on a long string to enable the cloth to dry. But they definitely weren't suited for the planet's climate.

"We'll get you some proper clothes tomorrow," Janet said. She'd stripped off herself at once, without a qualm, even though the other girls had been hesitant. "And I suggest that you remember this in future. You won't have a government-issue nursemaid here."

Not that we had one before, Kailee thought, sourly.

Janet reached into a cupboard, produced a handful of towels and tossed them to the girls. "There are dressing gowns in here too," she added. "You can wear them for dinner tonight, when you are introduced to local cooking. Wristwatches too; it's early afternoon, by local time."

Kailee blinked. It still felt like early morning to her.

"That's the starship lag," Janet explained, when Kailee asked. "The starship operated on Galactic Standard Time; Meridian operates on its own 25-hour day. Right now, your body still thinks it's on GST. You'll get used to it after a good night's sleep."

Privately, Kailee hoped that she was right. Her mind felt...weird.

But then she noticed that the smell was gone. She'd get used to the rest of the world in time.

CHAPTER
SEVENTEEN

In the meantime, the teachers continued to face problems that just wouldn't go away, no matter which fad was currently in vogue. Class sizes were huge; teachers were unable to give individual pupils the attention they needed. Kids who fell behind were left to struggle on their own; teachers simply didn't have the time to help them catch up.

- Professor Leo Caesius, *Education and the Decline and Fall of the Galactic Empire*

"So," Samantha said, once Janet had left the room, "what does everyone think of the colonial boy?"

Kailee wasn't sure what to say. She knew how colonials were portrayed on Earth, either as barbarians in need of a good thumping or desperate refugees eager for help – and true civilisation – from Earth. But Austin hadn't struck her as either. He'd been calm, polite...and he'd carried a weapon. What did that mean?

"Handsome," Honey said. "And strange."

"Healthy," Li added. "Very healthy."

Kailee couldn't disagree. Austin was definitely healthy, healthier than any of the boys from Earth – healthier, perhaps, then the crewmen on the starship. There was something about him that the boys she'd known on Earth lacked, a sense of healthy confidence that outshone them as the sun outshone the moon. She had to admit that she *did* find Austin attractive, even though she had rarely allowed herself to feel attraction for anyone. And yet there was something about his willingness to carry a weapon that bothered her. In her experience, backed up by countless entertainment flicks, someone who carried a weapon willingly was almost certainly a bad guy.

She finished towelling herself off, then reached for one of the dressing gowns and pulled it on. It felt oddly scratchy against her skin – she couldn't imagine what material had been used to make it – but it covered her up nicely. She tied up the belt, then strode over to the door and peered through into the next room. There were six beds, neatly placed against the wall; beyond, there was a slightly smaller room containing a large tub. It looked like an oversized sink. Kailee stared at it for several moments before realising that it was actually a bathtub, one large enough to take two girls at the same time. There were baths in the CityBlock, she knew, but she'd never dared go. The only girls who went were those assured of powerful protectors.

"The guys in the spaceport looked healthy too," Samantha said, as Kailee came back to face her. "It must be living here."

Kailee nodded in silent agreement. To Austin, she guessed, the Earth-born must look pallid and pale. Even the dark-skinned Abdul might look...*odd* in sunlight. She remembered the muscles she'd seen under Austin's shirt and wondered, absently, just how he'd come by them. He didn't *look* like a bodybuilder – or someone who patronised the body-shops. It was quite possible, she decided, that muscles had been engineered into him before birth.

Janet stepped through as soon as the last of the girls had finished drying herself and donning her dressing gown. "If you will come with me," she said, bluntly, "we will get something *proper* to eat."

The girls smiled as they followed her through the curtain and into a larger chamber that seemed to be lined with wood. A large fire – a *real* fire – burned in a fireplace; Kailee hadn't seen one of those outside historical fantasies. A colossal wooden table dominated the centre of the room, with two wooden benches on each side. It had to be hugely expensive, she told herself, as she looked around. The entire room was largely wood. And they were even burning it in the fire!

She hadn't really cared for the rations on the starship, although they were closely related to foodstuffs she'd eaten on Earth. Algae-based products always looked and tasted of cardboard anyway; they were bland, utterly inoffensive. But the food on the table was...strange, barely recognisable. There were meats, vegetables, breads...Kailee's family had never been able to afford off-world food, even on their birthdays. An entire fortune was sitting on the table, waiting for her.

"I picked a wide selection of food," Austin said. He sounded pleased with himself. "All from the local markets, naturally."

Kailee stared at him. How rich *was* he? There was no one in her apartment block who could have purchased so much food, certainly not to honour guests from another world. They'd serve algae-based foodstuffs, perhaps with some flavouring if the guests were lucky. It was staggering wealth, wealth beyond the boundaries of comprehension. She wasn't the only one staring at Austin either. Several of the girls were obviously considering trying to seduce the colonial boy.

Yates surprised them all by laughing. "How much do you think this is worth?"

Gary tried to answer. "A hundred thousand credits?"

Kailee saw surprise clearly written on Austin's face. "Not that much," he said, sounding rather stunned. "A bare handful of credits at most."

Yates nodded, motioning for the girls to sit. "The food here is simple, but plentiful," he said. "And it is *real*. There aren't any algae-farms on the surface of the planet."

Kailee sat down, eying the meat dubiously. It looked...odd. One of the girls let out a yelp as she saw a fish lying on the table, its sightless eyes staring at nothing. Austin picked up a knife and a long fork, then started to cut into the fish, revealing its innards. He seemed rather surprised by the expression of disgust on Yuki's face.

"There isn't any packaged food here either," Yates informed them. He took a huge chunk of meat, then cut it into long stripes and started to hand it out. "The food here is all *natural*."

"But healthy," Janet added, softly. "And you may even feel yourself becoming more energetic after you eat."

Kailee hesitated as Yates put a piece of meat in front of her, then cut herself a slice and nibbled it carefully. It tasted...rich. The flavour was strange to her taste buds after years of eating algae-based products, but it wasn't displeasing. She chewed it, then swallowed and reached for a glass of orange liquid. Unlike the drinks they were given at school or after-school care, it was thick and slushy. But it tasted heavenly.

"Most of the food you will eat in the CityBlocks has been heavily processed," Yates said. "I believe that even the *real* foodstuffs, imported from the nearby systems at great cost, have also been treated. Here, the food is all natural. Humans have eaten this kind of food for centuries without ill-effects. Indeed, a proper diet of natural food does wonders for the human system."

Austin sat down at the head of the table and smiled at them. Kailee found herself smiling back, even as she studied him thoughtfully. Was his rude health merely the product of eating and drinking proper food? It wasn't a concept she knew enough to understand, not when the sole lessons she'd had on basic human foodstuffs had focused on the wonders of algae and the importance of not wasting resources. Would *she* return to Earth healthier than when she left?

He is attractive, she thought, ruefully aware that most of the girls were also doing their best to stare at him without making it obvious. It was a survival skill on Earth. Looking at the wrong guy for too long could be taken as an expression of interest, which could go badly wrong if the man felt like being pushy. *But why?*

Kailee had never really been attracted to any of the boys – or girls – she knew in the CityBlock. Part of it had been her awareness that she needed to keep herself as pure as possible, part of it had been simple disdain; there was no real advantage in being boy-crazy and she knew it. Men were unreliable; no matter what the girl did, she would always be dependent on the man and helpless if he abandoned her. She'd seen it happen before, when a long-term relationship broke up. The girl's status had plunged from diva to whore within days. No, dependency on a man was dangerous.

And yet she found herself attracted to Austin.

She tore her gaze away from him and looked at the other boys. Gary seemed as nerdy as ever, although he'd managed the walk from the space-port to the city remarkably well. Darrin and Barry *still* smelled of cleaning fluids; Kailee had been careful to keep her opinion to herself, but she rather admired Yates for daring to actually *punish* the two brats. Neither of them seemed very impressed with Austin, although she caught Darrin throwing yearning looks at the colonial boy whenever he thought no one was looking. Could he be attracted to him too?

But it seemed unlikely. Darrin had cut a swath through the more available girls in the CityBlock, without touching any of the boys. Unless he was one of the weirdo boys who were ashamed of liking their own sex, she considered, but he'd never struck her as being that sort of person. The homosexual boys would be glad to have another and the straight boys would be delighted at having less competition for the girls. It wasn't as if anyone would pick on him for liking boys.

She pulled her attention back to her food and ate, carefully. The vegetables tasted funny; she discovered that she liked raw carrots – once she got over her instinctive revulsion at eating uncooked food – but actually disliked cooked carrots. Some of the meat was very good; the beef and lamb were excellent, the pork was rather fatty and she didn't like it much. The fish tasted appalling and she refused to take any more. But, on the whole, she found herself enjoying their first meal on the planet. It was definitely very different to anything they would have eaten on Earth.

And if this is cheap here, she asked herself, *how much does it cost to produce the wood?*

"We intend to take you on tour around the city tomorrow morning," Yates said, when the plates were finally clean. Austin stood up, without being asked, and gathered in the plates, carrying them over to a smaller table set against the wooden wall. "There will be time for you to see and admire the various occupations practiced on this world. Then, in two or three days, we will head out to a farm."

Kailee wondered, absently, just what *that* would be like. She'd been on holographic tours of algae farms and other such installations, but she'd never seen a proper farm outside of a handful of entertainment flicks. And, given that they'd all been frankly pornographic, she rather doubted they bore any resemblance to reality.

"You'll find watches in the drawers under your beds," Yates continued. "Breakfast tomorrow is at 0800 precisely, followed rapidly by departure at

0900. Anyone who doesn't get up in time will be dumped in a cold bathtub and woken up that way."

Kailee groaned. She wasn't the only one. The time they'd spent on the starship had spoiled them, breaking their habit of rising early to go to school. Yates hadn't been quite as bloody-minded as the school authorities, ready to ignore blatant bullying but come down hard on anyone who dared to be more than a few minutes late for school. And she wasn't sure how long they'd even *have* to sleep. They were still attuned to Galactic Standard Time.

"Do not fret," Yates said. "I rather doubt you will be sleeping in tomorrow."

He smirked at them, then motioned for them to stand up. "One other word of warning," he said, as they stood. "Behave yourselves. You are not on Earth, not now. There are different standards here and woe betide you if you break them."

Kailee was still puzzling over what he meant as Janet led them back into their side of the house and then into the washroom. Earth was all they had ever known; what other standards of behaviour could there be?

"This is a bathtub," Janet said. She briefly demonstrated how to turn on the taps, then how to shut them off again. Kailee was surprised at being told that the water was effectively unlimited until she remembered the rain pouring from the sky. If there was one thing the planet had in abundance, it was water. "I suggest that you take a bath now, before you go to bed, then shower in the morning."

The girls all looked surprised, but it was Honey who put it into words. "Why do you want us to wash and shower all the time?"

Janet gave them all a rather sardonic look. "This is not a clean environment," she pointed out, dryly. "You will be muddy, you will be sweaty... and believe me, being dirty is not regarded as very pleasant or healthy here. And since the water is available, you can use it all the time to wash yourself clean."

Kailee wondered, suddenly, if Austin thought they *smelled*. Water was tightly rationed in the CityBlocks and the starship hadn't been much better, even though Janet had told them more than they wanted to know about how dirty water – and other liquids – could be cleansed and recycled. Kailee hadn't really wanted to know such details. She'd had to force herself to drink again after discovering where the water had been. But it had been purified...

"We'll get you all proper clothes tomorrow," Janet continued. "I'd suggest that you check your bags, pull out anything that is wet – or even merely damp - and hang it up to dry. Other than that..."

She nodded towards the curtain. "Yates and I will be sleeping outside," she concluded. "If you need us – and it had better be important – feel free to call."

———

"So," Yates said. "What do you make of your new friends?"

Austin frowned as he washed the plates clean, one by one. He was mildly surprised that none of the newcomers had offered to do the washing up – it was regarded as a guest's duty, when staying at someone else's house – but they were tired after their long trip. And most of them had stared at him, their expressions hooded and unreadable. He didn't know what to make of that.

"They seem a little surprised to be here," he said. Some of them had even looked as if they wanted to turn down the food, preferring to starve. "And they seem...pale."

"They didn't grow up in the fields," Yates told him. He moved over to stand beside Austin and began to dry the plates. "And this is a *very* different environment to anything they have experienced beforehand. I'm expecting some of them to have problems when they discover just how wide and open Meridian actually *is*."

Austin shrugged in incomprehension.

"Other than that, I'm sure we'll get along," he said, when he realised that Yates was waiting for a response. "Why weren't they so keen on the food at first?"

Yates snorted, although Austin could tell it wasn't directed at him. "Most people on Earth cannot afford to eat anything more than algae-based products, like ration bars," he said. "It would surprise me if many of our charges had ever eaten something more natural. And even then, it comes in packets and they are often unaware of the source. Here...there is not only real meat, but it comes in chunks that were clearly once part of an animal."

"Strange," Austin said. He finished the last plate and moved on to the glasses. "And they all kept staring at me."

"Strangers can be dangerous on Earth," Yates said, neutrally. "It isn't a very safe place to live."

Austin looked at him in surprise. Everyone knew that Earth was the homeworld of humanity, the cradle of mankind. How could it *not* be safe? Meridian had hundreds of dangerous animals in the countryside, including some that had developed a taste for human flesh and others that were harmless to humanity, but dangerous to the local environment. He'd heard his father ranting often enough about the fools who had introduced rabbits to the planet's ecology. They'd bred like...well, rabbits.

He looked back at the sink, then finished washing the knives and forks. The newcomers hadn't had very good table manners either, he'd noticed. Most of the boys had eaten with their bare hands, something that would have earned Austin a clip around the ear if he'd done that at home. His mother would have told him that it was only acceptable when in the countryside. And the girls...

There was something about them that puzzled him. They were nothing like his sisters, or his brief girlfriends from school; they almost seemed weak and fragile to his eyes. It was easy to imagine them breaking if they fell, like glass dolls. There was little life in them at all. But it wasn't something he could *ask* about, not when there was no way the question couldn't be made inoffensive. Yates definitely seemed to take the safety of his charges seriously.

"I'm looking forward to showing them the farm," he said, although he wasn't sure if that were true. What would his father's farm look like to someone from Earth? Would they be charmed by the animals or disgusted by the manure? He'd seen the girls squirm when they'd ended up with mud on their clothes or even their bare skin. One didn't spend time on a farm without getting dirty at one point or another. "And showing them around the city."

"I'd like you to spend some time with Darrin and Barry," Yates said. It took Austin a moment to place the names. But Barry wasn't easy to forget, not when he was oddly-oversized. "They might find a place to fit in here."

"Yes, sir," Austin said. "I'll see what I can do."

CHAPTER
EIGHTEEN

This might have been solved if teachers were allowed to give honest feedback to the children (and their parents). This was not, however, permitted. The fads decreed that telling the children that they were failing would damage their self-esteem, thus teachers were forced to look for ways to compliment even the very worst of students.

- Professor Leo Caesius, *Education and the Decline and Fall of the Galactic Empire*

Gary jerked awake as he heard a noise – something screeching – coming from outside the house. For a long moment, he didn't even know where he was; the bed felt very different to his bed at home or the bunk on the starship. And then he remembered. Reaching for the watch – the sole piece of technology he'd seen in the house – he checked the time and blinked in surprise. It was barely 0700, local time, and yet he felt completely energised.

He cast a nervous look at where Barry and Darrin were sleeping – Barry snoring so loudly that it was a miracle that anyone else was asleep – then padded towards the washroom and closed the door. He'd never dared spend long in the shower on the starship, even without the water rations. Now, though, he locked the door and turned on the taps, marvelling at how the water came out and filled the tub. Before he'd come to Meridian, he'd never seen clean water in such large quantities. He'd certainly never dared to go to the public bathhouses.

The water was warm enough to make him relax, but he knew he didn't dare relax completely, not with Barry in the next room. He scrubbed himself clean, then stood up and dried himself with a towel, rather than the hot air they'd had to use back home. Outside, Abdul and Steve were stirring too; Gary pulled on his clothes rapidly, then walked through the curtain and down into the living room. Austin was already there, building up a fire in the fireplace. He turned around and smiled at Gary before Gary could decide if he wanted to slip backwards and hide.

"Good morning," Austin said. "Have you ever built a fire before?"

Gary shook his head, wordlessly. First the weapon, carried so casually, and now building a fire. They'd been taught, time and time again, never to play with fire, not even on the smallest possible scale. It was dangerous, they'd been told, and it could easily spread out of control. But Austin seemed to be building up the fire with easy competence.

"There's a handful of papers at the bottom," Austin said, pointing into the fireplace. "Above them are some twigs and other pieces of wood that should catch fire easily, allowing the flames to spread through them and up into the larger pieces of wood. Once *they* catch, the fire will continue to burn as long as it is fed with fuel."

Gary nodded. "What stops it from burning down the whole house?"

Austin give him an odd look. "The fireplace is made of stone," he said, finally. "Stone doesn't actually burn, so as long as the fire stays inside the fireplace the house is in no danger."

He held out a box of matches. "Would you like to light it?"

"I..." Gary hesitated. Part of him wanted to try, part of him was too scared even to touch the box. What if something went wrong? They'd all seen the videos showing the schoolchildren why playing with fire was so dangerous. And yet..."I'll try."

He took the box, opened it and regarded the matches doubtfully. None of the videos had been very clear on just what the user should do to start a fire; it took him several moments to realise that he had to rub the matches against the side of the box. The first time he did it, nothing happened; the second time, the match flared to life so brightly that he dropped it in shock. Austin hastily stamped on the match and suggested that he be more careful next time. It still took several tries before he managed to get a lighted match to touch the paper and ignite the fire.

"Watch," Austin suggested, as he took back the box of matches. The wasted matches were already dumped into the fire. "The flames are only starting to make their way through the fireplace."

Gary watched, feeling a strange sense of almost childish wonder. The flames were growing brighter as they consumed the paper, then slowly working their way up through a web of ever-larger pieces of wood until they reached the biggest pieces of all. Flames licked and crackled around them and slowly, very slowly, they began to burn.

"It's lighting the fire without a match that is really difficult," Austin said, as he stood up and led Gary through a small door. Behind the fireplace, there was a large metal structure and a colossal basin of water. "I had to do it before I won my first scouting badge."

He picked up a pile of plates, then passed them to Gary. "Put them on the table," he added. "And then help me sort out the food for you and your friends."

Gary nodded. He'd never really understood how much work went into cooking food, particularly on a primitive planet. It was so much easier to have blocks of algae-based material, even though they tasted of nothing in particular. Austin seemed to enjoy it; he produced great strips of meat, fried them in a large pan, then put it to one side as he fried large vegetables and pieces of bread. Gary felt his mouth watering as he smelled the cooking food, even though he had his doubts. They'd been warned, more than once, that cooking their own food was unhealthy.

"You'll have to get someone else to help clean up afterwards," Austin warned. "Can any of you cook?"

"I don't think so," Gary said. He'd known parents who had tried all sorts of tricks to make their rations taste more palatable, but he didn't know if that counted as real cooking. "It isn't something we learned on Earth."

"Odd," Austin commented. He gave Gary a thin smirk. "I'm afraid you're going to have to learn."

He picked up the large frying pan and carried it into the next room. Yates and most of the boys were already seated at the table, while the girls were drifting in one by one. Gary guessed that they were taking advantage of the bathtub, assuming that the girls had one too; they'd probably been reluctant to go to the public baths themselves. Everyone knew that girls who went there were easy. Or at least that was what Gary had been told.

Li stuck up a hand. "What is this, sir?"

"Fried bacon, fried potatoes, fried eggs, fried mushrooms, fried tomato, fried bread," Austin said. He seemed rather amused by her reaction. "Did I mention that it included fried bacon?"

He ladled out the food and watched them eat. Gary took a seat and gratefully accepted a large piece of bacon, with two runny eggs and a slice of bread. It tasted odd to him, but not unpleasant. The thought of eating real meat was no longer strange after last night. He finished his plate and looked around in hopes of more, but there was nothing left. Clearly, there was something in the planet's atmosphere that encouraged them to eat. He'd never eaten so much on Earth.

But then, the food was never very tasty, he thought, darkly. *Here, it tastes great.*

"Austin, please can you show Darrin, Abdul and Steve how to wash up," Yates said, when they were finished. "Everyone else, get ready to leave the house at 0900 precisely. That gives you twenty minutes."

Gary glanced at his watch. Yates was correct. Where had all the time gone?

Twenty minutes later, he heard the grumbling from the boys as they complained about having to do the washing up. None of them seemed to have enjoyed it, even though Austin and Yates had both pointed out that it was necessary. A dirty plate or pan couldn't be used again until it was cleaned. And, if the newcomers couldn't cook, they could damn well wash. Gary allowed himself a moment of relief that Yates was in charge; if it had been one of the teachers from Earth, he knew that *he* would have been doing all the washing up. It was much easier to make Gary do something than someone like Barry.

"Remember what I said," Yates reminded them, as they put on their hats and headed out the door. "Behave yourselves – or else."

Gary kept close to Yates as he led them through a series of streets, staring around at the buildings. Most of them were made of wood or brick, although there were a handful made of metal. The air was cool and smelled faintly of salt, but water dripped down from the side of the buildings and ran down the streets towards the sea. None of the locals seemed particularly bothered by the threat of another downpour from high overhead. But then, they were probably used to it.

He sucked in his breath as he spotted, for the first time, a pair of colonial girls. They were laughing and joking when they first appeared, then they stopped and stared with frank curiosity at the newcomers from Earth. Gary stared back, too impressed to be careful of showing too much interest; the girls were almost obscenely healthy. They wore simple trousers and shirts, yet they somehow managed to glow with life and health that none of the girls from Earth matched. Gary felt a stirring he quickly brushed aside. After he'd been beaten up by a boy in school for showing too much interest in his girlfriend he'd restricted himself to porn. But no porn matched the colonial girls.

Barry wolf-whistled. Yates rounded on him and glared him into silence, then nodded apologetically at the girls. There was a brief moment of pity in their eyes, then they walked off down the street. Gary watched them go, feeling another wave of envy. Their lives were safe, unthreatened by bullies or would-be rapists. How could they *not* feel pity for someone from Earth?

They resumed walking down the street until they reached a large market, with a number of stalls hidden under bright canopies. Gary found himself looking around with a strange mix of awe and disgust; there were stalls selling live animals, or animals so freshly killed that they still looked alive. One shopkeeper was actually cutting up a sheep in front of his customers, who were calling out orders and requests for pieces of meat. Another plunged his hand into a vat of water and produced fish, flipping and flopping in his hand, for another customer. There was a dull thump as he bashed the fish's head with a hammer, then dropped it into a bag and passed it to his customer. She gave him a handful of coins and walked off with satisfaction. Gary found it hard not to be sick.

There were stalls piled high with fruits and vegetables, followed by stalls selling cut meat and even a handful of paper books. Gary couldn't understand where they came from; paper books were rare on Earth;

almost everything was online anyway. Behind them, someone was frying meat and selling colossal burgers to men wearing overalls as they made their way down towards the shore. It didn't look very healthy, but the cook was doing a roaring trade. The men chatted amongst themselves and largely ignored the newcomers from Earth. It took Gary several moments to realise that two of them were actually women. But they didn't look very feminine at all.

"Girls, come with me," Janet ordered. She led them towards a large building at one corner of the marketplace. "Boys, stay here with Yates."

Gary obeyed, wandering over to the bookstall and examining the books. None of the titles seemed familiar, apart from a couple they'd been meant to read in school. He picked one of them up, then winced as he realised it was actually quite hard to read printed text. And to think that he skim-read text presented to him by a reader! He put the book down and picked up another with a garish cover, one featuring a bikini-clad woman carrying a sword that was almost larger than herself. Inside, the text was so small as to be almost beyond his ability to read.

He glanced up as a line of children walked through the marketplace, none of them bothering to hide their interest in the newcomers. They couldn't be any older than nine or ten, although it was hard to tell. By then, children from the CityBlocks would have learned that they couldn't trust anyone, sometimes even including their own parents. But these children seemed confident, their bright eyes unaware of any threat. Gary felt another stab of envy as he looked at their innocent faces. None of them would ever have to deal with someone like Barry. They'd grow up to be just like Austin.

"Look at this," Darrin called.

Gary sighed, but slipped over to see what had caught his attention – and that of the rest of the boys. The stall was selling *guns*! He stared in disbelief, unable to accept that someone would just *let* Darrin, Barry and the others just look at guns, let alone handle them. But the stall-keeper seemed to have no difficulty letting them pick up and examine the weapons, even though it was clear that they had no idea what they were doing. A cold lump of ice started to form in Gary's chest. If Barry and Darrin had been bad enough without weapons, what would they be like *with* them?

"That's a standard self-defence pistol," the stall-keeper said. "Not very easy to shoot precisely at long range, but a real killer at close ranges – unless, of course, your enemy is wearing body armour. Given the right bullets, they can even stop a charging hog if you hit the bastard between the eyes. But if you want to go hunting, you'd be better off with a standard rifle."

Gary felt sick. Desperately, he turned away and threaded his way between the stalls until he finally came to the edge of the marketplace and looked down on the docks. They didn't seem very spectacular at first, but the sight of so many boats impressed him. There were kids on the boats, he saw, some of them no older than himself – and some definitely younger. He tried to tell himself that they were getting work experience, something that had been largely unavailable on Earth, but he didn't believe himself. Those kids were actually doing something worthwhile with their lives, already. Even in the best possible case, Gary knew that *he* would have been condemned to at least four more years of schooling on Earth before he could get a proper job.

A voice spoke from behind him. "Trying to run away?"

Gary jumped, then turned around. Yates was standing there. His voice had sounded different, somehow.

"No," Gary confessed. He wasn't sure, really, what to make of Yates. "I was just contemplating a wasted life."

"You're not the only one," Yates said, briskly. He nodded down towards the boats as they headed out to sea. "I understand that you helped this morning?"

"I think so," Gary said. Yates quirked an eyebrow, inviting Gary to continue. "I wasn't sure how helpful I actually *was*."

"Someone like Austin would have learned how to cook from a very early age," Yates said, softly. "Someone like you would never have been expected to cook, or clean, or do anything else for yourself. Parents here teach their children the basics as soon as they can; parents on Earth are legally forbidden from putting their kids to work outside school, even something as minor as cleaning the dishes. Learned helplessness has been ingrained into most of you after years of schooling."

Gary scowled. "But why?"

"You tell me," Yates said. He turned and started to walk back towards the rest of the group, then stopped. "You're a bright boy, Gary. You scored highly in the exams on the ship, exams which are nowhere near as... tainted as exams on Earth. You tell me why you have never been taught to take care of yourself."

He led Gary back to the group, then led them all into a large warehouse crammed with clothes and other supplies. A dark-skinned man measured Gary carefully, then produced a series of shirts, trousers and shoes that were perfect for the environment. According to him, they could be washed thoroughly and then dried without risking any damage at all. Gary remembered just how many clothes had been ruined during the walk to the city and wondered, helplessly, why he hadn't thought to check the requirements. Yates had been right. The information had been written down in the briefing notes they'd been given.

Back outside, they met up with a handful of other colonials, all of whom looked just like Austin. "You can spend the next hour or two exploring the city," Yates said, pairing them up into groups. "I've given your escorts money for food, but report back to the house at 1600 for dinner. Don't be late or there will be no food until late evening."

Gary nodded. Everyone knew, now, that Yates meant it.

He feared that he would be partnered with Darrin and Barry, but instead he was matched with Steve and a colonial boy who seemed a younger version of Austin, with a brighter smile.

"My father works down at the docks," the boy said, without even bothering to introduce himself. "Let's go see the boats, shall we?"

He seemed rude, Gary thought, then it struck him that the locals would probably know just about everyone in the city. There was no way to be sure, but Sabre City seemed smaller than a single CityBlock on Earth. The boy might not even realise that the newcomers wouldn't know his name. How many visitors from Earth did they get anyway?

Sighing, putting the thought aside, Gary followed him and Steve down towards the docks.

CHAPTER
NINETEEN

Without clear feedback, students were unable to understand their own weaknesses, let alone come to grips with them. Students who might have had the native ability to advance never made the effort because they never realised that the effort had to be made. They believed they were doing fine, right up until the moment they left school – and at that point, it was too late.

- Professor Leo Caesius, *Education and the Decline and Fall of the Galactic Empire*

Darrin had to admit, as he and Barry followed Austin, that he was bored. Sabre City was a strange new environment, but it simply didn't look very interesting. The girls were attractive, yet they were strange, strange enough to make him wonder how they would react to *any* attempt at courtship. And there were the weapons most of them carried, either on their backs or on their belts. None of the locals seemed to find carrying so many weapons anything out of the ordinary.

The only interesting sight had been the gun stall. He'd listened with genuine interest as the seller described the weapons he sold, each one a fascinating hint of a power Darrin had never been allowed to touch. A real live weapon? Darrin knew that there were soldiers who were never allowed to touch weapons, even though they were in the military. The thought of knives and makeshift spears simply didn't compare to firearms. How could they?

"So," Austin said, once they were some distance from where Yates had been standing, "what do you want to do?"

"Guns," Barry said, at once. Their thoughts had obviously been running in the same direction. "I'd like to shoot a gun."

Austin didn't seem to find anything wrong with it, even coming from Barry. Darrin found that surprising; a child who confessed to violent thoughts on Earth would often be sent to the psychologist, who would do absolutely nothing of any value. Like so much else, the whole system was absurd. The truly violent like Barry and Moe, for example, were left alone, while those who couldn't fight were harassed. Instead, Austin merely turned and led them through a maze of side-streets until they reached a large building at the edge of town.

"The shooting range should be nearly empty now," Austin said, as they walked up the steps and into the stone building. "Most of the users will either be at work or at school."

He was right, Darrin discovered. There was hardly anyone in the building, apart from a bored-looking man seated in front of a rack of weapons. The absence of any visible security puzzled him; on Earth, firearms were so tightly restricted that no ordinary citizen could hope to lay hands on one. Austin spoke briefly to the man, who eyed them both with some interest, then picked up a pair of long rifles and handed them to Austin.

"Most newcomers from Earth come here within the first week," Austin explained, as he led them through a pair of heavy doors. Inside, there was a long room with a set of targets at the far end. "There are classes on weapons-handling for everyone, just to make sure that they know the basics. A weapon can make the difference between life and death out in the countryside."

Darrin looked at him, interested. "Why?"

"Lots of nasty creatures out there," Austin commented. "And quite a few runaway indents."

"So you shoot them," Barry grunted. "Is that allowed?"

"Kill or be killed, at times," Austin admitted. "It's quite legal to shoot an intruder on your territory, although it is generally considered a good idea to shout a warning first."

Darrin shook his head in disbelief. He'd heard of people who had resisted muggers and rapists on Earth...and they'd often been worked over by the Civil Guard, who hated the idea of *anyone* showing resistance. And that had been before the gangs had extracted revenge for their dead or wounded fellows. But if everyone in the CityBlock was armed...he found himself silently trying to calculate just how much blood would flow in the endless corridors. It was hard to imagine anyone holding back if so much power was put into their hands.

Or maybe the gangs would just continue to dominate, he thought, dryly. *The gangs are organised.*

"This is a fairly basic rifle," Austin said, retrieving a set of cartridges from a cabinet and showing them how to open up the weapon. "You can slot six bullets into the magazine, then fire them one by one. Naturally, you have to keep the weapon clean at all times...which I imagine is something you'll cover in the weapons classes you'll get later."

Darrin rather doubted that was true. There had been nothing about weapons of any kind in the schedules they'd been given. Maybe new settlers from Earth received such training as a matter of course – he knew next to nothing about operating a weapon – but they were only going to be on the planet for a couple of months. It was quite likely that Yates had no intention of teaching them anything about weapons. After all, having such knowledge might get them in trouble on Earth.

He took the rifle and slotted in the bullets, one by one. Austin talked them through basic range safety – never step beyond the line, never point a weapon at someone – and then motioned for Darrin to take a shot at the target. Darrin lifted the rifle and pulled the trigger, which clicked. Nothing else, as far as he could tell, happened.

"Take off the safety," Austin said, shortly. "You have to have it on at all times, except when you actually intend to fire."

Darrin flushed, carefully clicked off the safety and took aim again. This time, there was a loud CRACK as the rifle fired, the bullet slamming into the far wall, leaving a red mark to the left of the target. Barry let out a faint snicker as Darrin realised that he'd missed. And yet he'd thought he'd aimed perfectly...

And he'd fired a gun. The thought made his body start to shake. He was no stranger to violence, even before he'd battered Fitz and knocked him out...and yet firing a gun made him tremble. The gun had turned him into...what? A killer? And yet he had come very close to killing a man before ever laying eyes on a weapon. For the first time in years, Darrin was actually *frightened* by the prospect of violence. What did physical strength matter when one had a gun?

I could have shot Fitz, he thought. *And Fitz could have shot me.*

"Take another shot," Austin urged. Absurdly, the colonial didn't seem to be the slightest bit worried about being too close to a loaded weapon. But it was all perfectly normal for him. "Or let Barry have a shot."

Darrin hesitated, then lifted the rifle, took careful aim and fired a second shot. This time, the bullet struck the man-shaped target in the right shoulder. If the man had been real, he would have been seriously injured. Darrin let the weapon fall to point at the floor as he staggered in realisation. The gun had to be taken seriously or never touched at all.

"You might not kill him," Austin observed, as he took the gun back. "Firing to wound might work in the movies, but it doesn't work so well in real life."

He passed the weapon to Barry, who seemed disturbingly eager to try it. The larger boy cycled through all four of the remaining bullets, hitting the target three times. Darrin winced inwardly, unsure what to make of it. A weapon would make Barry far more dangerous and unpleasant, just like the baddies in the entertainment flicks. But they'd never actually been able to hit the hero or heroine, no matter how many rounds they'd fired.

And they never had to reload either, Darrin thought, as Austin patiently showed them how to reload the gun. What sort of weapons had infinite bullets? Somehow, he had a feeling that the depiction of unlimited ammunition was also unrealistic. *What else did they get wrong? Or lie about?*

It grew easier to fire as he practiced with the weapon, time and time again. Austin seemed pleased with their progress; he even picked up a couple of other weapons and demonstrated how to use them. Darrin discovered that he liked the pistol, but its accuracy – at least in his hands – was definitely awful. Austin, on the other hand, could hit the targets reliably with each hand.

"So," Barry said, when they were taking a break, "what were you doing with the guns before you came here?"

Austin smiled. "I was taught how to use one as soon as I was old enough," he said. "It was my job to pot rabbits and birds for my mother to cook. You never know when you might need a weapon to hunt, particularly when the food is running short. And besides, hunting teaches you to be cunning."

Barry leaned forward. "Did you ever actually *kill* someone?"

"Not yet," Austin said. He didn't seem alarmed by the question. "Having a gun doesn't give you a licence to kill."

"But people are killed here," Barry said. "Why?"

Darrin shivered. The line of questions bothered him – but, as far as he could tell, Austin didn't seem to find it anything out of the ordinary. Maybe it wasn't out of the ordinary for him, Darrin wondered; maybe he'd actually discussed killing with his friends and family, dissecting what had happened to others and learning from their experiences. Darrin had had to undergo a few such sessions himself in school, although they'd been tedious and consisted largely of the teachers telling them what others had done wrong. There had been no room for debate.

"Every so often, bandits attack farms and have to be beaten off," Austin said. "Then there's the immigrants from other worlds who don't realise that no means no."

Surprise sex, Darrin thought, remembering the jokes the boys had made about taking the girls by surprise. It had seemed funny at the time, a way of proving their dominance over the women. But if there had been a very real risk of death, he asked himself, would it have been so amusing?

They went back to the shooting range and tested several other weapons. Darrin found himself watching Barry carefully, noting how the boy's entire demeanour seemed to change when he was clutching a weapon in his oversized hands. Silently, Darrin cursed the events that had conspired to throw him and Barry together. Maybe he should have made friends with one of the other boys, maybe even Gary. Sitting next to Barry was like sitting next to a tiger, desperately stuffing food in its mouth in the hopes that it would be too full to eat him next.

"Tell me," Barry said, after firing off another six shots towards the targets. "How do you actually *get* a weapon?"

"You buy it, generally," Austin said. He seemed rather puzzled by the question. "Take your money to a stall, buy the weapon you want and then take it away. My father threw a fit when I brought home the first rifle I'd purchased with my own money. I'd forgotten to buy ammunition to go with it."

Darrin shook his head in disbelief. His mother would have been horrified if he'd come home with a live weapon – at least if she'd been sober at the time - although Fitz would probably have stolen it. The thought of shooting the bastard was very attractive; surely, Austin had to be joking. Didn't the colonials ever have homicidal desires against their fellow men? There were so many hatreds in the CityBlocks that adding weapons would merely have led to a bloody slaughter.

Gary might take a shot at Barry, Darrin thought. If a gun gave anyone the power to kill, what would it do to Gary? There were weaker boys who fought like mad bastards when attacked, even though they couldn't hope to win. What would *they* do with guns? And would it really be a bad idea if Barry died?

The thought nagged at his mind. He'd known that Barry and Moe would always be there, at least unless they ran afoul of the gangs. But that was unlikely; they'd probably leave school at seventeen and go right into the gangs, serving as enforcers. He tried to form a mental image of them being killed by their superiors for molesting girls or otherwise threatening the protection rackets, but that was unlikely too. They were just too promising as thugs to be thrown away so easily.

"Really," Barry said. Darrin had to think to remember what they were talking about. "What did your father do?"

"Refused to buy any ammunition and said I would have to wait until I earned more allowance before I could fire the gun," Austin said. "And told me off for carelessness."

He shook his head. "Dad was right," he admitted. "A weapon is useless without ammunition and not particularly helpful unless you know how to use it."

Darrin pulled his mind all the way back to the conversation. "How many rounds do you fire off?"

"Hundreds, every time I come here," Austin said. "I'm practicing for the trials to become a Bush Ranger. You have to be an expert shot, as well as a hunter, a basic doctor and quite a few other skills. Being in the city isn't really helpful."

"I can see why," Darrin said. "Where do you normally live?"

"On my father's farm," Austin said. He shrugged. "It's fairly common for youngsters to take a year or two working somewhere else, just to give them a taste of other occupations. I spent four months on the boats and discovered I hated it. Fishing is the one sort of hunting I dislike."

Darrin had to smile. At least Austin had *some* limitations. It was funny, but finding out that there was something Austin couldn't do made him like the other boy. He'd seemed too perfect, particularly since he'd cooked breakfast and then had the girls staring at him whenever he'd been looking the other way.

"Take your final shots now," Austin added, glancing at his watch. "We don't want to be here during lunch break."

Barry laughed. "Why not?"

"Because a few dozen people will come here for lunch, eat their sandwiches and hold a small shooting contest," Austin said. "And while I can take part, you two cannot – at least, not yet. You'd need months of practice before you were ready to take part in a shooting contest."

"There are such contests?" Darrin asked. "Why...?"

"Fun," Austin said. "My sister Judy won the last sharpshooting contest for teenagers."

Darrin blinked. Judy? No, the name was a coincidence; it couldn't be anything else. And yet, he remembered just how desperate *his* Judy had been to ingratiate herself to him, even opening her legs as soon as he'd asked. She had been willing to offer him everything in exchange for protection. Somehow, he couldn't imagine Austin's Judy doing the same. If she could shoot – and win a contest against others with a similar background – she had to be able to take care of herself. He'd never met the girl, yet he found himself certain that she was just like her brother. Everyone here had grown up in a very different environment.

Austin waited for Darrin to fire the final shots, then led them both back into the reception room and spoke briefly to the bored-looking man. Darrin watched him for a long moment, then jerked in surprise as Barry poked him with a long finger. He was still carrying the rifle, pointing it out the door towards a large vehicle. Darrin saw the grin on his face and knew, beyond a shadow of a doubt, just what Barry had in mind. He opened his mouth to say something, but it was already too late. Barry squeezed the trigger and the gun fired.

Austin spun around. "What the fuck...?"

Darrin barely heard him, even though it was the first time he'd heard Austin swear. The bullet had struck the vehicle's windscreen, shattering it. An alarm sounded a moment later, the vehicle's lights flashing on and off in time with the honking horn. Someone started to shout in outrage, the words blurring together; several pedestrians were drawing weapons of their own and taking cover...

Austin ran forward and grabbed the gun in Barry's hand, forcing it down towards the ground. Barry giggled and held on to the weapon, despite the clear anger in Austin's face. The colonial boy didn't hesitate; he poked something that looked like a silver pencil into Barry's arm. Barry jerked, as if he'd been zapped with something, then collapsed to the ground. Darrin opened his mouth to speak, then gaped as the bored-looking man – no longer looking quite so bored – pointed a pistol at his face.

"Keep your hands where I can see them," he snarled. The tiny pistol muzzle looked large enough to swallow the moon, a black hole consuming Darrin's attention. "Up in the air."

Darrin obeyed, shaking. He'd never felt so close to death, not even during his first real fight, when he'd been determined to win to force the older boys to find easier targets. He didn't even dare to move as his hands were yanked behind his back and something hard and plastic was wrapped around them, keeping him firmly trapped.

But it was the look in Austin's eyes – a strange mixture of betrayal and disappointment – that left him feeling shaken and cold. They could have been friends, he saw now, friends and allies, even if they came from very different worlds. But Barry had ruined it, just like he ruined everything.

It took all his remaining determination to keep from crying.

CHAPTER

TWENTY

Worse, as teachers were no longer in charge of the schools (if they had ever been) they were not able to maintain effective discipline. Children need rules and boundaries; the teachers were simply not permitted to write the rules or even enforce them.

- Professor Leo Caesius, *Education and the Decline and Fall of the Galactic Empire*

The prison cell was a dark and dismal place.

Darrin had to admit, as he sat on the bunk, his hands still cuffed behind his back, that the architect was a genius in his own way. He'd designed a cell that made it very clear to the inhabitant that he or she was in deep trouble. The walls were made of dark stone, the front of the cell was sealed with iron bars and the bunk was firmly fixed to the floor. And the less said about the toilet, the better. With his hands cuffed, he wasn't even sure how he was meant to use it, when the time came to finally go.

He silently cursed Barry under his breath as he waited, knowing that there was nothing else he could do. The man at the shooting range had handed him over to a burly man in a blue uniform, who had marched him through the streets, into a smaller building and dumped him into a cell. Being exposed to so many stares had been humiliating, even if he didn't know any of them personally. It had been mere luck, he suspected, that none of the others from Earth had seen him. And then he'd been told to wait.

Time seemed to have slowed down to a crawl. Darrin had no idea how long he'd been in the cell, but somehow it seemed preferable to wait rather than face the music. They'd been warned that this wasn't Earth, yet Barry hadn't listened. And nor had Darrin, not really. They hadn't really understood what they'd been told. He tested the cuffs – again – and cursed inwardly as he realised they were unbreakable. There was no escape.

He looked up as he heard someone come into the room. Yates was standing there, his face grim. Darrin cringed inwardly, knowing that it was going to be bad. Very bad. If Yates had made them scrub the decks for months after a minor bullying incident – very minor, compared to some of the incidents on Earth – who knew what he would do to them now? And, coming to think of it, where *was* Barry?

"So tell me," Yates said, as he unlocked the cell and stepped inside. "Just *what* were you thinking, really?"

Darrin swallowed. "I didn't mean to do anything," he whined. "I...it was Barry who fired the shot!"

"Yes, I suppose it was," Yates agreed. "So tell me. Why didn't you do anything to stop him?"

Darrin swallowed again. He could have said something, or done something, but the truth was that he'd done nothing, that he'd been too intimidated by Barry to stand in his way. Maybe he could stand up for himself better than Gary, maybe he *had* beaten Fitz to within an inch of his life, yet he'd still been reluctant to risk Barry's anger. But his failure to stand up to his...acquaintance had cost him dearly. The memory of the look in Austin's eyes made him shudder. They could have been friends.

"No answer, then," Yates said. "Did it not occur to you that letting him vandalise property might upset people?"

"But the gangs do it all the time on Earth," Darrin protested, finding his voice. "And the schools are vandalised regularly..."

"That's because Earth's government doesn't punish the gangs for their actions," Yates informed him, coldly. "And because the block residents don't stand up for themselves, not even slightly. Do you think they know, I wonder, that quite a few CityBlocks have been pushed to the limits by vandals, vandals who have smashed or damaged air circulation subsystems?

You should be grateful that there are so many redundancies built into your block's systems. Without them, you would all have suffocated to death by now.

"But this isn't Earth. You damaged a vehicle belonging to a resident of this planet, who is demanding recompense. And you will have to pay."

"I want a lawyer," Darrin said. Each of Yates's words felt worse than a blow from Fitz, even the ones that had left him bruised and bleeding. "It wasn't me who fired the shot."

He gathered himself. "I shouldn't even be in jail," he added. "I'll sue..."

Yates laughed at him. "Sue who?"

Darrin found himself scrabbling for excuses, even though he knew what he was doing. "He shouldn't have parked the car there," he protested. "And they shouldn't have given us guns. And I..."

Yates strode forward, caught him by the collar and hauled him into the air. "Are you suggesting that the victim is to blame? Do you imagine that he hung signs all over his car inviting you to shoot it? Or that merely giving you the opportunity, without having the slightest idea that he was doing so, made him the guilty party?"

His voice became mocking. "Oh, it was *such* a tempting target," he sneered. "I can't be blamed for taking a shot at it."

Darrin winced as Yates dropped him back onto the bunk. "That is the logic of a coward, the logic of a man who cannot accept responsibility for his own actions – or his failures to act."

"I'm no coward," Darrin protested. "I..."

Yates ignored him. "There's a girl showing legs that go all the way up to heaven," he continued, in the same sneering tone. "I didn't mean to rape her; she seduced me into raping her by wearing such revealing clothes. That man's wallet in his pocket was just begging me to steal it. The teacher whose leg I broke was such an unpleasant guy he was practically demanding to be hurt. *It's not my fault!*"

He glared down into Darrin's eyes. "That's what I've heard, time and time again, from people just like you. People who are unable to admit that they were responsible for their own actions. Those people are *cowards*."

Darrin gathered himself. "I am not a coward!"

Yates's held his eyes. "No?"

Darrin hesitated. He hated the thought of being considered a coward, but...the thought nagged at his mind. How many times had he chosen to go along with Barry, just to avoid the bigger boy's dislike – or to avoid making himself a target? How many times had he surrendered to Fitz, in hopes it would save him from a beating? How many times had he seen someone smaller and weaker than himself get picked on and done nothing? And how many times had he picked on someone himself? He hadn't ever picked a fight with someone bigger than him.

"You could have stopped Barry," Yates said, quietly. "Or you could have stopped talking to him on the ship. Why didn't you?"

"Because I was scared," Darrin admitted. The words tasted like ashes in his mouth. "I was scared, all right?"

"We make progress," Yates said. "Answer me a question. What do you want to do with your life?"

"I don't know," Darrin said. There was literally nothing beyond the end of his schooling. "I can find a job, perhaps."

Yates snorted. "You know, your teachers aren't really allowed to keep proper records of your progress through the school system," he said. "On the face of it, there's nothing to separate you from the thousands of other young brats in your class. But I can read between the lines – and I've been testing you on the ship. Your reading level is staggeringly poor; you cannot write at all."

"But I don't need to read and write," Darrin objected. "The reader does all that for me."

"Yes, in school," Yates said. "But not being able to read makes it impossible for you to learn material your teachers don't select for you. It also makes it impossible to hold down a worthwhile job. But even if that wasn't a problem, your maths skills are pretty basic, at least outside gambling. You can calculate the odds quickly, but little else. And your levels of general understanding of science, history, biology and current studies are almost nonexistent."

"But those are boring," Darrin protested.

"And necessary," Yates said. "In short, you lack even the knowledge to understand just how badly off you are. You may stay in the school system until you are twenty-one, unless you decide to leave early, but what will you do after that? You are not even thuggish enough to join the gangs. No, you'll stay in your apartment, eat algae bars and start helping some poor bitch to turn out the next generation of CityBlock residents. And, if you are lucky, you'll live long enough to see your grandchildren before you die."

He stepped backwards. "You're not the only one in the same boat," he added. "Tell me, how much do you actually *know* about Kailee?"

Darrin considered it. "Ice princess," he said, finally. "No one has ever had her."

Yates scowled at him. "Is that all you think about?"

He went on before Darrin could answer. "Kailee wants to become an actress," he said. "Do you think she has a chance?"

"She's beautiful," Darrin said. He remembered all the actresses he'd seen. They were all staggeringly beautiful – and utterly untouchable. Word on the street was that they wouldn't put out for anyone unless he had at least a million in the bank. "I think she could make it."

"Let's see," Yates said. "The current population of Earth is roughly eighty billion. How many of them are girls?"

Darrin hesitated, then shook his head. He had no idea how to answer the question.

Yates let out a loud sigh. "Half of them," he snapped. "Forty billion, to be precise. It is a number so vast as to be utterly beyond your comprehension. Of those women, how many do you think are Kailee's age?"

"I don't know," Darrin said. He wanted to work it out for himself, but he didn't know where to begin. But if male and females came in equal numbers, maybe age worked the same way, with the forty billion women distributed from zero to...what? He didn't even know how long a person lived! "Divided up between the ages..."

"At least you're *trying* to think," Yates said, unsympathetically. "For the record, the age of actresses entering the entertainment industry falls between seventeen to twenty-five. After then, the actress is generally considered to be well past her prime. And Kailee isn't the only girl with dreams of stardom. I looked it up, after Janet told me her dream. Every year, millions of girls start trying to find themselves an agent. Tell me, gambler, what does that tell you?"

Darrin gritted his teeth, but answered. "Her chances are very poor."

"Indeed they are," Yates agreed. He gave Darrin a thin smile that sent a burst of pride flickering through his mind. "Kailee will be one of millions – and not one of the best, at least going by educational achievements. Her reading skills are only slightly above yours. She will literally be unable to read her scripts, should she get that far. And there are other problems too, Darrin. Most of the really famous actors and actresses have contacts in the guilds, or family connections. The chances are that Kailee will be directed into pornographic productions, where there is no lack of demand for nubile young women, if she gets anywhere at all. She would have to be very lucky to start the climb towards stardom."

Darrin remembered watching such productions. He'd never given any thought to the girls, either about how they'd joined or what happened to them afterwards. But Yates pushed on, coldly and utterly remorselessly.

"Girls who take part in such productions are often burned out by the end of their first year," Yates said. "They have been had, literally, in every possible way. The lucky ones might just have made a nest egg; the less lucky ones will go straight into prostitution and never see the light of day again; the really unlucky ones will die on set, murdered by their fellows. And no one will remember them, no one at all.

"Of all of you, Gary is the only one with any real hope of gaining a proper job," Yates continued. "He's mastered reading and writing, he's learned how to study for himself...he might not go back to Earth at all. But you and Barry...you're going to have to decide what you want to make of your lives."

"But why?" Darrin asked. He felt too stunned to feel anything, any longer. "Why is the world like this?"

Yates laughed. "I could tell you that the Grand Senate prefers to keep you ignorant, rather than give you the tools you need to figure out just how badly you've been screwed," he said, darkly. "Or I could tell you that your superiors hate you so badly that mere death isn't enough for them, that they prefer to trap you in the CityBlocks and let you manufacture your own monsters.

"Or I could tell you that *no one* is to blame, that that government really is incompetent, that you're all victims of processes that had been weakening the Empire for centuries and those in power have no better idea of how to stop the decline than yourselves. What answer would you like?"

"The truthful one," Darrin snapped.

"There's truth in all of them," Yates said, quietly. One hand started to play with a golden cross hanging around his neck. "I wonder...do you know how lucky you are to have won the contest?"

"I didn't really write anything," Darrin confessed. "And I'd bet that Barry didn't either."

Understanding clicked. "Someone selected us, didn't they?"

"In a manner of speaking," Yates said. He looked Darrin in the eye. "Do you know what the term 'self-selected' means?"

Darrin shook his head.

"When someone chooses to sign up with a colonising consortium and leave Earth, it means that they are selecting themselves as colonists," Yates explained. "It means that they have enough awareness to understand that Earth is doomed and enough determination to try to make a home on a new colony world. But you...you and your comrades were all picked at random, just to see if you could make it out here. None of you selected yourself for this; in fact, I don't think that any of you actually *wanted* to win."

"But here we are," Darrin said. He rattled his handcuffs mournfully. "Trapped."

"Maybe," Yates said. "Your teachers have been forbidden from speaking bluntly to you, or saying anything that might impact on your self-esteem, or even disciplining you for your minor offences. In doing so, they have taught you and your fellows that there is no discipline and the law of the jungle – might makes right – rules supreme. Unsurprisingly, you lack even the awareness to understand why *you*, as well as Barry, are in trouble here.

"I *can* speak bluntly to you and I will. Being on this trip, if you choose to make use of it, is the best thing that has ever and will ever happen to you. On Earth, you have no future – and I think you know that, don't you? Here...you can make a new life for yourself, if you choose to put in the effort. But you have to have the determination to try.

"No one here is going to push you forward or do the work for you," he added. "But no one is going to hold you back either."

Darrin felt a strange mixture of hope and fear. Part of him wanted to try, remembering that Fitz – assuming the man had survived – would want to kill him the moment he returned to Earth. The other part of him doubted his ability to do anything – and knew that the colonials now had good reason to distrust him. And, by extension, everyone else from Earth.

"They hate me," he whined. "And I can't pay for the vehicle."

"No, you can't," Yates agreed. "I have spoken to the owner. The vehicle will be repaired using funds I brought with me, for various reasons. However, you will not be allowed to walk away unmarked."

Darrin swallowed, but listened.

"Austin didn't realise that you had no experience with guns," Yates said. "It was careless of him, but the local culture here frowns on denying anyone access to weapons. And in any case, he was not responsible for you and Barry screwing around with them. However, the end result was that you caused damage – you could easily have killed someone, whereupon I couldn't save you – and you have to pay.

"This isn't Earth. Petty criminals are not given a slap on the wrist. You and Barry will have to take a whipping before you rejoin us, after which the affair will be considered closed."

"Oh," Darrin said. He remembered Fitz lashing him with the belt while he'd been in a drunken rage. The welts had taken weeks to heal. "And if we refuse?"

"While the rest of us are exploring the planet, you will spend the rest of your time here," Yates said. "And then you will be either shipped back to Earth or assigned to an indent work team. It will not be a pleasant experience."

"I'll take the whipping," Darrin said. He could handle pain, thanks to Fitz. "But can I really make a living here?"

Yates hesitated. "I was just like you once," he said. "I grew up in the lower levels of Brit-Cit and, like you, I had few prospects. I sneaked to the upper levels and stole whatever took my fancy, right up until the day I was caught by the Civil Guard. They beat the shit out of me and threw me into a cell. It turned out that the Imperial Army was having a recruiting shortfall, so the recruiter gave me the choice between signing up or being exiled as just another indent."

He smiled. "If I'd known that there *was* fighting going on...

"But I did make it," he concluded. "And you can do the same, if you're prepared to work at it. Because no one can make you a success. You have to do it for yourself. And if you fail...at least you will have tried."

CHAPTER
TWENTY-ONE

Should a teacher clash with a student, the student would not only have the full support of the system, but an advocate willing to stand up and speak for him. The teacher, on the other hand, would not only be forced to stand alone; he would also face an automatic presumption of guilt. Unsurprisingly, students were able to get away with almost anything.

- Professor Leo Caesius, *Education and the
Decline and Fall of the Galactic Empire*

Gary was not surprised that Darrin and Barry had managed to get themselves into trouble.

What *had* surprised him, when he and Steve had returned to the house – which James had told them was called the lodge – was that they had both been arrested and thrown into a prison cell. Gary had seen the two bullies scrubbing the decks, but he'd assumed that Yates had only been able to punish them so effectively because they were onboard ship. But they'd been arrested on Meridian...

"This is not Earth," Yates told them, after a terse explanation of what had happened and why. "The rules are different here, as your friends have just found out. Tomorrow, they will be publicly whipped to make the point clear. I suggest that the remainder of you bear it in mind at all times."

Gary shook his head in disbelief. What sort of idiot would let Darrin and Barry handle a loaded weapon? Gary had seen Barry and Moe damaging large parts of the school – including Gary's work – simply because they could. From what Yates had said, it was pure dumb luck that no one had been injured or killed. And yet the hell of it was that a whipping was much more punishment than either of them would have gotten on Earth.

"After the process is completed," Yates continued, "you will not mention it to them or anyone else. The whole affair will be considered closed. Do you understand me?"

"Yes," Gary muttered, when Yates's gaze fell on him. "I understand."

He wouldn't dare mention the whole affair to anyone, but that wouldn't stop him enjoying the thought of the two bastards finally getting what they deserved. Gary allowed himself to imagine them being lashed, wondering if the person holding the whip would strike them hard enough to draw blood. It wasn't a nice thing to wonder at all, he knew, but he remembered everything they'd done too clearly to do anything other than delight in their misfortune. And maybe it would be *good* for them.

The thought kept dancing through his mind as they ate dinner – a meat stew served with crusty bread that tasted so much better than school food that Gary silently promised himself that he would never return – and went to bed. It was astonishing how much better he felt without the two bastards around, Gary knew; he washed himself, settled into bed and fell asleep quickly. Normally, he would lie awake for hours, just knowing that they were near him. He had never had a comfortable night.

He arose the following morning, took a long bath and slipped downstairs. Somewhat to his surprise, Austin was lighting the fire again; the colonial boy looked oddly pensive when he saw Gary. Gary had never seen Austin show any real doubt before; he'd just faced whatever the world had offered him and tackled it. But, when Austin nodded to him and turned to walk into the kitchen, it was clear that he was moving oddly, as if he were in pain.

Gary followed him, worried. "Are you all right?"

Austin nodded, one hand rubbing the seat of his trousers. "I'll be better soon," he said, shortly. "Is it really true that there are no guns on Earth?"

"The one you carried at the spaceport was the first I'd ever seen," Gary admitted. "Why did you teach Barry and Darrin how to shoot?"

"I never even thought about it," Austin confessed, as he started to heat the oil. "Basic weapons safety is so ingrained into us from an early age that I didn't think they'd be so stupid. They could have been shot! Or shot themselves!"

Which wouldn't be a bad thing, Gary thought. Barry was a thug; Darrin picked on Gary because there wasn't anyone else. But he kept that thought to himself.

"Father told me that Earth-folk just do as they're told," Austin added. "And you're never allowed to succeed or fail on your own."

"No one really cares," Gary said. He cursed the easy confidence he'd seen in Austin's eyes. "There are more people in our school than there are in the entire city" – the briefing notes had said as much, when he'd reread them to see what else they'd missed – "and most of them are absolutely hopeless. You can do nothing and still get by with a degree. It just so happens that the degree is worthless."

"Sounds awful," Austin said. "Why do you put up with it?"

Gary hesitated, then admitted the truth. "Because we don't know how to take care of ourselves," he said. "And because we're scared."

He found himself wondering, again, just what would have become of his long-term plan if he hadn't won the contest. Yates had pretty much hinted that Imperial University wasn't as well-regarded as Gary had thought, although some of its courses were required for promising careers. But his studies of the starship's database had suggested that the courses actually had nothing to do with the career, whatever it was. They'd merely been tacked on to please the educational bureaucrats.

"No wonder no one wants to go back," Austin said. "Even the indents wind up fitting into our society. Or dead."

Gary blinked in surprise. "There's no one who wants to go back to Earth?"

"No one," Austin confirmed. He hesitated. "I won't say that there aren't a few people who have doubts, but they generally stay here and eventually fit in."

He finished frying the bacon, then started to crack the eggs, one by one. "This world is pretty tolerant of what people do, provided that other people aren't hurt or seriously threatened," he added. "You should consider staying here."

Gary hesitated, then asked the question that had first came to him in the dead of night. "Can you teach *me* how to use a gun?"

Unsurprisingly, Austin took a long time to answer. "Yes," he said finally, "with the proviso that I will personally kill you if you mess around with it. I was not expecting your friends to mess around and...and I could have got someone killed."

"I understand," Gary said. Somehow, he was sure that Austin wasn't joking. "What would have happened if Barry had killed someone?"

"Barry would have been sentenced to hard labour, if someone didn't shoot back in the first few seconds," Austin said. "There are a handful of work gangs for true criminals where they work hard and pay off their debts. If the person he'd killed owed money, either to the consortium or someone else, they would also have to pay those debts off too. Darrin might have been in trouble too, even though he didn't fire the fatal shot. And I, the idiot who gave someone from Earth a weapon and then turned my back..."

He shook his head. "I heard on Earth people can get away with murder," he added. "How do you keep the murder rate down?"

"We don't, I think," Gary said. People were murdered all the time, even in school. One day, he'd always feared, Barry and Moe would actually kill him for good. "But I don't know for sure."

"Ask your supervisor," Austin said. He flipped the eggs into a plate, then carried them into the next room. "Eat up quickly, mates. You don't want to miss the whipping."

———

Kailee felt sick as she picked at her food, even the tasty aroma failing to encourage her to eat properly. They were going to watch as Darrin and Barry were whipped...the thought was appalling, even though she rather felt the two boys deserved it. After all, for all their efforts, they had been unable to earn enough credits to replace the destroyed or soiled underwear while they'd been on the ship. And there had been no place to buy proper underwear either; she'd looked while they were being fitted with colonial clothes and hadn't seen anything more fancy than basic cloth panties and bras. Earth's vast selection of frilly lingerie simply didn't exist on Meridian.

Maybe I should start an underwear shop, she thought, sardonically. *Bring the benefits of proper underwear to the natives.*

"Eat up," Janet urged. As always, the older woman had devoured a colossal plate of food. "You need to keep up your strength."

Kailee didn't dare make a face, although she wanted to glare. Janet had told them, in no uncertain terms, that they *were* going to see the whipping. She'd refused to listen to excuses, just repeating the same thing over and over again. The whole group had to see just what crime and punishment was like on Meridian, at least when the criminals were actually arrested. Their escort from yesterday had told them, without any dissembling at all, that it was perfectly legal to shoot a rapist if one was attacked.

She finished enough of the food to satisfy Janet, then found herself roped in to help with the washing up. The whole effort of scraping congealed oil, fat and eggs off the plates disgusted her. She honestly didn't understand how Aunt Lillian could spend so long keeping the entire apartment clean and tidy. Austin supervised, ensuring that the plates were cleaned to his satisfaction. Kailee reluctantly obeyed, even though she resented it. Besides, as Janet had pointed out on the first day, if the plates weren't cleaned quickly, they would be eating off dirty plates in the evening.

"Get changed, then follow us," Yates ordered, once the dishes were finished. "We leave in twenty minutes, precisely."

Kailee clenched her teeth. Such precise timetables were annoying. It was almost like being stuck in school, although she had to admit that Meridian was a more attractive environment than the CityBlock. Perhaps, when she was a famous actress, she could hold a movie shoot on the planet. If some of the girls decided to stay, as they'd suggested they would, she might meet them again...she pushed the daydream aside, then walked back into the bedroom and hastily changed into proper clothes. She would have liked to take a bath or shower so she could scrub herself clean, but there was no time. Instead, she merely washed her hands and headed back to the door.

Outside, the sky was overcast, threatening rain. Kailee looked up at it nervously, then tugged at her hood, making sure that it was there. The people on the streets glanced at them, their eyes following the Earth-born as they walked down towards the centre of town. After Barry had proved himself so careless, Kailee realised, the townsfolk simply didn't trust the others not to be equally careless. And yet, they didn't seem inclined to punish the entire group, no matter how wary they were. Kailee didn't really understand what she was seeing.

A small crowd was gathering in front of a wooden stage, all sheltered under a large overhang. Some of them looked younger than Kailee herself, others looked older; she felt a flicker of disgust before remembering just what material kids on Earth learned to access before they even reached their first decade. She'd actually downloaded flicks herself that had consisted of someone pretending to be beaten to death. It had all been pretence and yet it had been staggeringly real. But the flicks could do astonishing things with special effects, she knew; she'd read all about them. It was easy to create an illusion of almost anything, with a little effort.

She found herself shivering as a cold gust of wind blew in from the ocean, bringing with it the scent of salt water and fish. Their first trip on a boat had been hair-raising, even though their escort had sworn blind that they were perfectly safe. Kailee had panicked and hidden in the bottom of the boat, utterly convinced that they were going to flip over and drown at any second. There might have been locals swimming in the sea, but Kailee couldn't swim. It hadn't been one of the skills she'd been taught in school. And even if it had been, she'd heard enough about the public baths not to dare go to the swimming pools.

A man wearing dark clothes stepped up onto the stage and glared at the crowd until it fell silent. When he spoke, his voice echoed naturally across the square; it took Kailee a moment to realise that he was speaking normally, not using any form of amplifier like the teachers at school. And the crowd was letting him speak!

"There are two young miscreants to be punished," he said, shortly. "One has been sentenced to ten lashes for vandalism and acts likely to put lives at risk. The other has been sentenced to five lashes for carelessness and failing to stop the first from acting. Once the punishment has been completed, the incident will not be discussed again."

It had the air, Kailee realised, of something being stated for the record. What did he mean when he said that the incident would not be discussed again? It was hard to get anything noted down in one's permanent record on Earth – but once it *was* noted down, it was...well, *permanent*. Barry and Darrin wouldn't be able to get away from being whipped in front of a gawking crowd, would they? Would they even be able to face their fellows afterwards?

She watched, feeling an odd mixture of emotions, as Barry and Darrin were brought out, wearing nothing above the waist and with their hands cuffed in front of them. Their faces were very pale; Barry seemed to be trying to glare at the crowd, while Darrin looked lost in his own thoughts. The men escorting them ordered them to kneel, then stepped backwards. A moment later, one of them produced the whip.

Kailee felt sick the moment she saw it. It wasn't quite what she'd been expecting; instead, it was a long thin stick that swished unpleasantly as the man spun it through the air. She found herself wondering just how much harm it would do if it struck her bare skin, then pushed the thought aside. This was wrong...

And yet, what else did they deserve?

———

Darrin didn't dare look up as he heard something swishing through the air. It had been an uncomfortable night in the jail cell, followed by a small breakfast and a brief explanation of what they had to do. They could make as much noise as they liked, the sheriff had explained, but once they were ordered to kneel they were to remain as still as possible. If they had a problem with that, he'd added, their hands would be cuffed to the ground and there would be extra lashes.

He tried to ignore the crowd – they'd been told that their fellows would be witnessing – as he braced himself. Pain he could handle, he told himself. But as the whipping man stepped up to stand beside him, he felt his resolve leaking away. Yates had been right; he *was* a coward, endlessly making excuses for himself.

"You can wallow in your own filth, if you like," the man whispered, too quietly for anyone apart from Darrin to hear. "Or you can learn from the experience and make something of yourself."

Darrin sensed, somehow, the whip rising, then it cracked down over his exposed back. For a long moment, he felt nothing...and then he screamed as a line of fire seemed to burn into his skin. The pain was excruciating, worse than anything he'd endured from Fitz; he started to move, to leap to his feet, before realising that it would only bring more pain. Four more strokes followed in quick succession, leaving him lying on the stage with his back on fire. He no longer cared about the watching crowd; all he cared about was enduring the pain. And then, moments later, he heard Barry howling in agony.

Had Barry ever been hurt? Darrin honestly couldn't say he knew the bigger boy all that well, not when they hadn't had much to do with one another before leaving Earth. Had he been beaten by his father or stepfather...did he even *have* a father? But in the end, it didn't really matter. All that mattered was that Darrin had made a mistake when he'd effectively befriended Barry, whatever his motivations. And that he would have as little to do with Barry as possible from then onwards.

Strong hands gripped him and helped him to his feet. Darrin looked around to see the crowd slipping out of the square, now the show was over. His back still hurt, a throbbing that felt worse than anything Fitz had ever doled out, but he allowed himself a moment of relief as the cuffs were removed. He turned and caught sight of Gary, standing at the edge of the square to get one last look at the whipped boys. Gary looked...*pleased.* And how could Darrin blame him?

There is always someone stronger, he thought, remembering how easily Yates had picked him up, despite his size. No *wonder* Gary had been so pleased to see them hurt. If he couldn't fight himself, he could at least enjoy their suffering.

"I should warn you of something," the sheriff said. Darrin noted, through the pain, that Yates was standing behind the man, his face unreadable. "This is your one chance to redeem yourself. Act badly again and you'll be sent to the chain gang. And few people ever return from the chains."

Somehow, Darrin found himself believing each and every word.

CHAPTER
TWENTY-TWO

This seems particularly absurd when one realises that, as long as a teacher kept his or her head down, they were guaranteed life-time employment. Trying to be a good teacher, by pushing kids forward, could result in losing their jobs; doing nothing, or even actively harming students, went unpunished.

*- Professor Leo Caesius, Education and the
Decline and Fall of the Galactic Empire*

Austin had been told, more than once, that quitting in midstream was the worst possible thing a person could do to himself. It would make him a quitter, his father had said, someone who could never embark on a project for fear of being unable to complete it. And his father had more than lived up to his own words. He'd pushed Austin hard, but he'd pushed himself harder. Austin still remembered the old man's single-minded determination to make the farm succeed, even if he worked himself into an early grave. Even a minor illness had not been allowed to stand in his way.

And yet Austin had seriously considered abandoning the Earth-born and going back to the farm. He had never considered, not really, that someone his age would be so careless with a weapon. Such carelessness was often rapidly cured at school, with liberal applications of corporal punishment if necessary. Going to the shooting range was a common activity among people his age; hell, kids of nine or ten were allowed to go without their parents, as long as they had their shooting badge from school. He'd honestly never realised just how stupid – or ignorant – Earth-born people could be.

They're children, Uncle Ramos had said, as he'd undid his belt. *Children. You have to treat them as kids.*

The thought had stung almost as badly as the belt. Austin was sixteen, but he'd been responsible and mature for years. He'd learned how to work on the farm, how to take care of the animals and how to cope with problems; after all, help was hours away at best. He was no *child*! Children were fools who couldn't be trusted outside without a leash, who didn't know the difference between safe and dangerous – and who didn't know who to ask, if they needed to learn. Austin hadn't been a child since he'd turned ten years old and, by then, he'd been helping on the farm for years.

But the Earth-born were still children.

He'd known a couple of boys who had had a kind of learning disability, one that had made them oversized children and kept them permanently immature. They hadn't been *bad*, they'd just never really understood anything. But the visitors – the *children* – from Earth had no such problems. They were just *ignorant*. But the universe didn't really care about the difference between ignorance and stupidity, not when the crunch came. They'd be killed either way.

They didn't know how to cook. They had to be forced to clean. Chances were, they hadn't even realised that their bedding needed to be changed every so often. They didn't know how to drive a truck or fly a light aircraft. They didn't know what was edible and what wasn't, no matter what they'd been taught. Austin had learned the hard way that some seemingly safe plants were actually quite dangerous, if one didn't cook them properly. The Earth-born wouldn't even know where to begin.

He looked up as he heard someone at the door, expecting Gary. But it was Darrin, standing there as if he expected to be told to get lost. Austin was tempted to do just that, particularly after the thrashing he'd received from his uncle. Basic politeness, on the other hand, told against it. He could at least wait to see what the young man – the *child* – from Earth had to say.

"I wanted to say sorry," Darrin said. He didn't come any further into the kitchen. "I didn't mean to get you in trouble."

"I'm sure you didn't," Austin said. He had dealt with the situation as his father had taught, quickly and efficiently, but afterwards he'd started to shake badly. Barry could easily have shot someone, merely for laughs. But he wouldn't have found the aftermath very funny at all. If someone blamed Austin for it and managed to make the charge stick, he might well have been indentured until the debt was paid. "You're just a child, aren't you?"

Darrin didn't look as if he intended to dispute it. "I don't know what to do," he confessed, slowly. There was a frustrated hopelessness in his voice that sounded more than a little irritating. "Going back to Earth seems pointless, but what can I do here?"

"Learn basic firearms safety, for one thing," Austin snapped, feeling his temper flare. Darrin seemed to have recovered quickly from the neural whip, although he was probably still aching. Austin *hoped* the immature idiot was still aching. The marks his uncle had left on his buttocks would take days to fade completely. "Do you realise just how close you came to getting shot?"

"Yes, I know," Darrin said. He looked as though he meant it. "What can I do on this planet?"

Austin considered it for a long moment. Most settlers came to farm, although a handful found themselves working other trades. The craftsmen in the city were always looking for apprentices and quite a few of the newcomers preferred the chance of becoming a craftsman rather than working on a farm. But someone completely on his own?

"You could hire onto a fishing crew," he said, after a moment. The normal crews were composed of families, keeping the boat safely in their hands, but there would probably be openings for someone who was willing to learn. "Can you swim?"

Darrin shook his head, wordlessly.

"I learned to swim when I was four," Austin told him, remembering Silver Lake. It had been a great place for young boys and girls. "You really do need to learn, particularly here."

He wondered what else Darrin could do. "There are apprenticeships for vehicle mechanics," he added, after a moment. "It's dirty work, but I'm told it is very rewarding. Or you could try to sign up with a butcher or baker. They'd certainly give you a chance."

"But...what if I failed?" Darrin asked. "I don't know what I can do."

"There's always grunt labour," Austin said, tiredly. He was here because he wanted to improve his chances of becoming a Bush Ranger. There was no point in whining just because he had to pay his dues before earning the reward. "It pays well, really."

He turned to look at the Earth-born boy. "I don't know how things work on Earth," he said, "but you were really quite lucky. Here, you would count as an adult. You were lucky not to be punished as one."

————

Gary watched Darrin and Barry with quiet amusement, keeping his face carefully blank. Neither of them looked comfortable, despite the lack of marks on their skin. Gary had risked a glance at their backs after they'd returned to the lodge and discovered that they were almost completely unmarked. It made no sense to him until he'd looked up the information in the briefing notes and discovered that a neural whip left almost no marks on the bare skin. But they were still definitely aching and that was enough for Gary.

"We will be leaving from the landing strip after breakfast," Yates reminded them. He'd told them to pack last night, leaving half of their clothes and supplies in the lodge. "There will be a four-hour flight to the farm, where we will be spending the next week. It will also give people time to forget us."

He cast a look at Darrin and Barry that would have made Gary cringe, if it had been directed at him. Darrin looked subdued – he'd sat well away from Barry – but Barry looked mutinous, as if he was on the verge of doing something else stupid. Gary silently prayed that he would do something that could get him thrown back into jail – or worse. He had no doubt that Yates could handle anything Barry might throw at him, then hammer him into the ground.

Breakfast passed quickly, allowing Gary to get a quick wash and check his bag before leaving the bedroom. He didn't trust Barry not to try to take out his clothes and leave them behind. Once he'd checked the bag, he added his reader to the top. There was enough material loaded onto the device to keep him happy for years, if necessary. And besides, it included a full copy of the briefing notes. He didn't want to be caught by surprise again.

"Check everything," Yates reminded them, as he walked back outside to the door. "And then check again."

Gary nodded, then followed Yates and the others back onto the streets. This time, the sky was a perfect blue; high overhead, he could see birds wheeling in the morning air. It wasn't quite hot yet, but he knew that the temperature was going to rise rapidly as the morning turned into afternoon. He lifted an eyebrow when he saw Darrin walking next to Austin, chatting to the colonial boy in hushed whispers, then grinned as he realised that Kailee was walking right next to him. It wasn't much, compared to what the other boys boasted of – normally before mocking Gary for being a virgin – but it was something. Kailee gave him a sharp glance, then looked away. Clearly, she wasn't so impressed by walking beside him.

They reached the outskirts of the city and turned into a large grassy field. The aircraft at one end of the field looked tiny, smaller than the shuttle that had carried them down to the surface of the planet. Gary sucked in a breath as he saw it clearly; it looked surprisingly old and fragile, as if it needed more than just a coat of paint. The briefing notes had warned that colonial technology was deliberately kept as simple as possible – it would be impossible to repair one of the heavy-lift shuttles on Meridian – but there had to be limits, surely?

The colonials minimise risk as much as possible, he thought, remembering something that Yates had said. *But that doesn't mean they try to render it completely non-existent. They know that is an impossible dream.*

"Captain Flint," Yates called, as a burly man emerged from the aircraft. "These are my charges."

Flint gave them all a long look. "Welcome to Old Lace, as I call her," he said, nodding towards the aircraft. "She may be old, but she'll get you wherever you want to go."

"Good luck," Janet said. She waved and turned to walk away. "See you when you get back."

Gary blinked in surprise – she wasn't coming with them?

"No," Janet said, when Kailee asked. "I have to go smooth some ruffled feathers at the spaceport."

Inside the plane, the cabin was surprisingly cramped and the seats were small, too small for someone like Barry to sit comfortably. Flint buzzed around them, issuing seat assignments; Gary grinned to himself as he got both a window seat and Kailee sitting next to him. Barry and Darrin were carefully separated; Barry at the front, Darrin at the back of the aircraft.

"Listen up," Flint barked, once they were all sitting down. "Stay in your seats unless you absolutely have to go take a piss." He pointed towards a small door at the rear of the plane. "If you have to take a piss, go quickly then come back and put your seatbelt back on. If I tell you to stay in your seats, do as I say even if you have to wet yourself. And if I tell you to brace, sit like this" – he demonstrated – "and pray. Any questions?"

Gary wanted to ask if he could get off, but he didn't quite dare. Flying in the aircar had been bad enough, yet Old Lace made the aircar look completely safe. Flint walked to the front of the aircraft and took the controls. A dull roar echoed through Old Lace as she came to life, Flint calling out strange words as he ran down a long checklist. Gary found himself wondering just how many of them were really necessary.

He gasped as a hand caught his and squeezed, tightly. Kailee looked as nervous as Gary felt, reaching out for comfort even if it came from him. Gary stared at her for a long moment, then turned his hand around to clutch hers tightly. Moments later, the aircraft started to move, juddering forward inch by inch. Flint cried out something that sounded like "Tally Ho," then hit the accelerator. The plane lunged forward with terrifying speed – Gary remembered, suddenly, the fence at the edge of the field – and clawed its way into the air. Moments later, the shuddering started...

"We're not going to have a comfortable flight," Flint called. He didn't seem worried. If anything, he seemed delighted. "But don't worry. We're perfectly safe."

Gary didn't believe him. Outside, he could see the aircraft's wings; they seemed to be moving up and down in line with the turbulence hitting the craft. He felt sick to his stomach as the plane shook again, even as he left the city behind. Somehow, he managed to look down and see just how small the city actually was, certainly when compared to a CityBlock. If Yates was right, there were more people in the average CityBlock on Earth than there were on the entire colony world.

There was a final shudder, then the turbulence started to fade away. Gary felt Kailee relax slightly, although she didn't take her hand from his. It wasn't sexual, he realised; it was nothing more than the desire for human contact. He looked away from her, ashamed of his own thoughts. In a way, he really was little better than Darrin or Barry. The only real difference was that he didn't have the nerve to push a girl into sex.

But that would be dangerous here, he thought. *They could legally kill someone who was trying to rape them.*

"As you can see, if you look to the right," Yates said, "there are large steamboats on the Jordan heading northwards. Those boats carry most of the supplies from the spaceport to the various new settlements. Right now, the Governor is opening up a whole new county for settlement, while the other settlements are maturing and starting to expand on their own."

Abdul stuck up a hand. "Are there no roads?"

"None that go far from the city," Yates told him. "The local ecology fights back savagely against attempts to cut roads through the trees and forests, so right now it isn't worth the effort of building them. Later, the colonial authorities intend to start building proper roads to link together the various settlements, but that will need another fifty to one hundred years. As it is, what roads there are need to be cleared time and time again."

Gary nodded, looking down onto a jungle. It seemed thick, utterly impenetrable. The only gap in the trees was the winding river. It looked small from high overhead, but the boats suggested that it was actually quite large. A thought struck him and he held up his hand.

"Why did they put the city there?" He asked, when Yates nodded at him. "The forest makes it difficult for anyone to get out to the farms, doesn't it?"

"It's the easiest place to access the river," Austin said. "There are actually quite a number of settlements on smaller islands; they were established first, during the early years. Boating and fishing was well-established before they set up the first farms inland, using the river to transport goods. Later, they just moved the spaceport to the mainland and burned enough of the forest away to keep it clear."

Time moved by slowly. Gary watched as the forest gave way to something else, a pattern that looked almost like a very scrubby desert. But there was no way to know for sure, not with his very limited experience in geology. Earth's geology had been largely immaterial for a very long time, according to the starship's files. The giant megacities were utterly untouched by earthquakes, weather or anything else that had once bothered the planet's inhabitants. But inside, they were boring. And traps for humans too weak or ignorant to try to climb out.

I won't be going back, he promised himself, as he started to doze off. The sound of the engine was almost hypnotic; besides, Barry was several seats away, behind him. *Whatever happens, I won't go back to Earth.*

A dull thump ran through the aircraft suddenly, followed by an abrupt lurch to one side. Gary felt himself shocked completely awake as an alarm sounded, followed by a torrent of swearing from Flint. The dull roar of the engines grew louder, then faded away to nothingness. Gary realised, as the swearing grew louder, that the aircraft was in real trouble. They were practically falling out of the sky...

"Stay in your seats," Yates bellowed, so loudly that Gary jumped. Everyone was starting to panic, even Barry. Gary had never seen the oversized boy panic before. "If you unstrapped yourself, strap yourself back in now!"

The aircraft twisted again, then fell. Gary clutched at Kailee, holding her hand tightly as panic threatened to take over. Outside, he saw flickers of light...and smoke streaming from one of the engines under the wing. What the hell had gone wrong? The aircraft lurched – for a moment, Gary was convinced it was going to heel over completely – and then righted itself. But the ground was coming up alarmingly fast.

"Brace," Flint snapped. The note of alarm in his voice chilled Gary to the bone. "Get into brace position now, damn you!"

A dull beeping echoed through the cabin as the lights failed. It sounded like the end of the world. Gary found himself praying, although he wasn't sure who or what he was praying to; somehow, he managed to let go of Kailee's hand long enough to get into the right position. Moments later, there was a thunderous crashing sound...

... And Gary fell into blackness.

CHAPTER
TWENTY-THREE

This ensured that many public schools within the Empire became nightmarish hellholes for their inhabitants. Bullying, rape and even murder were common. Gangs stalked the corridors, searching for victims...and recruiting for the larger gangs that ran criminal operations within the CityBlocks of Earth. In fact, during the final years of the Empire, there were war zones that were less dangerous than Undercity schools.

- Professor Leo Caesius, *Education and the Decline and Fall of the Galactic Empire*

Darrin fought his way back to awareness slowly, through a haze of pain that made it hard to think. The dull ache from his back, made worse by the chair...he tried to remember where they were and what had happened, but his memory refused to cooperate. He forced his eyes open and looked out upon a scene from hell. Tangled metal lay in front of him, the front of the plane smashed open; a body sat next to him, blood pouring down towards the ground.

He'd been on an aircraft, he remembered, suddenly. The thought seemed to galvanise his mind. He'd been on an aircraft and the aircraft had crashed. And he'd been sitting next to Yates...

Somehow, he managed to undo his straps and stand upright. He appeared to be uninjured, as far as he could tell, but his entire body was shaking. Yates was bleeding from a nasty wound to the chest, a piece of metal having rammed itself through his body, pinning him to the seat.

Darrin felt sick, then horrified; a couple of inches to the left and it would have been he, not Yates, who had been badly injured. He stared at the older man, unsure of what to do, then stepped past him and out into the aisle. Yates wasn't the only one who'd been badly injured.

Austin pulled himself to his feet. Darrin felt a flash of relief – he didn't have the slightest idea what to do – then caught sight of Honey. Her head had been smashed to a pulp, leaving a bloody stump sticking out of her chest. Darrin's chest heaved and he turned away, a moment before he was violently sick. He'd seen entertainment flicks far gorier, but this was real. It had an impact far beyond the worst of the snuff flicks he'd seen. Beside Honey, Harold was also dead. The boy had barely made an impression on Darrin; he'd been quiet, rarely speaking to anyone. Now, he was dead.

"Stand up," Austin ordered, raising his voice. In his stunned state, it took Darrin several moments to realise that he was addressing everyone else. "If you can move, stand up."

Darrin let out a sigh of relief that surprised him as Gary and Kailee managed to stand up. Kailee had a nasty-looking scratch on her forehead – blood was trickling down her face – but she otherwise looked intact. Gary was holding her hand, surprisingly; the nerd looked as shocked as Darrin himself. Austin looked down at Li, who seemed to be injured. One of her legs was bent out of shape.

"Help me get her out of the plane," Austin ordered.

Darrin hastily took Li by the shoulders and tried to get her to stand up. Austin slapped his arm, hard enough to force his mind to focus, then motioned for him to unbuckle the entire seat. Between Austin, Gary and Darrin, they managed to use the chair as a makeshift stretcher to carry her out of the plane. Thankfully, Li seemed to have been knocked out completely. It would have been much harder to move her if she'd been screaming at the time.

"Stay here," Austin ordered, when they had put several metres between themselves and the crashed plane. "If you know how to bandage her leg, do so. And wait for me."

Darrin watched helplessly as Austin walked back towards the plane, then turned his attention to Li. She looked fragile, one leg clearly broken and hanging off the seat. Darrin found himself exchanging helpless glances with Gary, unsure of what to do. Did they bind up the leg and prevent the bones from separating still further or would that merely make it worse? On Earth, they had been warned – many times – not to give medical aid without the proper qualifications and waivers. After all, someone could sue, either for impersonating a doctor or for providing bad medical care.

Li whimpered suddenly and Darrin came to a decision. Pulling off his shirt, he started to use it to bind up Li's leg. If she wanted to complain, she could do so later. Kailee stood next to him as soon as she realised what he was doing and held Li's leg still. Darrin pulled the shirt as tight as he could, then tied the arms together. It wouldn't stay in place for very long, but hopefully it would last long enough for Austin to come back and tell them what to do. Or for help to arrive from the city...

He looked around for the first time, taking in the desolation of the surrounding landscape. He didn't know anything like enough to tell where they were; all he could see were scattered trees and something that resembled grass. In the distance, he could see mountains rising up towards the sky. Birds – clearly disturbed by the crash – were flocking away from them as fast as they could go.

Darrin sat down, feeling faint. They were far from civilisation, far from anyone who might help them...and they were completely alone.

––––––––

Austin gritted his teeth as he made his way back into the plane. The Earth-born hadn't realised it, as far as he could tell, but one of the engines had definitely caught fire. If the flames spread to the fuel tank, the entire aircraft would explode, taking the bodies with it – and Austin too, if he were still onboard. He heard someone moving and blinked in surprise as he saw Barry, stumbling to his feet. The oversized kid was bleeding from several minor wounds, but he looked generally intact, if stunned.

"Get out and walk away from the crash site," Austin ordered. He was prepared to slap Barry if necessary, but Barry nodded and started to totter towards the hatch without hesitation. Austin opened his mouth to point out that there were plenty of gashes in the hull, then pushed the thought aside. Barry was too badly stunned to notice "Hurry!"

He turned and started to work his way through the rest of the craft. Steve and Abdul were both trapped under a piece of fuselage; cursing his decision to send Barry away, Austin pushed and pulled at it until the two boys could wriggle free. Like Barry, they had cuts and bruises, but seemed largely intact. Austin pointed them towards the nearest gash in the hull, then checked Yuki and Honey. Both of the girls were definitely dead. In front of them, Samantha was stunned, but alive. Austin shouted at Steve and Abdul to carry her out, then kept moving forward. Flint's body was so badly wounded that Austin knew there was no point in checking for a pulse, while Yates was trapped.

Austin swore as he looked down at the older man. He'd come to respect Yates, in the handful of days he'd known him; seeing him wounded and trapped was horrifying. And there was nothing he could do; the piece of metal pinning him to the seat was also the only thing keeping him alive. Maybe a proper medical team could have kept him alive while cutting him free of the plane and shipping him to a hospital, but Austin knew that no such team could arrive in time. Yates was dying right in front of his eyes.

"No hope," Yates said. He had to say it twice before Austin heard him properly. "Get them back home for me, all right?"

"Yes, sir," Austin said. He knew it would be difficult, almost impossible. But he wasn't about to simply quit. Besides, his thoughts pointed out, where was he going to go? "I don't dare move the piece of metal..."

"Internal damage," Yates said. His voice was very quiet, almost a whisper. "Don't worry about me, son. Just get them all home. Keep an eye on them. And watch that Barry. He's trouble."

"I know," Austin said.

The thought made him scowl. He'd heard enough to know that the others all had potential, but Barry didn't seem to have noticed repeated wake-up calls. But then, he *had* been taught bad habits from a very early age. Austin knew precisely what his parents would have done if they'd caught him bullying another child, assuming he survived the experience; he wouldn't have been able to sit down for a week. Perhaps there was someone worthwhile inside Barry, but no one had ever given him the discipline he needed to bring it out.

He hesitated, unsure of what to do. As a younger child, he'd watched helplessly as one of the indents suffered an accident and bled to death, despite everything his fellows could do to help him. Austin had already known that death came to everyone – his grandmother had died when he was old enough to miss her – but seeing the indent die had taught him that death could come suddenly. And, no matter what some people claimed, there were times when one could do nothing, apart from making sure that the dying didn't die alone.

"You can't stay here," Yates said. His breathing was starting to fail. "Get the hell out, son."

His body shuddered one final time, then fell limp.

Austin took one final look, then stumbled to his feet and headed towards the nearest gash in the hull. It tore at him to leave the bodies in the aircraft, where they might be burned or eaten by wild animals, but there was no time to bury them now. Cursing his own oversight, he stopped, walked back to the pilot's seat and retrieved the medical case from under Flint's body. It wouldn't do the pilot any good, but it might help save other lives.

Outside, he walked around to look at the engine. It was smouldering darkly, suggesting that the fire was on the verge of going out. Austin wondered briefly if they could drain the remaining fuel from the plane's tanks, but failed to come up with a practical way to do it safely. Instead, he turned away from the aircraft and hurried back towards the rest of the group. They all looked relieved to see him.

Darrin caught his eye. "Where's Yates?"

"Dead," Austin said, shortly. He saw the look of astonishment – even panic – in their eyes and scowled. This was why he'd been taught, right from birth, never to grow too dependent on anyone. "What have you done to Li?"

"Bandaged up her leg," Kailee said. Her forehead looked to have stopped bleeding, thankfully. "Is she going to be all right?"

Austin considered, briefly, what he should tell her. Someone from Meridian would know basic emergency medicine as a matter of course; they'd know that Li needed better medical care and attention than they could provide. But someone from Earth...for all Austin knew, they were as ignorant about matters medical as they were about everything else. Li would be fine if she had a proper doctor, but the closest doctor was at least seventy miles away.

"I think she needs treatment," Austin said, shortly. He knelt down beside the girl and started to feel her leg. It was broken in at least one place, he decided, wishing that he had more practical experience. But he'd never been interested in devoting himself to medicine full time. "We'll have to make her a splint."

He looked around, crossly. They could probably scavenge everything they needed to make one from the plane, but he didn't dare go back to the hulk until after the fire had gone out completely. A glance at the sky told him that it was likely to rain, sooner rather than later, and that might put out the fire, yet being drenched to the skin was unlikely to be good for any of them. He snorted inwardly a moment later. There was no prospect of shelter unless they went back to the plane.

"Leave her for the moment," he added. They'd have to build a make-shift stretcher too, if they had to trek cross-country to the nearest settlement. He opened the medical kit and produced a set of cloths. "Kailee, let me see the cut on your forehead."

A girl from Meridian might have protested – foolishly – that there were others who needed medical attention more. Kailee just stepped over to him and bowed her head, allowing him to see the cut clearly for the first time. Blood had stained her dark hair, dripping down over her clothes and skin. Austin wiped the cut clean of blood, then examined it quickly. Thankfully, it didn't look deep enough to be dangerous.

"I'll put a plaster on it," he said, retrieving one from the pack. "It should heal on its own."

He moved to Steve and Abdul, both of whom had cuts and bruises too. Gary and Darrin looked fine, apart from bruises; Barry looked mutinous at the mere thought of allowing someone else to inspect his wounds.

Austin rolled his eyes, then left Barry alone where he was sitting on the ground, staring at nothing. At least he wasn't causing trouble. But then, living through a crash would be enough to stun anyone.

Kailee caught his arm. "Austin," she said, "how long will it be before they find us?"

———

Gary had been eying Barry nervously, but when he heard Kailee's question he turned to hear the answer. On Earth, everyone was told that the emergency services responded promptly to any distress call, but everyone *knew* that there were places in the lower levels where the emergency services never bothered to go at all. They were just too dangerous, Gary had heard; thugs like Darrin and Barry attacked the medics whenever they made an appearance.

"It may be a while," Austin hedged. It was curiously imprecise for the colonial boy, imprecise enough for alarm bells to start ringing in Gary's head. "They may never come."

Darrin looked up, shocked. "But...but we crashed!"

Austin sighed. "There are precisely ten light aircraft like that one" – he nodded towards the crashed aircraft – "on the planet," he said. "Nine now, I suppose. They're scattered over the mainland, apart from one based on the islands. In order for them to start looking for us, they would have to first know that something had gone wrong, then be dispatched over here – assuming, of course, they have a rough idea of where we were. We might easily have been blown far off course."

He sighed, again. "And they won't know what happened to us," he added. "They might just hesitate before sending out another aircraft, let alone all of them."

Gary felt something cold and hard congeal in the pit of his stomach. "What about the satellites? Surely they would have seen us crash."

"This isn't Earth," Austin said, not unkindly. "There isn't total surveillance of the planet's surface. They might well have missed us completely."

In the distance, Gary heard a peal of thunder. Dark clouds were drifting towards them from the mountains. He shuddered as he realised, for the first time, just how wide open the planet was, compared to Earth. There were no towering CityBlocks, just endless landscapes, with forests, rivers and animals. He silently promised himself that, when he got back to the spaceport, he would get his spacer's ticket and never set foot on a planet's surface again.

He shivered inwardly as he looked over towards Barry. The bully was oddly subdued after his whipping and then the crash, but Gary had no illusions as to how long that would last. It wouldn't take long before Barry realised that Yates was dead, that...

Gary swallowed. He'd found Yates intimidating, a strange cross between a teacher and a bully himself. Yates had never given him the answers, or lied to him; he'd pushed Gary into discovering things for himself. And he'd held open the door and shown Gary a new world he could step into, one that would allow him to leave Earth behind forever. But now he was gone. Gary wouldn't have believed that *anything* could kill Yates if Austin hadn't told him the news. Austin was the one person in the group Gary trusted not to lie.

Yates had intimidated Barry. Gary would have sworn that was impossible, but Yates had somehow made Barry behave himself, at least when Yates was in the same room. Now, without Yates...Gary remembered how Barry had entertained himself at school and shuddered. It wouldn't be long before Barry realised that there were no restraints on his behaviour any longer, except perhaps for Austin. But which way would the colonial boy jump? Gary knew how it worked on Earth – the other boys abandoned the weakest to the mercy of the bullies – but what would happen here?

And Austin had implied, strongly, that there wouldn't be any help coming from the city.

Gary pulled himself to his feet and looked over at the crashed aircraft. Yates's body was inside, along with the other bodies...and what few supplies they'd brought with them. He wished, desperately, that he had a weapon, but there had been no time to learn how to use one, even if he'd been allowed to carry a gun. After Barry, he had a feeling that Austin might be reluctant to let others play with his weapons. And how could Gary blame him?

He shuddered, helplessly. Maybe it would be better to walk off into the countryside now, before Barry realised that there were no longer any restraints on his behaviour. But he'd only wind up dead soon enough...

Moments later, the first drops of rain started to fall.

CHAPTER
TWENTY-FOUR

One would imagine that the bureaucrats would realise that something had gone badly wrong. Maybe some of them, as individuals, did. But they were unable or unwilling to halt the decline, simply because of how many vested interests there were in maintaining the system as it stood.

- Professor Leo Caesius, *Education and the Decline and Fall of the Galactic Empire*

Kailee was almost relieved as the rain started to fall, despite the fact she knew that she would be soaked to the skin within minutes. The blood – *her* blood – had stained her hair, leaving her feeling disgusting and unclean. Now, she ran her fingers through her dark hair, watching as the blood slowly washed out and pooled on the ground. The water was warm, thankfully; it almost felt like taking a shower, except she was still wearing her clothes.

She scowled as she realised that her clothes were clinging to her skin, showing off her curves to the world. It wasn't the first time that had happened, she knew, remembering the walk from the spaceport to the city, but Yates had been there...now, she and the other girls were alone with a bunch of horny men. She wished, desperately, that Janet had accompanied them, but she'd stayed behind in the city. Kailee and the others were on their own.

Li moaned as the water splashed down on her face, finally stirring. Kailee wondered, guiltily, just how much pain the smaller girl was actually in, now she was finally coming back to life. Li might have been lucky that she'd been knocked out by the crash...she watched as Austin knelt down beside Li, ignoring the water splashing on the ground. If he hadn't been there, they would have *really* been in trouble.

A thought struck her as she moved to help him. "Do you know where we are?"

Austin blinked in surprise. "Only vaguely," he said. "This isn't anywhere near my home..."

Darrin snorted, speaking loudly to be heard over the falling rain. "I thought you knew this planet," he snapped. "We were told that you were our native guide."

Austin laughed, although there was little humour in the sound. "Planets are *big*," he pointed out, sarcastically. "I know the land around my father's farm like the back of my hand, and I've explored the city many times, but here...? I've never been here before, ever. I know it about as well as you do."

Kailee swallowed, her throat suddenly dry. Austin was right; on Earth, they'd all been familiar with their part of the CityBlock, but they'd never known much about the rest of the planet. They certainly didn't know how to navigate outside the CityBlock. How could Austin be expected to know every square inch of his homeworld? She tried to work out how long it would take him to explore the entire continent, then gave up in irritation. It was impossible to even guess at the answer.

She shuddered as a thought struck her. They could *die* out here.

The prospect of a violent death had been ever-present in the CityBlock. It was part of the reason she wanted to leave. Even if she was one of the lucky ones, she would still waste her life; marry someone boring, have his children and watch them remain trapped in the CityBlock, just like herself. And there were worse fates than death for women in the CityBlocks...

But here, they could die too.

"I'm sorry," she muttered, as she knelt beside Li and took her hand. "I didn't think."

"Don't worry about it," Austin said. For a moment, he seemed to be peering down at Li's chest with chilling intensity, then Kailee realised that he was trying to use his body to give Li some cover from the rain. "I dare say that you have plenty of time to learn."

Kailee doubted it, but watched as Li slowly stumbled back into full awareness. The moment the pain hit her, she started to scream. Austin produced an injector from the medical kit and pressed it against her neck; moments later, Li quietened down, relaxing slightly. But her eyes were still fearful.

"We crashed," Austin said, without bothering to shelter her from the news. "And you have a broken leg. Lie still."

Kailee looked over at the other boys. Darrin, Abdul and Steve were watching the water splashing over the crashed aircraft, while Gary was standing some distance from them, eying Barry nervously. The bully was squatting on the ground, staring at nothing. Kailee muttered a silent prayer that he would remain out of it completely, but she doubted that they would be that lucky. Why couldn't Barry have been killed instead of Yates? *Yates* would have known what to do.

"I can't feel my leg," Li gasped, drawing Kailee's attention back to her. "What did you give me?"

"Strong painkiller," Austin explained. "It won't last forever, I'm afraid."

Kailee listened as he explained the situation, then looked up into the dark sky. It seemed impossible that *anything* could fly in this weather, she told herself; the rainstorm alone might prevent aircraft from even taking off. Wind blew raindrops into her face as she started to pace, feeling her clothes growing heavier and heavier. For a long moment, she looked down at the water on the ground and wondered if they were about to be caught in a flood.

The rainstorm stopped as abruptly as it had begun. Kailee looked up and watched as the sun came out, then sighed in relief as she realised the heat would dry their skin and clothes. Li still looked miserable – water had pooled around her, drenching her broken leg – but everyone else started to cheer up. Kailee rolled her eyes inwardly. As far as she could tell, their situation hadn't really improved at all.

"Darrin, Barry, you're with me," Austin ordered. "We're going to go empty the plane. Everyone else, stay here."

Barry looked up, suddenly. "And just who put you in charge?"

———

Darrin felt himself awash with water, even after the rainfall finally came to an end. There had been no shelter, nowhere to hide from the water; his clothes felt heavy and uncomfortable against his skin, even after he started to squeeze the cloth to expel the water. The bright sunlight might help them to dry, he told himself, but it was also dangerous. What would happen if they got burnt?

He winced as Barry asked the dreaded question. Barry wasn't the sort of person to take orders calmly, at least unless the person issuing the orders had proved his willingness to slap Barry down hard. Perhaps, Darrin realised suddenly, that was why Barry hadn't argued to Yates's face about scrubbing the decks, no matter how much he'd grumbled to Darrin while they'd been working hard. In his brutish mind, Yates had been strong enough to impose himself on Barry and thus was his natural superior.

Austin gave him a dark look. "Because I know how to survive out here and you don't," he snapped. "If you want to set out on your own, feel free. Good luck to you. If not, I suggest you take orders and *learn*."

Barry glared at him for a long moment, then looked at Darrin, clearly seeking support. But Darrin knew that Austin was right; even if he'd trusted Barry, he knew the larger boy was no more knowledgeable about surviving than Darrin himself. Bracing himself for a fight, he shook his head firmly. Yates had been right about one thing. Spending time with Barry, letting Barry lead him wherever he wanted to go, was asking for trouble. But would Barry pick a fight with all four boys? Which way would Abdul and Steve jump?

There was a long dangerous pause...and then Barry nodded, reluctantly. Austin nodded back, then led the way towards the aircraft. Up close, Darrin decided, it was a miracle that any of them had survived. The hull was broken beyond repair; it looked as though it had melted slightly, then been left to flow into a new configuration. Both wings were badly battered, but there was no longer any sign of smoke.

"Shit," Barry said.

Darrin followed his gaze. India's body lay on the ground, broken and torn.

"She must have fallen through a gash in the hull," Austin said. For the first time, he sounded shaken. "Poor girl."

We never even noticed she was gone, Darrin thought.

Austin made them walk around the hull twice, looking for any other signs of trouble, before they stepped into the interior of the aircraft. Inside, it smelt of blood, shit and death. Darrin forced himself to breathe through his mouth as Austin started to recover their bags and pass them to the others. Barry took four bags at once and carried them outside, then came back for the others. Darrin couldn't keep himself from looking at all that remained of Yuki's body, shuddering at how easily death had come for her. Honey's body didn't look any better.

He drew in a breath when he saw Yates. The older man looked surprisingly peaceful, but he was very definitely dead. Darrin reached out, despite himself, and touched the man's forehead, then looked up as he heard a snicker. Barry had come forward and was looking at the body himself, gloating inwardly over Yates's death. Darrin shuddered, then stepped back, away from the body. There were quite a few other bags they needed to remove from the plane.

"The radio is broken," Austin said, from the cockpit. "And the GPS too. The flares aren't likely to work unless rescue is quite close."

Darrin nodded, feeling helpless. Austin passed him a coil of rope, then two red boxes; tiredly, Darrin carried them outside. The ground was already drying rapidly after the rain; he placed the boxes beside the bags, then turned to slip back into the hull. Barry was standing beside Yuki's body, one hand inside her shirt. Sickened, Darrin looked away.

"There's no time to bury them," Austin said, shortly. Darrin couldn't tell if he'd seen what Barry had been doing or not. "We may have to set fire to the plane ourselves just to send up a smoke signal."

Outside, Austin carried some pieces of metal and rope over to where Li was lying. "I'm going to bind up your leg properly," he said, shortly. "And then I'm going to put together a very basic stretcher. We can carry you quite some distance, if necessary."

He looked over at the others. "Go through the bags, all of them," he added. "Sort out what we have, then we can decide what to do with it."

Once, Darrin suspected, he might have enjoyed going through the bags. Now, it was the only thing they could do. He found himself a new shirt, then dug through the rest. There was a small pile of clothing, a reader – Barry laughed when he realised that Gary had brought his reader with him – and little else. He briefly considered changing clothes, but judging by the weather they'd seen over the past few days he suspected that it would be a waste of time. The downpour would start again, soon enough.

The emergency supplies were limited, he realised numbly, as he sorted them out one by one. A handful of ration bars, a coil of rope, a handful of knives, a small medical kit, the flares, a handful of devices he didn't recognise...and little else. Apart from whatever Austin was carrying, he suspected, they didn't have much in the way of ammunition for the rifle either. Was there even a second weapon?

"Give that a try," Austin ordered. Abdul and Steve picked up the makeshift stretcher and carried it a couple of metres. Li looked weak, but relieved. She'd probably thought that they'd simply abandon her by the aircraft. "Good. We can carry you with us, if necessary."

Kailee looked up, her damp hair clinging to her face and making her seem waiflike. "Where are we going?"

Austin looked down at the ground, then back up at her. "If we head east," he said, holding a compass in one hand, "we should cross the Jordan. After that, we head down the bank until we reach a settlement – or hail a boat, should we see one. The alternative is to head south and try to make it to the coast, but there's no guarantee of finding a settlement. I'm not sure just how far off-course we were when the plane crashed."

Barry grunted. "How far do we have to walk?"

"I'm not sure," Austin admitted. Darrin suspected that he was deliberately not giving Barry a better answer. "It will take us several days, at the very least."

"So we stay here," Steve said. "They're bound to come looking for us, eventually."

"Eventually, yes," Austin said. He looked from person to person. "We have enough food for one meal, just one. If we stay here, we will be lucky to survive long enough to be rescued – assuming that they locate us quickly. But, as I said, the odds are against it. Our best bet is to try to walk to the Jordan."

"Li won't make it," Steve said.

"Then we leave her," Barry said. "She's *useless*."

"I don't know how you do it on Earth," Austin snapped, "but we don't abandon people here."

But they did on Earth, Darrin knew. No one would stop to help someone in need, for fear it might prove contagious. Or that the person they tried to rescue would sue them afterwards.

"I can stay with her," Steve offered. "We can take shelter in the plane and wait for rescue."

Austin considered it. "Even if we left you all the ration bars," he said. "We..."

"Wait," Barry said. "You're going to leave him all the ration bars?"

"We can find food along the way," Austin said, sharply. Darrin wondered just how strong the temptation was to shoot Barry and swear it was an accident. "I know how to hunt, how to fish, how to do a great many things you need to learn if you want to survive. But if you keep talking about abandoning people...I'll damn well abandon you."

Barry glared at him for a long moment, then shut up.

"We would definitely make better time without carrying the stretcher," Austin mused. He gave Steve a long considering look. "You do understand the risks?"

"I think so," Steve said.

Darrin doubted it. Steve hadn't seen the interior of the crashed aircraft. It might keep out the rain, but it had a number of dead bodies inside...bodies that would rapidly start to stink. He remembered the day when several bodies had turned up in a side corridor, abandoned by the murderers; the stench had been horrific until the gangs had finally dragged the bodies away and dumped them somewhere else. Darrin had no idea what had happened to the victims – or their bodies, after that.

"I'll write you out a note for the rescue party, assuming one arrives," Austin said. "And I need to talk to you about a few other things before we go."

———

Gary had seriously considered asking to remain with Steve and Li, even though one was badly wounded and the other was an unknown factor. He couldn't be as bad as Barry, surely. But he knew that Austin would refuse, if he asked; there just weren't enough ration bars to keep three people alive for more than a couple of days.

He left Austin and the others organising their supplies and walked into the broken aircraft. The stench struck him at once, a ghastly stench that reminded him of the school toilets on Earth. Steve was not going to have an easy time of it, he saw, as he wrapped his shirt over his nose. The bodies would start to decay rapidly in this weather, forcing him to either bury them or abandon the aircraft completely. But it was the only shelter for miles around.

Bracing himself, he walked up to where Yates had died and looked down at the body. The older man, the one who had intimidated Barry so badly he'd barely even *looked* at Gary since he'd spent weeks scrubbing the decks on the starship, was dead. Gary hesitated, feeling oddly as if he was doing something wrong, then started to search the man's body. The gun was on the man's belt, where he had expected it. Carefully, feeling almost as if he had picked up a poisonous snake, Gary took the gun and hid it under his shirt. The two ammunition clips were wrapped up in a cloth and carried in his hand.

He should give it to Austin, he knew. The colonial boy would know how to handle it, while Gary wasn't sure how to do anything with the pistol. But he didn't quite dare let go of the weapon, not when he knew that Barry would be sleeping near him every night – and Yates was no longer around to protect him. Instead, he said a silent goodbye to the first teacher he'd met who'd actually stood up to the thugs and walked out of the aircraft. When Austin tossed him a bag, he placed the ammunition inside and slung the bag over his back.

"It's not going to be an easy walk," Austin warned, as he passed Steve the remaining ration bars and half of the flares. "We will have to pause long enough to search for food, then set up camp sites and fires. But people have survived in worse conditions before. And I'm sure they *will* be looking for us, once they realise we didn't make it to the farm."

Gary listened, wondering just how many of those people had good reason to hate and fear their fellows. The colonials seemed to trust one another, they seemed to feel *safe* with one another. But Gary knew that he didn't dare trust Barry any further than he could throw the oversized bully. Did Austin know just how dangerous Barry could be? Somehow, Gary doubted it.

He met, very briefly, Kailee's eyes. She clearly shared his fears. Hell, she had to feel *more* vulnerable, not less. Barry would find her a very tempting target for more than just bullying.

"Come along," Austin said, taking his position at the head of the column. "Let's go."

CHAPTER
TWENTY-FIVE

What this meant was that the average student, upon leaving school, would be lucky if he or she could read or write, let alone solve basic maths problems. About the only thing they could do with any competence was claim social support from the Empire (there were mandatory classes in claiming one's benefits). They were certainly ill-prepared to do anything else.

- Professor Leo Caesius, *Education and the Decline and Fall of the Galactic Empire*

Thirty minutes after they started to march, Darrin was already aching. The sun was beating down from high overhead, making them sweat as they walked eastwards. He'd already stumbled twice, somehow managing to keep going by telling himself that neither of the girls were complaining. Kailee and Samantha were actually walking quite hard, better than himself. And Gary was making a good job of it too.

The landscape changed as they walked onwards. There were more trees, coming in odd patches that seemed less than completely random. As they moved higher, they saw water running down the slopes, following long-established paths that seemed to lead down to small lakes and ponds. It was both beautiful and terrifying in a manner Darrin found hard to put into words. The environment was so full of life, compared to the CityBlock, that it was utterly overwhelming.

Birds flew through the trees; small animals, half-seen in the gloom, moved rapidly through the undergrowth, keeping their distance from the human interlopers. There was a faint buzzing sound that seemed vaguely mechanical, making Darrin hope that they were about to be rescued, before Austin told them that it was nothing more than insects buzzing in the trees. The sound grew louder as they moved deeper into the forest, rising and falling around them in strange, almost hypnotic patterns. It chilled Darrin to the bone.

"We take a break here," Austin said, as they reached a large pond. A small stream ran from the pond, heading back the way they'd come. "There's a place we can sleep there."

Darrin glanced at his watch and realised, to his surprise, that it was almost evening. The sun was already setting in the sky. How far had they walked? The aching in his body insisted that it had been thousands of miles, but common sense told him it couldn't have been more than ten at the most. Or was it more than that? There was no way to be sure, not like there would have been in a CityBlock. All he knew was that he had never walked so far in his life.

He unslung his bag and put it on the ground, then sagged down beside it. Kailee and Samantha sat too, their clothes stained with sweat that made the cloth cling to their bodies, but Darrin couldn't even muster the energy to be interested. Even Barry looked exhausted, although there was a nasty glint in his eye. Austin, on the other hand, looked unbothered by the walk. Darrin hated him at that moment.

"There's water," Kailee said, looking over at the pond. "Can't we drink it?"

"One moment," Austin said. He scooped up some water with a cup from the emergency supplies, then dropped a tablet into the liquid. "This water may not be safe to drink without some preparation."

Kailee looked at him in surprise. "Why not?"

Austin looked equally surprised. "Do you know how many animals have been drinking this water, washing in this water, pissing in this water...?"

Darrin was torn between amusement and dismay at Kailee's shock and disgust. It wasn't something they normally had to worry about in the CityBlocks, where the water was extensively purified before it was deemed fit for human consumption. But here...it was easy to imagine that something might have polluted the water. Kailee seemed undecided between refusing to drink or trying to gulp down the water without thinking of what might have gone into it.

"The tablet should do something about that," Austin assured her. "but we're going to have to boil the water once we run out of purification tablets. There's no other way to be sure that the water is safe to drink."

He ordered Barry and Darrin to collect firewood, while taking Abdul and Gary to clear the ground near the pond. Darrin obeyed, scooping up large amounts of fallen wood and piling it up at the edge of the clearing. Austin sorted through it, working half of the wood into a crude shelter and tossing the other half into the cleared patch of ground. The shelter looked pathetic, but tolerable. Darrin had a feeling that they'd be growing used to worse by the end of the trip, if they managed to survive long enough to reach the Jordan.

"If you need to go to the toilet," Austin said, digging through the bags, "dig a little hole in the ground for your shit. We don't want to attract animals to our campsite."

Darrin eyed him for a long moment. "Is there anything dangerous in the forest?"

"Yes," Austin said, shortly. "Would you like a list?"

Darrin shook his head. He hadn't paid much attention to the briefing notes, but he'd read enough to be sure that he didn't actually want to know. The terraforming package had included quite a few animals that were potentially dangerous, including wild pigs, foxes and goats. He couldn't recall if there was anything native to the planet that was considered dangerous, but it was a distinct possibility.

Austin smirked, then motioned for him to sit in front of the pile of firewood. "I'm going to cheat," he confessed. "I brought a small lighter from the aircraft's emergency supplies."

"Good," Gary said. "I was wondering how you meant to light the fire."

Darrin watched as Austin smiled at Gary, then pointed the device at the wood and clicked the trigger. There was a sudden wave of heat, followed by flames spreading rapidly through the small pile of firewood. Austin carefully positioned other pieces of wood over the fire, allowing them to dry in the heat, then stood upright.

"Make sure you keep feeding it, but don't let it spread too far," he warned. "The last thing we want to do is accidentally set the forest on fire."

Barry grinned, his face illuminated oddly by the fire. "Wouldn't that help them find us?"

"Only so they can indenture us for the rest of our lives," Austin said. He smirked, brightly enough that Darrin suspected that he was partly joking. "Burning down the forest would do a *lot* of ecological damage."

Darrin looked around. The forest wasn't particularly dry. It was hard to imagine a fire hot enough to spread rapidly through the damp wood. But if the lighter could set fire to the wood they'd gathered, what else could it do?

"I have a more pertinent problem," Samantha announced. "I'm hungry."

There was a dull rumble of agreement. "I'll see what I can find," Austin said. He picked up the water, took a sip, then passed it to Kailee. "Just keep an eye on the fire."

He stepped over to the pond and peered carefully into the water. Darrin had a moment to see him go very still, then plunge his hand into the pond and grab something below the surface of the water. A second later, he yanked a strange creature out of the pond and dropped it on the ground; it looked like a giant spider, only with nasty-looking claws at one end. The claws clattered madly as the creature attempted to escape, but Austin was holding it too firmly. He took one of the knives from the aircraft and shoved it into the creature's head. It fell still a moment later.

Silence fell, broken only by the sound of Kailee being noisily sick.

"Tell me," Austin said, as she hacked and coughed. "How do you *think* they kill the animals you eat every day?"

But we don't eat animals every day, Darrin thought. On Earth, they'd rarely – if ever – eaten genuine meat. *All we eat is algae...*

He watched with a kind of queasy fascination as Austin cut up the creature, pulling strips of pinkish meat from its shell. The stench was awful; he found himself wondering if he could even eat enough of the meat to stay alive. Austin directed Gary to find some suitable sticks and leaves, then carefully arranged the meat over the fire. Barry found himself roped in to keep the meat in place, where it would cook thoroughly without falling into the heat. Darrin shrugged and just kept feeding the fire with pieces of wood.

"This isn't the nicest critter to eat," Austin confessed, as he finished dissecting the creature, removed the top of its shell, then tossed the bones into the pond. "It's actually a terraforming mistake, I believe; the baseline crab actually prefers salt water. But some of them mutated and got into the land-based water ecology too."

"Oh," Samantha said. "And is it safe to eat?"

"Yes, if cooked thoroughly," Austin said. "The critters actually have relatives who have poison glands, but you won't find any of them this far from the sea."

Darrin shuddered. He'd never seen anything like the crab in his life and, somehow, he didn't want to sleep next to the pond any longer. Who knew *what* might come crawling out of the water at night? Maybe the crabs hunted for life above the surface...

"Don't worry about it," Austin said, firmly. "They only eat the smaller critters in the water."

Darrin nodded. Austin checked the cooking meat, then walked off with Kailee and Samantha into the darkening forest. When they returned, they were carrying a handful of nuts and green leaves that Austin swore were safe to eat. They were washed carefully in the purified water, then put to one side. Austin checked the meat again, then pronounced it cooked. He took the first portion from the fire and passed it to Barry. Darrin couldn't help wondering if Austin had picked his guinea pig deliberately. If Barry choked on it and died...well, it would be no great loss.

"Tastes smoky," Barry said, after a moment. "But edible."

"Glad to hear it," Austin said, dryly. He passed the pieces of food around, then looked up at the sky. "Eat up quickly, folks. We're going to have to go to bed soon."

Darrin took his piece and chewed, thoughtfully. It didn't taste very nice, but it was definitely edible. And it was nicer than algae-based food, which was largely tasteless. The nuts and leaves the girls had found helped to cool the meat, making it easier to eat. He took a sip of water to help wash it down and winced at the complete lack of taste. It was almost as tasteless as the water on Earth.

Kailee smiled, her teeth reflecting the light of the fire. "How come you're taking it so calmly if you've never been here before?"

Austin laughed. "I was – I *am* – a Scout," he said. "I've been on route marches before, even if they were nowhere near here. The basics don't change, really."

Gary looked up, interested. "What's a Scout?"

"It's a...club for young men and women, where we learn skills we will need in later life," Austin said, shortly. "We go walking, swimming, boating...just about everything we do on the farms and a little bit more. There's a scouting troop based around every large settlement, each one competing with the others to win the most badges every year. It's great fun, particularly after the harvest."

He smiled. "Don't you have Scouts on Earth?"

Darrin shook his head. It sounded like fun, but there was no way that anyone could or would operate such a system on Earth. There would be too much chance of someone getting hurt, he knew, and lawsuits that would bankrupt almost anyone. It was absurd, given how many people were injured or killed daily in the CityBlocks, but it was the way things were. No one could hope to even get permission to *try*.

"There were a bunch of settlers from Terra Nova who came here, two years ago," Austin said, with quiet amusement. "None of us had really grasped the fact that there were Scouts on other worlds – nor had they, which annoyed all of us. They'd set themselves up as the Scouts of Meridian while they were on the transport starship, complete with patrol leaders and badges. They were rather put out to discover that we were there first – and that we weren't interested in taking them on as anything other than beginners."

Kailee laughed, quietly. "I bet that didn't go down well," she said. "What did you do?"

"We ended up offering them the choice between joining us or setting themselves up as another troop," Austin said. "Most of them joined us, particularly the younger and newer ones. It was the older ones who wanted to cling to the badges and ranks they felt they'd earned. I don't suppose I can blame them for that."

"And you have campfire meals," Darrin said, feeling another flash of envy. What would life on Earth had been like if Barry and Moe had been allowed to channel their energy into nicer activities than bullying? "What else do you do?"

"We sing," Austin said. "I can caterwaul with the best of them."

He opened his mouth and began to bellow out the words of a song. Darrin felt himself caught between awe and horror. Few people on Earth would have dared to put themselves forward – and those who did weren't always the nicest of people. But Austin sang without embarrassment, without shame; Darrin looked at him and felt, once again, the sensation that his life had been deliberately kept bland. Yates had said as much, more than once. But Darrin hadn't understood until too late.

"There's a version of this song that is rather rude," Austin added, when he reached the end of the song. He didn't seem put out that none of them had joined in. "The Patrol Leaders all tell us not to sing it anywhere near the adults..."

Gary leaned forward. "Weren't the adults Scouts themselves?"

Austin grinned at him. "Of course they were," he said. "But they tell themselves that *their* children wouldn't *dare* to sing such a song."

He threw open his mouth and sung.

"There once was a Gallic minister's wife,
"And she had never a care in her life,
"Until she came into trouble and strife...
"And Oh! The minister's wife!"

"That doesn't sound very rude," Barry said. He hadn't seemed to be paying close attention to anyone. He'd just chewed his food, staring into the fire. "What's rude about it?"

"Everyone is supposed to make up additional verses," Austin explained. "They all have to share the same final line, which means that the ending words of each line have to rhyme with *wife*. And it all goes downhill from there."

"The husband said he wanted a change in his life,
"And then he started to fuck his wife,
"And everyone else, which just caused strife,
"And Oh! The minister's wife!"

He laughed, quietly. "Well, that and there are ministers on the planet," he added. "Good men, mostly, but they can stand on their dignity a bit too much."

"It doesn't scan properly," Kailee objected. "The words don't quite match."

"The secret is to just have fun," Austin said. "Just imagine it; sitting around a fire" – he indicated the burning embers – "cooking sausages or frying marshmallows, then sleeping out under the stars. You and your friends, singing together...you can't imagine it, unless you've been there."

His voice lowered. "But you haven't, have you?"

"No," Gary said, quietly. There was a bitterness in his voice that left Darrin feeling guilty, even though he had never been the worst of Gary's tormentors. "I haven't."

Darrin understood, even though he suspected that Austin wouldn't. Gary could never relax, not at school, not in the corridors, not even in his own apartment, given how wimpy and pathetic he was. It didn't matter how smart he was, even though Yates had said that Gary might just have the best chance of getting out of the CityBlock and making a new life for himself. There was no IQ high enough to stop a fist, no level of intelligence capable of beating someone far stronger than Gary himself. Even if the Scouts *had* been an option, Gary would never have dared join. He would just have spent their camping trips watching his back.

I'm sorry, he thought, inwardly. But he knew he could never say it out loud. Apologising was a sign of weakness. Everyone on Earth knew that...

But they weren't on Earth, not any longer. And he might just manage to stay on Meridian.

Austin sang them a couple more songs, one about a young girl who went to the stars and the other about a man who drank far too much alcohol and regularly swore never to touch the booze again, only to break his pledge the following night. The verses grew sillier and sillier as the man kept coming up with excuses, finally falling and breaking his neck. But the final verse said he found himself in heaven, drinking from a lake of booze.

"The shelter should give you some protection," Austin said, addressing the girls. "The rest of us will sleep outside."

Gary looked up towards the stars, high overhead. "What if it rains?"

"We get wet," Austin said, dryly. He looked down at the fire. "I'll take the first watch; Darrin, I'll wake you in a few hours to take over from me. Keep the fire going and don't hesitate to wake me if something approaches the clearing. And if you see an aircraft, use the flares at once."

"All right," Darrin said.

He found a reasonably comfortable place to lie down, then closed his eyes. Despite their position, sleep claimed him almost at once. But none of his dreams were pleasant.

CHAPTER
TWENTY-SIX

They had been told that they could simply walk into a job. This was untrue. They might have paper qualifications, but those didn't always translate into either competence or experience. Holding down even the most basic of jobs was a real problem. They were not even prepared for rote labour. Instead, they tended to claim their Living Allowances and stay at their government-assigned homes.

- Professor Leo Caesius, *Education and the Decline and Fall of the Galactic Empire*

When they were asleep, Austin decided, the Earth-born looked...different.

He studied Darrin thoughtfully, watching as the suspicion and fear slowly faded away, leaving someone who might have been considered handsome, if he looked like that all the time. Maybe not entirely *innocent* – Austin had once been told that no teenager could be considered *innocent* – but more human than the guarded persona Darrin presented in daylight, one that feared the worst of everyone. Barry too looked almost innocent, while Gary looked almost relaxed. But it was clear that Gary never relaxed completely.

Austin looked down at them, feeling a strange kind of pity. He was a product of an open culture that taught its kids to be responsible, trusted them to behave themselves and punished them when they went off the rails. They were products of a culture that taught them nothing, didn't trust anyone and considered punishment an outdated concept. Austin wasn't sure just how much of what Yates had told him about Earth was actually true, but it was quite possible that none of them would ever amount to anything once they got home. If, of course, they *did* get home. Darrin had certainly sounded like he wanted to stay on Meridian.

He stood up, peering out into the darkness. The light of the fire would help keep predators away, he hoped; it was also playing merry hell with his night vision. Larger creatures could be heard moving in the undergrowth, although none of them came out into the light. Austin walked to the edge of the forest, then turned back to peer into the shelter. Kailee and Samantha were cuddled together, snoring quietly. They too looked relaxed...

Austin shook his head in disbelief as he made his way back to the fire. If they did want to stay on Meridian, they would have to learn how to fit in – and how to behave. Barry was luckier than he deserved, lucky enough to tell Austin that strings had been pulled at a very high level. He could easily have been indentured for wanton vandalism, let alone gross carelessness. And Darrin and Austin might have been dragged down with him.

Yates had warned him to watch Barry. Austin had seriously considered tying him up for the night, even though it would have definitely turned Barry into an enemy. If he'd had one other colonial-born with him, he would have been able to sleep easier. But instead...he looked at Darrin and Abdul and winced, inwardly. Could he rely on them to look after their own interests, let alone those of the group? But they were so ignorant that they couldn't even be trusted to know what their own interests *were!*

Everyone is selfish, although just about everyone will try to claim otherwise, his scoutmaster had said, when discussing history and moral philosophy. *This is not actually a bad thing. A person who acts in his own selfish interests can be relied upon, a person who claims to act out of selfless motives may change his mind or break his word at any time, justifying it to himself with ease.*

Austin nodded to himself, looking down at Darrin. The colonials tried to act in their own best interests. No matter how tight-fisted someone was, he would keep his word – or acquire a reputation as a liar, which would make it impossible for him to do business in future. A bad reputation could destroy its holder. But Earth...the Earth-born had never been taught the advantages of honour, even the advantages of dealing openly with other people. Maybe that was why Earth was so damn legalistic. They couldn't trust their fellows at all.

The moon rose high in the sky, casting an eerie light over the campsite. Austin knew people who had gone there briefly, before returning to Meridian and admitting that a spacer's life wasn't for them. He knew how they felt. The lunar landscape was dead and cold, without a single scrap of life. There might be spacers who sneered at the planet-bound, calling them dirty-feet or worse, but space itself was lifeless. How could anyone live there?

And how, he asked himself silently, *could anyone live on Earth?*

He looked at the Earth-born and shuddered. They were cruel parodies of what a human being should be, but perhaps it was to be expected. They spent all their lives in little metal and concrete boxes, either preying on their fellows or being preyed on. There was little in their life that was sacred, nothing to live or die for. And there was no safety at all. He'd seen how the girls clung together, eying the boys with barely-concealed fear. On Meridian, a rapist would be lucky if he wasn't shot or lynched. But on Earth...

You are the product of a highly-individualised culture, Yates had said. *You grew up knowing that you had to respect your fellows, even if you didn't like them. You had responsibility hammered into your head from a very early age. My charges were not brought up like you.*

The thought was almost *alien*. How could someone be different? None of the colonists from Earth had been quite so...obnoxious. Yes, they'd made stupid mistakes and had to learn the hard way, but they'd not been unpleasant to the first colonists and their descendents. But they were the ones who wanted to build a new life. The contest winners hadn't ever *intended* to leave their world.

They don't understand that they're caught in a trap, Austin thought. *There's no way out for them.*

He shuddered, remembering the lobster pots fishermen used. They put the pots down in the morning and waited. When the lobster scuttled into the trap, it discovered that no matter how it struggled, it couldn't escape. The fishermen pulled the trap up in the evening and had the lobster for dinner. But Earth...Earth was a giant lobster pot for its inhabitants. For every one that got out, a thousand – perhaps more – remained hopelessly trapped on a dying world.

His watch bleeped softly. Austin muttered a curse under his breath, then looked over at Darrin. Did he *dare* put him on watch? Darrin hadn't fired the shot – his only crime hadn't been not stopping Barry – but who knew how he would act now, when everyone was asleep? And yet, Austin didn't dare sleep without leaving someone else on watch – or try to stay awake all night. The medical kit didn't include enough stimulants to keep him awake until they reached the Jordan.

Carefully, he knelt down beside Darrin and shook him gently. The boy's eyes snapped open at once. Despite his tiredness, Austin realised, he'd actually slept very lightly. Austin frowned – he'd known scouts who hadn't been awoken by thunder and lightning – before remembering what he'd been told about Earth. Sleeping too deeply could get someone killed.

"I need you to stay on watch," he said. He took a breath, then passed Darrin the rifle. "If you see something – anything – wake me up. Don't disturb anyone else."

Darrin looked pale in the moonlight, but nodded.

Silently praying that Darrin wouldn't do anything stupid, Austin lay down on the ground and closed his eyes.

———

Darrin held the rifle in one hand and looked down at Austin, feeling an odd wave of envy that threatened to overwhelm him. Austin slept so *easily*. There was no sense of fear, no worries about a cruel stepfather or a drunken mother; there were no worries at all. Darrin hadn't slept easily anywhere, not even on the starship. After all, even though Yates had been there, he had known that Barry might do something stupid anyway.

He felt a twinge on his back as he sat down, cradling the rifle. It didn't seem fair that he'd been punished for failing to stop Barry, yet whenever he thought about it he knew that the consequences could have been far worse. Barry might have taken a shot at a passing colonial – or even at Darrin himself. He knew that there had been times when Barry and Moe had thrown balls at their fellow pupils, just for shits and giggles. And they had been no respecters of anyone. Rumour claimed that the departure of one of the younger female teachers had come after the two of them had cornered her in a supply cupboard and had some fun...

Fun, Darrin thought. It had certainly seemed like fun, once. He'd enjoyed hearing the stories, laughing at the tales...but now they no longer seemed funny. His back had been lashed, and it had hurt, yet in truth he knew he deserved worse. Maybe not for failing to stop Barry, but for everything else he'd seen and condoned while he'd been on Earth. He looked over at Barry, who was snoring deeply, and shuddered. If Darrin had been stronger, strong enough to defy everyone else in school, would he have acted like Barry and Moe?

He wanted to deny it, but he knew the truth. The basic rule on Earth was simple; the strong dominated the weak. Gary had been the weakest of the weak, picked on even by others who weren't particularly strong; Barry and Moe had been the strongest, the lords and masters of the school and everyone in it. Darrin himself...he shuddered at the memory of picking on other students, then allying himself with Barry. He'd fallen into a destructive pattern without ever realising that the pattern was there, let alone that it might be wrong.

And then Yates had flattened Barry with a single punch.

The memory still made him cringe. He was used to watching teachers back down, submitting themselves to endless humiliations from the stronger pupils. Yates hadn't backed down; instead, he'd knocked Barry out, so effectively that the bully hadn't even been able to land a blow. Barry might not have learnt anything from the experience, or the weeks they'd both spent scrubbing the floors, but Darrin had learned that Barry was no longer the strongest of them all. And then he'd wondered if that would also have been true on Earth. Maybe Barry would not have lasted long outside the school...

He looked down at the rifle. It represented power, it represented the ability to kill...and Austin had *trusted* him with it. The colonial boy...even in sleep, he looked peaceful and relaxed, untouched by the nightmares of Earth. Darrin found himself caught between hatred, envy and a dull admiration. He *wanted* Austin to like him, even as he found himself envying the colonial boy for all the opportunities he'd enjoyed that had been denied to Darrin and his friends.

Bet he wouldn't last long on Earth, the resentful part of his mind muttered. But he knew, somehow, that a person as self-confident as Austin would manage to live anywhere. *Why couldn't we live like that?*

They'd been taught that the government on Earth provided everything they needed. It was clear to him now that the teachers had lied. None of them had ever been allowed to shape their students, to try to show them a better way of living...or to punish them when they stepped out of line. The pupils had never been taught right from wrong – or anything better than the law of the concrete jungle. Was it really surprising that they had reverted to barbarism?

The fire was starting to flicker and die. Darrin stood up and started to feed it with twigs, followed by larger pieces of wood. The heat started to rise slowly; Darrin let out a sigh of relief, then sat down next to the fire. He'd never been allowed to build a fire on Earth or do anything else that might be dangerous. There was too high a risk of lawsuits...or, for that matter, of someone like Barry using it as a chance to hurt a fellow student. Darrin felt shame burning through his chest as he realised that, if Barry *had*, he would have laughed. They would *all* have laughed, save for the victim. But who cared about him?

He looked back at Austin and sighed inwardly. Austin might have been thrashed by his uncle – that had been obvious – but it was clear that the colonial boy didn't bear a grudge. But then, Austin probably blamed himself for letting Barry anywhere near a weapon. Just as Darrin found it hard to understand the colonial mindset, Austin probably found it hard to comprehend just how ignorant and incompetent visitors from Earth had to be. If he had realised that there was something amiss with a visit to a shooting range, he might have refused to take them...

Darrin shuddered, remembering the last time Fitz had thrashed him. The man had been drunk, so blinded with alcohol that it was a miracle that he'd been able to walk, let alone wield the belt. God alone knew what Darrin had done to deserve it; there was no way that Fitz had ever punished him for anything that actually deserved punishment. But he'd been left beaten and broken, his skin marred with bruises where the end of the belt had struck his bare flesh. *Austin* had never had to worry about a drunken stepfather. He could just have shot the bastard if he'd had one.

But, in hindsight, perhaps it was easy to understand Fitz. Like Darrin, he would have gone to school – and probably graduated with no qualifications worth having. Darrin had never really understood why students like Gary busted their balls trying to score the highest possible marks, when all one really needed to do was turn in a paper to pass, but he understood now. Fitz wouldn't have been able to find a proper job, if he had even bothered to look. His life had been utterly wasted. He didn't even have good contacts with the gangs, something that might make his life easier, no matter what he claimed. No wonder he'd spent most of his time getting smashed out of his mind.

Darrin scowled, bitterly. He'd picked on Gary too – and a dozen other boys – in the hopes of finding a diversion from the boredom of school. Maybe Fitz had just done the same. It wasn't a reassuring thought.

He looked up at the moon, glowing high overhead. Earth had a moon too – they'd studied it in school – but he'd never actually seen it. Even if they had been allowed up to the very highest levels of the CityBlock, they wouldn't have seen the moon, not when the skies were permanently cloudy. Here, the wide open spaces both called to him and intimidated him. Part of him just wanted to run and hide from the emptiness...maybe he should have remained in jail until they'd shipped him back to Earth. He certainly wouldn't have flown on the crashed aircraft.

But what was there for him on Earth?

Maybe Fitz was dead, instead of waiting patiently for his stepson to come home. It was the best case scenario. Darrin had never loved Fitz. There were other fathers, he knew, who were equally unpleasant to their children, but they sometimes acted like real fathers. Fitz had never seen Darrin as anything other than a source of income – Darrin never saw any of his living allowance – and a whipping boy. If Fitz was dead, his mother would be free of him, at least until she found someone else to protect her. If she could...

Darrin swallowed. What *was* there for him on Earth? Nothing. He could graduate with a worthless degree and then...he'd become just like Fitz. Maybe he'd marry Judy, have kids with her, then watch helplessly as they became just like him. Hell, perhaps he'd start beating them too, hoping to relieve his frustration. Just as picking on the weak at school had made him feel powerful, picking on his children would make it easier for him to forget that he was trapped. And it would be worse, he realised as he peered into the darkness surrounding the campsite. Unlike Fitz, he would know what he was missing.

No, he told himself, firmly. *I will not go back to Earth.*

Austin had told him that there was no shortage of employment for someone willing to work hard. Darrin silently promised himself that he *would* work hard, as soon as he found a job – even simple brute labour might be more promising than living on Earth. He could find a place to live in the city, then perhaps marry someone who grew up on Meridian... someone who would stand up for herself and her children. Someone who wouldn't let him behave like Fitz.

He had no idea if he'd ever find someone suitable. How was one supposed to pick up a girl on Meridian? The methods he'd learnt on Earth seemed more likely to get him shot than into bed with a colonial girl. He'd have to ask Austin – or perhaps he should get established first. It was a dream, he knew, one he knew would be difficult to achieve. And yet, he had the feeling that trying would have made Yates proud of him. Winning Yates's respect would have made his life worthwhile, because his respect was worth having. He wished that he'd had a chance to tell Yates that before he'd died.

And the dream kept him awake as he waited, as patiently as he could, for the sun to rise in the sky.

CHAPTER
TWENTY-SEVEN

This created major problems for the Empire. The growing workforce was incapable of handling the tasks assigned to it. They could not be relied upon for anything serious, which ensured that the number of problems in the Empire's infrastructure grew too large to be fixed.

- Professor Leo Caesius, *Education and the Decline and Fall of the Galactic Empire*

Gary awoke with a jerk.

Something was poking into his stomach, hard. For a moment, he thought that Barry or Darrin had shoved a stone under his body while he was asleep, before he remembered the gun. He'd gone to sleep on top of the weapon, even though he'd feared accidentally triggering it when he rolled over. It had seemed dangerous, but it had also seemed the best way to keep the weapon out of sight. He didn't want anyone to know he had it.

The air was cooler than normal, he realised, as he stumbled to his feet, carefully concealing the weapon in his clothes. They'd been told at school that concealing a weapon on one's person was easy – it was the excuse for the extensive security measures – but it proved, once again, that the teachers hadn't really known what they were talking about. Gary suspected that hiding the weapon was going to be harder and harder as they progressed. If nothing else, he would have to strip off his shirt at some point or see it sodden with sweat.

"Welcome back to the world," Austin called. "Come and get something to eat."

He'd caught more crabs, Gary saw, as he walked over to the fire. The meat was cooking rapidly, while Austin and Darrin were using their shells to collect and boil water for their drinking. Gary hesitated when Austin passed him a knife, then started to saw into one of the dead crabs. Even touching the creature gave him the creeps.

"Not all of that is good meat," Austin warned. He'd been watching Gary with some amusement. "But not too bad, for a first try."

Gary found himself caught between embarrassment and pleasure. "Thank you," he said, finally. "There's more here than we can eat, isn't there?"

"Quite right," Austin said. It would have been sarcasm from anyone on Earth, but Austin seemed to genuinely mean it. "We're taking the opportunity to cook the meat and carry it with us. It can serve as lunch."

He snorted as he picked his way through the pile of meat, throwing the inedible material back into the pond. "Pity we don't have any salt to help preserve it," he added. "Without it, the meat will go bad quickly, no matter how thoroughly we cook it. But we will have to make do."

There was a crashing sound from behind them. Barry was dragging a large piece of wood into the clearing. It looked like he'd torn a large branch from a tree – or, more likely, picked one off the ground and dragged it back to them. Austin examined it quickly, nodded in approval, then started to slice the branch into smaller pieces with his monofilament knife. Once cut up, the pieces were placed by the fire to dry.

The girls awoke and stumbled out of their shelter, looking terrible. Gary kept his face as blank as possible, but Barry hooted and catcalled. Kailee and Samantha looked as if they hadn't washed their hair for a week. Their clothes were filthy and faces were bruised, although it didn't look as though they'd been beaten by someone. Gary felt a twinge of pain on his jaw and touched it, carefully. He'd been sleeping on the ground too and it had left a mark.

"Remember to bury your poop," Barry called after them, as they hobbled into the countryside. "We don't want wild animals digging it up."

Austin gave him a sharp look. "Be quiet," he said, tartly. "We're all in this together."

He plucked an oversized leaf off the rack, examined the meat quickly, then passed it to Gary and motioned for him to eat. It tasted different than it had the previous evening, although Gary would have been hard-pressed to say how or why. He picked at it with his fingers, washing it down with warm water. From what Austin had said, boiling the water was the only way to ensure that it was safe to drink.

The girls walked back into the clearing, looking a little better. Gary wondered just how well they'd slept; he never slept very well, even on his best days. It had to be worse for them, being alone with a handful of horny guys. Going to the toilet in the open had to be a terrifying experience. They would never be sure that they weren't being watched. The thought was disgusting, but he wouldn't put anything past Barry. He would do anything for amusement.

"I meant to ask," Abdul said, as Austin passed him a piece of meat. "Shouldn't we be going in the opposite direction?"

Austin blinked in surprise, then checked his compass. "No," he said. "Why?"

Abdul pointed at the stream running away from the pond. "Isn't that water going towards the Jordan?"

"No," Austin said. He hesitated, clearly trying to organise his thoughts. "We're on the wrong side of the incline. Water on this side runs down towards the lakes, not towards the Jordan."

Gary made a face. The explanation puzzled him, but then he'd never had a chance to study geography in any proper manner. There were no rivers left on Earth, as far as he knew, certainly not ones he was able to visit. And no one in their right mind would want to visit the heavily-polluted oceans. All he could really do was trust that Austin wasn't leading them astray. The colonial boy probably wanted to get them back to whatever passed for civilisation on Meridian as much as they wanted to get back there. If he'd wanted to abandon them, he could have done it at night. They wouldn't have realised that anything was wrong until it was far too late.

"We have to be careful around here," Austin added. "Sudden rainfalls and floods are common."

Barry snorted, rudely. "We *noticed*," he said. "And why are we constantly heading *upwards*?"

"It's the shortest path to the Jordan," Austin said. There was a hint of irritation in his tone. "If we had maps or a working GPS receiver, I might take a longer route that would be easier on untrained walkers. But we don't have either and I don't want to take the risk of getting lost."

"Should have one in the emergency packs," Barry muttered. "Or something else to call for help."

Austin passed him a leaf of meat, then settled down to eat his own food. Barry stared at him angrily for a long moment, clearly annoyed at being so openly dismissed; Gary watched him, nervously. Barry had always insisted on forcing his way into taking charge back at school, when they'd been instructed to complete projects as a group. Somehow, those projects had turned into group bullying sessions, where everyone had picked on Gary. It had been a relief when they'd moved higher up the system and group projects had been abolished. He wouldn't have been able to keep his grades if he'd had to work with others.

Barry isn't going to be able to keep his mouth shut, he thought, grimly. *He will want to challenge Austin again...*

He briefly considered asking the colonial boy how to use the pistol, before dismissing the thought. After Barry had messed around at the shooting range, it was unlikely that Austin would let Gary *keep* the pistol. Gary couldn't really blame him for wanting to keep it out of his hands, but he didn't dare risk losing the weapon. It was his only means of defence.

"There are a great many things I wish we had," Austin said, into the silence. "But we don't have them. We have to make do with what we have. If you have a problem with that, I suggest you complain when we get home. No doubt future plane flights will carry a comprehensive emergency kit."

He was mocking Barry, Gary realised. But would Barry realise that he was being mocked?

"No doubt," Barry said, darkly. "We could sue, couldn't we?"

Austin ignored him. "Gary, go looking for more edible plants," he ordered. "Girls, help me to pack the meat into one of the packs. Everyone else, pack up the remaining packs, then dig a large hole for the waste. We don't want to leave any signs that we were here."

Barry scowled as Gary stood. "Surely they will have sent someone after us," he said. "Steve would have pointed them in the right direction, right?"

"Maybe," Austin said. "But if they start looking for us, they'll start from the air. They won't have the manpower to search for us on the ground."

He nodded at Gary. "Go."

Gary obeyed, walking away from the clearing and looking for edible plants. Thankfully, a handful were easily recognisable, although he knew that they had to be careful with mushrooms. Some of the ones they'd found yesterday had been inspected by Austin, then hastily discarded as being unsafe to eat. Gary wondered, absently, if Austin's time in the scouts had taught him to recognise dangerous plants by instinct. No matter how carefully *Gary* looked at the mushrooms, he couldn't tell the difference.

"They did," Austin said, when he returned and asked. "Do you know what we had to do to earn the badge for Middle Survivalist?"

Gary shook his head.

"They flew us to a forest, not too different from this one, and dropped us off," Austin said, cheerfully. "We were completely naked, save for our belts and a handful of tools. All we had to do was make it back to camp alive."

He scowled. "It took three days."

"Naked, you say," Barry said. "It sounds like fun."

He leered at the girls. "Come on, get naked."

"It wasn't," Austin said, quietly. "There was no protection at all for our feet, let alone the rest of us. And for those who went on to do Advanced Survivalist...well, *they* weren't given tools at all, just told to get out there and find everything they needed."

Darrin gave him an odd look. "Why didn't *you* do it?"

"I came to the city for a year's experience of something apart from the farm," Austin said. "I was planning to do it once I returned home, although dad might have forbidden it. Only a handful of people have ever completed Advanced Survivalist and most of them went into the Bush Rangers..."

Gary stared at him. "What happens if you *die* out there?" He looked down at his bruises merely from sleeping on the hard ground. "Or if you get injured?"

"There's an emergency signal," Austin told him. "All you have to do is trigger it and they come pick you up. But you don't pass the test if you do."

He shrugged. "There was a big argument a few years back, while I was a Beaver," he added. "Someone got seriously injured and his partner triggered the distress beacon, then insisted on remaining in the forest and completing his test. Depending on how one looks at the rules, that's cheating, even if the evacuation crew didn't give him any actual help. Lots of outraged fist-shaking over that!

"In the end, they ruled that he hadn't really had a choice. But it still irked the people who *had* passed without calling for help, even if the help wasn't for them."

"That's stupid," Darrin said. "He couldn't have left his friend to die, could he?"

Gary blinked in surprise. *Darrin* was arguing in favour of helping someone? On Earth, helping someone was a mug's game. If you helped someone, you could be blamed for anything that went wrong and sued... assuming, of course, that you didn't put your own life in danger trying. Gary hated to admit it, but he probably wouldn't have tried to help someone, no matter how desperately they needed it. And the thought of Barry or Moe helping someone was absurd.

"That was the point his supporters raised in the debates," Austin confessed. "But it still annoyed a great many people."

Kailee turned suddenly and ran into the forest. Gary watched her go in some alarm, then looked back at Austin. The colonial boy didn't look surprised, merely...concerned. But he made no move to go after her.

"Get the packs on your backs," Austin said, instead. "Once Kailee is back, we'll start moving."

———

Kailee hadn't felt right since she'd woken up, unsure of where she was. The shelter had seemed nightmarishly weak in the early morning light. One strong gust of wind, she told herself, and it would have collapsed on top of them. Instead, her body had ached mercilessly when she got up in the morning...and then, when she'd eaten her share of the meat, her stomach had started to burn. She'd barely been able to hold herself together long enough to run into the forest and find a bush to hide behind while she did her business.

Afterwards, she stumbled forwards and collapsed on the ground. She felt utterly filthy, far worse than she'd ever felt on Earth. It was worse, in fact, because she now knew what it felt like to be actually *clean*. If there was one thing Meridian was not short of, it was water – and the endless showers and baths had been a luxury in and of themselves. All of the girls had simply luxuriated in the water, washing themselves again and again. Now...they seemed like a distant memory.

She didn't dare bathe in the pond. Even if the boys hadn't been there – and she knew that Darrin and Barry would certainly try to peek – she knew that there were animals in the water, animals that could pinch or bite her. Shuddering, she reached for a leaf and wiped herself as best as she could, cursing under her breath. Her stomach still hurt, badly. All she could do was lie on the ground, her pants around her knees, and pray.

The meat wasn't good, she decided, remembering everything they'd been told about the advantages of algae-based products. It was true enough that she'd never had a tummy ache after eating ration bars, or even Aunt Lillian's attempts to make the food more palatable by adding various kinds of flavourings and sauces. Indeed, they'd been told, time and time again, that real meat was unhealthy. She'd wondered if that was merely an attempt to convince them not to eat it, but now...now, she wasn't so sure.

And yet she hadn't felt unwell after eating meat the first time...

She heard the sound of someone crashing through the bushes and frantically pulled herself to her feet, yanking up her pants to cover herself. The girls toilets at school were forbidden to the boys, but that hadn't stopped them from coming in from time to time; Kailee had often forced herself to just keep it in, rather than walk into the toilets. Even when the boys weren't invading the room, there were girls who were almost as bad.

Austin came into view and she relaxed, slightly. Her tummy still felt uneasy and she didn't want to go far, but at least he wasn't Barry. And she wasn't clean...one of the few pieces of advice they'd been given about preventing unwelcome male attention was to piss on them in hopes of putting them off. But Kailee had heard of several girls who'd done just that and then been beaten to within an inch of their lives. Boys didn't take sexual frustration very well.

"That does tend to happen, if the meat isn't perfect," Austin said. "How are you feeling?"

Kailee glared at him. "Does that happen to your glorious scouts too?"

"It's been known to happen," Austin agreed. He ignored her tone, thankfully. She'd known boys who had beaten their girlfriends for speaking to them in anything less than a respectful voice. "I'm sorry it had to happen to you."

"Thank you," Kailee growled. She rubbed her belly, angrily. "Is there nothing we can do about it?"

"Not until we get home," Austin said. "We're stuck out here."

Kailee stared at him, then sagged to the ground, wrapping her arms around her legs. She just wanted to go home. Even being with Aunt Lillian would be better than being in the forest, eating poisonous food and being eyed by four boys who had nothing to restrain them, but their better instincts. And boys, she knew, had *no* better instincts. They were creatures of lust and desire, barely maturing until they were too old to chase girls. There were few things she would ever have in common with Aunt Lillian, but one of them was a certain wariness of untamed boys.

She flinched as Austin knelt down and put a hand on her shoulder. "I know how you feel," he admitted. "I felt the same way too once, when I ran into the countryside. I got lost, rather badly. If I hadn't found my way to another farm, I might well have died out there."

Kailee looked at him. "You?"

"I was five," Austin said. "I'd had a row with my mother. It was just a petty little argument, but it felt like the end of the world. After that...I started learning more about the countryside. Dad signed me up for the Beavers and the rest is history."

He stood, then held out a hand to help Kailee to her feet. "The difference between survival and death is often a matter of will," he said. He sounded as though he was quoting someone he'd heard once. "If you want to give up, you can stay here and wait for death to find you. Or you can spit in the old man's eye and keep going, whatever the world throws at you."

"That's stupid," Kailee objected, as she stood. She didn't take his hand. "I could be shot in the head and then I'd be dead. No amount of willpower would keep me going."

"I said that too," Austin said. "And I got told that whatever didn't kill me would make me stronger."

He turned. "Come on," he added. "It's time to start moving again."

CHAPTER
TWENTY-EIGHT

Does this seem absurd? Everything from replacing processor boxes to navigating starships required (at the very least) the basic ability to read. The Empire was forced to simplify its infrastructure as much as possible, yet even the most simple repair jobs required years of retraining before a potential worker could handle them.

- Professor Leo Caesius, *Education and the Decline and Fall of the Galactic Empire*

If anything, Darrin discovered, the second day of walking was even harder than the first. His body began aching within minutes, while Gary and the girls were clearly held back by their own aches and pains. Only Austin seemed unbothered; Abdul and Barry were also in pain, but trying to hide it. Darrin couldn't help wondering if they were ever going to make it to the Jordan. At this rate, they were all going to collapse at the end of the second day.

The landscape changed too, becoming more mountainous. Trees pushed in around them, casting long shadows over their path, while small animals ran past them constantly. Abdul lost his footing at one point, falling down the slope and almost banging his head against a rock. Barry sniggered, of course, but Austin climbed down and helped Abdul back to his feet. Darrin felt oddly guilty about not trying to help himself, even though he was carrying a heavy pack. Austin was definitely stronger and nimbler than he looked if he could scramble down without removing the bag from *his* back.

He found himself becoming thirsty, but struggled manfully not to stop and demand water. The medical kit could serve as a makeshift water carrier – Austin had filled it back at the first campsite – yet it couldn't actually carry very much. Darrin forced himself to ignore his body's demands, even though he knew he should probably request help. He didn't want to waste what they had.

Samantha stumbled past him, her eyes half-closed and sweat pouring down her back. Darrin found himself staring at the shape of her ass, allowing it to draw him onwards even as he felt like falling down and collapsing in a heap. Behind him, Gary fell behind slightly, until he was walking next to Kailee. Barry brought up the rear, no doubt feasting his eyes on Kailee while resisting the urge to grumble. He'd grumbled loudly as they'd walked until it had proven too much for him and he'd quietened.

He reached up and brushed his sweaty hair away from his eyes. His entire forehead was damp, sweat dripping down to the ground. How long had it been, he asked himself, since they'd started to walk? It felt like they'd walked for days! Austin had said, in a rather droll tone, that they would have to pass their hump before they grew used to walking, but Darrin had no idea what that meant. It was probably an expression unique to Meridian.

Once they passed through a small bunch of trees, the semi-path – Darrin hadn't been able to decide if humans had made it or if they'd just been lucky enough to find a usable route – lurched, then headed downwards. There was a large lake lying at the bottom, far larger than the pond they'd rested beside on the first night. A mountain rose up beside the lake, covered in green bushes and plants; on the other side, a small river flowed out from the lake and headed down the valley. Darrin silently hoped that it headed towards the Jordan, although he wasn't so sure. Further down, it seemed to twist and turn out of sight.

"Look at the lakeshore," Austin said, holding up his hand to stop them. "What do you see?"

Darrin tore his gaze away from Samantha's chest and looked towards the lake. There was a muddy shoreline, marred by animal tracks. Beasts came to the lake to drink, Darrin realised slowly, including some that might well be dangerous. He looked around, nervously. Who knew what might be lurking in the undergrowth, watching them through inhuman eyes?

"Animal tracks," Barry said. He sounded pleased at answering first. But Darrin knew that it was only a matter of time before he challenged Austin directly. "There are animals here..."

"Look," Kailee squealed.

Darrin stared. In the trees, a four-legged shape was standing in the shadows, watching the humans through glinting eyes. He'd heard the sound of animals in the underbrush, but this was the first time he'd seen something just looking back at them. The animal looked like a small horse, yet it was hard to make out the details. It seemed unsure what to make of the humans by the lake.

Austin lifted his gun in one smooth motion and fired, once. The animal started, staggered, then fell to the ground. Kailee let out a cry of protest, which Austin ignored. Instead, he walked towards the animal, gun at the ready. Darrin and Barry exchanged glances, then walked after Austin. The colonial boy stopped in front of his target, then reached down and snapped the creature's neck. If it hadn't been dead before – Austin had hit it in the head, he saw – it was definitely dead now.

Up close, it *did* look a little like a small horse. Brown fur covered its body, oddly soft and warm to the touch. Austin checked the body, then motioned for Darrin to take one end and Barry to take the other. There was an odd glint in Barry's eye as he helped pick up and carry the creature back to the lakeside. Barry, Darrin realised, had never seen anything die before, apart from the crabs. This...was something far larger.

"You bastard," Kailee said, when she saw the creature clearly. "You..."

Austin gave her a surprised look. "You do realise that you've eaten venison before?"

Kailee stared at him, then stormed off looking sick. Samantha gave Austin an unreadable look, then followed Kailee. Austin shrugged, then opened his pack and produced the knives.

"Gary, go set up a fire," he ordered, shortly. "The lighter is in the bag. Darrin, Barry, watch carefully. I'll show you how to slaughter a deer."

Watching him dissect the crabs had been unpleasant, Darrin knew. This was worse. The deer's blood pooled on the ground, summoning flies and other insects that buzzed around the dead animal like boys around a girl. There were no such insects on Earth, Darrin knew; they'd been wiped out long ago, at least in the CityBlocks. But on Meridian, they were still part of the environment. He couldn't keep himself from trying to swat them as Austin carefully skinned the deer, then checked Gary's fire. It was already burning brightly.

"Set up the meat above the fire, as before," Austin ordered. "We need to make sure we cook it thoroughly."

"Got it," Darrin said. He looked over at Austin. "Shouldn't someone go after the girls?"

"I'll go," Barry said, standing upright. "I'll bring them right back here."

"I think that would be a bad idea," Austin said, shortly. He stood himself. "Just keep watching the fire and cooking the meat. I'll go after them."

Barry glared at him, then squatted down next to the fire. Austin gave Darrin a long unreadable look, then turned and walked after the girls. Darrin suspected that the girls had good reason to be relieved, although *he* wasn't. Barry wasn't good company at any time.

"I'm thoroughly sick of him," Barry announced, as soon as Austin was out of earshot. "Who does he think he is?"

"He thinks he knows what he's doing," Abdul said. "And he's probably right."

Darrin winced, looking at Barry. Barry was going to explode, he just knew it. And when he did...he looked at Gary and saw the same apprehension written over his face. Gary was a good observer, if only so he knew when to try to escape. But there was no escape from Barry now...

He sucked in his breath – and tasted the meat in the air. "The meal should be good," he promised. It might help divert Barry from his planned rampage. "Better than the crab, I think."

"Oh, definitely," Abdul agreed.

Barry looked from one to the other, then shut up.

Darrin kept the surprise off his face. Barry *never* shut up, let alone left people alone. He was up to something...but what?

———

Kailee wasn't sure quite why she'd reacted so badly to the death of the deer. She *had* been the person who'd first seen it, but she hadn't fired the fatal shot. But, up close, it had been clear that the deer had been a beautiful creature. And Austin had shot it and started to gut it without a second thought. She'd been disgusted when he'd started cutting up the crabs, but the deer was something else. Somehow, its death had affected her badly.

She stumbled to a halt some distance from the dead creature and sat down on the muddy ground, feeling – once again – the urge to cry. Samantha came up and knelt down beside her, her blue eyes sympathetic. Kailee looked up at her, then started to cry openly. Samantha wrapped her arms around Kailee and held her, gently. Moments later, Kailee felt the tears starting to fade away.

"I don't think we have a choice," Samantha said, quietly. "We have to eat to live."

They looked up as someone else came crashing towards them, making no attempt to conceal his presence. Kailee let out a sigh of relief as she saw Austin. If he hadn't tried anything when the two of them were alone, she told herself, it was unlikely that he would try anything when Samantha was there too. But it was possible that he didn't find either of them attractive, she had to admit. The colonial girls she'd seen had been strong and self-confident in a way neither Kailee nor Samantha could match.

"You shouldn't go wandering off alone," Austin said, as he looked down at them. "There are dangerous creatures in the countryside."

There were dangerous creatures gathered around the fire, Kailee knew, but she kept that thought to herself. Instead, she sighed. Her entire body ached in places she hadn't known she had, not before they'd started their march of death. It was growing impossible to believe that they had a hope of making it to the Jordan, let alone back to the city. And if they couldn't get back to the city, she couldn't hope to get back to Earth.

"Go back to the campsite," Austin ordered Samantha. "I'll talk to Kailee."

He waited till she was out of sight, then gave Kailee a long considering look. "Tell me," he said. "Why did you run?"

Kailee stared up at him. "I don't know," she said, finally. It was the safest answer, particularly when asked difficult questions at school. "Why did I run?"

Austin – no school psychologist – snorted. "How am *I* supposed to know?"

He smiled at her for a second, then looked away. "Let me guess," he said. "You've never seen such a creature killed before?"

"No," Kailee agreed. Tears prickled at the back of her eyes. The deer had been...cute, almost enchanting. And he'd killed it. "Why did you kill it?"

"We need the food," Austin said. There was a hint of sympathy in his voice, but nothing that might suggest that he would change his mind. She'd met teachers who could be swayed with a hint of feminine tears, yet Austin seemed to be immune. "We've already had one bad reaction to the food we found. I don't really want to risk giving you more crab."

Kailee hesitated. "You shot the deer for me?"

"Not just for you," Austin told her dryly. "But it is clear that you reacted badly to *something*."

"I know," Kailee said. The pain in her belly had faded as they walked, but the memory was still vivid. "Is all the food here unsafe?"

Austin tossed a question back at her. "Do you expect the world to be *safe*?"

It wasn't, Kailee knew, even for louts like Barry. No matter how much risk was eliminated, it was always there – and it was worse for a woman. She remembered clumping together with the other girls, fearing for her virginity and her life whenever she was alone with a boy...and knowing that nothing would ever be done to make her safer. Oh, they could try to *make* her feel safe, but she knew better than to believe it. There was no real punishment to deter outright rapists, let alone boys who thought that no meant yes, or that any resistance was only for show.

"... No," she admitted, finally.

"We can try to make it safer," Austin told her. "But there are never any guarantees. You might well have had a reaction to something without ever knowing what it was, because you never ate it before now."

Kailee shuddered. "I want to go home."

Austin looked surprised. "Do you *really* want to go back to Earth?"

"I...I don't know," Kailee said. "I just don't know."

She wanted to be a famous actress, she knew that much. If she wanted to be famous on a galactic scale, she knew, she would have to start on Earth. There were no actresses, as far as she knew, who came from anywhere outside the Core Worlds. She would have to find an agent, then work her way up before she lost her good looks. But...Earth wasn't safe; Earth wasn't even *remotely* safe. Meridian might be wild and untamed, but it was far more civilised. And...

Barry and Darrin had been *punished*. Kailee had never seen the attraction of videos showing men and women being beaten to within an inch of their lives, but there had been something attractive in watching the two of them actually paying for their crimes. No one on Earth was ever punished, no matter what they did. She hadn't enjoyed the sight, yet it had reassured her that there *was* justice in the universe, even if it wasn't on *Earth*.

If she stayed on Meridian, she would have to give up her dream. It was unlikely that any famous actress had ever come from Meridian. She didn't even know if the city – which was smaller than any CityBlock – had a theatre. What could she do on Meridian?

Austin considered it when she asked. "There's no shortage of employment prospects," he said, seriously. "It depends on what you want to do with your life."

He smiled. "You could work in a shop," he said. "Or you could work in a bar. Or, if you don't mind working very hard, you could become a farmer's wife. That would be very rewarding, but it would be hard work."

Kailee blinked. "Just like that?"

"There's a program to recruit women from Earth to serve as wives," Austin told her. "The women spend at least five years living on the farm with their husband, then they can decide if they want to stay with him or move elsewhere. If they have kids, they get the same rights as any other kids. I think some of the women are – well – indents. They chose to be wives rather than go into the labour pool."

"Oh," Kailee said. The thought made her feel sick, yet...was it really any different from the way women on Earth had to seek protectors? "What happens to them?"

"Most of them make it as wives, I think," Austin said. He shrugged. "It's generally considered rude to ask them what they did to be expelled from Earth. Here, people can make a new start. That includes you, if you want to stay."

He held out a hand. "But you can't keep acting like this," he added. "I know you're not used to life here – and you had no reason to expect to crash. But you're holding us all back now."

Kailee scowled at him. "And Barry isn't?"

"Barry is walking with the rest of us," Austin pointed out. "And if you hold us back again, I'll spank you in front of everyone."

Kailee met his eyes and realised that he wasn't joking, then took his hand and allowed him to help her to her feet. "And will you take a wife from Earth?"

"We shall see," Austin said. He nodded towards the lake. "If you like, you can take a swim after we eat lunch and wash yourself clean. The sun is bright enough to dry you out afterwards."

He grinned at her, then turned to walk towards the fire. "Don't worry about the meat," he added. "Once you get back to the city, you can pretend it was grown in a vat instead."

Kailee glared at his back as she walked back towards the fire. Samantha and the boys were sitting around it, chatting as they ate strips of meat. Austin stopped in front of the fire, took a piece of blackened meat and blew on it to cool the food down. Kailee took it when he offered it to her and took a careful bite. It tasted surprisingly good.

"We can have a swim afterwards, then resume our march," Austin said. He nodded towards the mountainside. "I'm afraid we're going to have to head upwards again."

Barry gave him a challenging look. "And wouldn't it be easier to walk through the valley?"

"The valley bends in the wrong direction," Austin pointed out, mildly. "It will be easier to get up while we can, then make our way towards the Jordan. We don't want to go too far off course."

"But it gives us a harder climb," Barry protested. "Why not go the easier route?"

"Because we would no longer be on a direct line for the Jordan," Austin snapped. "And if they are looking for us, that's where they will look."

Kailee swallowed, eying the two boys nervously. It was easy to imagine that they would start fighting – and who knew what would happen then? What if *Austin* lost?

She met Barry's eyes as he lifted them from her chest and knew the answer.

CHAPTER
TWENTY-NINE

And the drive required to handle those jobs was lacking. The graduates believed that they had finished their schooling and were simply unwilling to put in the commitment to gain more qualifications, particularly when it became clear that they would literally have to start from scratch.

- Professor Leo Caesius, Education and the Decline and Fall of the Galactic Empire

By the end of the fourth day, Gary knew, even Austin was reaching the limits of his endurance. Darrin and Abdul snapped at one another, while Barry challenged Austin at every point, demanding that he explain the reasoning behind his orders. Gary did his best to stay out of the arguments, hoping and praying that Austin stayed in charge. He knew better than to think that any of the others would be so tolerant of his presence.

"So tell me," Barry said, as they found a place to stop. "How much further do we have to go?"

"As far as we need to go," Austin said. For once, he sounded less than patient. "The Jordan cannot be that far away."

"We might be going the wrong way," Barry jeered. "What if we're wrong?"

"I have checked constantly with the compass," Austin snapped. "We are heading in the right general direction. All we have to do is keep walking."

"And if we're going the wrong way," Barry said, "we'd keep walking the wrong way."

Gary gritted his teeth. Couldn't Barry tell that Austin was their only hope? He knew how to navigate, while none of them even knew how to read a map! Navigating in the CityBlock was far easier than navigating in the wide open countryside. But instead, Barry kept snapping and sniping at Austin, as if he intended to try to claim leadership for himself. Gary felt the gun's reassuring presence at his belt, then felt cold ice running down his spine. What if he tried to fire and the gun refused to work?

Austin bunched his fists. "If you have a useful skill to share with us," he hissed, "why don't you share it instead of carping and criticising?"

"I can shoot," Barry snapped back. "But you won't *let* me shoot."

Gary was silently grateful that Austin rarely let go of the rifle. He didn't trust Barry with it any further than he could pick up and throw the entire CityBlock. Barry would use it to threaten the rest of them, of that Gary was sure. Kailee and Samantha, at least, would be useful to him. Gary would probably be shot just to encourage the others.

"You decided to fire a weapon recklessly into the streets," Austin said. "Why the hell should I let you anywhere near a weapon? You're damn lucky someone didn't return fire and kill you that day."

I wish they had, Gary thought, bitterly. But, once again, Barry had escaped the consequences of his actions. *He survived to torment me.*

Austin looked around, examining the latest clearing. There was only a small stream to provide water. It didn't seem large enough to hide edible fish or crabs; Gary wasn't sure if he should be pleased or upset. Austin had fished for crabs yesterday and then forced the boys to take turns slicing them open and cutting out the meat. Gary had felt unwell even *looking* at the crab. If Austin hadn't told him that the creature's ancestors came from Earth, Gary wouldn't have believed it. The crab had looked thoroughly alien.

"Kailee, Samantha, start looking for edible plants," Austin ordered. "Barry, Abdul, go find as much wood as possible. We need to build a fire."

"And do you think," Barry said, "that I am going to keep taking orders from you?"

Austin met his gaze squarely. "If you want to walk off into the countryside, alone, you may do so," he said. There was an icy resolution in his voice that made Gary cheer inwardly – and fret at the same time. Austin was not Yates. "I will not stop you if you want to leave. But you will have almost no chance of survival."

Barry stood upright, clenching his fists. "We are not your damned scouts," he snapped. "We are not here to take orders from *you*."

"Oh?" Austin said. "Would you like me to explain the reasoning behind them?"

His tone became mocking. "The girls have to collect edible vegetables because we need to eat," he said, sardonically. "You need to find wood so we can build a fire – *you*, in particular, because you are strong enough to carry large pieces of wood. Darrin and Gary are going to unpack the bags so we can get at our food supplies, I am going to hunt, to see what I can find."

He met Barry's eyes, a hint of challenge clearly visible in his expression. "Does that answer the question?"

Barry started to splutter. "You have no right to give us orders!"

"Then do nothing," Austin said. "Stay here. Starve when you run out of food. A few hundred years from now, they'll find your remains and wonder just who you were."

He looked from face to face. "Let me make something clear to you, if four days of being stranded *hasn't* taught you this already," he added. "I know what I'm doing. I have years of experience – as a farmer, as a scout, as a trainee Bush Ranger – to help me keep us all alive. You have less than two weeks experience on the surface of this planet, while all of your experience from Earth is useless at best and downright harmful at worst. If I wasn't with you, belly aches would be the least of your worries."

Gary knew that Austin was right. If he hadn't been there, Barry would probably have killed the others by now and taken the girls for himself. And then they would all have starved, if they hadn't been rescued...and they'd heard nothing to suggest that search parties had been dispatched from the city. Austin had pointed out that there wasn't much the city could do – they didn't have the aircraft or manpower to carry out a proper search – but it still chilled Gary to know that they'd effectively been abandoned. If they didn't make it back on their own, they would never make it back at all.

Austin's gaze came to rest on Barry. "Do as I tell you and you might just get back to civilisation to complain about me," he added, coldly. "Or go off on your own and good luck to you."

"Perhaps *you* should go," Barry snapped back. "You're not listening to us!"

Gary felt his blood run cold.

————

Austin had been told, once, that stupidity was a capital crime. The universe issued the punishment and nothing, save only the compassion of the smarter, would stand in the way of the sentence being carried out. He hadn't really believed it at the time, but then he hadn't really met anyone genuinely stupid. The Scouts had been more argumentative than he liked to admit, yet there had been good reasons for their arguments. None of them had picked fights while struggling to survive.

But we could have called for help, he knew. They'd always had emergency beacons. It would have been quitting – Austin would sooner have been beaten half to death than acquire a reputation as a quitter – but at least they would have survived. Sometimes, knowing that they could have quit was all that had kept them going. Here, though, there was no emergency beacon, nothing to call help. They were completely on their own.

He looked at Barry and wondered, absently, just what sort of evolutionary pattern had allowed him to be born. None of the other immigrants to Meridian had shown so much raw stupidity...but then, they'd *known* that they were coming to set up a new home. If they had failed to learn how to overcome their new environment, they would have died. But Barry didn't seem to care about anything, apart from being in charge. What was the point of taking command if one didn't know what one was doing?

Maybe the incest taboo no longer holds strong, he thought, nastily. His uncle had told him that no one from Earth could be trusted completely. Their way of life was poor, to say the least, and completely incomprehensible to people who actually had to *work* to survive. The explanation he'd been given – too much insistence on rights rather than responsibilities – made no sense. *Maybe Barry's mother is also his aunt.*

But how could Barry think that *he* should be in charge?

Austin had been a Beaver, then a Scout, then a Scout Leader. He'd earned the latter through hard work, proving himself to the scouts he was supposed to lead. Other scouting branches might have the leaders appointed by the adults, but Meridian insisted on competitions that proved the leaders actually had what it took. Austin wouldn't have minded – much – if he'd been beaten, provided the defeat was actually *fair*. Barry, on the other hand...if he had done anything more than harassing his fellow students on Earth, Austin would have been very much surprised.

The nasty part of his mind pointed out that he *could* quit. He knew how to survive. It wouldn't take long to put a considerable distance between himself and the Earth-born, then hole up for the night and sleep. He could set out to reach the Jordan the following morning, leaving them to make it or starve on their own. It might torpedo his chances of becoming a Bush Ranger – abandoning people in trouble would be frowned upon by the older Rangers, who got to choose future candidates – but there would be no other consequences. He hadn't accepted an obligation to keep them alive.

There will come a time, his Scoutmaster had said, *when you will find yourself unable to continue. It will not be your fault. Sometimes, you will lose no matter how hard you struggle. At that point, you need to know how to fold them and learn from the experience.*

"Let me put it as simply as I can," he said, staring at Barry. God, he was ugly. Austin was pretty sure that he was the result of a flawed engineering program or poor breeding. "I know more than you about remaining alive out here. Why – exactly – should I listen to your whining?"

He felt his temper flare, but somehow managed to hold it in check. "You know nothing," he snapped, coldly. "If you are too stupid to learn from the person who does, you are too stupid to live. Do you understand me?"

Barry's face purpled. For a moment, Austin genuinely thought he was going to have a heart attack. "I am not your slave," he said. "I think we should all decide on what to do."

Austin snorted. "And how many of you know what you're doing out here?"

He watched Barry carefully, wondering if the oversized thug would throw a punch. Barry didn't *look* to have any training – although Austin knew better than to take that for granted – but if half the stories about Earth were true, Barry probably knew a lot about dirty fighting and nasty tricks. He was strong, definitely; Austin had seen him carrying huge pieces of wood back to the fire, his rippling muscles standing out against the thin shirt. If he wanted to fight...

But Austin had plenty of experience of his own. The Scouts had learned martial arts as well as more basic skills. Austin knew he wasn't the best – he still remembered with some embarrassment the Scoutmaster offering a large reward to anyone who managed to knock him down, back when he'd felt the troop was getting overconfident – but he was ready to fight if necessary.

I could kill him, he thought. It would be easy, once he unslung the rifle from his back. A quick shot through Barry's head and then...they could dump the body somewhere in the forest, leaving it for the wild animals to eat. And yet...he had no idea what would happen when they got back to civilisation. Killing someone in self-defence was no murder, but would it be considered self-defence? And besides, did Barry really deserve death?

"I can learn," Barry said, stubbornly.

Austin sighed. "All of you," he said, sharply. "Listen carefully."

He'd told them again and again, but it seemed that he had to repeat himself one more time. "I know what I'm doing," he said. "If you want to stay with me, you are welcome – but you will have to work to help us all survive. If not, you can go. Choose."

Once, years ago, the scoutmasters had made them read a book that featured a group of scouts who had crash-landed on an alien world. Austin had enjoyed it; the scoutmasters had told them, afterwards, to read the book with a critical eye and point out all the mistakes. The writer, it was clear, had known little about the dangers of unknown worlds; the scouts ate and drank without taking even the simplest precautions. But they'd never faltered in their determination to survive, even when attacked by alien cannibals. By the time they had finally been rescued by the Marines, they'd built a large settlement of their own.

But they'd never had any real internal conflicts. None of them had ever argued amongst themselves, let alone come to blows. It was funny, he realised, that the scouts had picked out all the bad habits – eating and drinking without testing first – and yet they'd missed the single greatest implausibility of all. How *could* the scouts *not* argue from time to time? And, coming to think of it, they'd had no girls. How could their settlement have survived?

He pushed the memory aside and faced the off-worlders squarely.

"Choose," he said.

———

Darrin watched in horror as Barry and Austin almost came to blows. Barry was wrong, he knew; there was no way they could survive without Austin. And yet...Barry would sooner fight than take orders, no matter the sense behind them. In hindsight, it was yet another problem with Earth's schools. They didn't teach children that there were times when they should obey orders.

"You can go," Barry said. He didn't seem concerned about anything, but his own determination to stay in control. "We'll stay here and survive."

"No," Darrin said. It took all he had just to say the word. His body was shaking, reluctant to move, but somehow he stepped forward until he was standing next to Austin. "You can go, if you like. We are going to stay."

Barry stared at him in shocked incomprehension. Had he thought that Darrin would support him, no matter what happened? Darrin felt a flicker of shame at just how often he had supported Barry over the past few months; he'd helped Barry play his tricks on the girls – and Gary – and then scrubbed the floor beside him. Barry had learned nothing from the experience – or from the whipping. Darrin...liked to think that he'd learned something, even if it was just a healthy prudence.

And besides, he *liked* Austin.

On Earth, someone with knowledge wouldn't share it. Fitz had grumbled, more than once, about co-workers who kept vital information to themselves, rather than sharing it with people who might need it. But Austin...he'd told them what he was doing, even tried to teach them how to cut up animals and survive in the wild. He wasn't using the knowledge to lord it over them, no matter what Barry thought. Austin was genuinely trying to help them survive.

And Barry...? All *he* wanted was power. Power to tell people what to do, power to make the girls bend to his will...he didn't even have any long-term plans. Even a gang lord was more inclined to think beyond his own selfish desires. Darrin cursed himself for spending time with Barry on the ship, time he could have spent getting to know the other boys – even Gary, nerd though he was. At least Gary had some common sense. Barry had none. Besides, Darrin might have shared interests with the other boys.

Abdul stepped up and stood beside them. A moment later, Kailee and Samantha joined him; in the end, even Gary stood with them. Barry glared at them, clenching and re-clenching his fists. Darrin braced himself for a fight – Barry was solid muscle, strong enough to take a great deal of pain without breaking down – but Barry stopped.

"Very well," he said, tightly.

Darrin stared at him. Giving up was not something Barry did often. Normally, he would prefer to fight even if there was no hope of victory. Now...Darrin had no idea how capable Austin or Abdul were, but if Barry fought he might win. Instead, he seemed to be backing down.

"If you stay, do as you are told," Austin said. There was no give in his voice at all. "Or go."

Barry nodded, silently.

Darrin watched as everyone relaxed, even though he had his doubts. Barry never showed common sense – and besides, if he did have any common sense, why pick the fight in the first place? He pushed the thought aside as Austin started to issue orders, sending Barry to find firewood alone. Maybe Austin thought that it had been suspiciously easy too; Darrin could imagine him trying to tire Barry out before they had to sleep. Perhaps they could do something to immobilise Barry...

He sucked in a breath, suddenly aware of his heartbeat pounding desperately in his chest. It could easily have turned into a fight – and Barry was still there, still waiting. It had been far too easy. Somehow, he was sure that trouble was still lying in wait for them.

High overhead, the skies began to darken. Moments later, he heard the first peal of thunder in the distance.

CHAPTER
THIRTY

They knew what the Empire owed them; they knew their rights. They believed they were entitled to food, drink and a place to live. But they didn't understand their responsibilities, or even the simple fact that the Empire could not take care of the billions of unemployed citizens on Earth indefinitely. Taking care of one person was easy; taking care of billions was pushing the Empire to breaking point.

> - Professor Leo Caesius, *Education and the Decline and Fall of the Galactic Empire*

Kailee looked up as the rain started to fall, cascading down on them in great droplets of cold water. It had been warm last time, she recalled, feeling oddly betrayed. Now, it was freezing cold. There was no point in trying to light a fire; instead, the ground was starting to turn to mud very quickly. They'd picked a bad place to set up camp for the night.

She eyed Barry as he stared up at the sky, water dripping down his face. Watching him confronting Austin had been the most terrifying thing she'd ever seen, knowing that she and Samantha would be the prizes of whoever won. Austin could have taken advantage of them and hadn't; she knew better than to think that Barry would show as much consideration of their feelings. Girls talked about boys; she knew enough about Barry's habits to know that he wouldn't respect her wishes, let alone be gentle. No girl ever wanted to be alone with him.

"We have to go to higher ground," Austin shouted. It was hard to hear him over the constant drumming of the rain, let alone the thunder. "We can't stay here!"

Kailee winced as brilliant light flashed high overhead, followed by another peal of thunder. From what Austin had said, the longer the delay between the lightning and the thunder, the further away the storm actually was. It sounded as though they were right in the midst of the storm. The clouds were so dark that it looked as though night had come early, rather than two or three hours away. Austin always insisted that they rest early enough to set up a fire and hunt for food while it was still light.

Gary stumbled to his feet, half-bent over as though he were trying to protect something. His reader, Kailee guessed; the small computers were meant to be waterproof, but no one took that for granted any longer. They'd certainly never even been out in the rain until they'd come to Meridian. She followed him, feeling cold water dripping through her hair and down onto her shirt; her nipples hardened at the touch. Cursing her own body, she scooped up her bag and wrapped her arms around herself, hoping to conceal her breasts. The last thing she needed was one of the boys taking it as an invitation.

The deluge only grew worse as they stumbled up the side of the mountain, trying to get out of the forest. Lightning flickered constantly overhead, casting eerie flashes of light over the scene. Brief moments of visibility were followed by moments of absolute darkness, leaving her terrified to move for fear of slipping and sliding down the hill. They kept moving upwards, but the trees still seemed to be surrounding them. For a moment, she was convinced that they were creeping closer in the darkness, before dismissing the entire thought as stupid. Trees didn't walk on their own, at least not outside bad entertainment flicks.

She gritted her teeth as she heard small animals running through the storm, always staying out of sight of the human interlopers. Squeaks and hisses echoed out of the darkness, scaring her at first before she forced herself to ignore them. Something big crashed through the forest and across their path, vanishing back into the darkness before Kailee could get more than a brief glance at it. The creature looked to be about the size of a large dog.

The landscape changed as they moved higher and higher, becoming a slope. Mud cascaded down from high overhead, making them slip and slide as they fought their way upwards. Kailee saw rocks and cliffs far below, just waiting for anyone unwary enough to fall down into the darkness. Water dropped from high overhead, then pooled on the leaves and fell down towards the ground. It splashed across her face, making her cry out in shock. For a moment, she'd been sure that someone had thrown water at her deliberately. It was a favoured trick of the boys at school.

A deer ran down through the woods, looked at them for a brief second, then ran onwards. Kailee wondered if Austin would take a shot at it, but the colonial boy seemed as miserable as the rest of them. Besides, she asked herself, would his rifle even *fire* in this weather? It seemed absurd to think that a weapon was useless in the rain, but her life was full of absurdities. Barry's attempt at challenging Austin was merely the latest in a long line.

"Keep moving," Austin shouted. The ground wasn't just turning to mud, it was turning into a swamp! "Don't stop for anything!"

Kailee forced herself onwards, keeping her eyes on the ground. It looked worse with each flash of lightning, leaving her wondering how long it was going to be before the mud started sliding in earnest. She looked at Abdul instead and saw him drenched, his clothes and bag soaked to the skin. He looked back at her and managed a tired smile, but nothing else. They were all pushed right to the limit. Even Barry seemed tired and drained.

They stopped when they came to a stream. Normally, Kailee suspected, the stream would be easy to jump across, but now it was a raging torrent falling down to the valley below. Austin hesitated, then forced his way across the stream and stopped on the far side. Gary followed him, looking more like a drowned rat than ever. If they hadn't already been drenched, Kailee realised, the tiny stream might have forced them to walk miles out of their way.

If we're not already out of our way, she thought. Austin hadn't been looking at his compass when he'd directed them to higher ground. *We might be retracing our steps.*

She stepped into the cold water and shivered, then forced herself to walk across the stream. It might have been small, but the running water pressed against her ankles, warning her to be very careful where she placed her feet. The slightest misstep might send her falling down the stream to her death. On the far side, she waited for Samantha and the others, then resumed the trek after Austin. Lightning seemed to be flaring almost constantly now, as if the sky was ablaze with brilliant arc lights. She lowered her gaze as the rain – somehow, impossibly – intensified.

Darrin stumbled past her and caught Austin's arm. "Shouldn't we find shelter?"

Kailee thought that was a very good idea, but Austin shook his head. "There's none to be found," he shouted back. Thunder blocked whatever he'd said next from Kailee's ears. "We have to keep moving."

The climb seemed to grow harder as they walked higher, the rain beating down against her exposed face. Kailee found it hard to care, now, that her shirt was clinging to her breasts, or that Barry and Abdul were behind her. All that mattered was somehow keeping going until the rain came to an end, if it ever did. It felt as if the entire ocean was being dumped on their heads.

There was a cry behind her. Kailee turned, just in time to see Samantha slip and fall down the slope. The mud moved beneath Kailee's feet, forcing her to scramble away before she could be caught in the growing mudslide, but she couldn't take her eyes off Samantha falling into the darkness. A slap struck her buttocks, concentrating her mind. Austin pulled her up towards him, then shouted in her ear.

"Keep moving," he snapped. "I'll go after her!"

Kailee hesitated, then stumbled up the slope after Gary.

———

Darrin watched in horror as the mud started to slide down the slope, taking Samantha with it. The ground kept shifting beneath his own feet, as if he was about to fall too; somehow, he kept himself on his feet long enough to see Austin turn and head down the slope himself. He was going after Samantha! Darrin hesitated, unsure of what to do, then followed Austin down the slope. Halfway down, he slipped and landed on his bottom, then started to slide the rest of the way.

"Idiot," Austin shouted at him. "Get back to the others!"

"I'm not leaving you here alone," Darrin shouted back at him. He wasn't sure where *that* feeling had come from, apart from the simple desire to ensure that Austin – and Samantha – were safe. But Samantha had vanished somewhere in the darkness, while the mudslide was gathering speed. He had a brief vision of rocks, illuminated briefly by the darkness, waiting for him. Then the mud seemed to alter course and he fell...

He struck water hard enough to make him cry out. He'd only tried to swim once, in the lake after they'd killed and eaten the deer, and he'd been naked at the time. Now...he kicked and thrashed, forcing his way back to the surface. The pool seemed deep enough for him to drown, if he didn't manage to make it out. His clothes, utterly waterlogged, were pulling him down towards the bottom...

A hand caught him and hauled him to the poolside. "That was damn stupid," Austin's voice said. Darrin was too busy coughing and hacking to take any notice. Austin slapped him on the back, hard enough to force him to cough up the remaining water, then helped him to his feet. "Can you see Samantha?"

Darrin looked around. The ground was muddy; for an insane moment, he wondered if he'd somehow been moved far from the pool because he couldn't see it. And then he realised that the pool was covered with a thin coating of mud, enough to make it invisible to anyone who wasn't looking for it specifically. He could have walked right back into it without noticing. But, in the gloom, there was no sign of the girl.

"No," he said, softly. Had *he* distracted Austin from looking for her? "Where is she?"

"I wish I knew," Austin said. He started to inch forward, testing each footstep as he moved. "I think she will have been pushed down the gorge, but I'm not sure."

Darrin winced. In the half-light, they might be utterly unable to find the missing girl; she might be stunned, her body buried under the mud, or she might be dead. They'd be better off waiting for daylight, except that leaving her alone for so long might ensure she was dead when they finally found her. He found himself praying as he followed Austin, praying that they found Samantha alive and that it wasn't his fault that Austin had been delayed. But he knew that the latter prayer was unlikely to be granted.

The rain seemed to lessen for a long moment – long enough for him to hope that it was over – then started to cascade down, heavier than ever before. Visibility shrank to a bare metre or two ahead of them, whenever the lightning flashed. Austin almost fell down the gorge when the ground moved beneath his feet; Darrin barely caught him in time. The mud was covering very nasty-looking rocks, he realised suddenly. They were in danger of falling and breaking bones.

"This is useless," Austin shouted at him. "Where *is* she?"

Darrin looked up. The slope was hidden in the darkness – and so were the rest of the party. He wondered, briefly, if Steve and Li had been rescued, before deciding that it was unlikely. Surely, even if only one aircraft had been assigned to the search, they would have heard *something* and fired off the flare. He looked back down the gorge and caught sight of something red. His blood ran cold when he saw it. Samantha had been wearing a red shirt when she fell.

Austin glanced at him, then led the way down to where Samantha's body was lying. At first, she seemed merely stunned, but up close it was clear that her neck had been broken. Darrin felt a chill running down his neck as he saw her sightless eyes, staring at nothing. She was dead.

He shuddered. He'd barely known Samantha; like the other girls, she had tried to keep herself to herself, or at least away from the boys. And who could blame her, really? But he knew almost nothing about her and that felt wrong. Had she liked the same bands he'd liked? Had she had dreams for the future, like Kailee and Gary, or had she thought that she could just drift through life like himself? He wondered, helplessly, if she'd had a boyfriend or a protector – or if she'd tried to keep herself pure.

Her death bothered him. But, oddly, not having known much about her bothered him more.

She'd been attractive, he knew. He'd certainly stared at her. He'd...

He shook his head. She'd been more than just a pretty face and excellent body. But now she was dead.

"I'm sorry," Austin said, quietly. The colonial boy hadn't known Samantha at all, but he sounded broken up too. "She deserved better."

Darrin wondered, absently, why Austin felt that way. Had he talked to Samantha, even though the girl wouldn't have willingly spent time alone with another man? Or did the locals place more value on life than the Earth-born? The latter was probably the answer; Darrin knew, as well as anyway, that life was cheap on Earth. Rowdy Yates CityBlock alone had more residents than Meridian. But here...

"I know," he said, understanding – finally – all that had been stolen from the children of Earth. Yates had tried to tell him, but Darrin hadn't really understood. Not until now. "She deserved much better."

Austin reached down and closed Samantha's eyes, then looked back up the gorge. Darrin followed his gaze. Water was cascading down, heavier than ever. Climbing back up, Darrin realised, was likely to be hellish, but what other choice did they have? If they followed the gorge down, wherever it went, they would wind up miles from the rest of the group? He looked over at Austin and saw grim resolve written over his face. The colonial boy, apparently, had no intention of giving up.

"We may have to wait here until morning," Austin said. "God alone knows where the gorge will come to an end."

Darrin winced. Night was coming on rapidly. Even if the storm came to an end and the clouds faded away, they would still be trapped in darkness. There wouldn't even be any flickers of lightning to guide their footsteps. They would have to wait until morning before trying to find the rest of the party. Darrin wondered, suddenly, if the rest of the party would survive the night. They were with Barry, while Darrin and Austin were somewhere else. Barry would have his chance to take over...

Abdul will stop him, Darrin told himself. But he didn't really believe it.

"There's nothing we can do about that now," Austin said, when Darrin told him his fears. Somehow, falling down the gorge together had removed the last barriers between them. "Tell me; why do you tolerate such people on Earth?"

Darrin shook his head, wordlessly. He had no answer. They'd been lectured, time and time again, on the importance of not discriminating between people, but the whole series of lectures had just seemed a waste of time. Wasn't there a difference between picking on someone for something they couldn't help and picking on them because of their actions? Barry could have been taught the error of his ways long before he'd become a hulking brute, if someone had cared to try. But no one had bothered.

"It just seems stupid," Austin confessed. "What does Barry have to offer the world?"

"I know," Darrin whispered.

Barry had nothing to offer...but he could do damage. Gary had been broken by him – Darrin shivered when he remembered just how little resistance Gary had offered, even when he'd been humiliated – while the other boys had just been glad it wasn't them who had been targeted. And he might damage the girls too, given half a chance. Darrin was sure that most of his boasting was nothing more than lies. No one had time to have that much sex, not when he was also spending time bullying the weak, but being forced into sex had to be bad for the girls. Maybe *that* was why his mother spent so much time drunk out of her mind. She had no real freedom and independence and she knew it.

From the outside, Earth had to look like a nightmare, a place where common sense had been forgotten and the strong were allowed to run wild, bullying the weak. Maybe it had all made sense at one point, but it didn't now. How could it?

And yet, how could it be changed?

"I'm sorry," he said, unsure of just what he was apologising for. Not stopping Barry from using a gun to vandalise a car? Or for not taking Austin seriously at first. "I didn't know."

"Learn from the experience," Austin said. he clapped Darrin on the shoulder, then motioned to a rocky overhang. "We'll hide here until the sun rises, then start looking for them. They can't have gone *that* far."

Darrin privately hoped that he was right. He certainly wanted to believe it. But if Barry had decided to act up, the group might have scattered into the darkness. And then they would be impossible to find, even in broad daylight.

But they had to *try*. After all they'd been through, Darrin no longer wanted to give up.

CHAPTER
THIRTY-ONE

Furthermore, the Empire had few scientists who were pushing back the boundaries of research and development. There were relatively few minds willing to question and fewer societies and universities willing to assist them.
- Professor Leo Caesius, *Education and the Decline and Fall of the Galactic Empire*

Gary pulled himself to his feet and looked around, wearily. They'd climbed through the darkness until they'd finally found a clearing, just as the rain had finally come to an end. The ground had been muddy, but they'd just collapsed anyway, even Barry. They'd been too tired to do anything else. He felt a dull pain in his stomach, reminding him that none of them had eaten since yesterday lunchtime, as he moved. And then he looked around. There was no sign of Austin or Darrin.

He felt his blood run cold as he looked at Barry. The bully was asleep, but that wouldn't last – and when he awoke, who knew *what* he would do. Barry wasn't the type of person to learn from experience, no matter how harsh; Austin convincing the others to follow him would be something to avenge, not something to accept. Gary felt the gun at his belt, wondering if he dared shoot Barry now. But experience had taught him that the forces of law and order were never on *his* side. He could kill Barry and no doubt he would be punished for it.

Shoot him anyway, a voice insisted, at the back of his mind. It was the safest course of action, wasn't it? But what would Abdul do? Or Austin, when he finally caught up with them? Gary refused to believe that the colonial boy was dead. Austin, whatever else one could say about him, was a survivor. It wasn't true of anyone from Earth.

Gary pushed the thought aside and opened Kailee's pack. The girls had been tasked with carrying the food, giving them a lighter load than the boys. Inside, the cooked meat seemed to have spoiled. Gary took a sniff, then shook his head firmly. The exposure to water probably hadn't done it any good at all. He took the meat out of the pack and eyed it dubiously, then froze. Barry was awake and looking at him.

"Ah...the meat isn't edible," Gary said, before he could stop himself. He cursed inwardly a moment later. If the meat was definitely no longer edible, Barry eating it would solve a great many problems. "It stinks."

Barry pulled himself to his feet and stamped over to Gary. Like Gary, his clothes were damp and covered in mud. There was no point in changing, Gary knew. There was nothing to change *into*. All their other clothes were dripping wet too.

"So it would seem," Barry growled. He took a long sniff of the meat, then dropped it on the muddy ground. "Go look for plants we can eat."

Gary obeyed, surprised. It was such a *reasonable* order. If the meat was inedible, they would starve if they couldn't find enough edible plants. Austin had warned them that plants alone wouldn't keep them going, but there didn't seem to be any choice. *This* clearing didn't have a stream, let alone a pond. Pushing the thoughts aside, he worked his way through the forest, picking up plants he thought were edible. Some of the mushrooms tasted lovely when cooked, he knew, but he didn't dare take chances. Austin might be able to tell the difference between poisonous and safe mushrooms; Gary knew better than to take the risk. He simply couldn't say for sure about anything.

When he returned, he discovered that Barry had managed to light a fire and start drying their clothes. Abdul and Kailee were awake, both watching Barry carefully. Gary met Kailee's eyes and saw the same fear he felt himself written on her face. They both knew that it was only a matter of time before Barry reverted to type.

"Not good enough," Barry proclaimed, as he examined Gary's findings. "Go find some more."

Gary obeyed, glad of the chance to escape. He considered, briefly, just walking away completely, but he knew he didn't have the nerve – or the survival skills. Austin would have been fine on his own, Gary was sure, yet he knew that *he* didn't have the skills to remain alive on his own. He walked through a different part of the forest, picking at edible leaves and plants, silently praying that he would hear Austin coming towards them. Even *Darrin* would have been welcome. After Darrin had stood up to Barry, Gary had realised that there was something worthwhile hidden under the boy's skin. But it had been very well hidden.

He stopped as he saw something moving under a bush. Curiosity led him to take a look; he peeked under the bush and saw a small animal struggling, its head caught in a vine. A rabbit, if he recalled correctly. He caught the animal and pulled it free, then held it firmly against his chest as he walked carefully back to the campsite. Barry laughed, then took the rabbit from Gary's unresisting arms and snapped it's neck like a twig. Gary looked at Barry's face and shuddered. He'd *enjoyed* killing the helpless creature.

"Cut this...thing up," Barry ordered. He nodded towards the pack holding the knives. "And then cook us breakfast."

Gary forced down his disgust as he started to work. He hadn't had much luck slicing up the crab, or taking pieces of meat from the deer they'd killed, but the nasty look in Barry's eye told him that he'd better do a good job. Barry was striding to and fro, his gaze moving from Gary to Kailee. Somehow, Gary was sure that things were about to become much worse.

"We can survive out here," Barry said, as Gary hung the strips of meat above the fire. He was painfully aware that Austin would have done a much better job. As it was, he had to stay close to the fire, just to make sure that the meat didn't fall into the flames. "Why should we go back at all?"

He'd cracked, Gary realised. The experience of finally being balked, of finally being told that he would be held to account, had shattered what remained of Barry's common sense. Gary knew that they'd been immensely lucky to get the rabbit – he wasn't sure how the creature had managed to trap itself – but they couldn't survive out in the wild indefinitely. Sooner or later, they would eat the wrong thing or injure themselves and then they would need medical attention.

"Civilisation," Kailee said. She hunched slightly, her damp clothes clinging to her skin as she leaned closer to the fire. "Everything we need to survive."

"Everything we need to survive is right here," Barry said. There was an unholy confidence in his voice that sent chills running down Gary's spine. "Food, drink, fire...why go back to the city, let alone back to Earth?"

"You can stay here if you like," Abdul said, as Gary started to divide up the rabbit. "I want to get back to the city."

Barry walked back to the fire, then glared down at Gary. "Make sure that Kailee gets the best portions," he directed. "She's going to need to keep up her strength."

Shaking, Gary agreed. The rabbit didn't taste bad at all – he would have been pleased with it, under other circumstances – but he could barely swallow. He knew what was coming and it wasn't going to be pleasant. Barry gulped his down with every evidence of enjoyment, then tossed the leaf he'd used as a plate onto the fire. Gary watched it burn up like his hopes, time and time again. He silently cursed whoever had decided to send Barry away from Earth to the deepest, darkest pits of hell. They deserved far worse for what they'd done to him...and to Kailee.

He met the girl's eyes and knew that she knew what was coming.

"We can live out here," Barry said. "All of us, working together."

"Under you, of course," Abdul sneered. "What do you know about keeping us alive...?"

Barry threw himself at Abdul with staggering speed. Gary stared in horror; Barry had shown a sadistic precision whenever he'd picked on Gary, but now he was fighting savagely, pummelling Abdul into a pulp. Abdul was bigger and stronger than Gary had ever hoped to be, yet he was tiny compared to Barry. Barry hammered him into the ground, fists moving backwards and forwards like pistons. Blood spurted and splashed down onto the muddy ground.

Gary watched, unable to move, as Abdul's body hit the ground. His face was a bruised and bloody mess, one of his arms was definitely broken and he was coughing up blood. Barry stood over him, smirking openly.

Gary had always known that Barry wasn't just bored when he picked on someone – he actually enjoyed it – but this was worse. Barry, without any restraints on his behaviour, had beaten Abdul to death.

"Well," Barry said, as he raised his foot and held it above Abdul's head. "*That* was fun."

He pushed down, hard. There was a crushing sound and a final spurt of blood, then nothing.

Gary vomited, violently. He threw up the rabbit he'd eaten, then whatever had been left in his stomach from yesterday, then...it felt like he'd thrown up everything he'd eaten since the day he was born. His stomach hurt badly as he hacked and coughed, spewing up...he wasn't sure *what* he was spewing up. And Barry looked at him and laughed.

"Stay there," Barry ordered. He picked up one of Abdul's shirts and used it to wipe the blood off his hands, then looked around. "Where is she?"

Gary blinked in surprise. Kailee was gone.

————

Kailee had known that Barry was going to try something as soon as she realised that both Austin and Darrin were gone. One skill that girls learnt in the megacities was how to read boys – and she knew that Barry lusted for her, even though he was too scared of Austin to risk starting a fight. Not that he would ever have *admitted* being scared of Austin, she knew; Barry had probably told himself that he was biding his time. He wasn't the sort of person to admit to being scared.

She watched in horror as Barry started to pummel Abdul, knowing that it meant he believed that the last restraints on his behaviour, such as they were, had vanished. And then she pulled herself to her feet and slipped into the forest. Being eaten by a fox or one of the more dangerous creatures would be preferable, she felt, to spending any time with Barry. His mad delusions about living in the forest, away from civilisation, would get them all killed. Or, in her case, a fate worse than death.

The nightmare rent and tore at her mind as she ran. He might call her his wife, but she knew what she would be, just like most of the other women in the CityBlock. She would be his chattel, his slave. The schools might prattle on and on about female rights – the right to live as they pleased, the right to marry whom they wished – but she knew that the law would do nothing about an abusive husband. And not having a husband could be far worse. But now...

She ran harder, ducking and dodging her way through the trees, as she heard someone come running after her. Barry – it had to be Barry – was crashing his way through the branches, giggling to himself as he gave chase. Kailee pushed herself right to the limit, hoping that Barry would give up or they would run into Samantha, Austin and Darrin. Surely, they weren't dead. But if Barry found Samantha...he'd just set himself up with two wives. It wasn't as if anyone was going to stop him.

Something caught at her foot and she stumbled, then fell face-down into the mud. There was a shout of triumph from behind her as she rolled over, just in time to see Barry come up, his face twisted into a leer. The bastard wasn't even breathing hard. Kailee stared up at him, knowing that her luck had finally run out. She was going to be forced to let him have her, to violate her body, to invade her very core...every girl on Earth faced the same nightmare, even if they had a powerful protector. After all, that protector had to be paid something for his services.

She wished, desperately, that she'd spent more time listening to Janet – or that the older woman had come with them on the flight. But she hadn't. And even if she had, what could she have done? Barry was stronger than Janet, certainly stronger than Kailee. And his reputation suggested that he wouldn't hesitate to beat her bloody if it was what it took to make her surrender and open her legs.

Barry's leer grew wider. "Get undressed," he ordered. "Now. Make a show of it."

Kailee swallowed. She had prided herself on never being naked with a boy, never allowing them to touch her body. It had been kept pure for her planned career, but now...she hesitated, unsure of what to do. Surrender to him and hope he didn't make it hurt, or fight, knowing that he might make it hurt anyway. Sex didn't have to hurt, she knew, there were girls who claimed to enjoy it. But there were also boys who delighted in making the girls hurt, enjoying the power they wielded over their victims. And Barry was very definitely one of *those*.

I will not let him use me like this, she vowed, mentally.

"Come on," Barry said, impatiently. "I want to see your body."

Kailee glared at him, but stood and started to remove her shirt. Midway through, she remembered some of the odder sex education videos they'd been shown and began to move her hips, drawing his attention to her chest. She lifted her shirt briefly, then lowered it; a moment later, she removed it completely. Barry's eyes were fixed on her breasts, admiring them. Kailee shuddered in revulsion at the naked lust on his face. He snickered; she realised, in horror, that he was fully aware of her feelings. But the fact she didn't want to undress only made it more exiting for him.

She pushed her hands into her pants, then hesitated. Barry's expression urged her to continue, mocking all of her dreams of remaining untouched until she became an actress. Feeling a sense of bitterness that merged with her vulnerability, she unsnapped her pants and lowered them to her knees. The panties she'd brought all the way from Earth were already damp, clinging to her flesh. Part of her wondered if that was actually good for her.

But the rest of her knew it didn't matter.

Barry hastily undid his pants as she pulled down the panties and stood, naked, in front of him. She wanted to cover her breasts and groin, but she knew that he would only take it as a sign of fear and enjoy it. Instead, she forced herself to stand upright, proudly displaying everything she had. But as his eyes left trails of slime over her body, she knew that it wouldn't be enough to stop him. He wanted everything she had.

He stepped up to her...and she saw her chance. She brought her knee up as hard as she could, but Barry twisted to one side, just in time. Kailee realised her mistake an instant before his hand slapped into her face, knocking her to the muddy ground. The pain and blood in her mouth mocked her. Barry was *fond* of taking girls against their will. He knew all the tricks. He'd probably known that she was biding her time from the moment she'd started to undress.

"Slut," Barry said. Kailee tasted blood as he rolled her over, pushing her face-first into the mud. "Bitch. Ice Princess. Let me show you what a real man feels like."

Kailee forced herself to speak. "You can never get a woman to make love to you willingly," she said. "You..."

She gagged as he pushed her face-first into the mud. It was suddenly impossible to breathe...did he mean to *kill* her? Maybe that would be better than being his 'wife.' She thought for a moment of Aunt Lillian, of the bitterness that echoed through her voice whenever she talked about men, and wondered if her family would ever know what had happened to her. Had they even expected her to come home?

And then Barry pulled her head out of the mud. She cried out as he felt his fingers between her legs, then he mounted and entered her from behind. Kailee couldn't struggle any longer, even when it began to hurt. All she could do was lie there and take it. A deep burning shame spread through her as he spent himself. He'd *used* her, just like an object, just like something that didn't matter. She felt filthy and violated and knew that she would never be clean again.

Barry rolled off her and stood up, donning his trousers casually. Kailee just lay there, wishing that the ground would open up and swallow her. She hated him at that moment, she wanted to kill him...but she knew that she could never beat him in a fight. It wasn't as if weapons that might even the odds were available on Earth. Rape might not be a crime, or at least a crime that was actually *punished*...and yet owning a weapon was considered a serious offense.

No wonder Austin finds us so disgusting, she thought, bitterly.

"On your feet," Barry ordered. He reached down, pulled Kailee up and slapped her ass hard when she stumbled and almost fell again. "Don't bother to get dressed. We're going to have some more fun soon enough."

CHAPTER
THIRTY-TWO

In effect, the Empire was not only stagnant, it was regressing. Much of its technology would be familiar to someone from the early days of space exploration, while the promise of everything from gravimetric technology to focused force fields was largely unfulfilled.

- Professor Leo Caesius, *Education and the Decline and Fall of the Galactic Empire*

Barry was going to rape Kailee.

Gary watched him run into the forest, hoping that Kailee would manage to escape, but knowing that she would not. Kailee wasn't anything like as fast or tough as Barry – and besides, she had nowhere to go. None of them had anywhere to go. The compass had been lost with Austin and, even if they'd had it, Gary had no idea which way to go. They'd been forced right out of their way by the thunderstorm. For all he knew, they might accidentally start walking back towards the crash site.

Fear kept him immobile for long minutes. Barry had told him not to move. Gary even found it hard to breathe. Long experience told him that it was always worse if he didn't do what he was told, even if it was just standing still and waiting for the pain to begin. Submission had been beaten into him, time and time again, until Barry could expect him to sit and wait for him to return. He could run; he hadn't been tied to a tree...

But he was held in place by mental bonds that held him tighter than any rope.

Why was he so weak? He barely remembered the first day of school, but surely he hadn't been so isolated then...or had he? The government mandated that all children had to start school from the age of four; earlier, perhaps, if both parents worked. He recalled entering a large room and trying to play with the other kids, only to discover that he was isolated and picked on by the bullies. What had happened to make Moe and Barry such effective bullies when they were children? And what had happened to make Gary so *weak*?

Pain, he thought, as he looked over at Abdul's body. Barry was normally precise, hurting his target with the minimum of effort, but when he'd fought Abdul he'd lost control completely and beaten the other boy to death with his bare hands. Gary felt sick, wondering bitterly if Barry was going to come back and kill him too. If he did...could he resist? But resistance was always futile.

He heard...*something* in the distance, something human. A cry for help, perhaps, barely audible over the ever-present insect buzzing. Kailee was being hurt, he knew; he'd heard enough to know that Barry *liked* it to hurt. He shuddered and stared down at the muddy ground, then up into the fire. Barry had gone completely mad. Did he really believe that they could hide out in the countryside indefinitely?

A chill ran down Gary's neck as he realised that Barry might be right. Meridian's settlements were expanding slowly, slowly enough to allow Barry to hide in the undeveloped countryside. He could feed himself, if he were careful – and if he had two others with him, serving as his servants. But it wouldn't be very pleasant or healthy. There were too many plants that might kill or injure an unwary eater. And...Gary shuddered, again. It would be a nightmare for all of them.

He felt the gun at his waist, wondering how he'd managed to forget it. If he'd used it, he could have saved Abdul's life...and then what? Could he have killed Barry? But he knew that Barry was not the type of person to be balked easily. If he'd threatened Barry, he would have had to carry out the threat. Carefully, he drew the gun out of his belt and examined it in the bright sunlight. It looked so small and simple, smaller than he'd realised. And yet it was a deadly weapon.

Yates could probably have told him chapter and verse about it, if he'd still been alive, or Austin could have taught him how to shoot. But he was alone. Gary had never thought to use Earth's datanet to study guns – why bother, when he'd known he would never see one in his life? He'd been wrong...the gun seemed simple enough, but he didn't even know if it were loaded. He peered down at it, trying to determine how it went together. The trigger was obvious, yet was there a safety? Something to keep the gun from firing?

Yates kept it in his belt, Gary told himself. *He could have shot himself in the balls if he wasn't careful.*

He heard, in the distance, someone scream. It had to be Kailee. Gary's imagination, aided by what he'd heard of Barry's boasting and some darker videos he'd watched on the datanet, filled in the details. Kailee had been beaten, then forced into submission. Or maybe Barry had...he shook his head, trying to banish the visions. It didn't work. He liked Kailee, yet he was a helpless witness to whatever Barry intended to do to her.

The gun suddenly felt heavy in his hand. He wasn't helpless. He could do something. But he would have to force himself to *move.*

He stood up. The motion seemed to tire him. Somehow, he managed to stumble over to look at Abdul's body, feeling an odd sense of loss. Perhaps he should have tried to be friends with the other boys, knowing that Yates would have stopped Barry from attacking them. But he'd lost the skill of making friends long ago, back when it had become clear that anyone who even spoke to him risked being attacked by Barry or Moe. Even if Barry *hadn't* won the competition, Gary knew he would never have been able to talk to the other boys. No doubt Darrin would have picked up the slack and bullied him remorselessly.

"I'm sorry," he muttered, although he wasn't sure if he was talking to Abdul or himself. "I'm truly sorry."

He froze. Someone was crashing his way through the trees towards him. Gary gripped the gun in one hand, holding it as if it were a talisman against evil. Somehow, it gave him courage and determination; he understood, finally, just why everyone on the planet carried a gun. They *knew* that there was no such thing as physical equality, no matter what the teachers told them; they *knew* that they needed guns and technology to even the odds. Gary had known the first part ever since he'd been picked on for the first time, but he'd never been taught to articulate the second. He silently cursed Earth's schools under his breath as he saw someone come into view under the trees. They'd ingrained helplessness into most of their pupils.

Barry stepped into the clearing, an ugly leer of triumph spread over his face. Behind him, Kailee was naked...and badly bruised. There were marks all over her body, mud dripping down to the ground, but he could see enough to know that she'd been beaten. He tore his gaze off her breasts with an effort – she'd been hurt enough that she didn't even *try* to cover them – and met Barry's stare. The look of self-satisfaction on the bully's face made him feel sick.

"That was fun," Barry announced. "Pack up the bags. We're..."

He broke off as Gary lifted the gun and pointed it at his forehead. "Where did you get that?"

Gary held the gun as tightly as he dared. The look of sudden fear in Barry's eyes was exhilarating. For the first time in his life, he held the power – not Barry, with his fists, or the teachers, threatening to mark down his grades if he didn't shut up and do as they wanted. He understood, suddenly, the impulses that drove Barry and so many others on Earth. They had no real control over their own lives, but as long as they controlled others, they could forget about having no control themselves. What did fists matter, he asked himself, when he held a gun?

"I found it in the bag," Gary lied, smoothly. "What did you do to her?"

Barry gave him a long considering look. "Do you want a turn with her?"

Gary almost pulled the trigger there and then. Barry, deliberately or otherwise, had touched a nerve. Gary had resented his virginity almost as long as he'd known what he was missing, but there had been no way to lose it. He was too isolated and unpopular to ever hope to get a girl into bed, while the brothels were too dangerous for someone like him. Did the gun give him enough power to simply *take* what he wanted?

The thought seemed natural for a long chilling moment, then his mind revolted against it. He was not Barry – but he was thinking just like the bullying bastard. How could he take Kailee against her will? It would be wrong, morally wrong...the look on her face told him just how wrong it would be. He would be better remaining a virgin for the rest of his life than doing that to *anyone.*

"No," he said. It was a lie. Almost a lie. "I don't want her."

Barry smirked. "Do you want me instead?"

Gary almost threw up at the thought. Homosexuals weren't discriminated against on Earth, but he had never been interested in other men. And, even if he had been, he would certainly not have been interested in *Barry.* The thought of Barry and sex was enough to put him off sex for life! He felt the gun shake in his hand, sweat staining his palms. How *could* anyone say something like that?

Barry's smirk grew wider. "So tell me," he said. "What now?"

"Shoot him," Kailee said, dully. The life and light seemed to be gone from her eyes. "Kill him."

"Shut up, bitch," Barry said. Oddly, his voice remained calm and even. "This is *men's* business."

He looked at Gary, holding his eyes. "What are you going to do now?"

The bastard was right, Gary realised. What *was* he going to do? Barry was too dangerous and untrustworthy to be kept around. But if Gary ordered him to run into the forest...Barry would come at them in the darkness, when none of them could see a thing. But, even after such a scare, there was no way Gary could relax near Barry. The moment he closed his eyes, Barry would jump him, take the gun and then...kill him. Or merely beat the living daylights out of him.

"Kill him," Kailee repeated. "*Please.*"

"You're not a killer," Barry said. He somehow managed to project reassurance into his voice, even though he had to know that Gary wouldn't believe a word he said. "Do you really want to see another person die out here?"

Gary shuddered. He'd seen violence – he'd been the target of violence – but he'd never seen anyone die until he'd come to Meridian. Yates and the others in the plane, Abdul...he shuddered again, wondering what had happened to Austin, Darrin and Samantha. Had they been killed too? Would they spend the rest of their days wandering the forest, unable to find their way back to the settlements? Or would they kill each other, here and now.

"Go," Gary said, jerking the gun. "Run. Leave us."

Barry smiled, although it didn't touch his eyes. "Do you really think you can survive out here without me?"

Garry felt a sudden upswing of bitterness that surprised him. It hadn't been *Barry* who had helped them survive. It had been *Austin*, who had stuck with them even though Barry had sniped at him constantly. Gary wouldn't really have blamed Austin for walking off and abandoning the Earth-born in the countryside, not really. It said a great deal about the colonial boy that he'd stuck with them. But now they'd been separated...

"I don't think we can survive out here *with* you," Gary said. Barry was strong, strong enough to help, but he could never be trusted. "Go."

"You just want Kailee all to yourself," Barry said. "Or should I take her with me? Or should she go off on her own too?"

Gary felt his anger flare again. "Shut up and go," he ordered. "Now!"

Barry met his eyes. "You're no killer," he said. "I've known you for *years*. You've never had the nerve to fight anyone, even someone as weak as yourself. You won't kill me."

He was right, Gary knew. Gary had *never* been violent, let alone a killer. But fighting had seemed so futile when he couldn't win. There were boys at school who would fight anyway, kicking and biting even though they knew they would lose, yet Gary had never been one of them. The gun seemed to waver in his hand...

Barry leapt forward. Gary pulled the trigger. There was a loud BANG and Barry let out a curse, staggering forwards and collapsing onto the ground. Gary almost dropped the pistol – the recoil had *hurt*, something that wasn't shown on the entertainment flicks – and stumbled backwards. Blood was leaking from a wound in Barry's chest.

Gary stared in disbelief. All the entertainment flicks had shown bullets missing their targets or causing instant death. Gary had never really questioned what he'd seen. But now, watching Barry thrashing about on the muddy ground, he found himself wondering just how many other lies they'd been told. But there was no one to ask. Instead, he watched as Barry started to pull himself forwards.

"Bastard," Barry managed. His breathing was becoming ragged. "Help."

There was a howl of incoherent rage from behind him. Gary looked up, just in time to see Kailee picking up a branch and bringing it down on Barry's head, time and time again. Barry let out a gasping sound and collapsed completely, but Kailee didn't stop until his head had been smashed into a bloody pulp. Gary watched, feeling a strange mixture of horror and gleeful pleasure, as Barry died. Blood spilled, dirtying the ground. It was over.

He'd never thought to see one of his tormentors killed. It had seemed unbelievable that Yates had flattened Barry with a single punch, stranger too to watch as Barry and Darrin were lashed. And yet...Barry was now dead. The horror faded away, replaced by a strange numbness that pervaded his body. It was definitely over. Barry would never torment anyone again.

Kailee dropped the branch and fell to her knees beside Barry's body. Gary stared at her for a long moment, then reached out and enfolded her in his arms. It wasn't sexual, even though she was naked. He wanted to reassure her, to tell her that they would be safe. But he couldn't find the words, even as she started to sob into his arms.

Barry was dead. The thought kept running through his mind. Barry was dead. Barry was dead. It was over.

He held Kailee tightly, trying to push away the memories. But they kept coming; Barry picking on him for the first time, then the second, then thousands of times, all blurring together into a nightmare that had lasted twelve years. He'd worked hard to escape the CityBlock because of Barry and Moe, because he had known that – one day – they would kill him. But he'd never dreamed that it would end on a planet thousands of light years from Earth. It sounded like a bad fantasy – or a banned entertainment flick. And yet it had happened.

Kailee stiffened against him suddenly, then pushed him away. Gary understood; he moved backwards then stood, giving her some room. He'd been through hell, but it would be far worse for her. Walking back to the fire, he pushed in some more wood, then picked up the crab shell and headed off to find water. There was a stream not too far from the clearing.

A weight seemed to fall off his shoulders as it sank in. Barry was no longer looming in the background, ready to pick on Gary the moment Yates or Austin were looking the other way. And Moe was thousands of light years away. There had been others – Darrin hadn't always treated him very well too – but watching Barry die had given him a strange kind of confidence. He pushed the gun back into his belt – somehow, he hadn't even been aware that he'd still been carrying it – and smiled to himself. Whatever else happened, he vowed, he would never let himself be bullied again.

The day seemed much brighter than before, he realised, as he knelt by the stream and scooped up some water. It *looked* clean, but he couldn't tell for sure. Carrying it back to the clearing, he placed the shell on the ground and added a purification tablet. A quick check revealed that there were only four tablets left in the emergency kit.

Next time, he told himself, *make sure you bring a full camping kit.*

It was funny, he realised, how the trip had turned from a nightmare to something almost enjoyable. Now Barry was gone...he understood, suddenly, just why Austin had had that light in his eye when he talked about the Scouts. Maybe there was a scout troop in the city he could join. Or something akin to it in space, if he managed to find a berth on a freighter.

Kailee was still huddled on the ground, almost curled up into a ball. Gary hesitated, then picked up the water and carried it over to her. She stared up at him blankly, then took it and started to drink. Gary watched her for a long moment, then walked back towards the fire. It was still cold and she was naked. She needed to warm up, he decided. And maybe eat something...

But he didn't know what else he could do for her.

THIRTY-THREE

The signs were clear centuries before the Fall of Earth. Even so, the bureaucrats not only ignored them, they actively sabotaged any attempt to come to grips with the situation. This wasn't surprising; the bureaucrats feared the results if their control over the educational system was shattered. In order to prevent other systems from engaging in competition and exposing their weaknesses, the bureaucrats waged war on them.

- Professor Leo Caesius, *Education and the Decline and Fall of the Galactic Empire*

Kailee lay on the ground, wrapped in her own thoughts.

Barry was dead. She had not only watched him die, she'd killed him. Gary might have shot him – and why hadn't he shot Barry earlier? – but Kailee had delivered the final blow. The damage he'd done to her body and mind had been savagely repaid. And yet...she found herself shaking helplessly, knowing that she had lost control completely. Even regaining it, even killing Barry, hadn't helped her recover.

The memories tormented her as she curled up into a ball. Barry had forced his way into her, violating her most private place and stealing her virginity. He would have done worse, she knew, if he had been allowed to live. Kailee had heard horror stories, each one worse than the last, about him and other boys who thought that they had the right to force themselves on girls. And yet, she had managed to stay pure...until now. She thought she would never be clean again.

Her body, she was dimly aware, was battered, bruised and covered in mud. She should consider herself lucky, she knew, that Gary hadn't taken her as well. He was supposed to be weak, but in her current state she couldn't have fought off a child, let alone a grown man. But he was a decent person, decent enough to bring her water...

She shook her head. It wasn't enough. She knew she could swim in the lake or shower for hours and yet she would still be able to feel Barry's touch on her skin. And she knew that she had been lucky, even though the very thought was repulsive. If Barry had survived, he would have done far worse than merely force his way into her. She felt defiled, yet she knew it could have been worse. The thought mocked her as she uncurled and sat upright, looking around nervously. She'd been careful before, just like the other girls, but now...

They would have done nothing on Earth, she thought, looking over at Barry's body. None of the boys at school had ever been held to account for rape, as far as she knew, certainly not by the teachers or the Civil Guard. There were classes and counselling sessions and other completely useless measures, none of which hid the fact that someone had shattered a girl's confidence, made her nothing more than a receptacle for his lust...and gotten away with it.

Here...rapists died. If they weren't killed by their would-be victim, they were killed by the rest of the population. Somehow, Kailee found that more reassuring than anything else. On Earth, girls had committed suicide because they had been raped, then had to watch their tormentors walking around school, free and clear. But on Meridian...she looked back at Barry's body and snickered, humourlessly. Who could say that she hadn't had her revenge?

Carefully, she stood and examined herself. Her body was bruised, bleeding in a dozen places; carefully, she touched between her legs and winced in pain. There was blood dripping down from where he'd torn her maidenhead...she fought down the urge to kick his dead body, then looked over at Gary. He was politely averting his eyes. Kailee felt an odd flicker of gratitude, then walked over to her pack. Thankfully, there were enough clothes left to cover herself.

"I need to wash," she said, once she was decent. It struck her, a moment later, that she should probably have washed before dressing, but she hadn't been at her best. "Is there a place to go?"

"There's the stream where I got the water," Gary said. "It isn't very deep, but it should do."

Kailee allowed him to lead her to the stream, then asked him to leave her alone for a few minutes. Once he'd retreated into the forest, she undressed and stepped into the stream, then lay down in the water. It was bitterly cold – she had to force herself to remain in the water – but it washed her clean. And yet, as she climbed out of the stream, she still felt dirty. His phantom touch kept stroking her body.

There was no point in trying to dry herself. Instead, she pulled on her clothes and walked back towards the clearing. Gary was already there, sitting in front of the fire and preparing a handful of green leaves. Kailee felt her stomach rumble and winced, grimly aware that neither of them knew how to hunt properly. Without Austin, it was only a matter of time until they starved to death.

"We need to decide what to do," Gary said, as they nibbled the leaves. They tasted faintly unpleasant, but they seemed to be edible. "Do we wait here, in hopes of meeting up with the others, or do we go onwards?"

Kailee gave him a sharp look. She would never have pegged Gary for a confident man, but watching Barry die seemed to have changed him. Perhaps, she decided, she was looking at the *real* Gary now, the figure who would have emerged if Barry hadn't kept knocking him down. He hadn't tried anything, thankfully, nor forced her to talk. She'd always hated being forced to talk about intimate matters, particularly with boys.

"I don't know," Kailee said, finally. She knew as little as he did about surviving in the wild. "What do you think?"

"I think that we should go on," Gary said. He nodded towards the fire. "If we stay here and they meet us, well and good. If not...we're going to run out of food pretty quickly."

Immediately, Kailee thought. Austin had plucked crabs out of ponds and shot deer – it struck her, suddenly, that there might have been crabs in the stream – but they didn't know how to hunt properly. All they knew was a handful of semi-edible plants. And how long would those keep them alive?

"I think that's the right direction," Gary added, pointing towards a distant mountain. "We should cross the Jordan fairly soon."

Kailee had no idea if he was right or wrong – or, for that matter, if they would recognise the Jordan when they encountered it. They'd already seen one river – barely two metres wide – that they'd mistaken for the Jordan, before Austin pointed out that it was nowhere near wide enough to take a canoe, let alone a steamboat. The Jordan would – logically – be much wider, but they knew little else about it.

She smiled, weakly. At least Gary was asking her opinion. Most boys would just make up their own minds and then expect her to follow them, without asking questions. And Barry...

"We should keep moving," she decided, pushing the thought aside. If nothing else, she didn't want to stay anywhere near the dead bodies. She stood up and reached for her pack. They'd have to go through the other two packs, sort out what they needed and abandon the rest. "And..."

She heard someone walking through the forest, a moment before he stepped into the clearing, weapon in hand. Kailee stared; she'd expected to see Austin or Darrin, not a complete stranger in ragged clothing. He looked as if he hadn't shaved for months; his companion, stepping out behind him, looked worse. Kailee felt her blood run cold as she met the first man's eyes and knew that he wasn't entirely sane.

"Well," the man said, in a voice that was so thick as to be almost beyond her understanding, "what are you doing here?"

He waved his rifle at them, threateningly. "Explain."

Kailee and Gary exchanged glances. "There was a plane crash," Gary said, finally. He didn't sound as if he had any idea who the newcomers were – or what they wanted. "We've been hiking towards the Jordan ever since."

"Really," the second newcomer said. His accent was oddly familiar. "You're from *Earth*?"

"Yes," Gary said, shortly. "And so are you."

Kailee felt an odd flicker of admiration. She'd known that the accent was familiar, but Gary had placed it as being from Earth. It was a large planet, which suggested that the newcomer had come from a nearby CityBlock. There wasn't, as far as she knew, a different accent for each block, no matter how insular they were. But she could easily be wrong.

"And you took a rabbit from one of my traps," the first newcomer said. "Why?"

Gary sounded annoyed with himself. "I didn't realise that it was a trap," he said, sourly. "I thought that the rabbit had trapped itself."

The second newcomer let out a bark of harsh laughter. "I believe you now," he said. He elbowed his older companion. "That sort of ignorance can only come from Earth's towering CityBlocks, where children know everything and nothing."

His gaze fixed on Kailee's face. It wasn't lustful, she realised in surprise; he seemed to be *assessing* them. "How did you even come here, children?"

Kailee flushed, then exchanged another glance with Gary. Gary scowled, then explained about the competition and how they'd been rewarded with a trip to Meridian. The two men snickered loudly when Gary reached the point where the plane had crashed, then exchanged significant glances of their own. Kailee realised, in a flash of insight, that they might have moved from the frying pan to the fire.

"Interesting," the second newcomer said. "Don't you think, Dave?"

Dave – the first newcomer – nodded, then pointed his rifle at Gary's head. "Put your hands in the air," he ordered. He jerked a nod at Kailee. "You too, young lady."

Kailee shivered. "What...what are you going to do with us?"

"If they're going to send you back to Earth," Dave said, "they might be willing to pay ransom for you. We can trade you back to the settlement government in exchange for money and supplies. Or...we can always find other uses for you."

He nodded to his companion. "Doug, search them," he ordered. "And then bind their hands."

Kailee gritted her teeth as Doug ran his hands over her body, then pulled her hands behind her back and wrapped a rope around them, tying them firmly in place. He did the same to Gary a moment later, removing the pistol and sticking it in his own belt. Once Gary was tied too, they were pushed to the ground and told to wait while the two men searched their bags, looking for anything useful. From the sounds they made, it was clear that they hadn't seen civilisation in a long time. Neither of them bothered to comment on the bodies.

Gary looked at her, then over at Dave. "Who *are* you?"

Dave gave him a brilliant smile. "Let's just say that we're political refugees," he said. "I think that sounds convincing."

His companion snorted, rudely. "There was an...incident with a shipment of blue-videos and an illegal copying machine," he said. "The Civil Guard arrested me, walked me past a judge and exiled me out here. I broke free two weeks later, then fled into the countryside."

"Not too bad," Dave said. "That's almost correct."

"Shut up," Doug said. He walked over to Gary and helped him to his feet. "You'll need to keep up with us. If you don't, we'll hurt you. Do you understand me?"

"Yes," Gary said, coolly.

Kailee almost smiled, then winced in pain as Doug pulled her up too. "Follow Dave," he ordered. "I'll be right behind you."

Dave turned and walked into the undergrowth, heading through the forest. Kailee tried to move slowly at first, but a series of slaps from Doug forced her to speed up. For someone who was clearly older than herself, Dave moved through the forest with a surprising nimbleness and Kailee had to move fast to keep up with him. Gary seemed to be biding his time; Kailee silently hoped that he wouldn't do anything stupid. The newcomers, whoever they were, didn't have any reason to harm them. But what would they do, she asked herself, when they discovered that there was no ransom? Somehow, she couldn't see any of the colonials paying for her safe return. And Yates, the only one who might have paid something for them, was dead.

She listened, saying nothing, as Dave peppered Gary with questions about Earth. For someone who hadn't seen it in years, he seemed very curious. Gary tried to answer the questions as best as he could, but his attempts to ask questions in return were met with either smiles or frowns – and no real answers. Kailee remembered the prisoners they'd seen on Earth, the men and women who had been sentenced to exile, and shuddered. If Doug hadn't adapted well to Meridian, he had to be as cracked as his older friend.

"Stumbling into our territory was not wise," Doug said, breaking into their thoughts. "Didn't you know *anything*?"

Kailee shook her head. No one had mentioned that there might be... runaway indents in the countryside, although she was sure that she had heard *someone* refer to bandits. But Austin hadn't seemed worried, even though they'd had to walk through the countryside to reach the Jordan. Had he thought that there was no danger or had he simply decided that there was no point in worrying about it? Either was possible.

"They gave us a full lecture on what we could and couldn't do," Dave added. "Weren't you paying close attention?"

"Not enough," Kailee admitted.

The two men seemed to find this hilarious and snickered together for several minutes. Kailee wanted to shout at them, but she didn't quite dare. Instead, she forced herself to keep walking, noting how the foliage had grown thicker and thicker. The pathways the two men took seemed well-hidden, although Kailee had never seen a forest before crashing on Meridian. It was quite possible that someone could search for a hundred years and never find their bodies, if the two men decided to kill them. She tested her bonds carefully, only to discover that they were quite firm. Escape wasn't a possibility.

They stepped through a line of trees and into a village. Kailee was almost charmed by how carefully the wooden houses were blurred into the trees and hidden under a canopy, but none of the other inhabitants looked pleased to see her. She couldn't help noticing that most of them were men, with only a handful of women. The women didn't even *look* at her, merely keeping their heads down as they shuffled through the village. A handful of kids followed them, wearing nothing more than torn shirts, if they wore anything at all. They chased a handful of chickens through the village, laughing merrily. They too took no notice of the newcomers.

"A word of advice," Doug said, as they stopped outside one of the houses. "Behave yourselves and you will be treated well. Don't behave yourselves and...well, we can start by breaking both of your legs, just to make sure you can't run."

He opened the door and shoved them both inside. Kailee glared at the door as it slammed closed, then looked around. The building was dark, illuminated only by light pouring in through slits in the walls. There was nothing inside, apart from a bench and a muddy floor. They hadn't even bothered to untie their hands...

"Shit," Gary said, loudly. Too loudly. "What are we going to do now?"

Kailee almost laughed. He was asking *her*? She had never thought of herself as a leader – and she wouldn't have been allowed to lead on Earth. She sobered, trying to think clearly despite the growing ache in her wrists. They were prisoners, prisoners of people who wanted to trade them for ransom...and who knew what they would do when they discovered that there was *no* ransom?

"I don't know," she confessed.

The door rattled before she could say anything else. She looked up, alarmed, as a tired-looking woman clattered into the room. There was a sense of beaten helplessness in her eyes, something that reminded Kailee all too clearly of some of the older women she'd known on Earth. The woman had been broken completely.

"They should have untied you," the woman said, as she started to work on Kailee's bonds. "I need to examine you."

Gary leaned forward. "Are you a doctor?"

"I used to be," the woman said. There was no emotion in her voice at all. "Now, I belong here."

Kailee shuddered as the woman started to examine her, gently poking and prodding at Kailee's body. Her touch wasn't anything like as bad as Barry's, but Kailee still shivered as the hands moved lower. The woman looked up at her, sympathy in her eyes; Kailee realised, grimly, that she'd seen worse.

"If they don't manage to ransom you, they'll put you to wife," the woman said. "There are more men than women here, in the camp. I hope you're worth a lot of money."

Kailee – absurdly – found herself giggling. They'd all found a place they could fit in on Meridian , apart from Barry. Now, they'd found *Barry's* place...and he was dead.

The woman looked at her as if she'd gone insane. "This is no laugh-ing matter," she said. "There's no proper medical care here, not even for pregnant girls. If you are married off, you may not even survive your first pregnancy."

She shook her head. "I'll bring you food," the doctor said. "And then you can wait."

Kailee looked down at her, then over at Gary. He seemed equally scared, but resolute.

She gritted her teeth. Whatever happened, she vowed, they were going to get out of the village and escape.

CHAPTER
THIRTY-FOUR

The colonies – even some of the Core Worlds, or Corporate Worlds – might have been able to cope with the crisis. Corporations funded schools that produced more intellectual children, while conditions on the colonies ensured that children learned to take care of themselves from a very early age. Indeed, as the Empire entered its last century, almost all of the skilled labour workforce was made up of people from the colonies.

- Professor Leo Caesius, *Education and the Decline and Fall of the Galactic Empire*

It had taken Darrin and Austin nearly an hour to pick their way out of the gorge, after splitting the useful remains of Samantha's pack between them and then burying her body as best as they could. Darrin had been surprised that Austin had taken the time to dig a proper grave, but Austin had pointed out that allowing the wild animals to get a taste for human flesh might have unpleasant consequences down the line. Besides, Darrin suspected that Austin felt more than a little guilty about Samantha's death. He'd been in charge when she died.

"So," he said, when they reached the top. There was nothing to suggest where the others might be waiting, if they had survived the night. "Where do we go from here?"

Austin looked around, his face grim. Darrin understood. The way they picked might not be the right one – and if they went too far from the others, they might never find them. He strained his ears, hoping to hear something – anything – but all he heard was the sound of insects buzzing through the trees. There was nothing to lead them towards the others.

"We head upwards," Austin said. He nodded towards the higher ground, where they might be able to look out over the trees. "I told them to head upwards, so we might run into them – or see something like a fire. Gary had the lighter."

Darrin nodded, although he wasn't too hopeful. Gary and Abdul would be alone with Barry, unless one counted Kailee. Gary couldn't fight and Abdul...he had no idea how well the other boy could fight. It was far too likely that Barry had already killed both of them – or at least beaten the other two boys into submission. He followed Austin as he walked up the slope, taking care where he put his feet. The ground was still muddy after the rainstorm.

"Most of the tracks will have been washed away," Austin commented. "In the Scouts, we used to try to track each other through the countryside. It was never very easy, but it was almost impossible after a big rainstorm. Even when they were leaving marks for us to follow the marks could easily be destroyed."

"It sounds like you had fun," Darrin said. He felt another flash of envy. Why – he asked himself once again – hadn't they had anything like that on Earth? "What do you *do* with all the training?"

Austin smiled. "Some of us go into the Bush Rangers," he said. "A handful try to join the military, although recruitment has been low for the last few years. Others go out to break ground..."

Darrin blinked at him. "Break ground?"

"You can't just set up a patch of ground and call it a farm," Austin explained. "Preparing a homestead and turning it into a proper farm is a complicated process. The Breakers help homesteaders from Earth get it right first time, or create new homesteads for the smarter or richer settlers. It can take years to start growing crops properly."

"Oh," Darrin said. He had already decided that he wasn't going to try farming. Fishing, perhaps, if brute labour wasn't option. "How do the homesteaders cope?"

"Depends on what agreement they signed with the settlement consortium," Austin said. "Those who pay their own way are assigned broken ground, which can be turned into a farm within one or two years. Those who sign themselves over to the consortium have to start with a raw patch of land, then break it themselves. They tend to take five years to start growing crops and ten before they can pay off their debts.

Darrin considered it, briefly. Debts on Earth were largely ignored, passed on to future generations or simply written off. On Meridian, he suspected, debts were altogether more serious. What would happen if someone couldn't or wouldn't pay their debts?

"It depends," Austin said. "Generally, it takes five years for someone to prove themselves a farmer – or not. If they failed through no fault of their own, they might be given an extension – at the discretion of the consortium representative. But if they failed because they didn't work hard enough, or properly, the debt would have to be repaid. At worst, they would be indentured and their labour contracted out."

He paused as they reached higher ground. "Look," he said. "That's a fire."

Darrin followed his gaze. A plume of white smoke was rising up into the air, some distance away. Austin fiddled with his compass, then led Darrin back down into the forest, heading towards the fire. It had to belong to Barry and the others, Darrin told himself firmly. There was no way that there was someone else wandering through the forest.

It took nearly forty minutes to reach the clearing – there were times when Darrin was sure that they had lost the smoke – and when they did, they stopped in disbelief. Abdul and Barry were lying dead on the ground, while the fire had been left to smoulder. There was no sign of either Gary or Kailee. Darrin looked down at Abdul and winced. It looked as though he had been beaten to death by someone's bare fists.

"Barry has been shot," Austin observed. Darrin turned, just in time to see Austin use a stick to lever Barry's body over. A nasty wound could be seen clearly on his chest. "A pistol, judging from the wound. It probably wasn't the actual cause of death."

Darrin looked at the bloody mess that had once been Barry's head, then up at Austin. "No shit, Sherlock."

Austin snorted. "The wound doesn't look to be fatal," he added. "There are bullets that inflict enough trauma to kill, even if the wound itself isn't fatal. But this doesn't look to be one of them. It was the blows to the head that killed him."

"So," Darrin said. "Who killed him?"

"Elementary, my dear Darrin," Austin said. "Gary or Kailee. Probably Gary."

Darrin lifted his eyebrows. "You don't think Kailee could have killed him?"

"None of you owned a gun, as far as I know, and I doubt you could have bought one," Austin said. "That means that the gun was probably recovered from Mr. Yates after he died. Gary was the only one who went to the plane alone, hence Gary had the weapon."

His face twisted into a scowl. "I should have checked," he said, grimly. "Yates would definitely have carried a weapon."

Darrin shook his head. It had never occurred to *him* that Yates would be armed. He'd been strong and skilled enough to knock Barry out with a single punch. Why would he need a gun? But there were more dangerous people than Barry out there...

"All right; Gary killed the bastard," Darrin said. He'd mourned Samantha and he would mourn Abdul in due course, but he knew he would never mourn Barry. Even his mother, if she ever found out what had happened to her child, wouldn't mourn him. Moe would probably regret the death of his playmate, then find someone else to share in the tormenting of younger and weaker students. "So where did he go?"

Austin stepped back, then started to pace the campsite. "Footprints," he said, pointing down towards the ground. "Two sets; one larger than any of ours. The other was barefooted. I think it was a man, probably older than either of us."

Darrin stared at him. "Someone else was here?"

"Yes," Austin said. He continued to pace the campsite. "Two people sat here, long enough to leave heavy imprints in the mud. They slept here, then walked to the fire. But in what order did these events occur? The marks aren't clear enough to be sure."

"No," Darrin agreed, impatiently. "Someone took them, right? So who?"

"Good question," Austin agreed. "Bandits, runaway indents...maybe even an independent farmer who genuinely came here to help."

He shook his head. "Every year, a small number of criminals or indents decide that they'd be better off in the jungle than working on farms," he offered. "They're a persistent problem along the forward edge of the settlement line, sometimes stealing supplies or enticing others to run away with them. I don't know how they will treat Gary and Kailee, but I doubt it will be kind."

Darrin swallowed. Girls were kidnapped all the time on Earth, unless they lived in a residency block where the gangs were bribed to keep the residents safe. Once kidnapped, they were taken down to the lower levels and...well, no one knew *precisely* what happened to them, but Darrin could guess. Sold to brothels, if they were lucky; rumour had it that they were even fed to escaped monsters from the Arena. What would the bandits do with them?

He looked over at Austin. "Are they alive?"

Austin was peering down at the ground. "They went into the forest here," he said, softly. "They were definitely walking on their own feet, so they probably weren't badly injured or otherwise mistreated. But there just isn't proof enough to say for sure."

"We have to go after them," Darrin said. "Can we track them all the way back to their hideout?"

"I think so," Austin said. He looked up at the sky, then back down at the muddy ground. "As long as it doesn't rain, we should be able to follow them."

———

Austin felt more perturbed than he wanted to admit as he led the way through the forest, following the tracks left by Gary, Kailee and the unknowns. They were nearing the Jordan, but there were still some distance from the edge of settled land – close enough for someone to raid the nearest settlements, too far for militia sweeps to locate and destroy bandit camps in the jungle. If they'd been closer, he might well have considered heading directly to the settlements...

He looked down at the tracks, marvelling inwardly at how *blind* Darrin was when it came to moving in the forest. The unknowns might as well have left a map pointing along their route; there were broken twigs and bushes as well as footprints, all there for the trained eye to see and understand. It had been harder following the aggressors in Scout hunting games. The only problem was that Gary and Kailee didn't seem to have dropped something that could be used to point in their direction.

It was odd. Dropping something was the simplest trick, one taught to all Scouts. Had it not occurred to them – or had they thought that they were *safe*? It was possible, Austin supposed, that they'd had a stroke of luck and run into a survey team, but it didn't seem very likely. There was no reason for a survey team to come this far from the settlement zone before they'd scouted out territory closer to established settlements.

He paused as the path seemed to shift, brushing along the edge of a number of thorny bushes. Someone could get caught in them, he guessed, wondering if they had been deliberately planted. The Scout Fort in Hundred Acre Wood, near his home, had been carefully hidden in the undergrowth. They'd been told that the adults didn't know where it was, although Austin was old enough to know that was nonsense. Most of the adults had been scouts themselves; they'd known about the fort, probably even helped build it. But this was different.

"We have to go around," he muttered. He still couldn't hear anything *human*, but his senses were warning him that something wasn't right. "And hope that this barrier doesn't block us completely."

The footprints seemed to walk along the bushes until they reached a gap, one that led through the bushes and into...what? Austin hesitated, remembering what he'd learnt when they'd practiced with paintballs and played at being soldiers. The entire pathway seemed designed to lead them into a trap. They'd *have* to come at the enemy from one specific direction.

He slipped backwards and motioned for Darrin to follow him, tapping his lips to indicate that he should keep his mouth shut. None of the Earth-born seemed to grasp the value of quiet, but if anyone inside the complex heard them, there was no hint of it. He waited until they reached a safe distance, then sat down and put his lips to Darrin's ears.

"Someone set those bushes up to hide their base," he said. There had always been stories of bandit bases, but he'd been told that most of them were exaggerated. Bandits rarely had enough sense to set up permanent homes. Maybe their leader was someone who had been born on Meridian, then indentured for some crime. "I think they're in there, held prisoner."

Darrin froze, then leaned forward until he could whisper back. "Are you sure?"

"I think so," Austin said. "The bushes are not planted randomly. They block access except through a pre-selected route. We'd need a bulldozer to break through anywhere else."

He briefly considered their options. They could try to sneak through in darkness, once night fell, and see what they found inside the complex. Or they could sneak away, find the Jordan and float down to the next settlement – and hope they could summon help in time. Austin had no illusions about what the bandits might do to their prisoners, particularly Kailee. It didn't seem right to leave a girl captive, even though cold logic suggested that rescuing her would be a long-shot at best.

"I intend to try to slip through," he said. They'd have to scout out the rest of the area, see if he was actually correct, but unless he was wrong there was no alternative. "Do you want to come with me?"

"Yes," Darrin said, shortly.

Austin hesitated. The Scouts had trained and exercised for all sorts of contingencies – and many of them had gone into the militia as soon as they were old enough to be considered adults. Austin had intended to do a term himself, if he didn't manage to become a Bush Ranger. But Darrin... Darrin knew almost nothing, apart from the basics of shooting. There was a good chance that including him was a mistake.

But a second pair of hands might just be welcome.

"We'll scout out the area, then slip back and catch something to eat," he said. He cursed inwardly a moment later. They didn't dare try to light a fire. It was quite possible to start one even without the lighter, but how could they risk it when the unknowns were so close? "What else can we do?"

He caught Darrin's shoulder as they started to worm their way backwards from the enemy base. "I want you to remember something," he added. He pointed a finger towards the east, where the Jordan had to be. "If I get caught – and you get free – head eastwards, get to the river and get downstream. I don't want you trying anything heroic, not if the rest of us are caught. You have to get downstream and call for help."

Darrin hesitated, long enough for Austin to tell that he was conflicted. "Should I go now?"

Austin felt equally conflicted. Cold logic said that they should *both* go now. The Jordan was far stronger than any river the Earth-born had seen – and it could be dangerous, particularly in the uncharted sections. Austin had been boating on the river with the Scouts; he knew that it could be tricky, even though there weren't any dangerous creatures this far from the sea. For someone from Earth...

"I think we should wait and see what happens," Austin said, reluctantly. He wished – how he wished – for another Scout, even someone from a rival troop. The other Scout could have headed to the Jordan to summon help, while Austin and Darrin tried to sneak into the complex. "And I think you should keep some distance from me when I start sneaking around."

They spent the next hour, despite steadily-increasing hunger, scouting around the bandit complex. Austin hadn't really doubted that they were dealing with bandits, but seeing how carefully the complex had been hidden confirmed it. Survey parties or independent-minded settlers wouldn't have bothered to hide so thoroughly. Only bandits – an organised group of bandits – would have bothered to hide.

He said as much to Darrin as they put some distance between themselves and the complex, then started to collect edible plants. "We must have stumbled into their territory in the rainstorm," he said. "They must have seen Gary and Kailee and decided to just snatch them; they probably don't know about the rest of us."

"They would have seen the bodies," Darrin pointed out. "They might think we're all dead."

Austin shrugged. They'd had their packs with them when the mudslide carried them away, splitting up the group. There shouldn't have been anything to indicate that there were more than four refugees, as long as Gary and Kailee kept their mouths shut. And Barry and Abdul were very definitely dead. He remembered just how scared Gary had been of Barry and smiled to himself. Gary had overcome his fears in time to kill his tormentor before he could be killed himself.

"Too many unknowns," he said. The scoutmaster had told him, more than once, that there was no point in trying to eliminate risk altogether. It was a good recipe for paralysis, but nothing else. "We just have to take care."

THIRTY-FIVE

However, they faced huge opposition from the bureaucrats. In order to operate on Earth (or within the Core Worlds) they had to pass the exams, most of which were completely unrelated to the subject at hand. (To give one example, a medical doctor was also expected to pass an exam in astronomy.) If they wanted to pass the exams, they had to study, thus wasting time. It was easier to find a job out along the Rim. If nothing else, there was no anti-colonial discrimination there.

- Professor Leo Caesius, *Education and the Decline and Fall of the Galactic Empire*

When the door opened again, it revealed the doctor and three older men. Gary watched, alarmed, as the doctor and one of the men escorted Kailee out of the room, then the other two turned to face him. He braced himself, expecting torture or worse, but all the leader did was pull a sheet of paper out of his pocket and hold it out to Gary, who took it in surprise.

"You will write a note to prove that we hold you prisoner," the leader stated. "If you can write."

Gary briefly considered trying to pretend he couldn't. It would be believable; on Earth, only one schoolchild in a hundred could write more than their own name, if that. *Gary* could write, but only because he'd spent years practicing after realising that reading and writing were the keys to a better future, or at least one away from the damned CityBlock. But if he didn't write the note, what would they do? Take a sample of his blood and send it to the city?

"I need a pen," he said.

His blood ran cold as the leader passed him a simple pen. Somehow, he doubted that the planet's government – about which he knew very little – would pay a ransom for their unwanted guests from Earth. Even if they had known that Barry was dead, they might still be reluctant to help. And why not? It didn't take a genius to realise that the planet's government hadn't been involved in making the decision to hold the competition in the first place. *They* didn't need reluctant immigrants from Earth.

Pushing the sheet of paper against the wooden wall, he scribbled a brief note explaining who they were and what they needed. He didn't mention any of the others in the note; if Austin, Samantha and Darrin were still alive, at least they weren't in the bandit camp. After a moment's thought, he addressed it to Janet. If Yates had managed to talk the planetary government into lashing Barry, rather than indenturing him, it was possible that Janet would have the contacts to convince them to pay the ransom. Or maybe she wouldn't bother either.

"There," he said, passing the note back to the leader. He'd been tempted to try to write something that might lead rescuers to the bandit camp, but he hadn't been able to think of anything useful. Besides, it was too much to hope that *none* of the bandits could read. "It should get a response."

"Excellent," the leader said. He inspected the note quickly, sounding out the words, then pocketed it. "We will slip it to the nearest settlement tomorrow."

He turned and started walking towards the door. Gary called after him before he could stop himself. "Where is Kailee?"

"Your friend is currently in the care of our doctor," the bandit informed him, testily. Gary, well used to people being annoyed with him, could tell that the bandit wasn't actually angry at *Gary*. There was a power play of sorts going on. "She will be fine."

Gary watched them go, then slumped down on the muddy ground. The bandits clearly hadn't bothered to install a proper floor...although if the hut was actually their prison, they probably felt they didn't need one. He inspected the floor, wondering if he could actually dig his way out, before deciding that it would be useless. The prison was too small to allow him to dig without being heard.

He shook his head, feeling utterly alone. What were they going to do now?

———

Kailee looked around with some interest as the doctor led her to a larger building in the centre of the complex. On one hand, the bandit camp appeared primitive; on the other, there was a definite sense of organisation that reminded her of Sabre City. Small animals and children ran everywhere, while older men carried buckets of water from the well to the various small houses. Each house, as far as she could tell, housed several families, but the men seemed to greatly outnumber the women. Did they share wives?

She shuddered inwardly as they entered the larger building. Families on Earth took many forms, but she couldn't recall encountering several men who shared the same wife. Male jealousy would make it hard for them to cope, she suspected. She knew boys who had nearly killed each other because one of them thought that the other had slept with his girl-friend. It was possible, she supposed, that *men* were more rational, but somehow she doubted it. Men were far more influenced by emotion than women, more prone to letting it guide their thinking.

Maybe they know they don't have a choice, she thought. On Earth, the numbers of male and female citizens was roughly even. Here, in the midst of a bandit camp, who knew?

Inside, there was an electric light, the first Kailee had seen since the crash. She felt an odd sense of relief at seeing it, as if they had finally made their way back to civilisation. The room it illuminated was clean, with a large table, a small chair placed next to it and a handful of wooden boxes piled against the wall. A smaller door led into a washroom which looked both primitive and very welcoming. Kailee found herself staring at it – at the chance to get clean – with more lust than she had felt for any man.

The doctor let out an amused snort. "Go wash," she said, dryly. "There's no shortage of water here."

Kailee nodded, feeling an odd surge of emotions as she undressed – leaving her clothes outside – and stepped into the shower. It was primitive, yet it was clearly also a labour of love. She felt Barry's ghostly touch on her – in her – as she twisted the tap, sending lukewarm water cascading down from barrels high overhead. It took her a moment to realise that they'd rigged up a system for reflecting heat into the water, warming the makeshift tanks. She took the cloth from the side of the chamber and scrubbed herself, using soap to wash her body clean. But, no matter what she did, she wondered if she would ever feel truly clean again.

She took the opportunity to examine her body carefully. There were bruises and scratches, but most of the damage seemed to have healed. She said a silent prayer of thanks for Aunt Lillian's insistence that she get a contraceptive implant fitted, remembering with some embarrassment just how badly she'd whined and screamed when her aunt had dragged her to the doctor. If she hadn't...teenage pregnancy was far from uncommon on Earth, but the thought of carrying Barry's child was repulsive. She didn't know how she would have kept herself from strangling the brat, if she didn't give the child up to a government orphanage.

"You look much better," the doctor said, as Kailee stepped back into the main room. "Lie down on the table."

Kailee swallowed, but obeyed. Examinations by doctors were to be dreaded, the girls knew, even if the doctors were female. There were so many waivers to sign that, by the time the doctor actually examined the patient, the doctor could do anything without fear of being sued or imprisoned. Kailee had always had Aunt Lillian in the same room, but she had heard stories of girls who had been molested by doctors - or accidentally poisoned by them. The stories had always seemed believable. On Earth, anything could happen.

The doctor didn't produce any scanners. Instead, she poked and prodded at Kailee's body, then nodded to herself and stepped backwards. "You're reasonably undamaged," she said, shortly. "Most of your bruises will heal quickly if you take it easy, just keep washing them clean. And you really need to eat and drink more. I'll have something sent into your cell."

Kailee blinked in surprise. "Why?"

"Because if you are not ransomed, you will be kept here," the doctor said. There was a curious deadness in her voice. "And you will have to bear children."

"No," Kailee said.

"You will not be offered a choice," the doctor informed her, still in the same dead tone. "If you are lucky, you will have a good husband and…"

"I will not," Kailee insisted, hotly. "I…"

"There were others who said the same," the doctor said. "They all loudly proclaimed their determination to remain independent, their refusal to surrender to their captors. And now they are part of this community."

Kailee gave her a long look. There was no guilt on the doctor's face. There was nothing at all, just…*deadness.* The doctor had long since lost all traces of human emotion.

"Why?" She asked. "How did you even *get* here?"

"There was an accident with medicine I prescribed," the doctor said, in a cold dispassionate voice. "It wasn't my fault. The factory that produced it needed to meet a quota, so they didn't bother with any actual quality control. I later discovered that I'd injected a young boy with effective poison. Turned out that the young boy's father was powerful enough to get me indentured, no matter what papers he'd signed. The consortium noticed that I was a doctor and made me an offer I couldn't refuse."

She looked up, meeting Kailee's eyes for the first time. "They made me a doctor here, tending to farmers who would otherwise have nothing," she continued. "And then I was kidnapped, like others, from the edge of the settlement zone. I am lucky. As a doctor, I cannot be beaten, merely… forced to watch as others are beaten. There is no way to resist."

"I'm sorry," Kailee said. She swung her legs over the side of the table and stood, reaching for her clothes. "How did the other women get here?"

"Most of them were indents, like me," the doctor said. "A couple were kidnapped from farms and stolen away into the countryside. And they know, now, that escape is impossible."

She watched, cruelly dispassionate, as Kailee pulled on her muddy clothes. "I am sorry for you," she added. "But you might have been safer on your own."

Kailee kept her mouth closed as the doctor led her back to the prison, but now she knew more about the bandit camp it was easy to see what she meant. The women were broken, beaten down, just like far too many women on Earth. Maybe the bandits were more honest, she told herself, even though she refused to accept that they were right. They never pretended that the women could become more than wives, mothers and cooks. Some of the men, too, looked broken. A couple were even limping badly, although she wasn't sure what was wrong with them.

"Hamstrung," the doctor said, when Kailee finally broke her silence and asked. "They can barely walk, let alone run. Escape is impossible. I have hamstrung women too, when they were too determined to escape. They gave me no choice."

Kailee felt her temper flare. "*You* did it to them?"

The doctor's eyes were expressionless as she turned to face Kailee. "I had no choice," she said, softly. "Just like everyone else in this camp. I had no choice."

They reached the prison. The guard looked Kailee up and down – she gritted her teeth as his eyes travelled over her body – then stepped backwards and opened the door. Inside, Gary was sitting on the ground, waiting for her. There was a nervous look in his eyes.

Kailee stepped inside, then surprised herself by giving him a hug. As soon as the door was closed, she put her mouth to his ear and started to outline everything she'd seen. Gary listened, then told her about the ransom note. Kailee wondered, absently, if anyone would pay for them...or if they would be trapped in the bandit camp forever. She had to admit that it seemed unlikely that *anyone* would pay...

We have to get out of here, she thought. *Whatever it takes, we have to get out of here.*

———

The best time to sneak into a fortified camp, Austin had been told, was in the early morning, before the sun rose in the sky. There was enough darkness left to conceal his movements, while the enemy guards would be tired and anticipating their sleep rather than being on full alert. It was why military units – the competent ones, at least, according to his scoutmaster –stood to and prepared to resist attack in the early morning. But he didn't have time to waste.

Absolute darkness shrouded the enemy camp as he crawled back towards the bushes. They'd slipped back as soon as darkness began to fall, but he hadn't dared take them any closer until it was completely dark. If the enemy had night vision goggles or anything else...he shook his head, dismissing the thought. Such equipment was very rare on Meridian, even though there were no laws against the private possession of weapons. It was unlikely that the bandits had anything other than the Mark I eyeball.

He prayed silently that Darrin would keep his distance as he reached the gap in the bushes and started to crawl through. There was probably a guard posted further inside, concealed enough to be impossible to see from the outside, yet positioned so that he could intercept anyone trying to get in before they saw the interior of the complex. Austin made himself as small as possible, then inched forward. His eyes had adapted to the darkness as much as possible – there was more than a little genetic engineering in his family's past – but there simply wasn't enough light for him to see much. Was that a building ahead of him?

The wind shifted, carrying the scent of human habitation to his nose. Austin allowed himself a moment of triumph – he'd been right – then he sniffed more carefully. Humans, chickens, pigs...someone seemed to have set up an entire hidden farm. He couldn't smell any sheep or cattle, but perhaps that wasn't a surprise. Sheep and cattle required wide-open spaces if they were to be bred properly. Chicken and goats required very little.

There was a snapping sound, followed by a flare of light. Austin threw up his hand to cover his eyes, but the damage had been done. He was blind, just long enough for someone to jump him from behind. Austin let out a grunt as the bandit landed on his back, then kicked out and struck human flesh. The bandit made an annoyed sound, then pulled back and slammed a punch into Austin's back. Austin gasped in pain and tried to move, but it was futile. His captor held him as efficiently as he'd held the crabs, days ago.

He winced as he felt a gun poked into his back. It probably wouldn't
kill him, he realised, but it would almost certainly break his spine. A harsh
voice, right next to him, told him to put his hands behind his back. Austin
hesitated, just long enough for the gun to be pushed right into his skin,
then obeyed. He would be no good to anyone crippled or killed.

Idiot, he told himself, as his captor – captors – tied his hands together.
You walked right into a trap.

The scoutmaster would probably kick him out of the troop, he
realised, as he was roughly hauled to his feet and searched. He'd watched
carefully for human guards, but he hadn't been as careful as he should
have been about tripwires. One of them had been linked to an emergency
flare, blinding him long enough for the guards to catch him.

One of the guards caught him by the ear, after tearing the rifle off his
back. "Are you alone?"

"Yes," Austin said – and prayed Darrin wouldn't be caught. Somehow,
he doubted the bandits would be happy if they caught him lying to them.
"I'm alone."

"What a fucking idiot," the other guard muttered. "Coming in here
alone."

"Get a search party roused," the first guard said. He produced a pair
of handcuffs and clicked them onto Austin's wrists. "I don't believe him."

He dragged Austin through the darkened camp – it looked more like
a village, Austin realised – and thrust him, still handcuffed, into a small
room. Inside, it was dark, but he recognised Kailee's voice as she awoke
and cried out. Austin felt a mixture of relief – at least he'd found the missing girl – and horror. Who knew what the bandits would do to them?

The guard thrust him to the ground and walked away, shutting the
door firmly behind him.

"Austin?" Gary's voice said, from out of the darkness. "What happened?"

"I tried to get in after you," Austin said, before either of them could
say too much. The prison didn't look even remotely soundproofed. "The
others are dead."

He tried to find a comfortable position, but it wasn't easy. There was
no way the other two could undo the handcuffs, even if they could see

what they were doing. Gritting his teeth, remembering the suggestions for escaping in the handbook, Austin tried to slip his hands out of the bracelets. Unsurprisingly, it was a great deal harder in real life.

"Get some sleep," he said, firmly. There was nothing else they could do – and besides, he didn't want to talk too much. "We can catch up in the morning."

And pray, he added, in the privacy of his own mind, *that Darrin makes it back to civilisation.*

THIRTY-SIX

Worse, the bureaucrats attempted to extend their system out to every last world in the Empire. The problems facing students and teachers on Earth were grossly magnified when faced by students and teachers on worlds hundreds of light years from Earth. Indeed, the bureaucrats even attempted to close the loophole permitting home-schooling on starships, which would have crippled the interstellar economy years before its final collapse.

- Professor Leo Caesius, *Education and the Decline and Fall of the Galactic Empire*

Darrin saw the flash of light ahead of him and realised, to his horror, that Austin had been caught. It seemed impossible. Indeed, he hadn't expected Austin, of all people, to be caught by the bandits. The colonial boy had seemed so confident, so certain of his ability to survive that Darrin had come to think of him as invincible. Surely, if he and Barry had come to blows, Austin would have won.

But he'd been caught by the bandits.

For a long moment, Darrin hesitated, caught between two imperatives. The part of him that wanted to impress Austin, that wanted to convince the colonial boy that they could be friends, demanded that he go in after Austin and free him. But the part of him that knew that anyone who could catch Austin could catch Darrin too had other ideas. There was no point in throwing himself into the dragon's mouth, not when Austin had told him to seek the Jordan and use it to escape.

Carefully, staying low, he crawled backwards until he arrived at where they'd hidden their packs and a small collection of edible plants. His stomach growled as he wolfed down the food, demanding that he find something more filling to eat. But there was no time to hunt for a rabbit or something else, let alone make a fire and cook. The fire alone would lead the bandits right to him. Instead, he pulled the compass out of Austin's pack and looked at it doubtfully. If he got it wrong, in the darkness, he was as good as dead.

"The needle always points north," Austin had explained. It had all seemed perfectly simple in broad daylight. Now, Darrin had to stare at the glow-in-the-dark compass, silently grateful to whoever had invented it. "You can use it to determine which way to go."

Darrin twisted the compass until 'N' was pointing north, which showed him which way was east, towards the Jordan. It looked right, he knew, but what if it was wrong? He hesitated again, seriously considering trying to slip back to the bandit camp, then shook his head. It would just get him caught for nothing. Donning his pack, he started to walk through the forest towards the east.

It wasn't easy going. The darkness seemed almost a living thing; it flowed around him, making him see things that weren't there on closer reflection. Austin had commented that there were all sorts of stories of *things* lurking in the woodlands, strange creatures hiding from the gaze of mankind; now, looking and peering into the darkness, Darrin could believe that there was something there. The forest was almost completely silent, the silence broken only by strange hooting in the distance. The first time he heard it, Darrin thought that it was the bandits, coming after him in hot pursuit. It wasn't until he saw a white form fly over his head that he realised that birds were making the sounds. He'd never even heard of a bird flying at night before.

They probably gave us a wide berth, he thought, as he paused to catch his breath. Walking in the dead of night was far more exhausting than walking at day – and his hunger didn't make it any easier. He was tempted to sit down and sleep, then start walking again when dawn broke, yet he knew he didn't dare. If he relaxed now, he wouldn't have the energy to move later – and besides, if the bandits did manage to get Austin to talk, they would know that Darrin had escaped them. They might come after him.

What would they do to their prisoners? Darrin had watched thousands of entertainment flicks, some better than others, and they offered a wide range of possible answers. It would be easy enough for the bandits to torture Austin to get him to talk – or maybe simply inject him with a truth drug. They wouldn't need anything sophisticated. Darrin hadn't heard of any drug problems on Meridian, but if they had a sample of Sparkle Dust they could use it to make Austin highly suggestible. And then he would tell them whatever they wanted to know, without even hesitating.

He froze as he saw – or thought he saw – a humanoid shape in the darkness. For a moment, his heart was beating so loudly that he was convinced the bandits would be able to hear it from miles away. And then the shape vanished, leaving him alone. Darrin stared at where it had been for a long moment, wondering just what it was. A bandit? Another refugee? Or had he simply imagined the whole thing?

Shaking his head, he walked onwards...and right into a river. For an insane moment, he thought he'd found the Jordan, before realising that the river was far too small for anything larger than a toy boat. Austin had told them about building model boats and sailing them on rivers; it was, once again, something rarely practiced on Earth. Darrin felt yet another flash of envy, then pity – pity for everyone stuck on Earth. *They* would never know the joys of walking through the countryside. But then, no one in their right mind would want to walk on what remained of Earth's surface, the handful of places that weren't covered by megacities.

Yates's voice seemed to echo in his head. *The people who leave Earth select themselves*, he said. *Those who remain don't have the determination to escape or the drive to succeed.*

He gritted his teeth, wondering if hearing voices was actually the first sign of madness. Yates had *cared* about him, he saw that now. He had even cared about *Barry*, cared enough to try to punish the boys rather than let them run riot. Was that, he wondered bitterly, what it was like to have a *real* father? Someone who cared, someone who tried to prepare his children for the future, someone who disciplined them when necessary? Fitz had never cared about Darrin, his unwanted stepson; he'd certainly never bothered to try to shape his life. And Fitz might well be dead.

Darrin shivered. Fitz hadn't cared about him. The closest he'd come to any form of encouragement was to point out that Darrin would have to move into his own apartment as soon as he turned seventeen, the legal age for living apart from one's parents. And he hadn't really cared about Darrin's mother either. As long as she let him do whatever he wanted, he didn't care. He'd just claimed the living allowances for himself and used them to drink...he would have drunk himself into an early grave, if Darrin hadn't beaten him first. Was he dead?

No way to know, Darrin thought. He would never see Earth again, he realised, and he was fine with it. *I can spend the rest of my life here.*

Your life was wasted, Yates seemed to say. The darkness pressed closer, as if it scented weakness. *You cannot read or write, compose an argument – or survive. You have nothing to live for, or to die for. You and those like you are hacking away at Earth's foundations, tearing your way into its heart. The planet is dying and fools like you are only speeding the whole process up.*

"That isn't true," Darrin said. His head spun. Was he imagining Yates's voice...or was something truly supernatural taking place? It didn't seem likely. "I didn't know..."

Of course you didn't know, Yates mocked. *You never chose to learn. Do you think that Gary is uniquely intelligent? A genius? A delicate flower born among the filth and grime of the lower levels? The curse of your existence is this; the resources you need to actually grow and learn were there all the time, just like the famous ruby shoes. But you needed to make use of them yourself.*

You didn't know. No one was allowed to tell you. None of your teachers were ever allowed to tell you that there was something wrong with you, let alone give you a smack when you needed it. Your self-esteem was considered more important than your schooling. No one forced you to start learning. You found it so much easier just to relax and go with the flow. But what do you have to show for twelve years of schooling? You can barely read a simple book, your writing is impossible for anyone other than a cryptologist to understand, your grasp of everything from history to political philosophy is effectively non-existent. You couldn't add one to ten without taking off your shoes.

It was easier to do nothing. And so you did. You fell into bad habits. When you were partnered with Barry, you slipped into minion mode. You did as he wanted until you learned better. But how much trouble would you have saved yourself if you had learnt that lesson earlier? How much respect would you have earned from Austin – or me – if you had stood up to him from the start?

Darrin let out a cry and started to run, trying to escape. But the voice followed him; it was in his head, echoing through his thoughts. He was imagining it, he had to be imagining it...and yet it seemed all too real. The sun started to glimmer on the horizon and yet he kept running. He ran past trees, their branches leaning out to trap him, then down a long woody slope. And, at the bottom, he saw the Jordan and stopped, dead.

It had to be the Jordan. The river was wide, wider than the giant assembly hall at school on Earth. It flowed rapidly towards the south, towards the sea. The shoreline was nothing more than jagged rocks. Darrin smiled in awe as the sun rose higher, then stumbled as he felt his stomach rumble angrily. He was hungry. But there was nothing to eat.

He looked around, desperately. There were a handful of tiny crabs, far smaller than the giants Austin had caught, scuttling down by the shore. At other times, it would have fascinated him to see them moving on the rocks, their presence only betrayed by their movements. He could have sat down next to them and never noticed, if only they'd kept still. But he couldn't see how to cook them...

Yates had suggested that they learn to swim, but Darrin hadn't thought much of it, not after spending so much time in the baths on Earth. They were fun places; the girls wore almost nothing, while the boys showed off in-between gawking at the girls. And there were private baths where a boy and a girl could be together, if they paid the additional fee. But he'd never realised what swimming actually meant until they'd crashed – and by then it had been far too late. A few splashes in the lake barely counted as swimming.

He struggled, trying to remember what Yates had said. The man had been giving them useful advice, yet he hadn't listened very hard. Yates hadn't forced him to listen – *of course not,* his thoughts mocked him, *Yates wasn't there to make you learn, merely to offer you the chance* – and he'd barely memorised any of it. How did people stay afloat when they couldn't swim?

A branch appeared, drifting down the river, and he nodded in understanding. They clutched onto something that floated, using it to keep their heads above water. Darrin looked around, then saw another large branch, broken off a tree by the rainstorm. He walked over, picked it up with an effort, then half-dragged it back to the river. Bracing himself, he strode into the water.

It was colder than he'd expected, cold enough to make him think twice about what he was doing. And, it occurred to him, a moment too late, that there might be larger and nastier creatures in the water than crabs. But he forced himself to pull up his legs and let the water sweep him onwards, down towards the sea.

The cold numbed his body and mind. He had to force himself to concentrate, trying to drag up what Yates had told them, then every last detail of his times with Judy. Absently, he wondered what had happened to her on Earth. She wouldn't have waited for him, even if he'd planned to go back to humanity's dying homeworld. He knew that she *couldn't* wait for him. She would need a new protector, someone who would look after her in exchange for her body. Silently, Darrin wished her well. There was no point in being jealous, even though he would be expected to be so on Earth. They would never meet again.

Men like you give girls the choice between surrendering to one person or surrendering to them all, Yates seemed to say. Darrin was *sure* he was hallucinating now, delusions brought on by hunger and the cold. *You think of them as nothing more than objects. You feast your eyes on pornographic material that would have shocked an earlier generation, then you set out to make it real. The rape porn you watched was an act, staged by actors. But the rapes that took place in your school and CityBlock were all too real.*

"I didn't rape Judy," he said. It was suddenly very hard to move his lips. "I didn't!"

Do you think, Yates accused, *that there is something virtuous in* not *committing rape?*

His voice seemed to harden as the cold seeped in. *Judy could never do anything for herself, ever. None of you, boys or girls, were ever taught to defend yourselves. She was never allowed to be truly independent. In order to remain even remotely safe, she needed a protector. Maybe you didn't take her by force. But tell me – was what you did not comparable to rape?*

"I don't know," Darrin answered.

He felt his mind start to wander as he looked at the shoreline. It seemed to be nothing more than endless forest. A handful of animals were standing by the waterline, drinking from the river. Darrin wondered, absently, what they made of the human floating down on a makeshift raft, then realised that he was definitely slipping into madness. He'd certainly never discussed Judy with the real Yates.

And yet the thought mocked him. He'd never really bothered about Judy; he certainly hadn't *loved* her. The realisation left an unpleasant taste in his mouth. He was disgusted at himself, not her. Boys shared tips and tricks for greater sexual enjoyment, for both men and women, but he'd never used them. All that had been important had been his own pleasure. He'd never given a damn about hers.

Be a better person, Yates advised. *And don't forget to learn.*

The shout caught him by surprise, pulling him out of an undercurrent that threatened to drag him down into madness and death. He looked towards the shore and saw a small village, a large boat and a handful of people, staring at him. Darrin twisted and tried to kick his way towards the jetty, but his legs refused to work. The watchers must have realised that something was badly wrong, for one of them jumped into the water and swam towards him. Darrin relaxed, just long enough to accidentally let go of the branch. He fell under the water a moment later and started to choke. His rescuer caught him just in time.

Darrin coughed and gasped, spitting up water, as he was towed back towards the shore and helped up onto the jetty. The villagers seemed astonished to see him; he realised, dimly, that they were right at the edge of the settlement line. They had no reason to expect to see someone drifting down from the north...in fact, he realised, they might have good reason to think he was a bandit. Who else would be that far north?

"Get the nurse," one of his rescuers ordered. He knelt down beside Darrin and started to cut his clothes away from his body. "What happened, son?"

Tell him, Yates urged.

Darrin tried to swallow. Someone undressing him wasn't a good sign, at least on Earth. On the other hand, he was grimly aware of his water-logged clothes pressing in on him. Maybe this was something else, not a prelude to theft or assault.

"We crashed," he managed to say. It was suddenly very hard to speak. "We..."

His mind blurred. When he recovered, he was sitting in front of a roaring fire, hot blankets wrapped around his body. Several concerned faces were peering at him, two of them wearing military-style uniforms. The others appeared to be civilians. One of them, a nurse, was supervising a tube that ran from a device down into Darrin's arm. He looked away hastily, unwilling to see his skin penetrated by anything. On Earth, it was common for even the simplest procedures to take place under general anaesthetic.

"We've been looking for you," one of them said. The others seemed to defer to him, so Darrin assumed that he was the leader. "What happened?"

Tell him, Yates repeated.

Carefully, piece by piece, Darrin began to tell the full story.

"We'll find your friends," the leader promised, when he had finished. "For now, rest. You'll be no good to anyone if you catch hypothermia and die."

Darrin tried to object, but then someone pressed a metallic object against his neck. His senses swam and he plunged back into darkness.

CHAPTER
THIRTY-SEVEN

The result played out on the micro and macro scale. Earth's towering CityBlocks were filled with hordes of unemployed and unemployable men and women, bringing millions more of the same into the world every week; crime was on the rampage, the global infrastructure was breaking down...the miracle is that it lasted as long as it did. But when it fell apart, it took the core of the Empire with it.

- Professor Leo Caesius, *Education and the*
Decline and Fall of the Galactic Empire

Kailee winced as she opened her eyes, half-wondering how much of the previous day had been a dream – or a nightmare. Abdul was dead, Barry had forced his way into her...and then Gary and she had killed him. Was it possible to have a dream that was also a nightmare?

She groaned as she saw Austin, lying face-down on the floor, his hands cuffed behind his back. It hadn't been a nightmare, then. They'd been caught by bandits and...she shuddered, as she forced herself to stand up. Who would have thought that a covered building was more uncomfortable than the forest outside? But then, it *was* a prison. Comfort probably wasn't in the job description.

Austin opened his eyes. "Are you all right?"

Kailee nodded. Complaining about her aches and pains wouldn't help, would it? Besides, she didn't like the look of Austin's hands. They were starting to turn purple, an unpleasant-looking colour that chilled her to the bone. But what was worse was the knowledge that they were completely alone. Or were they?

"The others are dead," Austin said. "I'm sorry."

There was something in his tone that warned her not to press any further. She squatted on the ground, trying to force blood to circulate through her body...and mourned, silently, Samantha's death. Perhaps she should have spent more time with the other girls...but she had been too used to keeping her distance. Other girls could be helpful – and they all walked home together, seeking safety in numbers – but they could also be a liability. In hindsight, maybe her dream of becoming an actress had left her deprived in other ways. She would have liked a real confidante, just one.

But she couldn't talk about Barry with either Gary or Austin.

Pushing the thought aside, she stood and walked over to Austin, then knelt beside him and started to massage his wrists. The metal cuffs bit deeply into his skin, leaving ugly marks and risking permanent damage. Once – it seemed like years ago – a young girl had been tied up and stuffed into a locker by a gang of older bullies. Kailee had watched when she tumbled out, still bound hand and foot, then turned away. It was dangerous to show too much compassion on Earth. She winced in pain and guilt. The damage had never quite healed, years later.

"I'm sorry too," she said. "What did they say to you?"

"Nothing," Austin said. "They just put me in here with you."

"They want to trade us for ransom," Gary said.

Kailee jumped. She hadn't even realised he was awake. But Gary would probably be a light sleeper too, just like her. Barry was dead, yet he still haunted their dreams.

"I doubt they'll get much," Austin admitted, darkly. "The government wouldn't pay ransom for you."

"I don't doubt it," Kailee said. She shivered, remembering what the doctor had told her. If she were lucky, she might have a husband or set of husbands who didn't beat her too badly while forcing her to carry her children. And if she were unlucky...she might be regretting killing Barry before too long. "What about you?"

"My father might pay," Austin said. "But I don't know what he can afford."

He broke off as someone rattled the door, then opened it. Three men stepped inside, four more waiting outside. The leader motioned Kailee aside, then bent down and removed the cuffs from Austin's wrists. He immediately sat up and started to rub at the bruised skin.

"There is only one way out of this camp and it is heavily guarded," the leader informed them, as he motioned for the prisoners to stand up. His comrades tossed clothes at them, which they scrambled to don. "If you try to run, we'll cripple you permanently."

Kailee nodded, remembering the crippled men she'd seen the previous day. There was no need to shackle their legs, not when they could simply be crippled, making it impossible to run fast enough to escape. She lowered her eyes, but glanced around from side to side as they were led out of the prison and down past a series of houses. The one right at the end of the row was easily twice as big as the others, with enough turf on the roof to keep it well hidden from prying eyes. Inside, there was a small table, with a selection of food. Kailee felt her mouth water as she looked at the meal. Her stomach rumbled, hungrily. She would have eagerly devoured ration bars, if they had been available.

"Please, sit," a new voice said. The man stood at one end of the table, studying them thoughtfully. His accent was...odd. There were traces of Earth, but also of something else, something maddeningly familiar. "I dare say letting you starve to death would not be helpful, would it?"

Kailee sat and stared at the food. The chicken smelt heavenly...she barely realised her hands were moving until she picked up a drumstick and began to eat rapidly. Beside her, Gary and Austin did the same, swallowing food as if they feared it would go out of fashion. The bandit leader chuckled and warned them not to eat too quickly or they would choke, but they ignored him. All that mattered was eating as much as they could.

"Now," the bandit leader said, when they were done. "Tell me about Earth."

Gary looked up at him, emboldened by the food. "Why do you want to know?"

"Because I do," the bandit said. He gave them all a thin smirk. "What is happening on the planet now?"

Kailee had learned to dread Aunt Lillian's interrogations. The woman had the nose of a bloodhound when it came to spotting lies and deceits, then slowly worming away at her victim until the truth was exposed, cringing in the corner and trying to hide from prying eyes. But the bandit leader was, if anything, even worse. He asked questions, listened to the answers and then asked more questions, poking and prodding away at the truth as a child might prod at a sore tooth. Kailee had never really appreciated just how little she knew of Earth, despite having lived her entire life on the planet. And even Gary couldn't answer *all* of the leader's questions.

"Makes you wonder, doesn't it?"

She looked up at the question. "Wonder what?"

"Meridian is supposed to receive a colonist shipment every month from Earth," the leader said. "For the past two years, however, shipments have been reduced. There was a gap of four months between the previous shipment and the shipment that brought you to the planet."

He smiled. "And the number of freighters visiting the planet has dropped too," he added, looking directly at Gary. "I wonder what it means."

Kailee tried a diversionary tactic she'd leant from Aunt Lillian. "What do *you* think it means?"

"I think that, one day, the starships will stop coming altogether," the leader said. "And who knows what opportunities will arise on that day?"

Austin leaned forward. "Opportunities to do what?"

"We shall see," the leader said. He nodded to his men, who hauled Kailee and the others to their feet. "Until then...we shall find work for you to do. I suggest you work hard. There are plenty of ways you can be punished without causing permanent damage."

Kailee was still mulling it over when she saw the doctor. "Come with me," the doctor ordered. "I need an assistant in the ward."

Calling it a ward, Kailee decided, was a sick joke. No one in their right mind went into a hospital on Earth, not when the doctors were often untrained, underequipped or forced to prescribe medicine that might not have been properly tested. From what she'd heard, *real* doctors were in such high demand that they never had to go into the CityBlocks. Even the ones who did insisted that their patients sign away all their rights before treatment. The danger of a lawsuit was just too high.

The three patients in the ward looked as if they would have preferred Earth. One man had a nasty wound, another looked as though he had been in a fight...and the third, a pregnant woman, appeared to be on the verge of giving birth. The room itself smelled funny, as if the doctor could no longer even be bothered to clean. Kailee remembered Austin's lectures on the importance of hygiene and shuddered.

"That will be your first job," the doctor said, when Kailee pointed it out. "Clean this room."

Kailee cursed her own tongue, but got to work. At least it was better than the alternative.

———

"Welcome back to the world," a feminine voice said. "How are you feeling?"

Darrin hesitated. In truth, he felt bleary. And yet he no longer felt hungry or tired. That was a plus, he told himself firmly, even if he couldn't recall eating. After everything he'd been through...memory flickered in his mind and he jerked upright. Austin and the others were still trapped, still prisoners!

"Relax," the voice told him. "How are you feeling?"

Darrin looked around. A middle-aged woman was standing at the head of his bed, examining him with calm eyes. She wore a white smock that made her look like a nurse from one of the *Naughty Nurse* flicks... no, she was a *real* nurse. He pushed that thought aside before it showed on his face and swung his legs over the side of the bed. They wobbled the moment he tried to stand up, leaving him feeling helpless, unable to move.

"You didn't eat very well," the nurse informed him. "I've injected you with various nutritional supplements that should start making up the shortfall, but I would advise you to remain lying down until you feel better. Thankfully, you didn't catch any form of illness from being in the river. Didn't it occur to you to walk down the side of the river instead?"

"I was too tired to move under my own power," Darrin said. His head spun a little when he tried to stand up for the second time, then stabilised. "I had no choice."

He looked up as a dark-skinned man stuck his head into the room. "Laura, can I speak to him now?"

"If he feels up to it," the nurse – Laura – said, tartly. "Young man?"

Darrin nodded, quickly. "I'm ready."

The man stepped fully into the room and walked over to Darrin. Up close, he reminded Darrin of Yates; he had the same easy confidence and inner determination that Darrin had so envied. But there was something about him that was less...*polished*. Darrin wasn't sure if the man was reassuring or intimidating.

"I'm Colonel Nick," the man said, shortly. "For my sins, I am the local commander of the militia. I need you to come with me."

Darrin nodded and stood up. Nick put out a steadying hand, but Darrin forced himself to stand on his own and walk towards the door. The colonel walked past him and led him out of the small building, then down towards a long low building at the centre of the settlement. A man carrying a rifle stood on guard outside, wearing a khaki uniform and glaring around him as if he expected to be attacked at any moment. Darrin wondered, as Nick led him past the guard and into the building, just why the planet needed a militia in the first place.

Stupid question, he told himself. *The people who captured Austin might threaten settlements.*

Inside, there was a large table, with a paper map spread out on it. Darrin had never even *seen* a map before coming to Meridian, but it seemed easy enough to understand. Sabre City was at one end, with the Jordan running past the city and flowing down into the sea. That meant, logically, that *they* had to be further up the map...he studied it for a long moment, then pointed to where he thought they were. It was the settlement furthest from the city.

"Good," Nick said, when Darrin explained his reasoning. "Which leads neatly to the next question. Where exactly is the bandit camp?"

Darrin looked down at the map – and swore at his own stupidity. Of *course* the goddamned camp wouldn't be marked on the map! Nick

315

bounced question after question off him, looking for landmarks or any-thing else that might have led them to the camp, but the best he could do was point to where he thought he'd found the river.

"I thought that orbital satellites saw everything," he protested. There'd been a pair of Stellar Star movies where her antics had been faithfully recorded from orbit. "Can't you simply find them?"

"Our network isn't exactly mil-grade," Nick admitted. "And it isn't comprehensive in any case. Otherwise we would have found you without needing to look hard."

He led the way over to a computer screen and tapped a switch. "We had to swing a satellite over to look for you, after we realised that your plane was badly overdue," he said. "It still took us some time to locate the crash site and dispatch another aircraft. We picked up your friends, but we couldn't find you."

Darrin found himself smiling. "Steve and Li are alive?"

"They're both suffering badly from malnutrition – in Li's case, her broken leg needed immediate medical attention," Nick said. "But they're both alive. We shipped them both back to the city."

"I'm glad to hear it," Darrin said.

"So show me," Nick said, turning the display so Darrin could see clearly. "Which way did you go?"

Darrin swallowed. They'd walked eastwards; they *had* to have walked eastwards or they would have missed the Jordan completely. That much he knew. And they'd swum in a lake at the bottom of a valley...it was hard to be sure, because everything looked different from high overhead, but he thought he knew which lake it had been. And then...there had been a rainstorm...

A thought struck him. "We left the bodies there," he admitted. "Can you find them on camera?"

"Maybe," Nick said. "Can you show me where?"

"A clearing," Darrin said. But there were hundreds of clearings. He tried looking for the gorge, where Samantha's body had been buried, yet it seemed invisible. It was buried deep under the treetops. "We'd just have to look for it."

Nick picked up a communicator and muttered orders into it. "We don't have many trained observers, nor do we have spy software," he admitted. "Everything the satellites show us has to be studied with the naked eye. It takes too long to get anything done."

Darrin shook his head in disbelief. They'd been told that Earth was the safest place in the galaxy, that a child could be found within seconds if necessary...but they'd all known that was a lie. It was common for people to go missing and never be found, ever. No one even bothered to look, as far as he knew. The Civil Guard would be more likely to arrest than help anyone who came to them, no matter who they were. But now, on Meridian, even the infrastructure to find someone didn't exist.

"Sit down and rest," Nick urged. He must have sent a signal of some kind, because two minutes later another uniformed man came in with a plate of sandwiches and a pitcher of orange juice. "Eat something, then relax. You've done fine."

"Well enough for the Scouts?" Darrin asked. "Austin was always telling us about them."

"He's a troop leader – he should," Nick said. "Tell you what; you join them when you get back to Sabre and try and qualify for the militia set of badges. If you get them all, I'll put in a good word for you at the recruiting office."

Darrin blinked. "The militia set?"

"Surviving, sharpshooting, camping...a handful of others," Nick said. "All skills the militiamen need. You get them, you get your chance to join us."

"Thank you," Darrin said. He would have to work to earn them, he realised, but it would mean more to him than something he'd been given, like the awards on Earth. Everyone knew that a student could graduate just by signing his or her name on the exam sheet, but in that case the exams were worthless. "I'll do my best."

Nick glanced down at his communicator. "Got something here," he said, looking over at the computer. "Two bodies; both in plain view."

Darrin peered over his shoulder, trying to recollect the path to the bandit camp. "I think they're here," he said, finally. "I think..."

"Close enough," Nick assured him. He smiled, brilliantly. "You can rest now, I think. You've done more than enough."

"I want to come with you," Darrin said. "I *need* to be there."

"You'd just get in the way," Nick said, but he seemed understanding. "Understand this; if you come, you stay at the rear and obey orders. If you get in the way, I won't hesitate to cuff you and leave you on the boat. You *don't* know what you're doing. My men do."

"I understand," Darrin said. He would have agreed to anything, as long as it kept him there to watch as the others were rescued. "I won't get in your way."

"See that you don't," Nick said. He glanced at his watch. "We leave in an hour. Get your shit together or remain behind."

CHAPTER
THIRTY-EIGHT

Was this the result of deliberate malice? Perhaps, to some extent; it certainly suited the Grand Senate to leave citizens unaware of how the Empire actually worked. But it seems far more likely that, in the words of the almost-forgotten Heinlein, that the whole system was created by stupidity and incompetence rather than malice.

- Professor Leo Caesius, *Education and the Decline and Fall of the Galactic Empire*

Darrin had seen the steamboats earlier, during their exploration of Sabre City, but this was the first time he'd ever actually *been* on one. It seemed bigger on the inside than on the outside, although that might have been because most of the militiamen were crowding the decks. The crew, a family who lived and worked on the boat, largely ignored the newcomers.

He felt like a fifth wheel as the boat made its slow way upstream. Most of the militiamen ignored him, choosing instead to check and recheck their weapons. Nick, their commander, spent most of his time poring over a map, speaking in hushed tones to his subordinate officers. Darrin couldn't tell if they were making genuine plans or if they were putting on a show for the benefit of the soldiers. There was something about the way they talked that bothered him.

The sun was slowly setting in the sky when they reached the place he'd entered the river, hours ago. It looked familiar, he decided, although he wasn't entirely sure it *was* the right place. He hadn't realised until he'd seen the map just how large the unsettled zone actually was, or how many places there were to hide. An entire army could camp out in the wilderness and no one would be any the wiser. From what Nick had said, while trying to draw specifics out of Darrin's mind, the bandit camp suggested that there were more than a handful of bandits in the area. It was too big for one or two people to build alone.

One by one, the soldiers stepped off the boat and waded to the shore, carrying their packs and rifles above their heads. Darrin had thought the pack he had carried ever since the crash was heavy, but the militiamen carried far more weight on their backs. The supplies they'd brought with them seemed enough to feed an entire army, not just a hundred men. And he honestly wasn't sure how they planned to crawl through the undergrowth with those packs on their backs. They'd look like giant turtles, he decided, as he was helped to the shore himself. The men certainly couldn't *hide*.

"You can go ahead," Nick said, addressing one group of men. They didn't carry packs, merely rifles, which were slung over their shoulders. "We will follow at a more sedate pace."

The men nodded and vanished into the forest.

Nick watched them disappear, then grinned at Darrin. "Silent running from here on," he added. "Don't say a word."

With that, he led his men into the forest.

It felt different, walking with a small army. Darrin had felt isolated even when surrounded by Austin and the others. Now, the forest no longer seemed so threatening. The militiamen kept a sharp eye out for trouble, but otherwise marched with an easy confidence that reminded Darrin of Austin, although considerably more practiced. They didn't look like any soldiers he'd seen on the entertainment flicks, but there was something about them that made the militiamen look reassuring. And they looked capable of marching for hours.

Thirty minutes after they began walking, Nick put a hand to his ear. He had to have a communications earpiece, Darrin realised; he started to use his hands to indicate orders moments after receiving the first message. The soldiers split up into smaller groups, then started to advance towards the darkness, towards where the bandit camp had to be.

Despite himself, Darrin felt cold. Nick had said enough to tell him that there were never any guarantees in hostage-rescue operations, particularly when combined with bandit suppression. They might carry out a successful mission...

... And his friends might still wind up dead.

———

Kailee slumped to the ground as darkness fell over the bandit camp. Austin and Gary looked tired, but she felt mentally drained as well as physically exhausted. The bandit doctor seemed to have decided that the best way to keep Kailee out of trouble was to work her halfway to death – and she was definitely succeeding. Cleaning the so-called hospital ward had been followed by a dozen other tasks; some disgusting, some appalling. By the time she had finally been allowed to take a break to eat, she had been too exhausted to even try to talk the doctor into helping them escape.

Not, she suspected, that the doctor would have *helped*. Kailee had seen women like her on Earth, women who had been so completely broken they couldn't have raised a hand to defend themselves, even if they had been faced with imminent death. They were so far gone that they didn't even bother to come up with excuses for their actions – or their failures to act. Instead, they just sleepwalked through life. Kailee had a feeling that, if she had asked the doctor for help, the doctor would have immediately reported them to her master. It was probably what she'd been told to do.

Or perhaps she would think she is saving us, Kailee thought. *The bandits did make it clear that escape attempts would be severely punished.*

She gritted her teeth, remembering the patients she'd helped examine. Her ignorance had been a blessing, she suspected, even though all she could really do was look at the wounds and express her horror. The pregnant woman seemed unharmed, but there was a look in her eyes that told Kailee that she had been abused – and abused badly. One of the men had been beaten bloody; the doctor, in a rare moment of candour, had admitted that he'd been fighting over something and his opponent had ended up dead. Their leader had been unimpressed with the outcome and threatened bloody murder if the bandit fought again.

The odd thing was that she might have *liked* medicine, if she'd been given half a chance. She'd helped the pregnant woman – and then the woman had given her a shy smile that had melted Kailee's heart. Helping people felt good. It might not have the glamour of being an actress, but perhaps it was more satisfying. And yet...who would want to be a doctor on Earth? Kailee didn't have to ask to know that medicine was one of the most stressful professions on Earth, no matter what legal documents were signed before the patient entered the clinic. Would medicine on the colonies be any better?

Don't be fucking stupid, she told herself, as she lay down on the floor. *You can't even read and write. Do you think they'd let you study as a doctor?*

She shook her head, feeling another of her dreams fade away into nothingness. Earth no longer held anything for her, not now. But would she be happy on Meridian?

It doesn't matter, she told herself, savagely. *At least I would feel safer.*

———

Nick leaned close to Darrin, pressing his lips to the younger man's ears. "You have to stay here," he warned, as he pulled a pair of goggles over his eyes. "If you can't promise me you'll stay here, I'll cuff you to the tree."

"I'll stay here," Darrin said, quickly. The moon was rising in the sky, but hardly any light filtered down to the undergrowth. "Good luck."

"Thank you," Nick said, dryly. "Stay here."

He turned and slipped away into the darkness.

———

"Charges in place, sir."

Nick nodded. He would never have admitted it to anyone, but he was privately impressed with both the bandit camp and the boy from Earth. The camp itself would probably have remained undiscovered for years if Darrin hadn't located it and then made his way to the settlement. And he'd survived four days in the wilderness. Surviving such a trek was impressive when one had so little experience, even if he did have a Scout as an advisor.

The bandits were *organised*, he'd realised, as soon as he'd seen the wall of bushes. That boded ill for the future. They couldn't hope to take over the planet, he was sure, but they might well be able to cause a great deal of trouble for the militia. He'd checked the reports from the edge of the settlement zone and noted a handful of disappearances, mainly indents. In hindsight, he decided, they should have checked more carefully.

But the bandit camp was far enough from the settlements to remain undiscovered...

Pushing the thought aside, he keyed his earpiece.

"Go."

———

Austin was used to hard work. He'd helped on the farm as soon as he'd learned to walk, taking on more and more responsibility with each passing year. By the time he reached sixteen, he was effectively doing a full share of the farming chores, including a number that needed brute force. In that respect, working for the bandits hadn't been too bad. But they'd definitely been trying to exhaust him and he had to admit that they'd succeeded.

He'd been looking for ways to escape, but found none. The village was impressive, he had to admit, yet there was nowhere to hide. None of his half-formed plans for escape had included a way to get over the bushes or through the entrance without being spotted. The only idea he could think of that had even a hope of working was digging a tunnel, yet it didn't take much imagination to realise that the bandits could hardly miss *that*. It seemed that they were trapped, for the moment. He could only be grateful that they hadn't been shackled to the wall and left there until the ransom was paid – if, of course, it *was* paid.

Austin knew little of Earth, save what he'd been told by various people, but somehow he doubted that Earth would bother to pay ransom for two kids. Janet was still at Sabre City, he recalled; *she* might make such a decision, if she had the funds on hand. And if she didn't...Austin suspected that the colonial government wouldn't advance her the money. They certainly wouldn't want to *encourage* hostage-taking...

He closed his eyes and tried to sleep. His entire body ached. Moments later, the ground shook violently, followed by a series of loud thunder-claps. Austin jerked awake, realising that the camp was under attack. The sound of shooting broke out moments later, coming from outside the camp.

"Stay down," he hissed. Gary had started to stand up, even though the wooden walls of their prison would provide absolutely no protection if the bandits or their attackers started firing into the building. "Keep your fucking head down."

He crawled over to Kailee and climbed on top of her. She let out a sound that was half-gasp, half-cry, then clamped her mouth shut. Austin felt her body shivering against his, as if she found his touch repulsive. But it was the only way to provide her with even a little protection.

Outside, the sound of shooting grew louder.

———

There was a brilliant flash of light in the sky, followed by a pearly white light that seemed to blaze down from high overhead. Darrin had to cover his eyes until they had grown accustomed to the light, but even when he could open them safely he couldn't see much. He could hear shooting, yet he couldn't see very much at all. All he could do was wait.

He forced himself to stay where he was, even though his instincts were telling him to run. It was common for violence to break out on Earth – and bystanders were often caught up in the fighting, no matter how innocent they were. Darrin knew he should run, yet he didn't want to flee the battlefield, even though he was no combatant. There was a level of violence being unleashed that was far outside his experience, no matter how many violent entertainment flicks he'd watched.

A loud voice bellowed through the trees. "THROW DOWN YOUR WEAPONS AND SURRENDER," it ordered. "WE WILL NOT KILL YOU IF YOU SURRENDER."

The sound of shooting grew louder. Darrin hesitated, hopping from one foot to the other, then dropped to the ground as a flight of bullets flashed through the trees above his head. In the distance, he saw a flash of light, followed by a massive explosion. Something had just blown...

He shuddered, then forced himself to lie still. All he could do was wait.

———

"Women and children in this room, sir," the report said. "Two of the dames are pregnant."

"Get them on the ground," Nick ordered. The bandits had been completely surprised, but it seemed the bastards slept with their weapons under their pillows. He didn't dare unleash his full firepower for fear of wiping out innocents along with the guilty, so they had to take the village house by house. Thankfully, none of the houses were built of anything that might stand up to bullets. "Then make sure you cuff them."

He ignored the mutter of protest. The militiamen liked to think of themselves as heroes, heroes in a way the Civil Guard had long since forgotten. Nick rather envied their closeness to the local population; hell, they *were* the local population. But it also meant that they sometimes took dangerous chances. The women had been held captive for years, assuming that they were all genuine captives. They might easily have bonded with their captors, which might lead them to turn on their rescuers. Cuffing them all was safer than trying to sort out the safe from the dangerous in the midst of a firefight.

"Got some of them making a break for the wall," another militiaman said. "Colonel?"

"Cut them off at the knees," Nick ordered. They'd catch the bandits or kill them. He'd read reports from older colony worlds, where bandits had grown into a major headache for the authorities. This particular bunch of bandits would never have the opportunity to become more than a local nuisance. "And try to take them alive."

He wanted prisoners. There would be complaints, of course, that the bandits simply hadn't all been shot, but he wanted to interrogate them to confirm that there weren't any other bandit camps. After that...there were islands where irredeemable criminals could be dumped, if they didn't merit the death penalty. They couldn't hope to escape – or hurt anyone who wasn't a criminal.

Slowly, the sound of shooting began to die away.

————

Gary felt oddly composed as he lay on the ground, even when a stream of bullets blasted through the walls and punched their way out the other side of the building. Someone could kill him by accident, he knew, yet he felt much calmer than when he'd faced Barry. His tormentor's death had taken many of his fears into the darkness with him. Even when someone started tearing at the door, he found it hard to panic. He waited, calmly, as two armed men stepped into the room.

"Keep your hands where we can see them," the leader snapped. He knelt over Austin, secured his hands behind his back, then hauled him off Kailee and dumped him to one side like a sack of potatoes. Kailee squawked in protest, which earned her a knee in the back as her hands were bound. Gary submitted without a fight. "Stay here until we come back."

Gary almost snickered. Where did the newcomers think they were going to go?

It seemed like hours before the men returned, hauled the prisoners to their feet and marched them outside. The bandit camp had been shattered, once-proud buildings had been ripped apart or burned to the ground. A number of women sat on the ground, their children sitting next to them, staring around with fearful eyes. Behind them, a handful of men were clustered together, their hands bound behind their backs. Gary saw a dead body lying in their midst and guessed that their new captors weren't inclined to take backtalk...

"Austin," a voice called.

Gary swung around to see Darrin, running towards them. Behind him, there was a tall black man and a pale-skinned woman. Austin let out a delighted chuckle. Gary shook his head in disbelief. Who would have thought, really, that one day he would be *pleased* to see Darrin?

He shook his head, inwardly. Darrin had grown up. They'd all grown up a little, apart from Barry. But Barry was dead and gone and wouldn't be tormenting anyone any longer. Gary wondered, in the months and years to come, if he would feel shame and guilt for what he'd done to Barry, then dismissed the thought. Barry had never felt any guilt for what he'd done – and Gary hadn't been his only victim. In the end, his victims had destroyed him. A fitting conclusion to his life.

"You made it," Austin said. "Well done!"

"These are my friends," Darrin said, addressing the black man. He seemed to be in charge of the newcomers. "They shouldn't be tied up."

"True," the black man agreed. He nodded to his men, who cut through the bonds. Gary immediately started rubbing his wrists. "We will need to ask you some questions, though."

Kailee groaned. "Not again."

"Don't worry," the black man said. "You're safe now. We'll fly you back to the city, where you can recuperate. You can probably even sell your story to the newspapers, if you feel so inclined. They'd be thrilled to hear from a set of real heroes."

Gary blinked in surprise. "We're heroes?"

"Yep," the man said. His face twitched into a grin. "A bandit camp destroyed, prisoners rescued...not a bad day's work. They might even give you the keys to the city."

CHAPTER
THIRTY-NINE

Those on the outside of the system never understood it; those on the inside were forced to play by the rules the bureaucrats had built up over centuries. Fixing even the slightest problems was impossible, as those who saw the problems had no authority to change the rules or even try something new.

- Professor Leo Caesius, *Education and the Decline and Fall of the Galactic Empire*

"I wish I'd been with you," Janet said. "It might not have made much difference, but I wish I'd been with you."

Kailee shrugged. They'd been flown back to the city and immediately transported to the hospital, where they'd been given separate rooms and told to rest. Kailee had forgotten how good it could be to sleep alone, even though she kept jerking awake every time she heard a sound in the room. The phantom touch of Barry's hand on her skin would fade in time, she'd been told, but for the moment she half-wished someone was sleeping with her. It might have made life easier.

"Overall, your health checks out as better than expected," Janet added. "Most of your wounds were healed without problems. Barry...did some damage, but it was repaired."

She hesitated. "Do you want to talk about it?"

"I killed him," Kailee said. Barry had raped her and she'd killed him. It was funny, but one seemed to cancel out the other. Would the rape victims on Earth have coped better if they'd been allowed to kill their rapists? "Will I have to go on trial?"

"Probably not," Janet said. The second day, they'd told their stories to a handful of visitors from the city – and Janet, who had listened quietly and said nothing. "Barry's death has been ruled justifiable homicide. There isn't anyone here interested in pursuing the matter further, no kin who might seek recompense or revenge. You should be fine."

Kailee relaxed, slightly. "Thank you," she said. "What happens now?"

Janet gave her a long considering look. "What do you *want* to happen now?"

"I want to find a career here," Kailee said. "Earth doesn't have anything for me now."

"Cool," Janet said. She smiled. It made her look years younger. "And what do you actually want to do?"

"I would like to study medicine," Kailee said. "But I don't know if that would be possible."

"Maybe, maybe not," Janet said. She looked pensive for a moment. "You cannot read or write, nor can you perform more than simple arithmetic. On the other hand, those are skills you can learn, given the right incentive. You'll have to work hard."

She smiled. "I can speak to the nurses here," she added. "They might agree to take you on as a trainee, provided you make a determined effort to master those skills. But this isn't Earth, Kailee. One screw up and you will be kicked out so hard you'll end up in next week."

"I know," Kailee said. On Earth, it was almost impossible to get rid of a doctor, no matter how dangerously incompetent. There had been a doctor, a level or two above her, who had earned the nickname Dr. Death. Few people wanted to go to him for treatment. "But I want to take the chance to *try*."

Janet nodded. "And so you shall," she said. "There are other options, of course."

Kailee nodded. Fishing didn't hold an appeal for her, nor did becoming a farmwife. Maybe she could become a shopkeeper...but what would she sell? Besides, Janet was right. Her maths skills were very limited.

"The doctor tells me that you should be discharged tomorrow," Janet said, finally. "They've assigned you all an apartment, so you can sleep there - I'd suggest you rest for a few days, which will give me enough time to set up the interview with the nurses. In any case, don't leave the city."

"Of course not," Kailee agreed. Right now, she wouldn't have left the city if she'd been offered money to do it. "I'll stay in bed."

Janet stood, then picked a reader off the table and passed it to Kailee. "You might want to download basic medical texts from the datanet," she offered. "There should be an outline of what you will have to learn if you want proper qualifications, although you can go quite some distance without them. Meridian *definitely* isn't Earth."

She smiled. "But you really should practice reading," she added. "You're going to need it."

Kailee watched as she left the room, then turned her attention to the reader.

———

"Colonel Nick was quite impressed with you," Austin said, as Darrin dressed in the clothes he'd been loaned. "And so were the councillors. There's talk of hosting a large banquet for you and your friends."

Darrin flushed. It was funny, but after years of worthless praise from teachers he found *real* praise embarrassing. Colonel Nick had years of experience, Austin had been a Scout...and yet they'd both praised Darrin to the skies. A banquet would be even more embarrassing, he suspected. And yet part of him enjoyed the feeling of knowing he'd done well.

"More practically, I have a form for you," Austin continued. "If you're still interested, that is."

He passed Darrin a sheet of paper and a pen. "Your standard application form for the Sabre Salamanders," he explained. "They're the local Scouts. You'll be older than most of the newcomers, but you have a great deal to learn. Once you win a few badges, you'll have your chance to try out for the militia. If, of course, that is what you want to do with your life."

Darrin glanced at the form. It seemed almost absurdly simple compared to the endless realms of paperwork on Earth. Going paperless might be environmentally friendly – it was the excuse for never allowing a *real* book inside the school – but it seemed to allow forms to grow and grow until filling them in took hours. Instead, the Scouts just wanted name, address and prior experience. But he didn't even have an address.

"The council has given you and the others an apartment," Austin said, when he asked. "There's also a cash reward, which you need to accept at some point. And there might also be gifts from others."

Darrin nodded. "Thank you," he said, and meant it. "When do I start?"

Austin smirked. "You will also need to get a job, as the money will not last indefinitely," he warned. "My father might decide to give you a chance, but I think you'd be better off working in the city. Take a few days to see what options there are and then make up your mind. You could earn a good wage simply chopping down trees or working on the boats. It's up to you."

"I'll make up my mind soon," Darrin promised. "And yourself? What are you going to do now?"

"Write a full report, then have it ripped to shreds by the Scoutmaster, I assume," Austin said, dryly. He didn't seem very worried at the prospect. "He'll probably say I should have shot Barry or something, right at the start. Hindsight is always so much clearer, isn't it?"

He shrugged. "Speaking of which, my uncle apologised for all the awful things he said about you," he added. "He was quite impressed too. I think he even plans to invite you for dinner."

"Thank you," Darrin said, sardonically. Austin's uncle sounded fearsome. "But shouldn't I get better first?"

Austin laughed. "You don't get to stay in bed on the farm," he said, snidely. "Get well soon."

————

Gary had been discharged from the hospital after the first day, although the doctor had warned him to take it easy for the next few days. He'd gone to the lodge, then to the apartment where he'd met Steve. The older boy had talked briefly about remaining with the plane, then left Gary to settle in alone. It had been easy enough. Most of his stuff had been lost along the way.

He looked around his room, feeling oddly unsettled. There was no computer, apart from the reader – and there was unlikely to be one, at least for some years. Sabre City's datanet was primitive, he had discovered;

it simply wasn't designed to become as pervasive as Earth's, where it could be found almost everywhere. There was little call for a computer technician on Meridian, although Janet had pointed out that he could get a job at the spaceport while he waited for a freighter to arrive that might be interested in a new crewman. It was, Gary suspected, his only hope.

Shaking his head, he walked out of the room and into the living room. Li sat there, her leg encased in plaster. Gary knew that modern medicine could have healed her quicker, but she wasn't classed as important enough to deserve the best. He wondered, briefly, if the doctors regretted that decision, before telling himself it might not matter. The economics of interstellar shipping meant that only limited supplies of advanced medicines and nanotechnology were available on Meridian. Li could afford to heal the old-fashioned way.

He nodded to her, then walked out of the door. The apartment was actually a double-storey house, although they only had the lower level to themselves. From what he'd heard, it had originally belonged to a family that had stayed in the city for several years, then migrated out to a farm. It was actually one of the largest new-built buildings in the city, surprisingly enough. Only the prefabricated buildings were larger.

And, compared to the megacities, it was so tiny that it didn't even register.

Gary had never liked crowds. The handful of people on the streets didn't make him uncomfortable, not like walking through the megacity and fearing anything from theft to assault and random murder. But he wasn't sure he could spend the rest of his life on Meridian. Darrin might enjoy the chance to work with his muscles, Kailee might make it as a doctor; Gary knew that he would never be happy on Meridian. But it was better than Earth.

He paused outside the shooting range, then stepped inside. The man at the counter eyed him suspiciously, no doubt remembering what had happened when Darrin and Barry had gone shooting before the crash. Thankfully, the settlers didn't seem inclined to blame *everyone* from Earth for the sins of a couple of fools. Gary stopped outside the counter, then took a breath and opened his mouth.

"I'd like to apply for shooting lessons," he said.

"Would you," the man said. "And how much do you know already?"

"Nothing," Gary said, honestly. If he'd known how to use the pistol he'd taken, if he'd had the confidence to trust in himself, he might have been able to save Kailee from being raped. "I need to start at the beginning."

He still had nightmares about his bullet slamming into Barry. Some of them had him missing, which ended with him being beaten to death like Abdul. Others had Barry's body exploding into a bloody mass as soon as the bullet hit home, leaving Gary and Kailee covered in blood. He knew he needed the self-confidence to learn to use a gun to protect himself and the only way to gain it was to take proper lessons. Whatever else happened, he promised silently, he would never be bullied again.

"Very good," the man said. He rose to his feet, then plucked a pair of rifles and a pistol from the rack. "We shall begin at once."

————

Janet had always disliked paperwork. The Imperial Army seemed to produce enough paperwork every day to wipe the bottoms of every enlisted man for years to come – which was, in her opinion, the best possible use for it. Even working independently for the Golden Cross, she still had to do paperwork. But at least it was more interesting than certifying that X number of rounds had been taken from storage, that Y number of rounds had been expended in training operations and Z number of rounds had been returned to the locked cabinets.

Overall, the results of the experiment were encouraging. Twelve candidates, selected largely at random, were taken to Meridian. Seven of them ended up dead, six through no fault of their own. (The plane crash that also killed Sergeant Yates was an unexpected incident.) Of the remainder, three of them may fit into colonial society, one wishes to become an independent spacer and one has no plans for her future. I believe that when her leg recovers she may find a place on Meridian.

Janet scowled. The next paragraph was harder to write. Yates hadn't held out much hope for Barry either, but he'd wondered if Barry would do better if he'd been separated from his fellows. But he had never had the chance to find out.

> *That said, Subject Three – Barry Sycamore (Earth ID/case file attached) – was particularly disappointing. Barry engaged in bullying behaviour on the starship, then committed an act of wanton vandalism on Meridian, scrabbled with his comrades during their march back to civilisation and finally raped Subject Six. Subject Three was punished heavily for the first two offences, but unlike Subject Two failed to learn from the experience. I saw no evidence of moral realignment prior to the aircraft crash. In short, I believe that future candidates comparable to Subject Three should be rejected – if this is impossible, they should be assigned to one-on-one mentoring with someone they can respect.*

And thrash them for every little misdeed, Janet thought. She rather suspected that Yates would have been wasting his time. Barry had been too far gone to be saved, just like Han and a number of other worlds across the Empire. They were teetering on the brink of chaos.

She shook her head. The Golden Cross wasn't in the habit of shooting the messenger, but she'd been in the military long enough to know that unvarnished bad news wasn't considered welcome. But at least there was good news to go with the bad.

> *Encouragingly, Subjects Two, Four and Six managed to grow during their ordeal. Subject Two – Darrin Person (Earth ID/case file attached) – managed to reach civilisation to summon assistance to the captured Subjects Four and Six. Subject Six – Kailee Singh (Earth ID/case file attached) – was responsible for the fatal blow to Subject Three, despite having been raped by him. She showed a resiliency that was quite unexpected. I must note that while I did try to train her, along with the other girls, she always did the bare minimum necessary to proceed. Subject Four – Gary Seaman (Earth ID/*

case file attached) – showed remarkable initiative for someone from Earth, including taking Sergeant Yates's gun and concealing it until it became necessary to use the weapon.

Subject Four started the trip as a shaking weakling, if I may be blunt. His self-confidence was non-existent. He was determined to score highly on the exams that would allow him to leave the CityBlock behind forever. Now, he is shooting regularly and actually seems to be on the verge of a relationship with Subject Six. (I have taken it on myself to counsel him to be careful. Subject Six's reactions to her rape are atypical.) Overall, I can honestly say that the development of Subject Four has been extraordinary.

And none of them want to go back to Earth. I am not surprised.

Janet allowed herself a smile. She hadn't been impressed with Kailee either, but the girl had managed to surprise her. So had Li. It was a shame that the others hadn't survived, though; who knew what they might have become, given time?

But there was a more serious issue she had to address.

I must add, however, that the decision to allow Principal Rico's blatant rigging of the competition results (at least enough to ensure that four candidates came from his school) was badly in error. It created unwelcome dynamics among the selected; Subject Two, for example, was pushed together with Subject Three, even though the relationship was bad for both of them. Subject Four had no reason to try to make new ties with the others as two of his tormentors were also assigned to the program. He simply believed that they would be impossible to form. I believe that he might have been right.

In future, we should exercise greater care in selecting the candidates or take enough candidates to ensure that no school administrator gains an advantage by rigging the results. If nothing else, we can recruit enough to shuffle the groups around and ensure that all prior ties are broken.

Overall, the experiment may be deemed a partial success. However, doing it on a large scale may prove impossible. For better or worse, the twelve subjects were landed on a planet where the settlers outnumbered them thousands to one. If we expand the program to meaningful levels, we will alter that dynamic – and not in our favour. This is, of course, quite apart from the other problems. If we wish to save Earth (or at least as many of her inhabitants as we can) we may need to find another approach.

"If we can," she muttered to herself, as she attached her electronic signature. The report would go back to the Core Worlds on the next starship, although it would be months before it finally reached Earth. By then, the next bunch of candidates might have already been selected.

She shook her head. Earth's population was widely believed to be somewhere around eighty *billion*. If every starship in the Empire were assigned to hauling people away from Earth, it would still take centuries to evacuate the planet. And, even though Earth could not have long to live, most of the population wouldn't want to go.

But at least the potential existed. Earth's children *could* adapt to a new environment, even when they hadn't selected themselves. The experiment had proved that much, at least. But would it be enough to save Earth? Somehow, she doubted it.

Sighing, she tapped SEND. The message vanished into the datanet.

CHAPTER
FORTY

In the end, the important detail is simple. The Empire, in refusing to prepare its children to face the future, ensured that they had no future. Nor did the Empire.

- Professor Leo Caesius, *Education and the Decline and Fall of the Galactic Empire*

"I confess I had my doubts about you, lad," the foreman said. "You were not as physically strong as I would have preferred. But I took you on and you've made me proud."

Darrin paused, wiping the sweat from his brow. Six months of hard labour and proper food had worked wonders on his body. Once, he'd thought himself strong. Now, he suspected he was actually stronger than Barry had been before his death. And, thanks to the Scouts, he was also a great deal more experienced. He had a long way to go, but he was getting there.

"Thank you, Bob," he said. The foreman insisted on informality, except when he was chewing someone out. Darrin had earned more than his fair share of lectures in his first two weeks of working. But he'd improved. "Shooting tonight?"

"Yep," Bob grinned. He looked around the lumberyard. "You've done well today."

Darrin grinned. The lumberjacks walked out of the city in the morning, chopped down a number of trees and then carried their prizes back to the lumberyard, where they were converted into planks of wood for building or firewood. There wasn't much to the job, but it paid well and it kept him from having to think too much. And being a local hero had encouraged Bob to give him some extra time to settle in. It had definitely proved worth it.

He joined Bob and the others outside the yard for a celebratory beer. It had surprised him to see the colonials drinking beer – it was something he associated with Fitz – and he'd been reluctant to join them, at first. But the colonials didn't have bad habits when it came to alcohol. Those who got drunk tended to regret it. Darrin couldn't help wondering what Fitz would have been like if he'd spent a month on the chain gangs after beating his wife into a pulp while he was drunk. But there was no point in fretting about a man who might be dead – and who definitely *was* thousands of light years away.

"There'll be a little something extra in your pay-packets for the week, boys," Bob said, once he'd quaffed his can of beer. "Old Smoky was very pleased with the last shipment of lumber; they're hoping to start work on building the new transit dorms tomorrow. Any of you who want extra experience in working on construction sites are welcome to apply for leave and join him for a bit."

Darrin snorted. The lumberyard wasn't formal. Someone could sign up, work for a couple of weeks, then leave to another job. It was quite a popular job for young men who were in the city for one reason or another. Darrin had been new when he'd started, obviously. Now, he was one of the old sweats. Only Bob and a handful of others had remained with the yard since Bob had opened it, largely because they owned stock in the company. Darrin wondered, sometimes, if it would be worth investing himself.

He pushed the thought aside. For once, he could pick and choose among potential careers.

"I'll see some of you at the shooting range this evening," Bob concluded. "Everyone else, have a good evening and I'll see you all tomorrow."

Darrin put the empty can in the bucket, then strode off down the road and into the city. Sabre seemed to have kept expanding, even though there hadn't been a shipment of new immigrants for six months. But the planetary birth-rate was surprisingly high and the population was expanding naturally. Darrin wondered, sometimes, what would happen if they ran out of space. Would Meridian become like Earth – or Han? Or would the birth-rate fall once the planet was completely settled?

He unlocked the door, then stepped into the apartment. One habit he had never lost was locking the door, even though half of the colonials didn't seem to bother. But then, they all believed that a colonial's house was his private kingdom. Even the elected sheriffs were reluctant to cross the invisible line that separated public land from private territory. On Earth, anything that wasn't nailed down and guarded 24/7 was certain to be stolen, sooner or later.

"Darrin," Pepper called to him. She was Austin's sister, who had moved to the city for her year away from the farm. Austin had introduced Darrin to her and they'd hit it off, immediately. She was so different from Judy that it hurt, sometimes. Would Judy have been as independent-minded if she'd grown up on Meridian? "Gary sent you a message."

Darrin blinked in surprise. Gary and he had become friends, of a sort, but they didn't spend much time together. Not that Darrin could really blame Gary. The maturity he'd gained over the months had taught him that he'd treated Gary badly, even if he hadn't been as bad as Barry. But he had no idea how he could even begin to make up for it.

"He said that you should come visit the spaceport as soon as possible," Pepper added. "Do you think there's news from Earth?"

"I have no idea," Darrin said. He'd planned to go shooting with Bob and the others in the evening, but he had a feeling that Gary wouldn't have called them unless it was urgent. "I think I'd better go."

"I'll come with you," Pepper said. She ran a hand through her short red hair, then reached for her coat. The skies had been noticeably darkening while Darrin had walked home, suggesting that there was another rainstorm on the way. "It should be a fun walk."

Darrin smiled, remembering how they'd bitched and moaned the first time they'd walked from the spaceport to the city. Now, it seemed like nothing.

———

"Push," Kailee said. "*Push!*"

The woman groaned loudly, then gave one final push. Kailee watched in awe as the baby emerged from between her legs, looking so small and tiny compared to his – no, *her* – mother. The midwife coughed meaningfully; Kailee picked up her scissors, quickly cut the cord and watched as the baby started to breathe. She'd seen five or six births since she had started working in the maternity ward, yet they never failed to awe her. The children were being born into a world that would treat them far better than Earth.

"It's a girl," the midwife said. "Congratulations."

The mother let out a snicker. "He was so sure that it would be a boy," she said. "The bastard just kept babbling on about how he would have a son to raise."

Kailee winced. The mother had been kidnapped from a farm and held captive by the bandits – and, inevitably, one of them had knocked her up. But she'd been rescued, while the father had been dumped on a penal island thousands of miles from the mainland. She could rebuild her life...or have her daughter adopted by someone else. Kailee had read a few rape textbooks while she'd been struggling to come to terms with her own emotions and they'd told her that children produced by a rape were often hated by their own mothers. Putting the child up for adoption might be the best course of action.

"Never mind what he thought," the midwife said. "Have you picked a name?"

The mother shook her head. "I never thought I'd have the chance," she said. "Can you suggest one?"

"Lillian," Kailee said. "She was a strong woman on Earth."

Afterwards, she went into the private rooms, showered and dressed in her everyday clothes. The midwife – Kailee's mistress, at least until she had proved she could handle the task – had warned her time and time again about basic hygiene. She'd also pointed out that while it was easy enough to keep clean in the city, it could be harder in the countryside. Trainee doctors tended to make the rounds from settlement to settlement, she'd been warned. On Meridian, it was often impossible to get a patient – or an expectant mother – to the hospital on time.

"Good work," the midwife said, when she came out. "There's a message for you on the datanet."

Kailee nodded and walked over to the computer. One of the few advantages of working at the hospital was access to the planetary datanet, even though her reading skills were nowhere near as good as her supervisors wanted. She found the message, then sounded out the words one by one. Gary was asking her to come to the spaceport as soon as possible. It sounded urgent, she realised. They had an unspoken agreement that they would not interfere with their workplaces.

She spoke briefly to the midwife, then took the keys to the medical car and headed out of the hospital. The only other advantage of working in the hospital was that she was allowed to use the car, even though it was a ground car rather than the aircars used on Earth. It had been great fun to learn how to drive; she still got a kick from realising that neither Darrin nor Gary would have been allowed to learn, even on Meridian. There just weren't enough cars for everyone to have one of their own.

Halfway to the spaceport, she spotted Darrin and Pepper, hand-in-hand. Naturally, she stopped to offer them a lift.

————

Surprisingly, Gary had come to enjoy his position at the spaceport. There was an astonishing amount of computer equipment in the building, including some that had never been installed because it had been deemed too advanced for Meridian. Gary had checked and rechecked the manifests, then dragged it out of storage and installed it himself. It didn't quite match the thrill of fiddling with Earth's datanet – or the fun of playing games with thousands of others on the network – but it had been interesting. Besides, several of the systems weren't designed to link together and getting them to do so had been a real challenge.

There weren't actually many official duties at all, his former boss had told him. Indeed, there was only *one* full-time worker at the spaceport – Gary himself. When a starship landed, he would call for volunteers from the city to help unload, but apart from that all he really had to do was monitor the displays and keep himself from becoming too bored. The shuttles were stored at the Orbital Station; the crew kept themselves to themselves, rarely even talking to the people on the ground. Gary understood. There were times when he didn't want to talk to anyone either.

But it still struck him as odd, from time to time.

When the message blinked up on his screen, he read it...and then swore out loud. It couldn't be true, could it? But the message was verified; it had all the right confirmation codes attached. He called the others and waited, grimly, for them to arrive in the empty building so he could tell them in person. The council could hear the news later.

"A starship made a brief visit to the system," he said, when Kailee, Darrin and Pepper had finally arrived. Steve and Li were on their honeymoon, exploring the Craggy Mountains. "The ship transmitted a long message to Orbit Station, then crossed the Phase Limit again and jumped back into Phase Space. By the time the message reached us, the ship was long gone."

"So they didn't want to wait around for a reply," Darrin said. He held Pepper's hand tightly, as if he was nervous. "What did they say?"

Gary met Kailee's eyes. Their relationship had surprised him, but perhaps it shouldn't have. They both understood the limits of intimacy, as well as sharing experiences that had bound them together. But this would test them to the limit.

"The message said that Earth had fallen," Gary told them. He'd skimmed the details, but the ending lines had made it clear that humanity's homeworld was no longer habitable. "The planet is dead. Everyone we knew is gone."

"Dead," Kailee said. She sounded as though she didn't quite believe her own words. "They're all dead."

Gary wasn't sure he believed it either. Earth had such a high population that it was literally beyond human comprehension. How could they all be dead? It was a crime that made the Tyrant of Macedon, a man responsible for the deaths of billions of humans before the Imperial Navy put a stop to his revolution, look like a naughty boy. He tried to think about what it all meant and failed.

But maybe, on a more personal level...he shuddered. Moe was dead. Everyone else who had tormented him at school was dead. The teachers were dead.

And his family were dead. Sammie was dead. His parents were dead. Earth was gone.

"The message concluded that Meridian...well, that *we* have effectively been abandoned," Gary concluded. "We're on our own."

"If we'd been there," Kailee said softly, "we'd be dead too."

Gary nodded, looking at the timestamp on the message. Six months, more or less, after they'd left Earth. Six months for the most densely populated planet in the galaxy to collapse into chaos.

"Yes," he said, finally. "We would be dead."

He'd had hopes and dreams to escape the damned Rowdy Yates CityBlock. Now, he knew that even if he had managed to make it to Imperial University, he would have died when Earth collapsed. Kailee had dreamed of becoming an actress; she too would have died, unless she was lucky enough to leave the planet before it was too late. And Darrin had had no real plans at all. He would have found an apartment and a girl and started churning out babies. And he would have died too when the CityBlocks fell.

God alone knew what was going to happen to the Empire now. Meridian was a very minor world. It didn't even have a cloudscoop to mine HE3 from the gas giant. Chances were that they would simply be abandoned by what remained of the Empire...or what? What were the other alternatives? Nothing he'd read had ever suggested that the Empire could fall...

"At least we're alive," he concluded. "And we should probably count ourselves lucky."

————

Janet had never intended to stay on Meridian. It wasn't part of her calling, not after leaving one farming world. Even though she was respected on Meridian, it wasn't the same as moving from world to world. She had only taken on the task of helping with the project because Yates, who had been her mentor as well as her friend, had specifically requested her help. Now, Yates was dead and she was stuck.

There was no way to know if the message she had sent had uploaded itself to the messenger ship before it had re-crossed the Phase Limit and vanished. Janet rather doubted it – and, even if it had, who would get it? The Imperial Communications Network had been fraying for decades, a long time before Earth finally collapsed. Maybe that too had been a factor in the Empire's decline. But then, there had always been a delay in sending the message and having it received on the other side of the Empire. It could go no faster than the starship carrying it.

She looked down, again, at her notes. She'd watched all of the Earth-born, offering advice where necessary. They'd become adults, slightly skewed by the standards of Meridian, but adults none the less. But now all of her notes were useless. No one was ever going to read them.

We didn't predict the collapse so soon, she told herself. But the Empire was – had been – vast. Who knew what spark had set off the blaze that had destroyed Earth? Perhaps it had been something small and simple, perhaps it had been something so large that it had shattered the Empire. But she had a feeling that she would never know.

Carefully, she saved her notes, then closed the computer. There was no point in collecting more data, not now. Earth was gone.

But she had a feeling that the galaxy's troubles were only just beginning.

EPILOGUE

Gary wasn't sure why he bothered to stay at the spaceport. It wasn't like there was nothing else for him to do, not since Orbit Station had been placed into long-term shutdown and the remaining crew landed on the planet's surface. Improving the planetary datanet had been a long-term project, one he was rather proud of having led. It was cruder than Earth's, but much – much – harder to control. But, every day, he came to the spaceport, glanced at systems that had remained quiet for years, then returned to his work.

He stepped into the sensor room and stopped, dead. A light was flashing on the display, indicating the presence of an incoming starship. Gary felt his heart leap into his mouth as he bent over the systems, trying to massage data from the remaining orbital satellites. No starship had visited the system since the message from Earth, not for five years. He'd always assumed that they had simply been abandoned.

But now there was definitely a starship in orbit. And it was hailing the planet.

He cleared his throat, then opened a channel. "This is Meridian Spaceport," he said, hoping that his Imperial Standard was understandable. Everyone was supposed to speak it, but there were hundreds of accents in the Empire. "Please identify yourself."

The reply came at once. "This is *Wolfhound*, a harsh male voice said. "We represent the Wolfbane Consortium. You are ordered to surrender at once or face bombardment."

For a long moment, Gary didn't understand what he'd been told. Bombardment?

"I will have to call the council," he stammered, finally. "What do you *want*?"

"Your world has been annexed," the voice informed him. There was a definite hint of mockery in his tone. "You belong to us now."

The End

AFTERWORD
ON EDUCATION

You are providing for your disciples a show of wisdom without the reality. For, acquiring by your means much information unaided by instruction, they will appear to possess much knowledge, while, in fact, they will, for the most part, know nothing at all; and, moreover, be disagreeable people to deal with, as having become wise in their own conceit, instead of truly wise.

-Socrates

It is customary for everyone from politicians to housemothers to give their opinions on education – and most of them are not worth the paper they are printed on. In order to make my credentials (or lack thereof) clear, I will outline my own educational history first. You can then decide for yourself if I'm talking sense or if I have just wasted a few hundred thousand electrons.

I have never been a teacher. The closest I have come to serving as an educator was when I assisted other students at university. However, I have been a subject – I might say a victim – of the British educational establishment. I spent seven years at a primary school in Edinburgh, four years at a secondary (boarding) school in Fife and two years in another secondary school in Edinburgh. After that, I spent three years in Manchester in a university, after which I emerged with a BA (HONS) that was largely worthless. I confess that I understand little of the pressures facing British teachers. But I do not consider such pressures an acceptable excuse for the poor education I received at their hands.

I left university in 2003. My experience may be outdated.

I should add to the above note to explain that I am largely referring to British schools. The statements I have heard about American public schools suggest that they suffer from many similar problems to British schools, but I have no direct experience to draw on. Handle with care.

I did not enjoy my schooling. Being what is called a 'special needs' student (I suffer from an odd form of dyslexia), I required special treatment to move ahead. I did not receive that treatment from my primary school, at least until my final year there. As it was, they sent me to a boarding school for (in theory) such children. Many of them had far worse problems than I, others were (in my rather biased opinion) actually *stupid* rather than dyslexic. (To be fair, one of the worst bullies played a mean game of Chess.) By the time I left there, I had six Standard Grades (O-Levels) and was something of a nervous wreck. The two years I had at the next school were perhaps the best years of my education, although it was far too clear to me that I was quite some distance behind my classmates. Suffice it to say that I had real problems in staggering away with four Highers (A-Levels) and was quite surprised when I actually got into university. By then, much of my course had already been set.

Looking back at my education, certain things become clear. Those of us who were considered 'special needs' children were not really expected to do well. The real objective was to keep us out of the regular schools while getting us the minimum necessary to pass onwards to further education. We were not, for example, granted the resources necessary to learn about more than the basics. For example, there was no internet and only a handful of computers. For someone with poor handwriting, like myself, it was a nightmare.

In hindsight, the real marvel is that I did as well as I did.

And, compared to students who undertook a more regular course of study, my achievements were bloody pathetic.

If a foreign nation had imposed this system of education on the United States we would rightly consider it an act of war.

-Glenn T. Seaborg

So, what is wrong with British schools?

There are a multitude of problems. Some of them stem from being 'good enough.' Some of them are caused by poor educational policies, often flowing from political correctness. Some are problems of scale, caused by classes sizes; some are caused by badly-chosen educational material. I have decided to examine the most common problems; you can tell me, if you like, if these problems exist or existed in your schools.

-Mixed classes.
I'm not talking about mixing male and female pupils together. Nothing I have seen in my educational journey has left me with strong feelings one way or the other about mixing the sexes. I'm talking about mixing children of different educational ability or aptitude. In every class, there will be 10% fast children, 80% average children and 10% slow children. Not *stupid* (although some people *are* genuinely stupid), but pupils who require additional patience and time from the teacher to go over the material.

Several things will happen in this class, none of them good. The fast children will be bored because they are not being tested to the limits of their ability. The slow children will either drain the teacher's time and energy or be left behind until they cannot really catch up. In the meantime, most of the average kids will be largely ignored by the teacher because he or she is busy tending to the fast or slow children.

It is *verboten* to suggest that children perform at different levels, even though it is self-evidently true. We sort classes by age because it provides an inarguable way to separate out different sets of children. But there are kids who could move a year or two ahead and kids who should be kept back, just to give them a chance to learn properly.

What do you think this does to both fast and slow kids? The fast kids will develop an exaggerated idea of their own capabilities. The slow kids will start to think of themselves as stupid. (I've been in both places.) And this tends to lead to other problems, such as...

-Discipline (or lack thereof).
The educational process exists for two reasons, only one of which is broadly acknowledged. One is to ensure that children are taught the basic skills they need to know to get on in life; the other is to socialise children,

to teach them how to fit in with other children and adults. Guess which one is acknowledged? It isn't the socialisation process, that's for sure. Indeed, the boarding school I went to seemed to specialise in turning out little barbarians, rather than good-natured adults.

Put bluntly, teachers do not have the power to effectively discipline their pupils. They are often put into the position of bluffing their charges – and, when the bluff is called, find that they are unable to actually carry it out. For the average student, being excluded from school for a week or two isn't really a punishment. When that student suffers no real punishment for bullying his fellows (or her fellows, as bullies come in both sexes) he will happily carry on bullying them.

In my experience, male bullies tend to fall into three categories; the stupid, the over- privileged and the psychopath. The stupid hates the smarter kids (often, he's from a poorer home) and since he can't beat them academically, beats them with his fists instead. The over- privileged was granted too much too easily (either from his parents or on the sports field) and consequently sees himself immune to punishment. The psychopath is simply sick in the head; he gets his fun hurting and humiliating his fellows and everyone else he can reach.

These pupils need discipline. They rarely get it.

Their victims need protection. They rarely get it either.

Failing to provide discipline does neither the bullies nor their victims any favours. The bullies generally discover that adulthood is far less accepting of their idea of fun than the schoolyard. Adults go to jail for stunts bullies can pull and get away with it. Their victims, in the meantime, withdraw into themselves or snap completely.

-Poor work experience/vocational training.
One of the things I love about being a writer is that I am effectively being paid to enjoy my hobby. My previous career as a librarian did not offer that sense of fulfilment. People who want a particular kind of job want it because they believe they will enjoy it. When you're a kid, making decisions that will affect your future, you rarely get a chance to really experience life in your chosen career.

I had precisely four weeks of work experience from my third school and another four weeks from university. As my luck would have it, I was ill for part of both courses. (In addition, there were a handful of visits to various places in primary school, which didn't even scratch the surface.) Neither of them was really enough for me to make a final choice, nor did they come in time for me to change my picked courses.

-Little Practical Work.

One of my pleasures when I was a child was playing with Lego bricks and building vast structures. As I grew older, I played with my father's Meccano (the modern plastic stuff is generally disliked by anyone old enough to see how condescending it is to kids) and learned a great deal about how machines actually worked. I often had to work out ropes, clockwork and suchlike for myself.

I didn't get to do that at school.

Some of my readers will probably point out that playing with toys isn't actually schoolwork, is it? To which I would reply that such 'toys' taught me the basics of physics and how to solve problems and puzzles. Further, what practical work I *did* have at school was very limited and often involved being told to follow the instructions, rather than figuring out the how and why for myself.

It doesn't just involve toys and games. I was rarely told why certain kinds of maths were so important, or what practical use they had beyond tormenting me. Had I been told, had my work been linked to something *practical,* I believe that I would have done better at school.

-Poor Book Choices

Reading is one of my great pleasures...but that was no thanks to school. The books I was expected to read were often too easy for me (I learned to read very quickly) or boring. My English course in particular insisted on us reading *Sunset Song,* which – although a genuinely important piece of Scottish literature – was quite boring to a young boy. I was lucky in that I was able to read books outside class, thus cutting my reading skills on books I actually *liked.*

I can understand why schools might frown on *Harry Potter*. The books are not great literature, but they serve an important purpose by shaping the reading muscles and encouraging future reading. One might move from *Harry Potter* to *The Lord of the Rings* and then to *Sunset Song*. It's harder to do it the other way around.

-Poor University Courses

My university degree was intended to prepare me to work in a library. Practically speaking, everything I ever actually used during seven years as a librarian could have been taught in six months, with the net result that all I really achieved was a considerable debt and a degree that was useless outside the field. (I don't think I exaggerate to say that I could have handled my job at eighteen, without going to university at all.)

I am told it is actually worse in the USA. The modules I did in university were related (sometimes quite loosely) to librarianship, although their practical value was somewhat limited. In the USA, course requirements include subjects that are of no value to the eager student – and, in fact, serve no other purpose than padding out the course.

-Political Correctness

Ah, political correctness. The fear that something, no matter how well-meaning, will be taken as offensive by *someone*. (It is contemptible at any time, but it is even more contemptible when measures are taken against it *before* someone has a chance to complain.) Anything can be taken as offensive, anything at all. In pursuit of the bland miasma of political correctness, schools have been forced into an endless series of 'compromises' and outright surrenders.

Let's see now. Discussing the Holocaust is hard; it might offend someone. Discussing the Crusades, or Islam, or any other controversial subject? It might offend someone. Books like *Huckleberry Finn*? Barred on the grounds they might offend someone. Discussing racial, sexual or political issues? Someone might be offended.

Kids aren't stupid. They can tell when they're been talked down to.

And believe me, there's only so many politically-correct lectures (or sensitivity training) you can take before you start developing those undesirable traits.

> "Treat kids like equals! They're people too! They're smarter than you think! They were smart enough to catch me!"
>
> -Sideshow Bob, *The Simpsons*

As a kid, if I had been asked to name my favourite TV show, it would have been *Thunderbirds*. Even by today's standards, it stands up well...and it was groundbreaking at the time. The magnificent machines (the true stars of the show), the tension of watching as everything that can go wrong *did* go wrong...and the genuinely mature storylines. *Thunderbirds* treated kids as equals; the handful of episodes that did feature kids had them as *kids*, not mini-adults or kids who have to save the world after the adults bugger it all up.

And imagine my horror when I saw the live-action movie directed by Jonathon Frakes. It managed to fall right into the pitfalls that the original series evaded quite neatly. (Frakes really should have known better. There is a reason the most hatred regular character on *Star Trek: The Next Generation* was Wesley Crusher.) The adults are useless, the kids save the day...and are rewarded with adult responsibilities that they are in no way prepared for.

Some people will say that this is a silly observation – or at least irrelevant. But I do have a point; if you treat kids as intelligent, capable humans, you will have kids learning how to think, question and develop into mature adults. On the other hand, if you talk down to kids and make it clear to them that you're doing so, the kids will act out. Why not? They're not being treated with respect.

With that in mind, how might we fix education?

First, we need to bear in mind that kids need discipline and boundaries. Teachers should have the power to discipline kids and, at worst, remove the truly disruptive children from the classroom permanently.

There is always someone who acts up, either because they haven't learned better or because they're genuinely not right in the head. Tragic as that is, it would be better to remove him rather than let him drag down the rest of the class.

Second, we need to organise classes by capability. Even separating out the fast kids from the slow kids will be genuinely helpful for both sides. The fast will not be held back and the slow will not be unable to catch up.

Third, we need to concentrate on core skills. Reading, writing, maths and (these days) information recovery. Teach kids to read, encourage them to choose their own books and actually *think* about the material. Maybe they'll pick something lowbrow like *Harry Potter* or *Superman*. You can still get them to *think* about the material. Believe me, kids will do what they *enjoy* and if they enjoy reading, they'll read. For maths, link the basics into daily living. Show them how to calculate their own income, spending and saving. (It's all too easy to get into money trouble simply by not being able to calculate interest.)

Fourth, in addition to the third, give them puzzles and see how they solve them.

Fifth, and perhaps most important, be *honest*. Yes, some subjects are controversial; yes, some people will be offended. Instead of nagging kids and telling them that this is wrong, wrong, wrong, why not discuss why people are offended? Then you can point out that whatever the issue is, people can still discuss it rationally and there is room for disagreement.

There are people who will say that some material is too advanced for Small Children (note the capital letters.) But I disagree.

There's a dirty little secret about politics that also applies to education and just about everything else. Only a handful of people *care*. For everyone who rants and raves about what the kids are being taught, there are thousands of people who don't pay attention, let alone make a fuss. Special interest groups generally succeed because they look loud, while their opponents rarely organise.

If you're a parent, take an interest in what your kids are learning. If you don't like it, talk to the teachers, then get organised. One voice is crying alone in the wilderness, hundreds of voices will be heard. Get out there and push.

The child is the father of the man, as the old saying goes. What sort of fathers are we growing?

Christopher G. Nuttall
Kuala Lumpur, 2013

POSTSCRIPT

I have a habit of writing these afterwords before actually writing the story itself. Normally, switching from writing fiction to writing factual articles relating to said fiction is harder than the other way around (at least for me). It was something of a surprise, therefore, to discover a case so directly related to the theme of this novel that I just had to write a postscript.

If one needed an example of the kind of lunacy school administers are capable of, one needs look no further than the case of Erin Cox. (Google is your friend; a good précis of the entire case is available on Mike McDaniel's blog.) To summarise the case as I understand it, Erin Cox was called by a friend and asked to pick her up from a party. Her friend was too drunk to drive. Erin, who hadn't even been at the party (and wasn't drunk, as a police officer attested), was threatened with arrest. (I don't understand the legal issues under US law, so I don't know how serious this was for her.)

What *was* significant was that her high school administration decided to punish her. They stripped her of her position (a Captain in the school's volleyball team) and suspended her for five games.

Let's look at this again. Erin helped a friend. She was not drinking (let alone drink-driving); she was not arrested. And yet she has been punished. Punished for doing the *right thing*.

Honestly, compared to this, does anything I wrote in *Reality Check* seem implausible?

I confess I know nothing of the school's legal rights over a pupil when he or she is not at school. Nor was I ever the type of person to put myself out to get onto a school team. But this is pretty much a flagrant failure of common sense. The message sent is simple; *don't try to help a friend. You'll only be punished for it.*

Pretend that you are in her position. What would you have done?

And what would you do now? Would you take the risk of helping your friend, knowing that you might be punished by an unreasoning, careless and generally imbecilic school administration that is utterly incapable of applying common sense?

I have no love for team sports; I certainly have never played in any competitions. But there are students (like Erin) who love sports, who work hard to be on the teams and do their very best to bring home awards. Those students have now been told that their achievements, which they prize highly, can be snatched away for trying to do the right thing. Maybe it makes sense to boot someone off the team for drunkenness or otherwise showing bad judgement, but Erin did neither.

The only people who showed bad judgement are the school administrators. I'd bet good money they will not be held accountable for it.

And then they will act all surprised when students lose all respect for them.

CGN

The Empire's Corps will continue in

RETREAT HELL

PROLOGUE

DATELINE – TWO MONTHS AFTER THE FALL OF CORINTHIAN

Admiral Rani Singh hated to lose.

She'd worked her way up the ranks through sheer stubbornness and native ability, forsaking all the shortcuts lecherous older officers offered her. She'd taken pride in not surrendering herself to the temptations, even when she'd been assigned to Trafalgar Naval Base by a particularly vindictive superior after she'd declined his advances. She'd even managed to turn a position that should have killed her career into a springboard to supreme power when the Empire started to withdraw from the sector, turning herself into a military dictator and ruler of a small empire of her own.

But then she'd lost everything, but her life and a handful of starships.

In hindsight, she saw – all too clearly – where she'd gone wrong. She hadn't taken the Commonwealth seriously, not at the time. It was a gathering of stars and human settlements towards the Rim, on the opposite side of her headquarters to Earth. The Commonwealth should not have been able to put together a challenge to her forces, not the sector fleet she'd snatched almost intact during the final chaotic days of the Empire's rule. But the Commonwealth had sent its people to Corinthian and undermined her rule. And when the ghost fleet had turned up, she'd panicked and lost everything.

Oh, she'd had plenty of time to think, she recalled, as the remains of her fleet had crept from hiding place to hiding place, fearful of an encounter that could have drained their finite supplies still further. Smaller and older ships had been cannibalised to keep the bigger ones operational, although she knew that even a victorious engagement could cost her everything;

her crews had grown more and more restless, their loyalty only assured by the looming presence of her security forces. One day, she'd known, they might rise up against her – and, if they took the ships, surrender them to the Commonwealth. She'd slept with a pistol under her pillow and armed guards at her hatch.

She'd known – she had never truly been able to lie to herself – that the situation was desperate. Battleships required constant maintenance and an endless supply of spare parts, which they no longer possessed. Sooner or later, she would have to abandon some of her crewmen or run out of life support. Maybe she could have found a world they could occupy – she did have far more firepower with her than the average Rim world could deploy in its own defence – but that would have been a form of surrender. And yet it had started to look like the only option. It had been then, when she'd been in the depths of despair, that they'd stumbled across the ship from Wolfbane.

Rani had known, vaguely, that another successor state was taking shape and form, coreward of Corinthian. She'd always known the value of good intelligence and her officials had interviewed the crews of every freighter that had made landfall within her territory. But she had always assumed that she would contact them from a position of strength, not weakness...not when weakness would invite attack. She knew that better than any of her former superiors, none of whom had realised the true scale of the looming disaster. And yet there was no choice.

She looked up from the screen as Wolfbane came into view, her ragtag fleet escorted by a handful of battleships. They weren't – quite – pointing their weapons at her ships, but she knew it would be a matter of seconds between the decision to open fire and the ships actually firing on her. She'd come to Wolfbane, after sending a message through the captured ship's crew, knowing that it could easily be a trap. But there was still no choice.

I do have cards to play, she thought, although she had no idea if they would be sufficient to win her a place on Wolfbane. *I have ships – and I have intelligence. And I have a few tools I dare not share...*

She gritted her teeth as the fleet finally entered high orbit. Wolfbane had been the most successful world in its sector, hence the Sector

Government's decision to base itself there. It was surrounded by orbital weapons platforms, industrial nodes and starships – hundreds of starships. The general economic decline that had presaged the Fall of the Empire, it seemed, no longer cast a shadow over the Wolfbane Sector. She couldn't help feeling a flicker of envy – even her work on Corinthian hadn't produced so much activity – which she thrust aside ruthlessly. There was no time to waste on self-recrimination.

Her wristcom buzzed. "Admiral," Carolyn said, "the shuttle from Wolfbane is making its final approach."

Rani nodded. Her aide was loyal – but she had no choice. Rani's security officers had seen to that, conditioning Carolyn until she couldn't even conceive of betraying her mistress. But the price for such conditioning was a reduction in the woman's intelligence and ability to act without specific orders. Rani was all too aware of the weaknesses in the system, but she dared not take the risk of leaving her aide unconditioned. It would be far too dangerous.

"Understood," she said. "I'm on my way."

She straightened up and studied herself in the mirror. Long dark hair framed an oddly fragile face, her dark skin and darker eyes giving her a winsome appearance that belied her inner strength. Her dress uniform was perfectly tailored to her slender form, tight in all the right places. It should have been no surprise when her former superiors had tried to seduce her, she admitted bitterly. The recruiting officers had never mentioned *that* aspect of the military when they'd convinced her to join up. Nor had it been a problem, she had to admit, until she'd graduated from the Imperial Academy with the rank of Lieutenant.

Absently, she wondered what Governor Brown would make of her. There had been little in the files on him, including a note that he had strong ties to a dozen corporations that presumably no longer existed. *That* suggested flexibility, Rani knew. It was rare for an official to be beholden to more than one set of masters. But Brown had clearly managed it long enough to reach the post of Sector Governor. His word would have been law in the sector long before the Empire collapsed.

I'll seduce him if I have to, she told herself. It was a bitter thought, one she resented after everything she'd done to avoid trading sex for favours, but she was damned if she would not use all the tools in her arsenal to claw her way back to power. *And I will have my revenge.*

CHAPTER

ONE

If you start by reviewing a generalised (and highly sanitised) history of the three thousand years of the Empire's existence, you could be forgiven for thinking that between the Unification Wars and the End of Empire there was no war. Certainly, no major conflict threatened the existence of the Empire. But was there peace?

- Professor Leo Caesius, War in a time of 'Peace:'
The Empire's Forgotten Military History

Darkness wrapped the landscape in shadow, unbroken by the merest hint of mankind's technology. The moon had yet to rise, leaving the stars as the only source of light. And it was very, very quiet.

Pete Rzeminski sat on the edge of the clearing, looking up at the stars and waited, patiently, for his contacts to arrive. The darkness – and the sound of nocturnal wild animals coming to life now the sun was gone – didn't bother him. He'd been in far worse spots when he'd been on active duty. But that had been a long time ago.

Pete wondered, absently, what his Drill Instructors would make of him now. Would they understand, he asked himself, or would they condemn him for making his choice? Once, he'd sworn an oath to the Empire that had defined his life and his service. It had once meant everything to him, even after he'd quit in disgust and retreated to Thule, where his family lived. But now the Empire was gone. What was the point, he asked himself, of swearing to something that no longer existed?

And yet, it had taken him years to take sides. In the end, only the death of his wife and family had convinced him to take up arms.

He wrapped the thermal cloak around him tightly as the temperature continued to fall, pushing his recollections aside. The youngsters had complained when he'd insisted on meeting the outsiders alone – not all of them trusted him – but Pete had been insistent. He did have training they lacked, training in escaping pursuit and – if necessary – in resisting interrogation. There was still the very real possibility that the entire operation was a loyalist trap. If so, it would be foolish to risk more than one life to make contact.

They called him the old man, he knew. And he *was* old, by their standards, even if he was in excellent shape for a fifty year old man. His hair was slowly turning grey, but his body was still strong, the result of exercise and genetic treatments he'd undergone in the past. And his wife had never complained about his performance before she'd died...

Memories rose up unbidden as he forced himself to relax, mocking him. There had been the Slaughterhouse, where he'd first known true companionship, and then a series of endless bloody battles, each one only a symptom of the Empire's steady decline. And then there had been the final bloody cataclysm...and his departure from the Terran Marine Corps. In the end, he knew, he'd failed. He hadn't been able to stay in the Marines, knowing that they'd become the Empire's bully boys, the people responsible for fixing problems the Grand Senate caused for itself.

He pushed the self-pity aside as his ears picked up faint sounds, blown on the wind. High overhead, something was descending towards the clearing. Pete tensed, one hand reaching for the pistol at his belt, as his enhanced eyes finally picked up the shuttle. Despite himself, he was impressed. Thule was hardly a stage-one colony world, utterly incapable of detecting a starship in orbit or a shuttle passing through its atmosphere. Their contacts had managed to slip through a detection system that was rather more elaborate than anything Thule really needed. But then, the government had attempted to spend its way out of the financial crisis by investing in the local defence industry. It was just a shame that the crisis had proven well beyond the planet's ability to surmount.

The shuttle came to a hover over the clearing, then dropped down towards the ground. It was a boxy shape, coated in materials that absorbed or redirected sensor sweeps from both orbital and ground-based stations. The contacts had refused to discuss precisely how they intended to avoid the local defences, but Pete's private guess was that they'd hidden the shuttle on one of the freighters in orbit. He'd taken a look at the listings and seen several dozen that could easily have carried the shuttle, hidden away in a cargo hold or even bolted to the hull. It wouldn't be detected unless the inspection crew was *very* thorough.

Not that the government bothers to examine off-world ships unless they're independent, he thought, feeling a twinge of bitterness. He hadn't realised how closely he'd associated himself with Thule until after his extended family had been affected by the first political shockwaves sweeping across the planet. A system that had seemed logical – and a change from the Empire's maddeningly hypocritical ideology – had shown its weaknesses as soon as the winds of change had begun. *The Trade Federation would complain.*

The shuttle touched down, a faint hissing sound reaching his ears as the warm hull touched damp grass. Pete hesitated, then stepped forward as the hatch opened. No light spilled out – it was impossible to be *certain* that an orbital satellite wasn't looking for anything that stood out on the ground – but his eyes could pick out a figure standing in the hatch, carrying a rifle in both hands. The figure wore light body armour and goggles that enhanced his eyesight. A long moment passed, then the figure waved at Pete. Bracing himself, Pete walked up to the hatch.

"Alpha-Three-Preen," he said.

"Beta-Four-Prime," the contact replied. He stepped aside, inviting Pete into the shuttle. "And may I say what a relief it is to be dealing with professionals?"

Pete felt his lips quirk in silent amusement. The underground movements that had sprung up in the wake of the financial crisis – and mass unemployment, followed by disenfranchisement – had a cause, but no real experience. Most of their secret passwords and countersigns had come from books and entertainment programs, both of which sacrificed realism for drama. It had taken him years of effort to teach the youngsters about the virtues of the KISS principle. Maybe it lacked drama, but it was certainly one hell of a lot more effective.

Inside, the shuttle was dark, the interior illuminated only by the light from a single display monitoring the orbital situation. The hatch closed with a hiss, then the lights came on, revealing a handful of metal chairs and a single control stick. Pete felt a moment of nostalgia – it had been years since he'd ridden an infiltration shuttle down into hostile territory – which he pushed to one side. He couldn't afford the distraction, not now.

"We have weapons for you, as per request," the contact said. In the light, he was a bland young man, someone who could have passed unnoticed on any cosmopolitan world. Not too handsome and not too ugly. "And some intelligence as well."

He paused, significantly. "You are aware, of course, that both the Commonwealth and the Trade Federation plan to expand their activities in this sector?"

Pete nodded. He'd heard rumours, some of them more reliable than others. Joining the Commonwealth had seemed the ticket to economic recovery, but the Commonwealth either couldn't or wouldn't buy most of the planet's produce. He rather suspected the latter. The planetary development corporation – and then the elected government – had invested heavily in industrial production equipment, citing their belief that the sector would continue to grow and develop under the protection of the Empire. Now, Thule had more industrial production than she could use. Even throwing money into the planetary defences hadn't solved the growing economic disaster.

"We would like to come to terms with you, after you take over the government," the contact added. "Would that be acceptable to you?"

Pete kept his expression blank. No one did anything for nothing, not even the ivory tower intellectuals who'd provided the ideological base for the Empire's growth, development and slow collapse. Long experience in the Marine Corps had taught him that anyone who supplied weapons to underground movements wanted something in return. Sometimes, it was cold hard cash, paid in advance, but at other times it was political influence or post-war alliances. He would have preferred to pay in advance, rather than have the terms left undetermined. But he knew the underground could not hope to purchase advanced weapons systems with cash in hand. The planet's currency was almost definitely useless outside its star system.

"That would depend," he said carefully, "on just what those terms *were*."

The youngsters, he knew, would have been horrified at his attempt to sound out the contact. They would have protested, perhaps rightly, that the underground did not enjoy the luxury of being able to debate terms and conditions. Without advanced weapons systems, the underground could not hope to prevail. If worst came to worst, they'd argue, they could always launch another uprising against the contact's backers. Pete's caution would not bode well with them.

He smiled, a little sadly. Some of the underground might have made good Marines, once upon a time, while others were the kind of people the Marine Corps existed to defend. Now, they were forced to fight or accept permanent subordination...

The contact didn't sound offended. "We would like your political neutrality," he said. "If you do not wish to associate yourselves with us, you may avoid commitment, but you may not side with any other interstellar power."

Pete looked at him for a long thoughtful moment. He knew that the contact represented an interstellar power – no one else would be able to produce the weapons they'd offered – but he didn't know *who*. But the insistence on political neutrality suggested Wolfbane. There was no one else who had any interest in Thule remaining uninvolved. It was vaguely possible, he supposed, that the Trade Federation was covertly sabotaging the Commonwealth's operations, but it seemed unlikely. If nothing else, the Trade Federation benefited hugely from the current state of affairs. Why would they want to upset the applecart?

They wouldn't, he thought. Everything he knew about the Trade Federation backed up its assertion that it was not interested in political power, at least not to the extent of the Commonwealth or the vanished Empire. No, they were interested in interstellar trade and little else. They didn't benefit by upending the situation on Thule.

"Very well," he said, finally. "I cannot speak on behalf of every underground organisation, but my group will accept your terms."

"Good," the contact said. He turned to the collection of metal boxes at the rear of the cabin. "Once we have unloaded these, I will depart and you can begin your war."

Pete nodded. The youngsters couldn't think in the long term, but *he* could...and he couldn't help wondering if he'd just sold his soul along with the planet itself. But they had no alternative, no choice if they truly wanted to overthrow the government and create a new order. They needed outside support.

"Thank you," he said.

———

First Speaker Daniel Krautman, elected Head of State only weeks prior to the first financial shockwaves that had devastated the planet's economy, looked out of the Speaker's Mansion and down towards the empty streets. Once, they had been bustling with life at all hours, a reflection of the economic success the planet had enjoyed under his predecessors. Now, they were empty, save for passing military and police patrols. The city was under martial law and had been so for months. Even the camps of unemployed workers and students who had been evicted from their homes were quiet.

He shook his head in bitter disbelief, wondering – again – just what he had done to deserve such turmoil on his watch. He'd told himself that running for First Speaker would be a chance to ensure that his name went down in the planet's history, despite his comparative youth. He'd told himself that he would serve the fixed ten-year term, the economic boom would continue and he would retire to take up a place on a corporate board or simply write his memoirs. Instead, the bottom had dropped out of the economy only *weeks* after his election and nothing, no matter what he did, seemed to fix the problem.

Gritting his teeth, he swore under his breath as he caught sight of his reflection. He'd been middle-aged when he'd been elected, with black hair and a smile that charmed the lady voters – or so he'd been assured, by his focus groups. Now, he was almost an old man. His hair had turned white, his face was deathly pale and he walked like a cripple. The doctors swore blind that the constant pains in his chest were nothing more than the results of stress and there was nothing they could do, but he had his suspicions. There were political and corporate figures demanding a harsher response to the crisis and some of them might just have bribed the doctors to make his life miserable.

Or maybe he was just being paranoid, he told himself as he turned away from the window. He was lucky, compared to the men and women in the homeless camps, building what shelter they could from cardboard boxes and blankets supplied by charities. There, life was miserable and short; men struggled desperately to find a job while women sold themselves on street corners, trading sex for the food and warmth they needed to survive another few days. And the children...Daniel couldn't help shuddering at the thought of children in the camps, even though there was nothing he could do. Anything he might have tried would have been ruthlessly blocked by the conservative factions in the Senate.

But they might be right, he thought, numbly. *The founders set out to avoid creating a dependent society, like Earth.*

He shook his head, angrily. What good did it do to tell the unemployed to go get a job when there were no jobs to be had? What good did it do to insist that the government should create jobs when there was no money to pay the additional workers? What good did it to do to cling to the letter of the constitution when a crisis was upon them that had never been anticipated by the founders? But the hawks were adamantly opposed to any changes while the doves couldn't agree on how to proceed. And *he* was caught in the middle.

Daniel stepped over to his desk and looked down at the report his secretary had placed there before going to bed. It seemed that the only growth industry, even after contact with the Commonwealth and the Trade Federation, was government bureaucracy, as bureaucrats struggled to prove they were actually necessary. The report told him, in exhaustive detail, just how many men, women and children had been arrested at the most recent protest march, the one that had turned into yet another riot. Daniel glanced at the executive summary, then picked up the sheaf of papers and threw it across the room and into the fire. Maybe he should have offered it to the homeless, he told himself, a moment too late. They could have burnt the papers for heat.

There was a tap on the door. Daniel keyed a switch, opening it.

"First Speaker," General Erwin Adalbert said. "I apologise for disturbing you."

"Don't worry about it," Daniel said. He trusted the General, insofar as he trusted anyone these days. There were times when he suspected the only thing preventing a military coup was the simple fact that the military would have to solve the crisis itself. "What can I do for you?"

"We received an intelligence package from one of our agents in the underground," Adalbert said. "I'm afraid our worst nightmare has come to pass."

Daniel smiled, humourlessly. Protest marches, even riots, weren't a major problem. The various underground groups spent more time fighting each other and arguing over the plans to repair the economy – or nationalise it, or send everyone to the farms – than they did plotting to overthrow the government. His *real* nightmare was the underground groups burying their differences and uniting against him.

"They've definitely received some help from off-world," Adalbert continued. "There have been several weapons shipments already and more are apparently on the way."

"Oh," Daniel said. "Who from?"

"Intelligence believes that there is only one real suspect," Adalbert admitted. "Wolfbane."

Daniel couldn't disagree. The Commonwealth had nothing to gain and a great deal to lose by empowering underground movements intent on overthrowing the local government and reshaping the face of politics on Thule. Wolfbane, on the other hand, might well see advantage in trying to covertly knock Thule out of the Commonwealth. Given that the closest Wolfbane-controlled world was only nine light years away, they certainly had an interest...and probably the capability to do real damage.

"I see," he said.

"We can expect the various underground groups to start working together now," Adalbert added, softly. "Their suppliers will certainly insist on unity in exchange for weapons."

He paused. "First Speaker, we need to ask for assistance."

Daniel looked up, sharply. "Remind me," he said coldly, "just how much of our budget is spent on the military?"

Adalbert had the grace to look embarrassed. "We spent most of the money on upgrading and expanding our orbital defences," he said. "It provided more jobs than expanding troop numbers on the ground. We can expand our recruiting efforts, but we're already having problems training our current intake..."

"And we don't know how far we can trust the new recruits," Daniel finished.

"Yes, sir," Adalbert said. "And most of our new recruits are trained for policing duties, not all-out war. But that's what the underground is going to give us."

Daniel stared down at his desk. He'd wanted to go down in history, but not like this, not as the First Speaker who had invited outsiders to intervene in his planet's civil unrest. The Senate would crucify him, safe in the knowledge that *they* didn't have to deal with the situation. They'd voted him emergency powers, enough to call for assistance, but not enough to actually come to grips with the situation.

Damn them, he thought.

"Summon the Commonwealth representative," he said, finally. He honestly wasn't sure if the Commonwealth *could* legally help Thule. This was an internal problem, not an external threat. But there was no choice. "We will ask for help."

CHAPTER

TWO

No, there wasn't. Peace is merely defined as the absence of fighting. In actual fact, there were very few years in the Empire's long history when the Empire's military forces were not deployed into combat. They might face rebels or insurgents, terrorists or freedom fighters, but they were never truly at peace.
- Professor Leo Caesius, *War in a time of 'Peace:'*
The Empire's Forgotten Military History

It was raining the day they laid Lieutenant Elman Travis to rest.

Colonel Edward Stalker stood by himself, away from the handful of spectators, and watched as the coffin was lowered into the ground. Traditionally, insofar as 'tradition' had a meaning on a world barely a hundred years old, those who had died on active service would be buried in a military graveyard on the outskirts of Camelot, but Lieutenant Travis's father had insisted on laying him to rest in a private churchyard. Ed had raised no objections, knowing that the grieving needed time to come to terms with the loss. Councillor Travis, he suspected, had yet to truly believe his son was dead.

The preacher started to speak, his words barely intelligible under the driving rain. Ed had never been particularly religious – a life in the Undercity, then in the Marine Corps had never predisposed him to believe in God – but he understood the value of believing that the dead were gone, but not *truly* gone. Councillor Travis clung to the belief he would see his son again, drawing strength from his conviction. Ed privately hoped he was right. But he couldn't escape the feeling that dead meant *gone*.

It had been his fault, Ed knew. Lieutenant Travis had died on Lakshmibai, victim of a treacherous attack that had claimed the lives of over a hundred Avalon Knights. Ed had looked at the files, such as they were, and decided that there was no reason to object to Wolfbane's choice of Lakshmibai as a neutral world. And really, what threat could Lakshmibai pose to two spacefaring interstellar powers? It had never really occurred to him that the locals hated the outsiders so much that they would rise up against them, even under the threat of colossal devastation when the starships returned. If the Commonwealth Expeditionary Force hadn't been deployed to Lakshmibai, Ed knew that he would be dead by now, along with the representatives from Wolfbane. Who knew what *that* would have done to relationships between the two interstellar powers?

Ed was used to death, or so he'd told himself. Being in the Marines meant the near-certainty of a violent death – and no one, not even the most highly-trained Marine, was immune. He'd lost far too many people over the years, from Marines he'd considered friends to Marines who'd served under his command...and then Avalon Knights and others who had joined the military and helped make the Commonwealth a success. But those deaths had taken place before he'd screwed up, badly. And he *had* screwed up. In hindsight, always clearer than foresight, it was alarmingly clear that Lakshmibai was a disaster waiting to happen.

"Hindsight is always clearer," the lecture had said, when he'd gone to OCS on the Slaughterhouse. "You will always be second-guessed by people who will have access to a much more accurate picture than you had at the time. The trick is not to let those people get under your skin, because they will find it very hard to filter out the information they gathered in hindsight from what you knew before the disaster occurred."

He shook his head, bitterly. There were just too many unanswered questions over the whole Lakshmibai debacle for him to relax, even if he had been inclined to let the dead go. Had someone *aided* the locals, promising assistance that would prevent either the Commonwealth or Wolfbane taking bloody revenge for the slaughter of their people? Had the locals believed that the starships would never return? Or had they just been maddened fanatics, too enraged to consider the long-term consequences of their actions?

The preacher finally stopped speaking and nodded to the friends and family, who stepped forward, picked up clods of earth and started to hurl them into the grave. Ed watched dispassionately as the coffin was slowly buried, part of him wishing that he could join them and help bury a young man who'd died too soon. But Councillor Travis had made his wishes quite clear. Ed could attend the funeral, but not take an active part in the ceremony. He blamed Ed for his son's death.

It was a bitter thought. Ed had cared little for Earth's cadre of professional politicians, from the mayors and managers of the giant cityblocks to the Grand Senators, who were – in fact, if not in name – an aristocracy that had succeeded, long ago, in barring outsiders from rising within the Empire's power structure. They'd known nothing, but politics; their actions were considered purely in terms of how they would help or hinder their endless quest for more and more political power. It didn't take hindsight – as Professor Caesius had demonstrated years ago – to understand that Earth's politicians were certainly part of the problems tearing the Empire apart. And now the Empire was gone.

But Councillor Travis was different. Ed and Professor Caesius had written most of the requirements for political service on Avalon – and the rest of the Commonwealth – and Councillor Travis qualified. Indeed, part of Ed rather admired the man for what he had accomplished, even before the Marines had arrived on Avalon and deposed the old Council. He was no professional politician...which made his new opposition to the military – and Ed personally – more than a little heartbreaking. But there was no point in trying to avoid the fact.

I never had children, Ed thought, sourly. It wasn't uncommon for Marines to have children while on active service, but the children tended to be raised by their mothers while the fathers were moved from trouble spot to trouble spot. But Ed had never found someone he seriously considered marrying until he'd been sent to Avalon – and they couldn't marry, not while they were holding important posts. *What is it like to lose a child?*

Losing a Marine was always a tragedy, all the more so when he had been in command, responsible for the lives of his men. But Marines were trained to the very peak of human capability before they were set loose on an unsuspecting universe and assigned to individual Marine companies.

Ed had never been responsible for training his men. A child, on the other hand, was raised from birth by its parents. There was a connection there that even the most loyal and determined NCO failed to grasp with his men. How could he blame Councillor Travis for his grief?

He caught sight of the older man, leaning over the grave and shuddered. Councillor Travis was older than Ed, his body carrying the scars of struggle with the old Council's stranglehold on Avalon's economy. His hair had faded to white long ago, but there was a grim determination in his eyes that had carried him far. Now, that determination was turned against the military itself – and the Commonwealth.

Ed sighed, bitterly. The hell of it was that he believed that Councillor Travis was right.

———

It felt strange, Brigadier Jasmine Yamane considered, to be wearing civilian clothes. She hadn't been a civilian since she'd turned seventeen and walked right into the Marine Corps recruitment station on her homeworld. At Boot Camp, she'd worn the khaki outfits the new recruits were issued by the Drill Instructors, while the Slaughterhouse had expected them to wear combat battledress at all hours of the day. Even when she'd gone on leave, which had only happened once between her qualifying as a Marine and being exiled to Avalon with the rest of the company, she'd worn undress uniform.

But the instructions for the funeral had been quite clear. No military uniforms. None of the guests were to wear anything that could even remotely be construed as a military uniform. And, for someone who had never really considered how to dress herself for years, even picking something to wear had taken hours. It annoyed the hell out of her that she could react quickly and decisively on the battlefield, but found herself utterly indecisive when trying to decide what to wear. There was no way she could talk about that with the other Marines.

She caught sight of her own reflection in the growing puddle of water on the grass and sighed, inwardly. Eventually, she'd settled for a black shirt and a long black skirt that swirled oddly around her legs. It was loose, but it still felt constraining. The first time she'd pulled it on, she'd had a flash-back to one of the nastier exercises she'd undergone at the Slaughterhouse, when she'd been chained up and dropped into a swimming pool. It hadn't surprised her, afterwards, to learn that several recruits had quit when they'd realised what they had to do to proceed.

The preacher started to speak again, his words hanging on the air. Jasmine had once been religious, religious enough to understand why Councillor Travis and his family sought comfort from their belief in God. It had been a long time since she'd prayed formally, she reminded herself, although heartfelt prayers on the verge of battle were probably more sincere than anything she'd offered back on her homeworld. But listening to his words was a bitter reminder that over a hundred young men and women were dead – and most of them had died under her command.

I'm sorry, she thought, directing her thought towards the coffin, now buried under a thin layer of earth. *I'm so sorry.*

In the days of the Empire, she knew without false modesty, she would be lucky to have risen to Lieutenant by now. Promotion was slow, even within the Marine Corps – and a brevet promotion could be cancelled without affecting her career. It was worse, far worse, in the Imperial Army, where officers were often promoted based on their connections, rather than their actual competence. But Avalon needed experienced officers more than it needed to adhere to a strict promotion timetable and Jasmine had been promoted – faster, perhaps, than was wise.

She looked over at Colonel Stalker, standing on his own in the rain, and wondered how he managed to seem so impassive. Didn't the deaths bother him? He'd been in the Marines since before Jasmine had even entered Boot Camp, let alone the Slaughterhouse; hell, she rather suspected he'd been in the Marines long before Jasmine had even heard about them for the first time. Was he simply too experienced to truly *feel* each and every death? Or was he merely hiding his feelings and concentrating on the living?

Jasmine had known people died from a very early age, ever since her aunt had been killed in an accident on her homeworld. She'd served beside Marines who'd been killed in the line of fire, leaving their former comrades to mourn their deaths and move on as best as they could. But she hadn't had anyone die under her command until she'd been promoted for the first time. And yet, losing the young men and women of Avalon hurt worse than losing fellow Marines.

She puzzled over it as the preacher assured his audience, once again, that the dead had gone to a better place. Jasmine didn't doubt it. Lieutenant Travis had been a good officer, one of many young men to enter the army after the old Council had been sidelined...and his promotion had been well-deserved. Jasmine vaguely recalled meeting him once, during a review of the CEF's infantry companies. In hindsight, she rather wished she'd paid more attention to the young man. She'd had to look at his file to remember his face, before she'd even come to the funeral. The picture someone had placed on the coffin, before the pallbearers had lowered it into the ground, had been of the Lieutenant as a young child, smiling happily as he ran through the field. There had been endless promise in his smile, something that had made her start to tear up before she pulled herself firmly under control. Somehow, the picture hadn't been *him*.

He wasn't just young, she thought. *He was uncommitted.*

Maybe it wasn't fair, but *Marines* were committed in a way that few soldiers and civilians could grasp. She'd left her homeworld, spent seven months in Boot Camp and another two years at the Slaughterhouse, then signed up for a ten-year hitch as a Marine Rifleman. She had left her previous life behind, knowing that when she returned to her homeworld she would have nothing in common with her brothers and sisters. Hell, the Marines were her brothers and sisters now. But Lieutenant Travis could have gone home any time he liked – and no one would have looked at him as a potential monster in human clothing.

She shook her head, running her fingers through her short dark hair, cropped close to her skull. The Empire had had barely a percentage point of a percentage point of its vast population in uniform, even counting the vast number of uniformed bureaucrats and REMFs who added nothing to the military's ability to fight, but detracted from it at every conceivable opportunity. It was unusual for anyone on Earth to *know* someone who served or had served in the military personally, a pattern that was duplicated on most of the Core Worlds. Few of them had any real idea what the military was like, allowing themselves to be influenced by entertainment movies rather than reality. It had given them a skewed idea of what it was like to defend the Empire.

But on Avalon, almost everyone had served in the military, various local defence forces or knew someone who had served. There was little dispute over the value of the military...or the need to keep a formidable force at the ready. And yet...she couldn't help thinking that Councillor Travis was likely to cause real problems. What would it mean for the Commonwealth as a whole if the CEF concept was to be grounded without further exploration?

It was selfish of her, she knew, but she almost wished that she'd died instead.

When the service came to an end, she walked out of the churchyard and headed back to the apartment on the outskirts of Churchill Garrison. As the CEF's commander, she was expected to be near the base at all times, rather than sleeping on Castle Rock. And besides, it had other compensations. Some of them made sleeping away from her fellow Marines almost worthwhile.

———

Councillor Gordon Travis waited until the preacher shooed the remaining witnesses out of the churchyard, then walked over to the gravestone and knelt beside the hard stone. The muddy ground soaked his trousers, but he found it hard to care. His son was buried below the soil, his one and only son. What did a little discomfort matter compared to *that*?

Gordon knew he'd been lucky. His father's ticket to Avalon had been purchased by *his* father, who had gifted his wayward son with enough Imperial Credits to avoid the debt peonage that had blighted so many unwary colonists on Avalon. Gordon had grown up earning money without having to worry about it draining into an endless black hole of debt, money he'd swiftly invested in a shop when he'd finally realised he didn't want to spend his life staring at the back end of a mule. His father's farm might have been permanently hovering on the verge of bankruptcy, but Gordon's store had been a runaway success. It helped that he didn't have to save money to pay back loans he'd never taken out.

But when his father had been killed by bandits – and the old Council had done nothing – Gordon had sworn revenge. He'd joined the Crackers, funnelling money and resources to them, helping to keep the insurgency alive. It had seemed a dream come true when the Marines had arrived; they'd defeated the bandits, overthrown the old Council and come to terms with the Crackers. Gordon hadn't even raised any objections when his son had decided to join the Knights of Avalon. Every young man wanted to join.

I should have said no, he thought. God knew he'd had endless fights with his father over his reluctance to stay on the farm, fights that had resulted in them not speaking to each other for years. He'd known better than to bar his son from joining the military. How could he say no when the new elite were those who wore a uniform? But now...he knew he should have forbidden his son to join. Elman might have been mad at him, he might have stormed off and done something stupid, but at least he would have been alive.

Bitter hatred curled around his heart as he started to weep. Elman had been his only son and, as such, had been special in his eyes, even though his daughters had taken over the family business. Losing him *hurt*; somehow, Gordon knew he'd always assumed that he would die long before his son. But instead...he clutched the gravestone, feeling the cold stone against his bare skin. The Commonwealth had seemed a great idea at the time, one that would ensure that Avalon would never again be at the mercy of faceless bureaucrats thousands of light years away. But now... it wasn't worth his son's life.

And he didn't even die in defence of Avalon, he thought, bitterly. *He died on a world we should have known better even than to visit.*

Angrily, he stood up. It would not happen again, he vowed, as he marched away from his son's grave. *He* would make sure it never happened again, whatever it took. No more sons would die on foreign worlds.